PRAISE FOR *LORD OF THE SEA CASTLE*

'This lyrical novel is rich in history and evokes a wonderful sense of time and place. Great characters, strident battles and a story to be savoured.'

David Gilman, author of *Master of War*

'It's not just the grim gore of the Anglo-Norman battlefield that springs to life in Butler's skilful telling. Even better, he finds his way into the minds and spirits of those men for whom the ultimate prize was a nation.'

E.M. Powell, author of *The Lord of Ireland*

'From tourneys to treachery; from Welsh Marches to Irish marauders, Ruadh Butler propels us into the tumultuous times of the twelfth century. The clangour of swords and battle cries of knights echo from the pages of 'Lord of the Sea Castle', as Butler tells a gripping tale with skill, verve and gusto.'

Matthew Harffy, author of *The Serpent Sword*

'A bracing tale of lords and knights slugging it out for power and the chance to shape Ireland, Butler's vivid account of how the Norman's forged their kingdoms on these islands and their astute cultural amalgamation has a powerful resonance for modern readers post-Brexit.'

Anthony J. Quinn, author of *Disappeared*

PRAISE FOR *THE INVADER SERIES*

'*Swordland* begins with a vibrant and bloody set piece …
the beautiful but dangerous landscape of medieval Ireland
is well described, and the action scenes there are perfectly
pitched and handled with real expertise.'

Historical Novel Review

LORD OF
THE
SEA CASTLE

Ruadh Butler

Published by Accent Press Ltd 2017

www.accentpress.co.uk

Copyright © **Ruadh Butler** 2017

ISBN 9781910939277
eISBN 9781910939284

Printed in the UK by Clays Ltd, St. Ives

LOTTERY FUNDED

By the creek of Baginbun, will Ireland be lost or won?

Glossary

WALES

Abergavenny – castle controlled by the Braose family
Aberteifi – castle in modern Cardigan
Afon Wysg – River Usk
Brecon – castle in Powys
Castle Arnallt – Welsh castle in Upper Gwent
Ceredigion – Welsh kingdom on the west coast
Deheubarth – Welsh kingdom of South Wales
Gwent Uwchcoed – Upper Gwent
Afon Gwy – River Wye
Gwynedd – northern Welsh kingdom
Haverford – Haverfordwest
Melrfjord – Milford Haven
Nedd – modern Neath
Oystermouth – castle in southern Wales
Striguil – castle in modern Chepstow
Suðbury –Sedbury in Gloucestershire
Sweynsey – modern Swansea
Tyndyrn – Tintern Abbey
Usk – castle in modern Monmouthshire
Wentwood – forested hills in Monmouthshire

IRELAND

Banabh – Bannow Bay
Bearú – River Barrow
Uí Ceinnselaig – a tribal kingdom in modern County Wexford ruled by the Meic Murchada family
Cluainmín – Clonmines
Fearna – the modern town of Ferns

Dubhlinn – modern Dublin
Dun Conán – Duncannon
Dun Domhnall – Dun Donnell, modern Baginbun Point in County Wexford
Kerlingfjorðr – Carlingford
Laighin – the modern province of Leinster excepting Counties Meath, Westmeath, Longford, and Louth
Mhumhain – Kingdom of Munster
Osraighe – a tribal kingdom ruled by the Meic Giolla Phadraig family in modern Kilkenny and the southern part of Laois
Sláine – River Slaney
Siol Bhroin – Shelburne, a land including the Hook Peninsula in modern County Wexford
Siúire – River Suir
Strangrfjorðr – Strangford
Tuadhmumhain – petty-kingdom roughly equating to modern County Clare, ruled by the Uí Briain family
Uí Ceinnselaig – an Irish tribe led by Diarmait Mac Murchada
Veðrarfjord – Waterford; an Ostman city built on a "Windy Inlet" on the River Suir
Waesfjord – Wexford; an Ostman city built on mud flats with a name which means "Wide Inlet"

CHARACTERS

Alice of Abergavenny – a runaway
Basilia de Quincy – illegitimate daughter of Richard de Clare
Déisi – a tribe from modern County Waterford
Diarmait Mac Murchada – Dermot MacMurrough, King of Laighin
Donnchadh Ua Riagháin – Donnacha O'Ryan, King of the Uí Drona
Fionntán Ua Donnchaidh – Fintan O'Dunphy, an Irish warrior
Henry FitzEmpress – King of England
Harry the Young King – the heir to England
Hervey de Montmorency – uncle to Richard de Clare
Hubert Walter – a priest and court official

Máel Sechlainn Ua Fhaolain – Melaughlin O'Phelan, King of the Déisi

Máelmáedoc Ua Riagain – Malachy O'Regan, an adviser to Diarmait Mac Murchada of Laighin

Ragnall Mac Giolla Mhuire – Reginald MacGillamurray, King of Veðrarfjord

Raymond de Carew – a warrior in the retinue of Striguil

Richard de Clare – Lord of Striguil

Roger de Quincy – son-in-law to Richard de Clare, married to Basilia

Seisyll ap Dyfnwal – a Welsh chieftain

Sigtrygg Mac Giolla Mhuire – Sihtric MacGillamurray, a warrior from Veðrarfjord

Uí Drona – a tribe from the barony of Idrone in modern County Carlow

William de Braose– Lord of Abergavenny and son of Lord Bramber

William Marshal – a knight

Raymond's conrois

Gilbert Borard, Walter de Bloet, Asclettin FitzEustace, Amaury de Lyvet, Thurstin Hore, Denis d'Auton, Christian de Moleyns, Bertram d'Alton, Dafydd FitzHywel and William de Vale.

NOTES

The '**Fitz**' prefix is the Norman derivation of the Latin 'Filius' meaning 'son of'.

A **miles** (one of a number of milites) is a Norman horseman armoured similarly to a knight but not considered of the same noble rank.

The **Ostmen** (East Men) were made up of *Fionngall* (Fair Foreigners), presumed to be the descendants of the original Norse invaders who populated the cities of Dublin, Waterford, and Wexford (amongst others), and the *Dubhgall* (Dark Foreigners), who were Danes and arrived a century later following their conquests in northern England. The Danish Uí Ímair (the descendants of Ivarr) quickly became the ruling class in most of these settlements and founded the cities of Limerick and Cork.

Irish families were divided into clans (**tuath**) and septs (**finte**) thus Diarmait Mac Murchada was the King of the Uí Chennselaig (*tuath – the descendants of Cennsalach*) as well as the Meic Murchada (*finte – the sons of Murchad*)

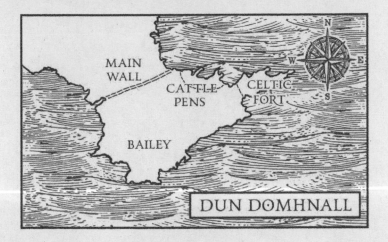

DUN DOMHNALL

MAIN WALL

CATTLE PENS

CELTIC FORT

BAILEY

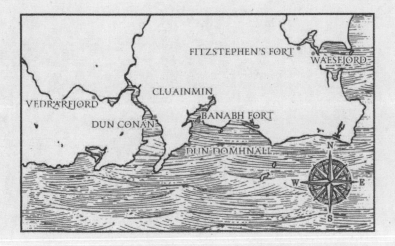

FITZSTEPHEN'S FORT

WAESFJORD

CLUAINMIN

VEDRARFJORD

BANABH FORT

DUN CONAN

DUN DOMHNALL

Part One

The Warlord of Wales

Prologue

Gwent, Wales - 1170

'*Diarmait Mac Donnchadh Mac Murchada, King of Laighin, to Sir Richard de Clare, Lord of Striguil, greetings,*' the letter began.

He blinked many times as he re-read the opening line of flowing script. 'Lord of Striguil?' he hissed through clenched teeth as he turned his eyes on the foreigner in outlandish garb who lounged by the hearth in the middle of the great hall. 'I am Earl of Pembroke and he would do well to remember that.'

The stranger did not blink as the lord of the castle admonished his king. 'I apologise on Diarmait's behalf, *Earl* Richard.' He bowed his head in equal reverence and contrition.

Over by the door an old bloodhound stretched his muscular legs, rustling week-old rushes on the floor, before clambering to his feet and plodding towards his master, where he bumped his nose on Richard de Clare's leg. The earl leant down and rubbed the dog's ear, and smiled as the animal stared up into his weary face. 'It is but a small affront, I suppose,' he told the stranger.

It had been a cold winter in southern Wales and there seemed to be no escape from the frosty weather, even in the great hall of Striguil Castle. The tired tapestries on the walls sagged and sank as a gusting breeze tumbled up the Gwy Valley to find holes in the aged plasterwork and mortar, scattering the cloying smell of damp around the

15

room. Candles flickered and swayed, as did the glowing fires in the brazier which warmed the shadowed face of the foreigner. Two of the earl's liege men huddled at his side before the flames.

'*My friend*,' Richard's study of the letter continued, '*the swallows have come and gone, yet you are tarrying still. Neither winds from the east nor the west have brought us your much-desired and long-expected presence. Let your present activity make up for this delay and prove by your deeds that you have not forgotten your engagements, but only deferred their performance.*'

The earl grimaced. He had not forgotten his promise to Diarmait Mac Murchada, but he had his reasons for delaying. Henry FitzEmpress, the King of England, was not a man to second-guess and Richard knew that if he made even the slightest move that earned Henry's displeasure, it could cost him his few remaining estates or even, depending on the King's famously unpredictable mood, his liberty. Henry had already taken Richard's holdings in Normandy and Buckinghamshire, but worse to Richard was the withholding of his father's title of Earl of Pembroke – all because he had backed the wrong horse during Henry's war for the throne against Stephen de Blois.

Richard looked down at the letter again, allowing his finger to trace the intricately winding and strange Irish lettering scratched on the thick vellum: '*The whole of Laighin has been recovered*,' he read aloud, '*and if you come in time with a strong force the other four parts of the kingdom will be easily united to this, the fifth. You will add to the flavour of your coming if it be speedy; it will turn out famous if it is not delayed, the sooner the better and all the more welcome. The wound in our regards which has been partly caused by neglect will be healed by your presence; firm friendship is secured by good offices and grows by benefits to greater strength.'*

Richard read the paragraph again and felt his heart leap. It seemed that Diarmait had now set his sights higher than simply recapturing the provincial throne from which he had been exiled four years before. He now wished to be High King of all Ireland and that meant that he would still require Richard's help. The earl turned his eyes heavenwards and thanked the Saviour for finally answering his prayers. There had been many occasions since Henry FitzEmpress' ascension that he had appealed to God for help. Denied royal patronage as well as the income from his forfeited estates for sixteen long years, Richard had quickly found himself deeply in debt. His remaining lands could not provide enough to pay both warriors and the king's taxes, and so, under pressure of his obligations to the distant monarch, he had limited his expenditure on his army. Many milites had left his service. It had not been long before Welsh raiders had sensed the weakness and targeted his borders, rustling sheep, cattle and goods whenever they could. Churches and monasteries which looked to him for protection had been attacked; villages and manors had been mercilessly pillaged; whole families had been carried off to be sold in the Danish slave markets in Ireland and beyond. All appealed to their lord for help and protection, but he could give none.

He wished his mother could be at his side to see him during his moment of triumph. Lady Pembroke had spent every waking moment working towards Richard's return to favour. She had forced her son to entertain many influential courtiers, those with the ear of King Henry, at great expense at feasts in Striguil where only the best foods were served, and the best garments and entertainment permitted. But nothing - not the expensive presents, the grand gestures, offers of friendship, bribery, coercion or

17

extortion - had worked to raise Richard de Clare in King Henry's affections. His mother had died the unhappy parent of a poor and pitiable man.

Then, one day, Diarmait Mac Murchada had come into his life and suddenly Richard felt he had stumbled upon a path to lead him back from ignominy. Word had arrived that Sir Hervey de Montmorency, his father's half-brother, was bringing an Irish king to Striguil with plans for a great adventure, one that promised vast wealth to anyone who helped him to regain his lost throne in the land of Laighin. He believed that even his late mother would have been proud of his efforts to organise all pomp and ceremony for the arrival of his royal visitor. No extravagance had been considered too much and he had borrowed a vast sum of silver from a Jew, Aaron of Lincoln, so that Striguil Castle could be adorned in splendour. New crimson and gold banners showing the arms of his noble family flowed from the walls of the great hall and everywhere were reminders of their ancient power and prestige. Two days of feasting had been planned and even the great Bishop of Worcester had promised to cross the Severn and attend the conference. Richard had brought in musicians from London to entertain the numerous influential nobles that he had invited at short notice. He wanted everyone who mattered to see the moment of his glory. He wanted to show them all that even kings attended the court of Richard de Clare. He wanted to see their jealousy with his own eyes. Everything had seemed to be taking a turn for the good.

Then Diarmait and Sir Hervey had arrived in his hall.

Both men could have been mistaken for beggars, such was the dreadful condition of their clothes. They had few warriors of note, no servants, and even the bearded harpers in the king's entourage addressed him as an equal. Richard had baulked in embarrassment and confusion at the sight of the pair, angry that his dream had been destroyed as quickly as it had formed in his imagination. Neither Sir Hervey nor King Diarmait looked like they could afford a sword, never mind help Richard to raise an army. There would be no glory or riches - or so he had thought.

As he sat reading Diarmait's letter, the earl recalled the mocking laughter of the gathered nobles echoing around the heavy stone walls of Striguil. He tried in vain to stop his ears and cheeks turning red. It was said that the whole March of Wales derided him and repeated stories that Richard de Clare entertained vagrants at his castle. Nobles scoffed and even mere villeins on the streets ridiculed him as he passed by.

Richard dragged a clammy hand through his thinning, dusty hair as he remembered his most recent humiliations.

While his servants had pulled the gaudy banners from the walls of the great hall and hounded the hired minstrels from the castle bounds without payment, Diarmait and Sir Hervey had cornered Richard and described their ambitious plans and his part in them. By then Richard had become angry and, despite his desire for the wealth and land which Diarmait offered, he had driven a hard bargain for even considering giving his help to their scheme. His disappointment had shaken free an obsession in Richard's soul – one that he would accomplish even if it claimed his life. He would recover his reputation.

Every proposal suggested by Diarmait and Sir Hervey had been met with hard bargaining until, in the end, the foreigner had offered something which Richard had not believed possible: a crown.

He had almost choked on his mug of wine when the exiled king had made the offer. Diarmait would marry his daughter to Richard and through her he would have claim to the throne of his reclaimed kingdom of Laighin after her father's death. That very night he had made solemn promises in the presence of sacred relics and churchmen that he would help Diarmait in his great cause, and since that day he had carefully plotted and contrived to make his dream come about; money had been borrowed, ships built, weapons forged and warriors engaged with the promise of knights' fees across the sea.

While he had organised his forces to invade, Diarmait Mac Murchada had lost patience with his slow progress and had journeyed further into Wales where he had found himself a small band of disreputable Normans to act as his bodyguard while he went ahead to Ireland. Those who he had employed were considered thugs and troublemakers by most civilised men, and Richard was no different. He had doubted that Robert FitzStephen and his mercenaries would be any benefit to Diarmait, unless the Irishman's aim was to raid, rape, pillage and steal from his enemies and allies alike. However, FitzStephen had led the small warband to re-conquer Diarmait's kingdom of Laighin, defeating the vast army of the High King of Ireland in the process. He had been rewarded with rule over the merchant town of Waesfjord and over two hundred thousand acres of land. FitzStephen, an illegitimate half-breed, now had a greater estate than Richard, a male-line descendant of the Dukes of Normandy and an earl of the realm! Distraught when he had heard of FitzStephen's success, Richard had convinced himself that he had let the best chance to rescue his reputation pass him by. But then Diarmait's letter had arrived in Striguil. The King of Laighin still desired his help and offered an even greater prize than before.

Diarmait had referred to FitzStephen's success in his letter and Richard carefully recited those lines: '*Our friend Sir Robert, son of Stephen, has led our forces t oa great victory over our enemies at the forest of Dubh-Tir.*' Richard frowned heavily, causing more worry lines to appear upon an already worried brow as he re-read the words. Hervey de Montmorency had been right, he decided. FitzStephen was trying to subvert him in Diarmait's regard. Could he also be aiming to assume his throne, he wondered?

'*We are now the master of our homeland, the lands of the Uí Ceinnselaig tribe,*' Richard stumbled over the peculiar words, '*and by our force of arms, we have been made king. But with your power beside ours we will conquer a greater kingdom still. I await your reply and your long awaited presence.*'

Richard carefully allowed the piece of parchment to fold. The heavy blood-red wax seal and white linen ribbon clattered on the wooden table top as the letter folded back into shape with a sharp hiss. For many minutes he said nothing. Instead he considered carefully the contents of the correspondence.

'Tell me, Master Ua Riagain, what do you make of this Robert FitzStephen character?' Richard de Clare finally asked the newcomer.

Máclmáedoc Ua Riagain gazed into the fire. It had been he who had borne the letter across the Irish Sea from his master's fortress at Fearna. He had been accompanied on his journey by Richard's uncle, Sir Hervey de Montmorency, and, from Máelmáedoc's side, the old Frenchman sneered at the mention of FitzStephen.

'He is a gambler and as ambitious a man as any I have met before,' said the bearded Máelmáedoc. 'FitzStephen will back his skill against any enemy, no matter their number. Eventually every gambler loses, and it is my view that he will ultimately fail when it will cost my king most.' Like many of the Irish ruling classes, Máelmáedoc could speak both Latin and French, Richard's native tongue, fluently and it was in that language in which they conversed. 'What Diarmait needs is an older, experienced warrior to rule his kingdom with a steady hand after he has gone. That is if the warrior's assistance is prompt,' continued Diarmait's emissary.

Richard raised a sandy eyebrow at Máelmáedoc's impertinence, but before he could retort his son-in-law Sir Roger de Quincy interceded:

'King Diarmait should not trust FitzStephen. He is a bandit proven capable of any underhand scheme. We should go to King Diarmait's side as soon as possible before that Welsh cur robs us of what we were promised. I could even go ahead with a small force of a thousand warriors?' Roger looked from face to face searching for support in this view, but received none. Everyone in the room knew that there was a dark history between Sir Roger and Robert FitzStephen, and even Máelmáedoc had heard the lurid stories about how Roger had betrayed FitzStephen to his enemies six years before. Richard de Clare, however, preferred to ignore such gossip about his daughter Basilia's husband.

'King Henry declared FitzStephen a rebel,' Roger exclaimed when no support for his opinion was offered.

'You raise a valid point, Roger,' the earl said and leant back on his chair, enjoying the heat from the distant fire upon his face. 'FitzStephen failed to get express permission from Henry to go to Ireland and if he ever falls into the king's hands he will suffer the consequences of that decision.' Obviously FitzStephen, a man who had been sprung from a Welsh prison months before his deeds in Ireland, had nothing to lose, Richard thought. 'I will have to get definite sanction from Henry *in person* before I do anything,' the earl stated, much, it was obvious, to the dislike of the three other men. 'The risk to my last estate … to Striguil … is too great and Henry FitzEmpress is not a man who can be so easily disregarded.'

'The king has been wintering in Poitou, nephew,' Hervey de Montmorency informed. 'It is dangerous to journey across the sea so late in the year. But if we could make for Ireland immediately ...'

'Before Robert FitzStephen becomes the power behind King Diarmait's throne?' the earl mused. If anything Sir Hervey seemed even more desperate than he for the great endeavour to go ahead. His uncle had been the first to see the potential in King Diarmait's plea for warriors, and thus could be assured of collecting a grand share of the spoils. But he was totally reliant on his nephew's participation. Not for the first time the earl caught Sir Hervey throw a hungry, wolfish look in his direction.

'I must visit King Henry. But you, Uncle, will return to Ireland with Master Ua Riagain and my answer for Diarmait. Tell him that I will come to his aid in the summer.'

Hervey stroked his hands over the long thin greasy locks which fell from his balding head and studied Richard's face. He seemed to be searching for an untruth in his nephew's words.

'What of Raymond le Gros?'

'Raymond?' Richard raised his eyebrows. 'I had completely forgotten about him. It is easily done,' he joked. The earl had indeed overlooked the man who commanded his household warriors, the man who Sir Hervey had scathingly called Raymond *the Fat*.

'He is a traitor to our cause, nephew. I have it on good authority that it was Raymond who directed King Diarmait to search out Robert FitzStephen last summer.' Hervey spat the words through his grizzled mouth. His eyes flicked towards Máelmáedoc.

'Raymond may be a blabbermouth but he certainly has

his uses,' Earl Richard replied with a smile. 'They are few, as well you know, but those that he has are valuable. Especially if fighting or food is involved.' The earl giggled at his small levity. 'In any event, I have no doubt that news of King Diarmait's offer would have reached FitzStephen's ears without his nephew's help, one way or another.'

'I don't know why you don't get rid of Raymond and make me captain of your conrois, Lord Father,' Roger de Quincy snorted. 'Raymond is a drunken oaf and if what Sir Hervey says is true, he is not to be trusted.'

'I expect that he simply did not realise the gravity of his chit-chat,' the old earl responded, side-stepping Roger's request as he had done many times before. 'Raymond doesn't think sometimes, but he is a demon in battle. And the men love him. He is a simple man.' *And no threat to my position*, Richard thought as he talked to his ambitious and graceful son-in-law.

Sir Roger de Quincy, looking extremely irritated, and mumbled that he was a much better candidate for high command than a lowborn man of mixed Welsh and Norman heritage like Raymond.

Richard ignored Roger's gripe and left his chair on the dais to stand before his Irish visitor. 'I am decided,' he told Máelmáedoc. 'I will visit Poitou and obtain royal permission to assist Diarmait in this great endeavour. Tell your king that I am coming and soon, Master Ua Riagain. Tell him that I will bring an army, the like of which he will never have seen. Diarmait's throne will be secured,' he said, 'and once that is done I will marry his daughter and he will name me his heir.'

Máelmáedoc nodded. 'That he will, Lord Strongbow.'

Strongbow; it was a name that spoke of the great power of Richard de Clare's family, and its mention made the earl lift his chin with pride to stare at his family arms which were chiselled in stone on the trusses of the roof beams above him. Where the name was mentioned men perished and great deeds were performed. Alone of his father's titles it was the one that the king could never take away from Richard de Clare. It was also the one which he had always struggled to live up to. But now he had the opportunity to outshine even his great father, who had first borne the name of Strongbow. His father had fought a hard battle of war and politics to become Earl of Pembroke. Could his son make himself a king in Ireland? If he succeeded the scorn which Richard had endured would be quieted and history would never forget him. His reputation would be saved.

But to do that he would have to travel to France and there convince Henry FitzEmpress, the most powerful, jealous, antagonistic, and autocratic monarch in Christendom, to let him go to Ireland. Strongbow had to persuade the man who despised him most to let him seek his fortune across the sea.

Chapter One

The race was on and the captain from Striguil was in no mood to come in second as he led his conrois up the slick valley beside the Afon Wysg. Down in the lowlands it had been easy for the Norman horsemen to follow the raiders' progress; dead men, burnt out homesteads, and the sorrowing wail of women and children had led the horsemen northwards towards Gwent Uwchcoed where Seisyll ap Dyfnwal was lord. Their pursuit had led them into disputed territory.

It was almost midday when the captain called a halt. The ten men from Striguil had exited the wooded valley moments before and come into a bright meadow bounded by evergreen trees on all sides. Close by was a small group of hovels, obviously Welsh - for no sane Norman would live this far from Usk Castle without a palisade to protect his home.

'We are certainly in Seisyll's lands now, Raymond,' tall Denis d'Auton told his captain.

Raymond de Carew gave no indication that he had heard the miles. Instead he leant downwards to investigate hoof marks on the ground. His chainmail hood shimmered as it tumbled across his wide shoulders. Like a hound confused by the scent of a wounded hind, Raymond's blond head bobbed from side to side as he scrutinised the marks. He then sat straight to survey the horizon, a large hand over his eyes to shield them from the hot sun.

His manner caused Denis to tense and like his captain

he began to scan the hilly landscape for possible threats. A large number of sheep and cattle had been grazing between the valley mouth and the Welsh houses, but, as Denis watched, they fled eastwards away from the Normans of Striguil who had stopped behind their captain.

'That's a large number of animals for such a small farmstead,' Raymond said, pointing his lance at the grazing animals. 'So where are the stockmen?' The beasts were the most valuable commodity on the March and should have been protected by a number of herdsmen. 'The hoof marks are wider-spaced than before,' he said as he turned his horse and pointed at the ground where the grass was flattened. 'They broke into a gallop here and made off towards those buildings. Something is not right.'

'I don't think there is anything to fear,' Denis replied with a dismissive wave of his hand.

It was an unfortunate statement to make because at that moment, with little more than a whinny and the solid thump of hooves on the heavy ground, fifteen horsemen emerged into view from between the Welsh hovels. Inscribed upon their red and blue surcoats were the three golden wheat sheaves of the Braose family. Their leader marshalled his force forty feet from Raymond's men.

'Abergavenny men,' Gilbert Borard, Raymond's most trusted lieutenant, whispered loudly in his captain's ear as he joined him from the back of the conrois. 'I reckon it must've been them who were thieving from Earl Strongbow's lands, not Seisyll and the Welsh. It might be a good time for us to leave.' Borard stopped talking when the leader of the Abergavenny men detached from his troop and trotted forward, his red and blue pennant fluttering from his long lance.

'What in seven hells does he want?' Borard muttered from behind his heavy black beard to Raymond.

'I've heard this is how they start a fight in England,' Raymond replied. 'He'll ask for our surrender, I will refuse and then he will set the rules. We'll have a scrap, but we aren't allowed to kill anybody.'

Borard sniffed a laugh and shook his head to show his disbelief at the unusual conventions of the nobility. In the March of Wales such frivolities were rare. Here, on the frontier, ambush was favoured and murder common. On the edge of the kingdom men scratched out a living from cold earth under constant fear of attack. You killed or feared repercussions. Life made men hard, women suspicious and warriors merciless. It was a place where the King of England's law did not reach.

Raymond clipped his heels to his courser's sides and walked his horse forward to meet his fellow Norman.

'I am Sir William de Braose, Lord of Abergavenny,' the armoured man dipped his head in greeting as Raymond and Borard approached. Two warriors flanked the young man in the red and blue surcoat. 'To whom am I speaking?'

Before answering, Raymond hungrily admired the newcomer's armour which covered everything except his young, red-cheeked face. His chainmail was a hard fish skin of shining steel circlets and not only wrapped his torso but also his forearms and shins. The nobleman even had long chainmail gloves and socks to protect those extremities. By comparison Raymond's hauberk was thin, with gaps between the links, and only stretched to his elbows. It was dented and had been mended in a hundred places, but it had saved his life numerous times. The skirts on his armour divided at his waist, covering only his thighs but allowing him to ride a horse comfortably, something Raymond doubted that Sir William could claim. But even still, the nobleman's mail was impressive. Below the hauberk Raymond knew that the knight would have a thick gambeson made of padded leather and stuffed tightly with wool for extra protection and comfort. On top of it all was the surcoat of his family, of the brightest reds, blues, and golds. Of course Sir William had a new-fangled great helm hanging from his expensive Spanish-made saddle.

Raymond's dented spangenhelm, cone-shaped and complete with bent nasal guard, would not have looked out of place amongst the warriors who had fought at Hastings a hundred years before. Likewise his shabby bucket saddle, which had belonged to his father, and his long leaf-shaped shield which bore no device. Sir William's lance was standard, but his sword's handle was inlaid with gold and wrapped in red cord to cushion the reverberations when it came together with another weapon. It matched his rich red leather scabbard and cushioned saddle. William de Braose looked every inch the Christian warrior, but he was out of place on the March of Wales. Apart from the few like Raymond who wore a surcoat bearing Strongbow's arms, most warriors in Gwent wore dull colours, greys and greens, so that they could mix in with the countryside. Few men of the March could afford the rich gaudiness of the English and French courts.

Even from five paces away Raymond could see the strength and power of Sir William's charger, which danced from hoof to hoof aggressively. The stallion was huge and was hidden beneath a long red rug bearing his master's famous family arms. It covered the whole beast, including its face, to the knees. Raymond rode a smaller, more manoeuvrable courser without any garish devices.

'My name is Raymond de Carew,' the captain finally answered Sir William de Braose's question, 'and I serve the Earl Strongbow of Striguil.'

If he recognised either name, Sir William did not show any interest. 'I am lord of these lands,' he stated simply, 'and you are either lost or trespassing. The second reason gives me the right to kill you and your men.'

Raymond raised his eyebrows at the sudden declaration, and chuckled. 'I believe you are new to the March, Sir William, so it is my duty to inform you that you are the one who is lost. These lands belong to Seisyll ap Dyfnwal of Castle Arnallt.'

William de Braose snorted. 'That Welshman is a rebel, and I will catch up with him soon. Then the raiding will stop.'

'It is funny that you would mention raiding – we were tracking a party about twenty strong who attacked one of Strongbow's manors above Usk. Have you heard anything about them?' He asked the question as innocently as he possibly could. 'They passed through this way extremely recently.'

'What exactly are you implying, Sir Raymond?'

'It is simply Raymond, Sir William,' the captain replied, 'I am no knight, only one of Strongbow's humble warriors. But in answer to your question, I am implying that you Abergavenny bastards were in my lord's territory; that you burned his manor house, and attempted to mask your skulduggery by leaving a trail that led into the lands of the Welsh. I am telling you that I am here to beat you bloody so that you will remember not to stray into Earl Strongbow's domains again.'

Sir William de Braose's response surprised Raymond: he laughed, dramatically and long. 'I will give your cheap sword to my son to use until I buy him a proper one when he becomes an esquire. Your little pony will be my daughter's pet. Your meagre ransom I will keep for myself.' Noting Raymond's confusion at the statement Sir William nodded back towards the valley mouth. 'You can surrender to my sergeant now, Master Raymond de Carew, while I take care of a little business in those houses,' he said and nonchalantly shifted his reins to direct his stallion towards the Welsh farmstead.

Raymond swung around in his saddle to see at what his opponent was indicating. What he saw shocked him for, at the mouth of the valley, were ten more mounted men in the same surcoats as Sir William de Braose. They blocked his escape route home.

He had been outmanoeuvred, Raymond realised. He was outnumbered and he was surrounded.

Sir William de Braose's men had indeed attacked Strongbow's uplands manors. They had stolen all they could carry and had then fled back over the hills towards Abergavenny. But somewhere along the way they had discovered that they were being followed and their leader had prepared a trap for his pursuer. And Raymond the Fat had bumbled straight into it.

All this Raymond understood in a moment and already he had decided what to do: he launched his lance into the chest of the nearest rider. The man, who had accompanied the smug and smiling William de Braose to the parley, tumbled from his saddle and dragged down his frightened horse with him. Luckily for Sir William his spooked mount swept him out of range or he would have been next to be attacked. His other warrior was not so lucky. Instead of fleeing, the Abergavenny man raised his sword and slashed at Raymond. But his blow never fell. Borard's spearpoint punched through the air to strike his midriff. A good-looking man of thirty with long black hair, Borard smiled behind his beard as he dragged the weapon from the dead man's stomach.

'Brainless bastard,' he said, sending a toothy grin in his captain's direction.

'We attack those men,' Raymond said. His horse skittered excitedly in small twists in front of his warriors who had quickly surrounded their leader. He pointed towards Sir William's men who gathered in front of the Welsh homestead. Sir William was already halfway to them and Raymond knew that speed was all if the men from Striguil were to survive a fight in the hills against the superior force. 'We kill them all and then turn around and deal with those bastards over by the valley.' He hoped that without Sir William's leadership the smaller number of men in the distance would not react as quickly to the change of events and that the Striguil men could take advantage by attacking the larger group.

'No ransoms,' Raymond commanded, knowing that some would be tempted to take prisoners. If they did that then they would be out of the fight and he could little afford to lose any of them. 'Then let's go,' he shouted as he hauled his courser, Dreigiau, around to look at the farmstead. The swift courser fought against the bridle for a second before he spotted the Abergavenny men in the distance. He then understood what his master desired and Raymond let the reins slacken so that the horse could take the lead. His legs still gripped Dreigiau's flanks, urging him onwards with a squeeze. As he rode Raymond realised that he had not recovered his lance from the man he had killed and so he drew his mace from his belt.

His milites fell in behind him, gnashing their teeth as they thundered towards the enemy. Wind whipped at their surcoats and, as they hoisted their weapons to strike, their crimson and gold pennants flickered like dragons' tongues. Some couched the eight-feet long lances under their armpits, but most held them over-arm, ready to stab down into the faces, chests and horses of their enemies.

The staccato crash as the two sets of horsemen collided

33

was stupendous and frightened the sheep and cattle into a hurried flight. Raymond's line of horsemen strafed across the front of the static Abergavenny men, prodding and provoking, stabbing, always moving as they defended their flanks from counters with their leaf-shaped shields. Spinning their horses, they retreated out of range before returning to send more warriors tumbling to the cold ground with gaping wounds.

'St Maurice!' Raymond bellowed his family's war cry as he barrelled through the centre of the enemy riders at full pace. Immediately he was lost in the tight throng as four Abergavenny horsemen surrounded him, and it looked like there was no way he could possibly escape unscathed from the circling mass of men, colourful shields and sweaty, grunting horses. But the men in Abergavenny blue and red began tumbling from their saddles to leave Raymond alone on horseback, looking for more targets. A smile was plastered across his face.

It was at this moment that Sir William de Braose collided with Raymond, throwing the Striguil captain from the saddle and onto the ground. His ringing lance had struck Raymond's shield plum on the boss, but it was the bone-crunching impact with the ground which ripped away Raymond's leather chin strap and sent his helmet skittering away.

'Raymond, you bastard,' the Lord of Abergavenny shouted as he circled his horse around and tapped his spurs to the flanks of his destrier. Raymond pulled himself to his feet, eighty pounds of chainmail and weaponry jangling loudly as his enemy thundered towards him. He was winded but unhurt and threw himself across the face of the horse at the last second to avoid the lance tip as it slashed past him. Sir William thundered away, sending clods of earth in the air as Raymond tumbled onto his shoulders and to his feet in one supple movement. He let his enemy go and sprinted towards Walter de Bloet, who was sheltering below his shield as another of the Abergavenny warriors pounded at him manically with stroke after stroke of his sword. The man cried out joyfully as every blow fell upon Walter's shield while his horse snapped and butted at his legs. Raymond let his shield swing onto his back by the guige, and dropped his mace so that it dangled from his arm as he ran. He pushed into the circling fracas of horses and grabbed the Abergavenny horseman by the ankle, using his strength to hoist him out of his saddle and onto the ground before he even knew that Raymond was there. He brought his mace down once to finish the enemy warrior.

Raymond had barely time to turn as Walter shouted a warning: 'Beware right!'

Another unseated man ran at him, screaming incoherently with his sword held over his head and blood streaming from beneath his wide-brimmed helmet. Raymond calmly swung his shield from his back and onto his left, sliding his arm into the tight enarmes on its rear. Crouched behind the leaf-shaped defence Raymond was protected from his eyes to his ankle. He took the first ringing blow on the steel boss in the middle of the shield. It was like striking a ton of wet sand and Raymond grunted as he shoved the Abergavenny warrior backwards a few steps with his shoulder before bringing the heavy shield up to horizontal and jabbing the man in the face with the pointed end. The man yelped at the unanticipated move and slashed wildly in his foe's direction. Raymond was ready and he danced out of its way, smashing the iron and steel mace straight into the man's face as his opponent's momentum took him forwards. The swordsman was unconscious before he slammed into the ground.

Amid the blood and carnage of the battle, Raymond began to laugh. He held his mace above his head in salute to the glory of the fight. His bare forearm already shone red and all around him men gaped at him as he whooped like a wolf at the sky.

Two more Abergavenny men came at Raymond. Pushing the mace into his belt, he drew his sword and attacked, his strokes a blur of grey steel that drove back both men. It looked odd that Raymond, short and stout, could perform such flawless swordsmanship against the two taller men who faced him, but his frame disguised his formidable fighting skills. He was twenty-four years old, a warrior and a captain. Those who did not know the portly Norman thought him too young to be captain of Strongbow's household warriors, too inexperienced to command. They saw him laughing and drinking with his milites and believed him to be a fool, too familiar with the men he was meant to be commanding. They dismissed him as insignificant and called him *Raymond le Gros*. But beneath the friendly exterior was a hard and skilful warrior of great renown on the March of Wales.

The two men struggled to hold off his attack as they backtracked. Their chainmail hauberks stopped Raymond's blows from puncturing the skin but could not prevent the power and weight of his sword causing severe bruising. Sir William's men fell back before Raymond's offensive.

'Come back,' he shouted as the two men finally fled his onslaught. 'You can't run away from Raymond the Fat.' He tilted his head back and laughed long and hard. 'Alright, maybe you can,' he shouted at the duo's backs as they sprinted away with the remainder of William de Braose's warriors. He watched as they made their way to regroup with the other horsemen at the mouth to the valley.

His courser was watching the fight from nearby, his ears twitching nervously. Raymond walked over and soothed

36

Dreigiau's nose. Horses whose riders had been unseated wandered listlessly around Dreigiau, as if awaiting his guidance.

'Good boy,' Raymond told his courser. The conrois' only casualty was Harald of Wallingford. He was pale, suffering from a vicious cut to his groin which was spouting blood that would not stop. Raymond knew that his miles would probably not survive, but he bound the wound tightly and then lifted Harald onto the back of a nearby horse on his stomach, stuffing his good leg into a stirrup.

Raymond then jumped up onto Dreigiau's back and looked across the grassy expanse at Sir William's men. He counted eighteen on horseback, almost double the number at his disposal, and they still blocked his path home through the valley to Striguil.

'What are we going to do?' Bertram d'Alton asked as he pulled up alongside his commander. 'Find a way back to Usk through the mountains?'

Raymond considered the question and studied the landscape for any advantage that he could use against Sir William de Braose. 'We ride hard and fast...' he began, but his warriors never heard the end of their captain's order. A new, distinctive sound interrupted his words and every head turned towards the valley mouth to the south.

Suddenly everything had changed.

The noise was like the wings of a hundred birds hurrying to the air. It was the twang of bowstrings, Welsh bowstrings, and it was Sir William de Braose's men who were the target of the arrow shafts. By the time that Sir William's men had even realised that they were under attack, the Welshmen each had two more arrows in the air and a fourth being nocked onto their bowstrings. Thirty of the best marksmen the March of Wales could offer had approached the Normans through the forest to the west and their arrows were tearing apart the Abergavenny horsemen.

And worse, Sir William hesitated.

The Lord of Abergavenny had learned to fight in England and France against well-ordered cavalry and infantry. Archers were an entirely different proposition to anything he had ever encountered before. Unsure of whether to advance or retreat further into the trees, he dithered as around him his men fell to the deadly arrow storm.

'The Welsh will deal with them,' the esquire, William de Vale, told Raymond with a happy glint in his eyes. 'And then we can escape!' Some others joined the mirth at their enemy's misfortune until Borard told them to shut up. He saw the look on his commander's face and it was not delight which he perceived. Raymond watched the attack on the men of Abergavenny in grave silence.

'New plan,' Raymond stated so that all his warriors could hear him. 'First, we get to those houses.' He indicated towards the thatched, squat rooftops of the Welsh homestead from which William de Braose had appeared before their fight. 'Dismount, stay low and go fast,' he commanded. A jangle of chainmail and weaponry accompanied the motion as the men leapt down from horseback. They crouched, shields swung onto shoulders, and turned their spears upside down so that the sun did not reflect off their bright blades and give away their position to the sharp-eyed Welsh archers. Raymond led them at a jog slightly north and westwards before looping south towards the Welsh wattle-and-mud buildings.

'Shut up,' he whispered loudly at William de Vale who had begun talking again. 'And don't you lose those spurs,' he warned the youngster. William, an esquire on the verge of ending his apprenticeship, had been given a set of cheap

38

spurs and told not to misplace them or face a forfeit. Of course the other horsemen had spent the rest of the journey from Usk trying to steal them from him, dreaming up ever worsening punishments when he found that they had taken.

It was only a few hundred paces to the houses and Raymond went quickly. There was no time to scout ahead, not if he was going to stop the Welsh from wiping out all of Sir William de Braose's raiders. Instead Raymond gripped his lance tightly and kept an eye firmly on the buildings as he approached. In the long grass he stumbled over the first body. It was a young Welsh boy.

'God's teeth,' William de Vale exclaimed. There was a gaping wound across the boy's face. Hoof marks dotted the ground around his prone body. One of the Abergavenny horsemen had cut him down as he ran for his life.

'Keep moving,' Borard hissed. He grabbed William by the shoulder as he stopped to stare at the body, and shoved him in the direction of the low, thatched houses which loomed a short distance ahead.

As they approached the first building, Raymond indicated that his warriors should stop and allow him to go forward alone. He handed his reins to Borard and hefted a crossbow in both hands, darting between two of the houses. The walls were made of twisted branches and cut turf which had been recently repaired with mud, smeared thick. Weeds grew tall in the crammed space. Flies careered around his head. The upland farmstead had probably been used for generations by the same family, visited only in the summer months to allow their winter pastures in the lowlands to recover.

It would never be used again, he quickly understood.

Still hidden between the buildings, Raymond stared into the small communal area in the middle of the group of buildings. His shallow breath stopped dead as he gazed between the upturned wicker baskets and forgotten cooking fires. He had feared ambush in the village, but he knew now that there would be none for the trap had already closed. It had claimed the lives of the Welsh family.

Raymond could see at least twelve bodies. The men had obviously attempted to put up a fight, but farmers could not hope to win against armoured warriors. Three women lay in disturbing, contorted positions. It was obvious what had happened. The men of Abergavenny had ridden north, away from Strongbow's sacked manors, when they had discovered that they were being tracked. Half the force had hidden downwind to the east while the larger group had taken up position amongst the houses. They had laid a snare for Raymond. To aid the deception, and to make sure that those who pursued them were not alerted to the trap, Sir William had silenced every voice in the village.

Raymond stepped out from beneath the shadow of the building, his crossbow still raised. There was not a sound within the farmstead, but he could still hear the shouts of the battle going on between Seisyll's Welshmen and Sir William de Braose's horsemen. For a moment he considered abandoning his plan to assist the lordly creature who had ordered the massacre.

'I should let Seisyll exact justice,' he muttered, his jaw set in anger as he looked down on the body of another child.

Movement to his right caused him to swing around, his considerations swept away by a surge of fear. A woman was tied by her arms to a spear staked deep in ground and had been muffled by a red and blue pennant. She kicked in a last, desperate effort to free her hands, her eyes frantic and locked on Raymond's crossbow.

'It's alright,' he told the girl in stuttering Welsh. 'I will not hurt you.' She was not the only person who still lived. Tied to the same stake, beaten bloody and purple with bruises, was a young man. The only reason that Raymond knew he was living was because he too was bound. The boy did not even need to be gagged, such were the extent of his injuries. The captain wondered who the girl was and why she and the unconscious boy alone had been spared death.

'The Devil take them,' said a shocked Borard as he came to Raymond's side and caught sight of the bodies. He produced a dagger from his belt and moved to cut the girl's bonds.

'Leave her,' Raymond told him, 'for now. This way.' The captain waved for Borard to follow him back outside the village where his dismounted milites awaited his orders. He took a deep breath before turning towards the bearded Borard. 'This is what we are going to do. Get each of our men to go into the village and find a body – tell them to do it quietly! They must bring one back and then get them up on a separate courser. They must be sitting straight up, not strung across on their bellies.' He raised his arm to vertical in front of him to emphasise his point.

'How will they stay upright?' Borard looked confused at Raymond's odd commands, but knew better than to question them; his captain had a plan and he was willing to trust that it was one that would bring the Striguil men victory.

'Slide a lance down through the neck of their shirts and then through their trouser leg,' he suggested. 'Then tie their feet under the coursers' bellies and their hands to the pommels. Bind the end of each lance to one of the stirrups so that it cannot fall out.' Borard nodded in answer and dashed off to complete his task.

Raymond watched his warriors' reaction as Borard delivered his orders. Most swapped confused glances with their fellows, shifting their weight from foot to foot as they attempted to comprehend. After a few seconds, the first few broke away and cantered towards the Welsh houses to carry out his instructions. The older men followed more soberly,

41

still questioning Borard about Raymond's plan as they disappeared between the buildings. Raymond did not follow. Instead he grabbed the bridle of the horse carrying Harald of Wallingford. The injured warrior whimpered and bit down on his lip to mask his pain. Blood dribbled freely from his right foot to the ground.

'Harald, I need one last favour of you today,' Raymond said as the first of men, Nicholas de Lyvet, returned dragging a dead Welshman towards the horses. Within seconds more of his men had passed by and begun their work.

'I am leaving you with our coursers,' Raymond told Harald. The injured man looked pained and pale but he nodded his head aggressively, his eyes screwed shut to mask the hurt. 'I want you to walk them northwards. The rest of the horses will be nervous, but they will flock behind you,' Raymond continued. 'Lead them north,' he repeated, 'and make sure the Welsh see you. Make them think we are retreating.' Raymond squeezed his friend's shoulder. 'Go north for five minutes and then circle back. Five minutes then wait for us to get back to the farmstead.'

'I can do that,' Harald replied.

Raymond smiled and squeezed Harald's forearm. He turned to find that his milites had accomplished his orders far more easily than he had imagined. Each of their nine horses had a body tied to their saddles. From close up they looked like the company of corpse-warriors from the nightmares of children, but Raymond knew that from this distance and in the fading light, the Welsh would only see tired Norman warriors, spear pennants fluttering above them, as they retreated in the face of an overwhelming show of force.

With a final glance towards the heavens, he slapped Harald's courser on the flank and watched as the Englishman rode away from the farmstead. Nine ill-at-ease

42

coursers with dead Welsh villagers strapped securely to their saddles followed him.

'Christ on his cross, Raymond,' hissed Walter de Bloet as he watched the coursers follow, 'you are sending them away with bloody Harald? He's half dead! How will we get away from the Welsh if they scatter?'

Raymond felt the all too familiar frustration rising in his throat. Not a day had gone by since his advancement to command of Strongbow's conrois ahead of Walter that he had not been the recipient of one of his snide comments. He had questioned every order. Every slip-up was reported.

'The captain knows what he is doing,' Borard answered sternly before raising a hopeful eyebrow at Raymond.

'I promise you that we will make it home,' Raymond whispered to his men who collected around him. 'I swear it to St Maurice,' he stated confidently. 'Shields, crossbows and sidearms,' he stated, giving his own crossbow a small shake. Each man nodded back to indicate that they were armed and ready. 'Follow me then,' Raymond said and gestured for his men to follow him back into the farmstead. 'Stay quiet,' he added. Despite the order his men were loud as they jogged through the buildings to the far end of the village. Chainmail rattled and weapons clattered off benches and walls. Wooden shields rang as they bumped together and one man cursed loudly as he caught his armoured knee on a cooking pot hung beside an open fire.

'Quiet, damn you,' Borard angered under his breath and forced the man onwards past the two people, still gagged and tied to the post.

Raymond reached the edge of the village first. There, he watched the fight going on between the Abergavenny men and the Welsh. It was, to Raymond's eye, less a battle than it was a bloodbath. Without crossbows or archers, Sir William de Braose's horsemen could not fight back. The

English lord had finally moved his men back under the shelter of the forest, but Raymond knew that the horsemen would still be taking damage from the arrows as they punched through the treetops and rebounded off trunks. Had it been he in Sir William's position he would've fled from the field as fast as he could, for the Welsh could not hope to keep up with the Normans on horseback. However, he suspected that the Lord of Abergavenny would think it dishonourable to follow that course of action.

The Welshmen, meanwhile, were lost in the mechanical action of unleashing their bombardment upon the hated invader of their lands. The marksmen did not even require order from their leader, but nocked and loosed arrow after arrow wherever a target presented itself. Some had even emerged from the forest and had turned their backs on the buildings where Raymond's men were hidden in order to get a better shot at Sir William's men.

Raymond turned on his heels and looked beyond his warriors, huddled behind him, and back over the thatched roofs. On the low ridge a quarter of a mile away, he spied Harald and his macabre column moving slowly away. He knew that the Welsh leader – perhaps Lord Seisyll for all Raymond knew – would've posted men to keep an eye on the smaller group of Normans while he destroyed William de Braose. He urged the Welsh scouts to spot his feint and to respond to it in an aggressive manner.

'Come on, see Harald. Move,' he whispered towards the woods which hid the archers. Moments later Raymond smiled as the Welshmen did exactly what he had hoped: believing the threat of the cavalry to be gone, they ran out of the trees to take up a better position to finish off Sir William de Braose and the men of Abergavenny.

'This is it lads,' Raymond whispered to his troops. 'We go forward quickly and quietly in two ranks. Do not stop or they will cut us down with their arrows.' Each of his men nodded their assent, their fingers dancing on their crossbow triggers.

The fields stretched southwards for less than a half mile to where began the forested pass back to Striguil. Thirty long-haired Welshmen streamed out of the forest into the meadow and began to loose their arrows again. From amongst the trees, screams sounded, more frequent than they had before.

The Welsh were now between Raymond de Carew's men and their home, but they had become completely distracted by their desire to destroy Sir William de Braose and were unaware that there were still Normans behind them; Normans who were now fast approaching their vulnerable backs. Raymond's men advanced quickly, hidden behind their teardrop shields, weapons in hand and their thigh muscles burning due to the crouched stance which took them forward. Only fifty paces remained between the Striguil men and their targets.

'Saesneg!' shouted a Welsh archer in the rear rank of their number. Immediately twenty bows swung around to point at the men of Striguil.

'Brace,' Raymond shouted to his men, all subterfuge forgotten. 'St Maurice will protect us!'

Behind him he heard men begin to inhale heavily in anticipation of what was to come. The first Welsh arrows flew in their direction with a sharp whistle of goose feathers. They smashed into the small Norman force.

'Faster,' he shouted, 'keep tight.' Raymond chanced a fleeting look over the rim of his shield but was forced to duck down when another arrow skimmed off his helmet. A grunt behind him told him that someone had sustained a wound from the glancing blow. The captain did not stop to check but dragged his men forward towards Seisyll's arrows.

'Hold your shape,' he roared. Another flight whistled as they arced towards the Normans. At thirty yards, the arrows partially punched through the wooden shields. Two steel arrowheads poked through close to Raymond's face, causing him a great deal of surprise. He knew that soon their shields would offer no shelter from the powerful Welsh longbows.

'Halt,' he shouted. All his men obeyed the order and then copied their captain, driving the pointed tip of their shields into the soft soil. 'Prepare,' Raymond commanded and watched as the men on either side removed their arms from the leather straps of their shield so that they could heft their crossbow in both hands.

'Aim for their guts!' he called and leaned over his shield. Dead ahead he saw a Welshman, his long brown shirt reaching to his bare knees as he stooped to pull an arrow from the ground. Raymond squeezed the trigger and felt the stock jump as the bolt disappeared and the bowstring snapped forward. All around him the staccato slap sounded as his men unleashed a volley of bolts towards the Welsh. Unlike the Normans, the enemy did not have shields and a clutch of men tumbled to the ground, including the man at whom Raymond had been aiming. Moments later their screams began to echo around the meadow.

'Shields,' Raymond called to his milites. He dropped his crossbow on the ground and drew his sword from his scabbard. 'Quickly - we cannot allow them to reform.' Almost immediately he felt a shield rim lock with his own and he turned to see Borard on his right, a hand axe ready. A second thump made him turn. Dependable Bertram d'Alton had taken up position on his left and beyond him Walter de Bloet, with a sullen look upon his face, made sure his shield overlapped that of his fellow miles.

'Forward!' Raymond commanded.

It was a tiny shieldwall, but it was strong and two ranks thick. Yet Raymond knew that he had to close the gap between his men and the Welsh or the next flight of arrows would cause casualties. He dared not raise his head to look at the enemy for fear that an enemy marksman pierce his eye with his sharpshooting. He knew that an archer could shoot an arrow every five seconds and he knew that if it was to come, the next flight would be soon. Raymond took a deep breath in anticipation and muttered a short prayer to the soldier's saint.

But the enemy's arrows never struck home. Instead a thunder of hooves and a cry of dread caused Raymond to call his conrois to a halt, earning him a questioning look from Borard. Gingerly, both men glanced over the rim of their shields.

A hoot of relief escaped Raymond's lungs as he watched the Welsh dashing towards the woods. Sir William, nestling in the forest, had watched Raymond's brave advance and, feeling the arrow storm lessen as the Welsh had turned to combat the more immediate threat from the men of Striguil, had charged the enemy position, scattering the bowmen. Few were quick enough to outpace Sir William's vengeful horsemen and, as Raymond watched, a number were crushed beneath their charge.

'Let's get them,' exclaimed Denis, pointing his lance at the fleeing Welsh.

'No,' Raymond countered. 'Remain in order. We retreat back to the houses. And keep your eyes on them 'uns from Abergavenny.' He did not want to get caught in the open by the horsemen who, although fighting beside the men of Striguil now, would certainly ride them down if they saw that they had the opportunity. For the moment Sir William's men were venting their aggression on the Welsh.

47

As his warriors edged backwards, Raymond watched the Abergavenny horsemen, so different to the style of his own milites. Strongbow's warriors, like all men of the Welsh March, valued flexibility and speed whereas those led by Sir William put more stock in a knight's ability to keep a secure seat, wield a heavy blade and crush his opponent. And what an adversary Sir William looked as he rode down the archers! A Welshman tumbled below his destrier and the young lord did not even break stride. After he had abandoned his twelve-foot lance in another bowman's spine, Sir William drew his broadsword, cleaving a man's head in two with a single sweep. After him came his milites and they tore into the scattered Welsh like bears.

Raymond's men retreated to the farmstead as the first Welsh survivors of Sir William's charge made it to the relative safety of forest. Raymond was sure he saw Seisyll's bearded face amongst those men, but he could not be sure. It would be a shame if the Welsh chieftain was dead, he thought. The few times they had met, Seisyll had proved a jovial companion, ready to make fun of one and all around him; a good man whether at wine or war.

'What is our condition?' he asked Borard as he entered the farmstead.

His friend didn't answer at once, instead nodding towards the wall of one of the houses where Harald of Wallingford sat propped up, his chin on his chest and his hands limp and bloody on his lap.

'He was dead by the time we made it back,' Borard told his captain.

'Well, at least he died a hero,' Raymond said as he returned his sword to its scabbard. A Welsh archer lay on his back in the middle of the nameless farmstead, a crossbow bolt standing tall in his chest. The bowman, it seemed, had fled the slaughter of the battlefield and made his way to the village where he had been shot by Harald's crossbow. 'We will write a song about his brave end when we get back to Striguil.'

'It wasn't Harald who killed him,' Borard said, lifting his chin towards the horses. Dead dead Welsh bodies still slumped upon their backs. Tending to the coursers was the girl who had been tied up in the village. Harald's crossbow was strapped across her back. She was stroking the coursers' muzzles and speaking to the frightened horses in soothing tones.

'Seems Harald knew that he hadn't much time left and that he couldn't defend our horses. He cut the woman free when he saw the Welshman headed this way,' Borard continued. 'She shot him dead. We found her there, standing over the body laughing and trying to reload.' He lowered his voice. 'She is pretty, there is no doubt about it, but she is possessed of the Devil,' he said with all the certainty of a bishop speaking of Christ's miracles.

'Madam,' Raymond addressed the woman, ignoring Borard's last comment. She immediately brought the crossbow up and pointed the weapon at his chest.

'We didn't mess with her,' Borard whispered from behind him, 'and neither should you.'

Raymond raised one hand in the air and smiled. For a long time he said nothing, but simply stared at the woman amongst the coursers. Eventually Dreigiau walked away from the conrois and nuzzled at his master's hand, encouraging affection and Raymond to hand over a treat.

'Who are you?' the woman suddenly spoke. She did not lower the crossbow.

'I am Raymond.'

'Are you with Sir William?' she asked, shoulder tightening on the crossbow stock. 'If not then why

49

did you help him?'

Raymond looked straight at her. 'He is from England and they,' he pointed a thumb in the direction of a scream which sounded behind him by the forest, 'are Welsh. One is my enemy while the other is merely a rival. Thank you by the way,' he added quickly.

'Thank me for killing that cur?' Her anger was vicious as she kicked the dead Welshman, still lying in the pathway. 'I thought he was one of Sir William's men. You all deserve worse than death.'

'Well, you did me a great service,' Raymond said with a smile so wide it matched her fury, 'and I thank you. Our horses are more important to us than anything else.' He rubbed Dreigiau's back. He knew why the woman was angry. It was a common enough occurrence on both sides of the Welsh-Norman conflict. 'And because of that service I will not stop until I have repaid my debt to you. Anything you ask of me, I will do.' The crossbow dropped an inch as Raymond pushed Dreigiau in the woman's direction. Obediently, his courser walked over to her and pushed his head into her shoulder, forcing her to set down the crossbow and stroke his face with both hands.

'My name is Alice,' she finally admitted, 'and he,' she indicated towards the insensible young man still staked to the ground, 'is Geoffrey, my brother. We are from Abergavenny, but we can never go home while William de Braose is alive.'

More questions were raised in Raymond's mind but he had more pressing matters than interrogating the woman. One thing he was sure of, though: she and her brother were the only people left alive in the village, and that meant that they were valuable to William de Braose and thus worth taking back to Strongbow.

'You should see to your brother. But will you also keep

50

my horses safe again for me, Alice of Abergavenny?' he asked. She nodded blankly and watched suspiciously as he bowed before her and left her amongst the coursers.

William de Vale was complaining and that was a good sign in Raymond's estimation. The esquire was propped up against the wall of a house on the far side of the compound. 'It hurts, it hurts, its hurts. Don't bloody touch it, you bastard,' he shouted at Walter de Bloet who prodded at the arrow shaft which poked from his shoulder.

'Stop bleating like a baby,' Walter replied. 'It was a deflection and it hasn't hit anything major. I have cut off the barb so we may as well get it out now. Grit your teeth and I will give it a tug.'

'You'll do no such thing until I get a mug of mead in my belly,' replied William.

'How is he?' Raymond asked Walter.

'He won't let me pull the arrow out, but you possess medical skills beyond mine,' Walter said as he climbed to his feet and walked away. 'So you can deal with it.'

Raymond ignored Walter's ire and knelt down beside the esquire to examine the wound. 'What's today's forfeit for losing the spurs?'

William's face dropped as if he was threatened with another arrow to the shoulder. 'Oh no,' he said and began desperately searching his clothes with his uninjured hand.

'Head shaved into a Benedictine tonsure, isn't it? Bertram is a right bastard for suggesting that penalty,' Raymond said as he produced the spurs from his own pocket. He clicked his tongue disapprovingly. 'But I think that you can do without the forfeit this one time. It'll be our secret.' He held out the spurs to William. As the esquire leaned forward to take them Raymond shot his hand out and tugged the arrow shaft from his shoulder in one swift movement. William screeched and leant forward, holding

51

his wound and cursing the woman who had given Raymond de Carew life.

'Good lad,' Raymond said, giggling at the esquire's expletive tirade. 'Get someone to clean it and bind it.' He turned to Walter, standing a little way off and watching him. 'Get those bodies down off the coursers. I suggest that you don't annoy the woman,' he warned, lifting his chin in the direction of Alice of Abergavenny.

'Horseman approaching!' The warning came from the edge of the settlement and it prevented Walter from arguing with his captain. Raymond walked slowly towards the rattle of hooves which came from beyond the farmstead's limits. The noise slowed as the rider came close and, as he cleared the buildings, Raymond was able to see that it was an esquire in the livery of Abergavenny who approached the settlement. Three more men waited outside crossbow range for permission to approach. Raymond, chainmail hauberk hood down on his shoulders, stepped out and nodded to the youngster, letting him know that it was alright for his master to approach. The lightly-armed boy turned around and cantered back towards his comrades with his answer. Moments later, Raymond met Sir William de Braose for the second time that day.

'Sir William,' Raymond reached up and took his destrier's bridle in his hand as he acknowledged the knight. Two warriors were with the young lord, still with Welsh blood wet upon their weaponry.

'Raymond,' Sir William jumped down from his steed, ignoring the captain's outstretched hand, staring instead into the heart of the farmstead. 'I owe you thanks, I suppose, despite you being a callous breaker of the peace. Still, you did save us from Seisyll's tricks,' he said and finally greeted Raymond by shaking his hand. In spite of his smile, there was something in Sir William de Braose's eyes that Raymond did not trust. He eyed the nobleman's two men-at-arms who had remained in the saddle and shifted uncomfortably. Raymond wondered why they were so nervous. Sir William's attempt to appear friendly was even more concerning, but he was not about to start another fight with the Abergavenny men, not unless it was unavoidable. He still needed a way back to Striguil.

'Can I offer you some mutton?' Raymond asked, inviting him to join him on a bench outside one of the buildings. 'My men have rounded up the animals that belonged to this farmstead. I suspect that their former owners will no longer need them.'

'Perfect. I'm famished. Killing Welshmen does build up a mighty hunger.'

Nodding despite his disgust, Raymond leant in close and whispered into Borard's ear. The miles, who had followed him to the parley, then walked back into the farmstead to organise food while his captain offered Sir William a stool in the shade of the houses. 'We had best sit outside the walls,' he told his guest, 'the stink in there is unimaginable.' He indicated back towards the centre of the village where his men were removing the dead Welsh bodies from the back of their coursers. Sir William looked momentarily discomfited, but Raymond quickly changed tack. 'So old Seisyll got away?'

'He did,' William de Braose replied. 'If I had been able to lay my hands on him I would have been awfully popular with my mother.'

Raymond laughed politely. It was said that Seisyll had murdered William's uncle, the former Lord of Abergavenny, Henry de Hereford, some years before and as Sir William reminded him of the story Raymond studied the young nobleman. A favourite of King Henry, Raymond remembered hearing, and heir to one of the most powerful barons in England. His mother had brought the powerful Welsh fiefs of Abergavenny and Brecon to her marriage bed and it seemed that her son had taken control of those lands in her name. What possible reason had brought William de Braose on this unimportant raid into Strongbow's lands, Raymond could not imagine. He suspected that it involved Alice of Abergavenny and her brother, Geoffrey, but as yet he did not know how they fitted into that story.

'Good, good,' Sir William smiled at Borard who returned a little while later with bread and mutton in carved wooden bowls. As they ate, the two men swapped news from around Wales and England. The biggest gossip was that Prince Owain of Gwynedd had died and his son, Hywel, was facing rebellion by his stepmother and half-brothers.

'I hear that Hywel has been forced to flee to Ireland by the savage woman and that she keeps her sons prisoner,' Sir William told Raymond with a laugh. 'Speaking of Ireland - what about that scoundrel Robert FitzStephen and decrepit old Maurice FitzGerald? I hear that they have done exceedingly well for themselves. They've managed to get their hands on a Norse town. I may put together an adventure of my own and get a bit of this land across the sea that seems so easy to take.'

Raymond nodded and smiled. It was obvious that Sir William did not realise that he was talking to the nephew of both men. He also knew that his reason for coming back to the farmstead was not to talk about mercenaries in distant Ireland. He waited for an opportune pause in conversation. 'So what can I do for you, Sir William? You are free to leave, or track Seisyll at your leisure. I am sure that you don't need my help for that.' He lifted the bony remnants of lamb from his own dish and pointed at the forest. 'But in case you do, he went that way.'

Sir William grimaced as he slowly finished his mouthful of oatcake and mutton. 'I have an offer for you, Raymond,' he said. 'We left two alive amongst these houses. I will give you ten marks for them both.'

'A lot of money,' Raymond nodded. 'So who are you getting for such a price?'

'No one of importance,' Sir William claimed. A nervous smile stretched across his face. 'Escaped prisoners only.'

'Expensive prisoners.'

Sir William's cheeks flared pink. 'I think you will find the toll to pass through the valley expensive also.' He nodded southwards. Raymond could see a number of fires which gave away the position of the Abergavenny warriors. 'Hand over my prisoners and I will let you go with my thanks and pocket full of silver.'

Raymond did not have the chance to answer. A scream behind them startled both men who jumped to their feet spilling their stew on the ground. Alice of Abergavenny burst from between the houses fumbling with her crossbow. In her haste she dropped the bolt and stooped to retrieve it. Behind her came young Geoffrey, her brother, heavily bruised but finally conscious and pleading with his sister to stop.

'You!' she yelled at Sir William, ignoring Geoffrey as the tears poured down her dirty face. Finally righting the crossbow, she brought it up and pointed it at the nobleman's chest.

Sir William raised a hand as another smile spread across his face. 'Alice, my love,' he managed to mumble before she squeezed the crossbow's release trigger. It was a point blank shot and he could not have done anything to stop the bolt. Not even a shield could stop a quarrel at that range, but in her anger Alice had not taken aim properly and the bolt seared through the surcoat and between his legs to become buried in the green grass at his rear. Not that Sir William realised immediately that he was not injured. He sprawled on the ground, only recognising that he was not hurt after a few seconds of searching his body for a wound.

'Kill her,' he commanded his two followers.

Alice was on her knees, crying and muttering incoherently. The boy, Geoffrey, stood over her, fists raised and fear evident on his bruised and swollen face. He tried to calm his sister and pulled the crossbow from her hands in an effort to defend her from the two advancing men-at-arms, but he did not have any crossbow shafts to shoot or the strength to load it.

In any event, Raymond stepped between William de Braose's warriors and the two youngsters, his bulk as intimidating as any castle. 'You will not touch her,' he said, all trace of friendliness and humour gone as he pointed the leg of lamb at them as if it was a weapon. Both men had watched Raymond in action earlier in the day and had heard the many stories of his prowess in battle, but they seemed doubtful as they watched the stout man with the friendly face place his hand on Alice's head. They may have been nervous but had been given a command by their lord and so they stalked forward tentatively, step by step, ready to strike.

'I wouldn't bloody try it if I were you,' a voice sounded behind the two men. It was Borard and he had Sir William on his knees, one hand gripping a bunch of the nobleman's long hair at the nape of his neck. The other held a dagger across his throat. Sir William tried to struggle but Borard held him still in a powerful grip. 'One move and he is dead.' Borard smiled as he spoke. Glancing at each other, the Abergavenny men lowered their swords and waited while Raymond's men, drawn out of the farmstead by the noise, gruffly took hold of their hauberks, throwing them to their knees in the dusty mud like their lord. Sir William grimaced at his warriors' meek compliance.

'I'll ask again,' Raymond rounded on Sir William. 'Who are these two that you so badly want dead?' The young lord licked his front teeth beneath his sweaty upper lip, but said nothing. A nod from Raymond brought a huge clout from Borard's forearm across William's head.

'The Devil take you,' Sir William shouted in shock. His two warriors frowned but could do nothing to assist their lord. After a few seconds of rubbing the back of his head, the Lord of Abergavenny finally acquiesced and told Raymond what he wanted to know: 'They are the bastards of Henry de Hereford, my uncle,' he said, aiming a murderous glance at Borard.

'That's a lie!' the young man, Geoffrey, exclaimed and jumped to his feet. 'Father Peter told you that our parents were married under the eyes of God.' His was an educated voice, like that of a priest or clerk.

Sir William laughed sharply to show his disdain for Geoffrey's opinion. 'I tell all my whores that I will marry them if they spread their legs wide enough,' he sneered and looked pointedly at Alice, who began bawling even more violently. Grinning, Sir William shifted his view back to Geoffrey. 'And if you had stayed in the monastery like a good little boy you would have had a fine life for a bastard.'

'Enough,' Raymond told them. He already knew what had befallen, or could guess it; a rival claimant to a great castle had been discarded as illegitimate and hidden in a monastery. It was not the first time such a thing had occurred; however, there seemed to be much more to Alice's story, a darker tale Raymond reckoned, and Sir William de Braose was central to it.

'I imagine that you do not want to return to your Holy

Order?' Raymond addressed Geoffrey, but he looked to Alice to answer.

'I am the rightful Lord of Abergavenny,' Geoffrey stood slowly, bruises and blood covering his face, 'as was my father, and I will no longer be an oblate at a monastery, but a warrior and a lord of a great citadel.'

Sir William laughed scathingly until Borard shook him to silence.

Raymond could see the tears glistening Geoffrey's eyes in the effort of holding his gaze. Half of him wanted to chuckle at this frail youth who wanted to challenge the power of William de Braose for a barony in the Welsh mountains. The other part of Raymond pitied the desperate young man who obviously had spirit and bravery to match that of his sister.

'If that is your wish then you have the protection of Raymond de Carew. You and the Lady Alice will travel with us back to Striguil where your case will be judged by Strongbow.'

Geoffrey allowed a long breath to release from his mouth while his sister bit her lip to hold back the tears.

'Thank you,' Geoffrey managed to say.

'What will we do with him, Raymond?' asked Borard as he gave Sir William a small kick. 'We could get a big ransom for this one. Those two might fetch something too,' he indicated towards the two men-at-arms who still stood in their midst.

Raymond considered the question. On the one hand it would make the journey a profitable enterprise, but he knew that it would not end there. William de Braose's father, Lord Bramber, was rich and powerful and would surely seek vengeance on those who had brought about the ignominious fall of his heir. Doubtless that would mean a determined assault on the lands and castle at isolated Usk.

58

Raymond did the calculation in his head and there was only one outcome that was beneficial to his master, Strongbow.

'We will release Sir William and his men. Take their weapons, armour and saddles. Then take their oaths that in return for their release they will not attack us,' Raymond told his subaltern. 'Then to make sure of that, take their clothes and send them on their way.' Within minutes Raymond's men had chivvied the three naked warriors of Abergavenny towards their horses at spearpoint. As soon as he was free Sir William, furious at such treatment of a knight, began spewing venom on the men of Striguil.

'You will be sorry for choosing a whore and a bastard over my friendship,' he shouted at the captain as he spun his horse on the dusty ground a few metres away. 'If we should cross swords again, Raymond the Fat, you will die painfully like the pig you are.' With a final spin and glare of pure rancour, the naked knight was gone back towards his troops in the forest.

'Well,' Raymond turned towards his troops standing silently at his back, 'that was dramatic.' As they giggled, the captain knelt and delicately lifted Alice to her knees.

'I am not a whore,' she appealed to Raymond. 'He is my cousin,' she moaned, 'and he said that he would help Geoffrey if I...' she began to sob again, 'but he lied.'

Raymond smiled and lifted her to her feet so that she could bury her head in his shoulder. He then gently hoisted her legs into his arms and carried her back into the farmstead. There, he laid her down on his cloak between the horses and the roaring fire and left her to whimper and to sleep. As he turned to leave she reached up and took hold of two of his fingers. She said nothing but looked deep into his eyes. He smiled and held her gaze. Alice let go as her brother approached and rolled up into Raymond's cloak.

'Thank you for helping us, my lord,' Geoffrey said softly.

'Call me Raymond, and you have no need to thank me,' he smiled. 'Thank your sister. She saved our horses and for that I will long be in her debt. I will take you back to Striguil with us, but do not expect a warm welcome from Earl Strongbow. Your presence could make the whole region unstable, especially if Sir William or his father gets King Henry involved.' The boy looked at Raymond, trying to understand how his squabble with his cousin could possibly involve the King of England. The captain smiled. 'Don't worry, lad,' he said, 'take care of your sister now and I will protect you both. We leave tomorrow before first light.'

'How will you get home if Sir William blockades the valley mouth?'

Raymond nodded the wall of the nearest house. Bows and bundles of Welsh arrows had been salvaged from the battlefield by his men. None had been left for the Abergavenny warriors to scavenge. 'The same way that Seisyll did it,' he described. 'But with a little more success, I would suggest.'

With that Raymond went back to his men and made sure that they were all getting some much-needed rest and food. He then congratulated them on their great skills during the fight, recanting the story of William de Vale's injury much to their delight. While they began their teasing of the esquire Raymond wandered towards the edge of the farmstead to take the first watch. There, alone with his thoughts for the first time that day, he passed the time planning the next day's adventure which would take him back to Striguil and to Strongbow, his lord.

Raymond smiled as the sun sank behind the hills. Munching on a large piece of mutton, he reckoned that it was good to be a warlord on the March of Wales.

Chapter Two

Strongbow stared out between the stone merlons that topped Striguil Castle as Raymond's conrois rode down from the hills of Wentwood. He espied a woman in the saddle behind Raymond, holding on tightly to his midriff, and that interested the earl far more than the lateness of his captain's return. Even from where he stood on the great stone keep, Strongbow could see that the woman was a beauty and how closely she gripped his captain's sides. Her head rested on Raymond's mailed shoulder and their blonde locks mingled as the wind whipped around them so that he could not tell where Raymond's hair ended and the woman's began. He could see her bare legs on either flank of the dark courser.

'Your friend Raymond seems to have found himself a *companion*,' Strongbow said to his daughter who hugged his arm to shield her from the gusts which rode up the steep white cliffs of the Gwy Valley. 'Obviously this woman is of a rank suited to his tastes.'

Basilia blushed at her father's suggestion. 'Raymond is a good Christian man,' she told him, 'and I am sure that he has been a perfect gentleman whatever her station.' From below her white linen wimple, she too watched as Raymond and the woman with the wild hair approached through the fields worked by her father's serfs. A sudden pang of possessiveness rose in her chest as she watched her childhood friend frolic with the newcomer, and Basilia scolded herself for the impulse. A long intake of air seemed

61

to wash away the wayward emotion and gave her a moment to reflect on her surprise that Raymond the Fat had caused any feelings like that to arise. Embarrassed, she turned her head away from the conrois and stared southwards towards the bridge in the distance. Basilia attempted to picture her husband, Sir Roger de Quincy, somewhere in the castle below nursing a horrid hangover, but her efforts and affections fell short.

'Raymond is late,' her father commented, 'exceptionally late. He was supposed to have returned three days ago. I wonder if he lost his way?' He raised a sandy eyebrow in his daughter's direction. 'Or could it be that something else waylaid him?' He giggled, enjoying the effect of his gentle teasing, as Basilia playfully punched her father in the side. In truth Strongbow was angry at Raymond's tardiness. A flurry of effort, early mornings and late nights, had allowed him to have everything ready to go to France to visit King Henry, but he had been unable to do so without leaving someone in command of Striguil. He had assumed that would be Raymond, but in the end, despairing of his captain, Strongbow had acquiesced to Roger de Quincy's request and agreed to leave his son-in-law in charge of his estates. Raymond would now join the earl on the journey across the sea, partially as punishment and somewhat as a necessity: France had been in turmoil for years thanks to the expansionist policies of the King of England. Henry had sought to impose his laws on more and more French lords, just as he had done in England, and stretch his rule beyond Normandy, Brittany, Maine, Anjou, and Touraine to Aquitaine and the Pyrenees Mountains. Dispossessed men who had stood against the king's authority were said to roam France causing trouble wherever they could, raping and pillaging, and waylaying travellers. The earl reckoned that Raymond's fighting skills would be far more use than Roger de Quincy's quick tongue if they stumbled into one of those gangs of bandits on their journey.

Strongbow stooped to test his knees. He groaned with the effort. He had spent the last few days at the great abbey of Tyndyrn, endowed by his grandfather's brother almost fifty years before. There he had prayed to St Benedict for a swift and fruitful end to what would be his most important journey in many years. Strongbow had already made a solemn promise that he would donate another large swathe of land to the Cistercian brothers if his journey to France was a success. It was a gamble for him to even appear in King Henry's presence and he reckoned that he could use every piece of good fortune available to him. He had prayed to each of the Trinity, begged the assistance of saints strange and familiar, from across Christendom and even from amongst the Welsh pantheon. Strongbow had beseeched holy icons for help, and had paid for the influence of priests, but it would all be worth it if they would intercede on his behalf. King Henry was known to be the most turbulent king ever to sit upon the English throne; constantly plotting, always suspicious. Nothing escaped his notice. And yet Strongbow had to make the journey so that he could obtain a definite licence from the king to invade Ireland and aid Diarmait Mac Murchada in the recovery of his throne. He felt sure that he had to meet Henry face to face and demand his independence in the presence of his bishops and nobles. That way the king could not consequently claim Richard had contravened his commands nor have reason to declare his estates in Wales forfeit. Strongbow's heart fluttered with nerves as he imagined his meeting with the king. He reached out and placed a hand on the wall of his castle. The damp stone steadied him and strengthened his resolve. The king had no claim over Striguil, he reminded himself. From his position atop the keep, the earl stared southwards towards the two towers which dominated the gates and beyond, over the deep fosse, to the weather beaten cliffs which defended one side of the castle.

You are the Earl Strongbow, he repeated over and over again.

'I am going indoors, Lord Father,' Basilia said suddenly and angrily, interrupting his thoughts. She curtsied once before crossing the heavy oak roof to the tower which led back towards the solar, main hall and the rest of the castle rooms.

Strongbow wondered momentarily what he had said to annoy his daughter, before dismissing the girl's irrational behaviour and returning to his vigil, watching Raymond as he passed through the town and then into the castle bailey. His warlord jumped down from horseback at the marshalsea before taking the young woman by her hips to help her from his courser. Both laughed at the small exchange and Strongbow felt his lips purse in anger at the sight of Raymond the Fat with a beautiful woman on his arm. The wind off the estuary buffeted Strongbow's gold and crimson surcoat and the slowly fading orange-red locks upon his head. He was jealous of his servant, he realised. He was carefree. He did not have to meet with King Henry.

The earl sighed, wishing that his mother was still alive to counsel him. She had always been confident and decisive no matter the circumstances, and her wise words would have been comforting to him now. He looked to the heavens and said another prayer to St Peter for his true hand of guidance in the coming weeks.

For the hundredth time he questioned whether he was indeed doing the right thing by going to France. His legacy, and possibly his life, depended on successfully convincing Henry to grant him licence to leave his service. Raymond's absence had meant that he had an excuse to delay the daunting journey, but his warlord had returned and so now Strongbow's great undertaking could begin.

'That was some tale, Raymond.' Strongbow told him when the captain had finished recanting his story. Raymond had to strain his ears to hear his lord over the victorious cheers that rose from those in the great hall.

'You strapped the villagers' bodies to your coursers to conceal your whereabouts from the Welsh?' Whether Strongbow was impressed, disgusted or disbelieving, Raymond could not tell. He had left out the part where he had stripped the Lord of Abergavenny of his armour though he did not doubt that his warriors' story would soon set tongues a-twittering in Striguil – especially when he appeared wearing Sir William's expensive chainmail and sitting on his expensive saddle. The rest he would sell in Gloucester or Hereford the next time Strongbow sent him on an errand to Goodrich Castle. His conrois hadn't been paid in two months and if the earl couldn't afford their wages, it fell to him to provide for them until their lord could.

Strongbow looked like he was going to address Raymond again, but seemed to think better of it and instead raised his hand to signal his harpers to begin playing. Raymond groaned internally. They had elected to play one of the earl's favourite songs, a lament based around the story of Lot, son of Noah. Raymond was in a good mood, and would rather that the troubadours would play a whimsical and jaunty tune – the one about the love between Tristan and Iseult at King Arthwyr's court, or, even better, the splendid Song of Roland and his glory at the Pass of Roncesvalles. That was Raymond's favourite and he knew every word of the great saga by heart. Instead the minstrels sawed slowly on their stringed instruments, accompanied by the mewing melody and dreary deeds about people being transformed into pillars of salt.

Dismissed, Raymond bowed and turned to leave the

dais when Sir Roger de Quincy's voice pierced the hubbub in the great hall. 'He tied bodies to the back of horses? I would have ridden down Seisyll's archers in a grand charge worthy of the Lord of Striguil,' he boasted to his father-in-law. 'I would not have needed to use trickery or allowed Sir William de Braose the pleasure of winning the victory.' Lounging at Strongbow's side at the top table, Sir Roger sneered down at Raymond.

The captain returned his jeer with a look of incredulity. He knew that Sir Roger had never faced a Welsh bowman in the open field, or, like Sir William, understood the damage that those marksmen could inflict on a horse or an armoured man who foolishly charged at them without the support of infantry or crossbowmen. He had once heard a Welshman boast that he could drive an arrow through an oak door. He might doubt that claim, but his experiences in Gwent Uwchcoed had made him even more impressed by the weapons borne by Seisyll's men.

Strongbow had caught the look on his captain's face and interjected before Raymond could make a joke at Roger's expense. 'I see you have brought back a lady from your *conquest*.'

Raymond's eyes flicked momentarily towards Basilia who sat on her father's left. Something in her father's tone made him think that Strongbow had insinuated a lack of propriety on his behalf. He held up his hands and began to deny any wrong-doing as far as Alice of Abergavenny was involved, but Strongbow stopped him short.

'So my old friend Henry de Hereford had his secrets?' the earl mused. 'Two bastards? What do we do about them?' He began drumming his long fingers on the table. 'What do we do?'

'They claim that they were accepted as Sir Henry's heirs before their cousin disinherited and imprisoned them,' Raymond described.

'It was Sir Henry's right as a Marcher Lord to dispose of his property as he saw fit,' Strongbow stated swiftly and reached out to take his daughter's hand. 'Bastard-born or not, it was their father's right and no one else's.' The earl made no secret about his intention to leave all his property to his only child. Denied King Henry's permission to marry a noblewoman of equal standing, Basilia was the illegitimate product of Strongbow's relationship with a merchant's daughter from Bristol. The king's aim in refusing the earl the licence to marry was so, upon Strongbow's death, the powerful Welsh fiefdom would revert to him. Strongbow disputed this. Striguil had not been the gift of any king, he argued, but won by the efforts of his family. In Striguil, Strongbow believed he was sovereign and no other. 'I will defend the independent rights of every Marcher Lord to my dying day,' the earl warned. His eyes glowed passionately.

Raymond bowed dutifully. 'Sir Henry's children were put in a religious house just outside Abergavenny by their cousin, Sir William de Braose. They escaped and were planning to seek out King Henry in London and to make an appeal to him to recognise the boy Geoffrey's claim. That's when they were recaptured by Sir William. I think that the attack on your manors was opportunist and that he was attempting to hide his presence and his reasons for being on your lands.' Raymond scratched his chin. 'Whether you believe them or not,' he admitted to his lord, 'I am sworn to protect the girl and she does not want to return to Abergavenny unless it is with her brother's rights recognised.'

Strongbow linked his fingers together and screwed up his eyebrows in concentration. 'Sir William's father will not stand for this. He will send someone for them,

Raymond. If his son was determined to get them back before, he will be even more desperate now.' He hummed and rested his lips on his hands, deep in thought. 'Rivals to Abergavenny,' he sighed. 'What, I wonder, would my father have done in this position?'

Sir Roger de Quincy had already made up his mind. 'We should ransom them back to Sir William,' he announced. 'If he wants them so badly he will pay a great deal of silver for their safe return.' Roger was drunk and his wife Basilia laid a gentle hand on his arm to stop him making a scene, but he ignored the advice and swatted his wife's hand away. 'If he wants to keep his fortress he should pay for the privilege,' he smirked at Raymond from behind his perfectly groomed beard.

Raymond was about to interject when another voice rang out over the mewing song and hullabaloo coming from the people in the hall below:

'My Lord Strongbow, you and my father were great friends and comrades in arms,' young Geoffrey of Abergavenny proclaimed. 'That friendship between Abergavenny and Striguil brought about a golden age for Gwent. My place is as your comrade in Abergavenny. Together we could oust the Welsh rebels from Castle Arnallt and secure our borders in friendship. I doubt that William de Braose would offer you the same.' Geoffrey swept into a dramatic bow before the earl which Strongbow returned.

'And your mother,' the earl replied, 'you have proof of her marriage to Lord Henry? It will be easier for you to convince the king of your rights if we have that evidence to hand.'

Geoffrey said nothing but dropped his eyes to the rushes-covered floor. 'The only proof we had was the word of the priest who married our parents. Sir William killed him and left his body to be eaten by wild animals in

Wentwood. But I will swear on any relic that they were legally married under the eyes of God.' The boy raised his chin, proud and defiant.

Strongbow said nothing. He knew as well as any in how precarious a position the Abergavenny claimants put him. William de Braose and his father, Lord Bramber, were powerful men who were said to enjoy the friendship of the king. They could make life difficult for Strongbow if they chose to do so. And at this moment in time, with his adventure in Ireland in the balance, that was unacceptable.

Raymond saw his lord's consternation and broke the silence. 'At any rate, my lord, your decision can await our return from King Henry's court. For now we should dance,' he raised his voice for the last few words and directed all eyes to the main body of the hall from where he received a bellow of agreement from many of Strongbow's warriors therein. At the same time he grabbed Geoffrey by the shoulder and leaned in close to speak: 'This is not the time to annoy Strongbow,' he whispered. 'Until it is you will serve as my esquire. When we were in Gwent Uwchcoed, you told Sir William that you would no longer be an oblate but a warrior. Well, I can teach you the skills to become a great fighter.' When it looked like Geoffrey would argue Raymond forced a wooden cup filled with wine into his hands. 'Drink up, Geoffrey of Abergavenny, Esquire of Striguil.'

Behind them, Strongbow rose from his wooden chair on the dais and signalled for all to be quiet. The huge tapestries showing scenes from Christ's life swayed in the wind which swept across the land of Wales. 'Tomorrow I depart for France and leave my son-in-law, Sir Roger,' he laid a hand on the shoulder of the man to his right, 'in command of my lands. Obey him as you would me or I will know why. But for tonight, enjoy this feast and before you sleep

69

please include those of us who will make the dangerous crossing of the sea in your prayers. I bid you good night.' And with that he bowed to his daughter before slipping off the raised platform and through the curtains towards his private chambers in the solar above.

Pressed by Raymond's gesticulations, the musicians began playing the Song of Roland. His milites, scattered around the hall, laughed as their captain bawdily sang along. Several people even stood up to dance but most kept their chairs to continue to eat, talk and drink their lord's cheap wine. Allowing the minstrels to take the lead in the song, Raymond led Geoffrey back to a table below the dais where Alice and Borard sat.

'Lord Strongbow seems to be in a shitty mood,' Borard said as his captain joined them. 'Something he ate? Or something Sir Roger fed him,' he added as Roger's drunken laughter echoed around the large hall of Striguil.

'The earl worries,' Raymond shrugged. 'He worries about his visit to King Henry's court, he worries about his daughter, he worries about Sir Roger ...'

'But not about Geoffrey and I,' Alice of Abergavenny leant forward as she spoke. 'It seems like we are on our own.'

'Alice,' exclaimed Geoffrey, embarrassed as his sister spoke out of turn. Normally a girl of her age would never have questioned an important man like Raymond when a guest at his master's fortress.

Alice scowled at her brother. Geoffrey did not know it but she had already saved his life by mollifying Sir William using the only weapon at her disposal. To make sure that he was safe again from the politicking of Strongbow and Roger de Quincy she needed a warrior's support. Her brother's future – her future – depended on Geoffrey earning King Henry's recognition of his claim to

70

Abergavenny, and that was why she had rescued him from the monastery and shepherded him across South Wales. If Sir William had not captured them both, she knew that she would've already been in Gloucester, and from there it would've been easy to make the long journey to the royal court in London in the company of traders or pilgrims. However, if what she had heard from Strongbow was true then the king was not in his English capital but across the sea. Alice recognised that she and Geoffrey had to get on board the ship to France so that she could find a way to get her brother into King Henry's presence. Alice looked at Raymond de Carew again, the man who had already saved her from certain death at the hands of Sir William de Braose. She smiled sweetly at him and leaned forward to talk. However, with a cry of joy, he bounded away from the table before she could speak. Annoyed, Alice turned to see what had drawn his attention away from her.

'Rat!' Raymond said joyfully as he planted a bear hug on a short, ungainly-looking man with auburn hair. 'Good to see you again! Alice, Geoffrey. May I introduce Milo de Cogan, my cousin and a scoundrel like you will never have met!'

Milo raised his chin to all at the table as he pulled his chape hood from his head and onto his shoulders. Alice thought him the oddest-looking man that she had ever seen. He was not the ugliest, but certainly little about him was handsome. His shoulders looked far too big for such a small man and they made him look hunched and old.

'Everyone calls him Rat,' Raymond said of Milo, 'and so should you.'

Milo raised an eyebrow in his cousin's direction as he sat down. 'Unlike you, some of us have been taught how to conduct ourselves in polite company. So I hear you are

71

going with Strongbow to France. How big is the boat exactly?' he asked and prodded Raymond in the stomach with his finger.

'Big enough,' Strongbow's captain laughed and turned towards Geoffrey and Alice. 'Milo leads a company of hobiler-archers and holds the castle at Goodrich for Strongbow.'

Alice nodded. 'What brings you to Striguil?'

'Strongbow's business in France,' Milo said as he munched on a leg of chicken stolen from Borard's plate. 'The earl wants me to babysit Sir Roger while he is overseas. It'll be nothing but boring garrison duty,' he conceded, 'but it pays better than trying to rustle cattle from Baderon of Monmouth and our old friend Seisyll.'

'Amen to that,' Borard added, raising his cup.

'Still, business could always be better,' Milo continued. 'I hear that there is land in Ireland,' his eyes lit up as he spoke of the kingdoms across the sea, 'pissing reams of it.'

'Milo de Cogan, you will find a better way to make yourself understood when in the company of ladies,' Basilia de Quincy scolded suddenly as she appeared unseen.

Raymond immediately jumped to his feet when he heard Basilia's voice. 'I am sorry, my lady. It will not happen again,' he babbled and bowed. As he turned towards Strongbow's daughter he spilled his mug of red wine all over Milo's crotch.

'Sweet buggering hell,' Milo shouted as he jumped to his feet. 'You'll pay for the cleaning, you dullard.' As he thumped his cousin hard in the arm the crimson liquid soaked through his shirt and trousers. Alice, Geoffrey and Borard burst into fits of laughter at his offensive remark while Basilia smiled and bowed her head to hide her embarrassment.

Raymond was like a cat caught stealing cream from a friar's table; he did not know how to react or which way to look and simply stared wide-eyed at Basilia, blushing and stammering for words as she admonished him with her eyes and shook her head in mock anger at Milo's words.

'I'm so, so sorry, Lady Basilia,' Raymond stuttered at his master's graceful daughter. 'You should not have to hear such profanities. I will never curse again. Never, I swear it,' he said as seriously as if he was making an oath to his king. Beside him a dripping Milo sniggered at his cousin's overly dramatic statement. 'And neither will Rat,' Raymond stumbled on, still staring at Basilia, who looked amused. 'I composed a ballad about you, my lady...' he began, wishing that someone would interrupt him as he turned redder than Milo's wine-soaked trousers.

Strongbow's daughter smiled and raised her eyebrows in sympathetic pity at his outburst. 'Raymond...' she began but whatever she was going to say went unspoken when a drunken Roger de Quincy rumbled over and threw an arm over his wife's shoulder.

'Raymond the Fat – the lord of dead horsemen and now a troubadour to boot,' he dropped down into an unsteady and sarcastic bow. He sank more of the red liquid from the glittering green glass as he rose, completely disregarding the other revellers at the table. 'I think we should all hear your song,' he paused, 'about my wife.'

'It is not finished,' Raymond stuttered, suddenly aware that many of those in the hall had turned to listen. To make it worse, Sir Roger silenced the minstrels in the corner and announced to the room that the captain was about to sing a love song to Lady Basilia.

'Go on, Raymond,' encouraged a drunken voice from the midst of the hall. 'Sing!'

73

'Well?' asked Sir Roger with a superior look. 'You don't want to let down your audience,' he added with a hiccup. 'So sing up.' At his side, Basilia blushed and shook her head apologetically in the face of her husband's brutish behaviour. It was that look that made up Raymond's mind.

'*Lady, I love thee*,' he began to warble, enacting the dramatic pose which he had often seen used by the minstrels he most revered, '*I love thee though your gentle touch would see me die. As the sun burns the grass that rises too high, I can approach your majesty but never touch it lest I die*,' he sang the mournful tune towards the woman he had loved from afar for so long. '*As Abelard yearned, and Lancelot won, or Paris saw his city undone, I am born, I exist and my love forlorn.*'

Silence accompanied the echo of his last word and Raymond slowly lifted his eyes from the reedy floor to meet Basilia's shocked gaze. Before he could apologise for his awkward manner and terrible singing voice, Alice of Abergavenny began to applaud and quickly her appreciation was taken up by those in the great hall of Striguil. Even Milo de Cogan, as hard-hearted a man as any on the March, slapped his heavy hand on the table top in ovation at Raymond's song, and bellowed for another verse. Only Sir Roger de Quincy did not join in.

'Well, well, well,' the knight said as he intently studied Raymond. His annoyance was obvious; the captain of Strongbow's army had not disgraced himself as he had hoped. 'Not bad, Raymond. But enough singing, for I need your input in another important issue. One in which I trust only your substantial expertise.'

'Go on,' Raymond replied suspiciously.

'The important issue is this...' he paused for theatrical

effect. 'What should I eat tonight?' he asked finally with a laugh. 'As I said, in this issue I trust only the judgement of Raymond the Fat.'

'Well...' Raymond began, his eyes flicking towards Basilia who shuffled uncomfortably as Sir Roger's arm moved down from his wife's shoulder to fumble at her left breast. Roger looked straight at Raymond as he moved, his eyes daring the warrior to tell him to stop his shameful act, which his wife tried unsuccessfully to fight off.

'The lamb is good,' Raymond continued through grinding teeth. Behind him, he could feel the disgust of his friends at Sir Roger's treatment of Basilia. All knew that Sir Roger would not have dared be so brazen had Strongbow been in the great hall. After draining his cup, the knight swept his eyes over the uncomfortable and embarrassed people who sat in silence at the table before him. His gaze finally settled on Alice of Abergavenny, sitting across from him and he flicked his hair from his face and licked his lips provocatively. His eyes bored into the beautiful woman and Alice wilted slightly under Sir Roger's heavy stare. He pulled his arm away from Basilia's breast and pushed Raymond out of his way so that he could see Alice properly. Behind him Basilia began to weep and fled back across the hall and out of sight, her colourful bliaut streaming behind her.

'Basilia...' Raymond called, but she did not stop.

'Lady Alice, we have not been formerly introduced,' Sir Roger said as he propped a hand on the table and leant towards her. He had not even noticed that his wife had gone. 'Before the night is through you will get to know me better,' he said. 'If it is coin you want, I have plenty.'

It was as if the whole hall had heard the exchange and went silent so that they could listen in. Alice gasped loudly, horrified, while Geoffrey shot to his feet to confront the knight, upsetting a candle. Sir Roger closed his eyes and laughed heartily as he leant forward on the table to insult Alice again.

Raymond had heard enough and swept the knight's hand from under him with one swift strike. All of Roger's weight had been propped on the table and in his stupor he was slow to react so that he cracked his head off the heavy oak with a sickening thud. The heir to Striguil grunted once before sliding under the table unconscious.

Raymond de Carew turned to the crowd in the hall. They had gone quiet again and many of them stood on their stools to get a better view of the encounter between their lord's son-in-law and the captain of his conrois. Beside Raymond, Borard was laughing uncontrollably at Sir Roger's prone body, his head in his hands attempting to muffle his mirth.

'That's what happens to any man who thinks he can drink more than Raymond the Fat,' the captain announced jovially before raising a mug from the table beside him. 'Cheers,' he saluted the men and women of Striguil before downing the coarse liquid. Alongside him Borard, finally free to laugh with the rest of the people at the feast, broke down in fits of good cheer while Raymond scowled at the minstrels in the corner of the room until they began strumming loudly on their harps.

Milo de Cogan poked Sir Roger with his foot. 'I think you've killed him,' he told his cousin as he calmly and leant down and robbed the knight of an emerald ring from his finger, secreting it amongst his wine-soaked clothes. 'Good riddance, I say,' he added, rising to his feet after patting the nobleman's pockets and finding nothing else to steal. 'Well, I should get back to the palisade. Have a good time in France, Raymond,' he said and leaned forward to shake his hand.

'I will. And you make sure that Sir Roger doesn't start a war while we are gone,' Raymond joked as he knelt to attend the stricken man.

Milo snorted a laugh. 'That depends if I think I can win or not.' And with that he disappeared into the midst of the people who still danced and gossiped in the great hall.

'Is he really hurt?' Alice of Abergavenny asked as she lured one of the many hounds of Striguil over to the table by waving a small scrap of meat in their direction. One big lolloping alaunt took the bait and trotted towards the woman who, instead of giving the dog the sliver of beef, threw it onto Roger's face. The dog leapt after the morsel and greedily scooped it off the nobleman's lips before licking them for their taste.

'Borard, Geoffrey,' Raymond beckoned his two companions. 'Get Sir Roger up into my quarters. Don't trouble Lady Basilia. Stay with him until morning. I don't want to find him choked on his own vomit tomorrow. That would put pay to Strongbow's voyage.' Both Borard and Geoffrey of Abergavenny looked annoyed at having to care for the insensible nobleman, but nodded their assent and then, not too delicately, manhandled Sir Roger de Quincy from under the table and out of the great hall.

'What a day,' Raymond mumbled as he dropped onto a stool and took another swig from a wine cup. Only Alice remained at his table and she watched him intently. She had perceived Raymond's affection for Strongbow's daughter, his gallantry in his treatment of the detestable Sir Roger de Quincy, and even the esteem in which the people of Striguil held him. Suddenly Raymond's eyes flicked up and caught her staring at him. He said nothing but simply smiled at her. If she needed one more reason to know that this was a good man, she had it.

'Will you see me back to my rooms, please?' she asked.

Five minutes later, Alice and Raymond were standing in the shadow of her room in the bailey of Striguil. Flickering firelight spilled from the donjon into the darkness where most of Strongbow's warriors lived. Alice had clung to the warrior's arm, though it was not especially cold, as they crossed the dusty expanse towards the guest quarters. To their left, a dog yelped suddenly at their appearance before a white-faced page appeared and calmed the hound.

Raymond giggled as Alice jumped in fright. 'I used to have the same job when I was esquire to the Lord of Raglan, Walter de Bloet's uncle. The dogs would keep you up all night,' he recalled. 'Still, it was better than being assigned to the lady of the castle. I had to do that for many years for the earl's late mother here in Striguil – extremely boring work, even for a seven-year-old.'

'What will become of my brother?' Alice asked suddenly, ignoring his recollections. 'What will become of me?'

'For the moment your brother will serve me as esquire,' Raymond answered. 'As for you...' he tailed off. 'I still am in your debt and will do whatever you ask of me. So what do you want?'

Alice pouted for a moment and looked up into Raymond's friendly face. 'I want my brother to be given back what is his.'

'I don't have the resources to capture Abergavenny.'

'I know,' she interrupted and laid a finger to his lips. 'However, you can take him with you to France. You could engineer a way for my brother to meet the king and argue his case directly.'

'I could?'

'And to do that he needs to be alive – I won't let

Geoffrey get himself killed chasing you into some stupid fight in the mountains. So I will have to stay with you, Raymond de Carew, to make sure that you don't put him in too much danger on one of your adventures.'

Raymond laughed in response, not knowing what to say, only aware that Alice was standing very close to him.

Moments passed before Alice spoke again. 'You are in love with Lady Basilia,' she told him.

'What?' Raymond stepped away from her. 'She is married to another man. She is a noblewoman and I am only...' he tailed off and shrugged. 'I am only Raymond the Fat,' he said with a sorry smile, 'and that will never be enough for someone like her, or her father.'

Alice smiled sympathetically. 'I told myself that I was in love with William de Braose,' she admitted and closed the gap between them. 'At least I had convinced myself that he would promise me marriage as well as keeping Geoffrey safe and I stupidly gave him my maidenhood to ensure he kept his promise. But like all men, he lied.'

'William de Braose is a fool.'

She nodded in answer but said nothing. Instead she suddenly grabbed Raymond by two clumps of his surcoat and kissed him hard upon the mouth.

'Wait,' he mumbled for a fraction of a second. 'Wait,' he appealed again. He needed time to consider what was happening.

'They say that I am not a noblewoman,' she told him as she withdrew from their kiss, 'and I won't be until we find a way to defeat William de Braose and reclaim Abergavenny. For now, you are what I want, Raymond de Carew.'

Seconds passed in the silence as their lips again came together. Suddenly Alice dragged Raymond into her room and threw the door shut behind them.

Chapter Three

Sir William de Braose was in no mood to be merciful. The men on their knees before him were Danes, their long-haired heads bowed as if resigned to the death that would soon take them. All of them, that was, except their leader who had to be tied like a hog awaiting slaughter. He still screamed profanities at the Lord of Abergavenny. The Dane was a giant of a man with bright red hair and a braided beard which sat like tusks on either side of his mouth. At his side were his axe and his fallen circular shield marked with the mask of a charging black boar.

'Would someone please quiet that damned pirate?' Sir William shouted at his warriors as the first light of the new morning spilled over the small hills to the east. Dull grey skies reflected in the puddled rainwater. In the distance cattle called for their morning fodder. 'Shut up, shut up,' Sir William mumbled in frustration as his men fought to gag their leader and avoid his attempts to bite them.

Sir William was learning to hate the Welsh March. He had thought that inheriting Abergavenny and Brecon would have meant liberation from an overbearing mother and an untrustworthy father, but it had brought nothing except violence and intrigue, problems, complications and obstacles. A day and a half in the saddle riding to Sweynsey had done nothing to improve his outlook.

It had been only a week since he had led a conrois of his warriors through the Gwent hills to recapture the bastards of Abergavenny, Alice and Geoffrey; a week since he should have secured his inheritance; a week since he had been embarrassed by Raymond de Carew. His anger at his treatment by Strongbow's warlord had driven him to cross Wales and visit John de London, the effete Lord of Oystermouth and Sweynsey, in the hope of an alliance which would allow him to attack Striguil from two sides. But nothing that he said or promised would compel Sir John to join him in his revenge, and Sir William had turned for home even angrier than he had been before. That was when the thunderstorm had struck, forcing his soaking conrois to seek shelter for the night in Nedd Abbey. The abbot had not denied them beds, but had pleaded poverty when Sir William had asked for food and wine. Ornate tapestries showing the lives of the saints adorned the walls of the chapterhouse as the abbot had deprived hospitality to the dripping and shivering men at his door. Sir William knew that the wall hangings were expensive and new, possibly even imported from Flanders, and that there was no way that an abbey with that wealth on display could possibly be as destitute as the abbot claimed. His first impulse had been to force his way into the pantry and see for himself what was available to eat, but one look at the abbot's rapacious face had stopped him.

'Would this make a difference?' he had asked, brandishing a heavy silver coin from his heavy purse. Of course it had been enough and the men of Abergavenny had gone to their beds happy and contented, if a little damp, with full bellies and the soothing effect of fine French wine.

God, it seemed, had been watching over the Cistercians of Nedd and their avaricious abbot. He had seen fit to send a storm to Wales and drive Sir William and his warriors to stay at the abbey on the very evening that the crew of Danes had come raiding.

Sir William could not remember the last time he had

heard of Danes pillaging a monastery in England, though he did not doubt that it was still a common occurrence on the dangerous March of Wales. The abbey had no defences other than a high wall and it seemed to Sir William that the local lord, Richard de Grenville, was a dullard, for the Danes were upon them without warning or response from the wooden castle a little way downriver. Nonetheless, it had been a short fight. The Danes – less than thirty in number – had been caught totally unprepared to combat anything other than squealing clerics, and had no idea that there were knights sleeping in the same dormitory as the monks; knights with weapons close to hand. Some of the Danes had died in the tight corridors of the abbey as William de Braose's warriors had spilled from the chapterhouse in full mail. Others had been killed in the open space and sanctity of the southern transept. Another group had put up a stiff fight in the grassy cloister, but all had eventually fled back towards the muddy river where their ship was moored. It wasn't even half a mile, but the land was boggy and the retreating Danes laden with all the treasures they could carry. Sir William and his men, on horseback, had no such problem and had quickly outpaced the retreating raiders using a short path pointed out by the abbot. They had cut the foreigners off from their ship and had killed four men left to guard the vessel.

The Danish captain should have surrendered. The enemy had no chance of fighting their way past the thirty men of Abergavenny, but their giant of a leader forced his warriors to lock shields and advance, their swords and axes silver above their helmets. That was when Richard de Grenville had turned up with four of his household warriors on horseback and twenty more men on foot. The encircled Danes had been ordered to throw down their arms and they had complied, except for their captain who had killed one of the local men before being felled by a ringing sword blow upon his helmeted head. It hadn't killed him, but while he was insensible Sir William had ordered him bound, knee and ankle, elbow and wrist.

'I'll kill you, *bacraut*!' the Dane shouted in Sir William's direction, having wrestled free of the gag. 'If you were a man you'd fight me.'

That the savage could speak French surprised Sir William, but he ignored the captive man's ire and turned to meet Sir Richard de Grenville. The Lord of Nedd was bearded and dressed like a Welshman, though he had chainmail and an elaborate Norman cloak which kept off the rain.

'I've never heard the like of it,' the old man coughed after swapping introductions with Sir William. It was cold and his breath turned to steam on the morning air as it escaped his mouth. 'Bloody brigands! Here, by God, at Nedd.'

His heavily accented French annoyed Sir William. 'You don't watch the river at night?'

Sir Richard laughed, the rain spitting off the end of his nasal protector. 'Who would? There hasn't been an attack like this since my father was a boy. When my steward awoke me I thought it must be the bloody Welsh and that I was in real trouble. But this lot?' He kicked the legs of the Danish captain, earning a wolfish snarl from the bound man. 'They are good for nothing unless you want somebody murdered.'

His words echoed around Sir William's head. 'They do that sort of thing?' he asked.

The Lord of Nedd shrugged. 'They get up to all sorts for the right price.' He scratched under his mail coif and began counting the Danes. 'I'll return the abbey's belongings and you can have anything that is in the ship.

I'll take the ship itself. Agreed?'

'And the crew?' asked Sir William without assenting to his claim over the spoils of the fight. 'What will become of them?'

Sir Richard took a long swig from a wineskin. He had thought to allow the younger man to take whatever trinkets the Danes had in the belly of their great ship, and leave him the merchandise of real value: the crewmen themselves. 'I'll hand them over to the sheriff in Cardiff, of course,' he lied and wiped the wine from his lips. The truth was that the Danes would fetch a huge price in the great slave market of Dubhlinn in faraway Ireland and he needed their vessel to transport the captured men across the sea. 'Unless you would prefer to hang them here and now?' he chanced and held his breath.

Sir William did not answer immediately. Instead he turned his back on Sir Richard de Grenville and stood over the Danish raiders as if doing his own calculations of their worth. All had been ordered to sit down and their hands had been bound, but only their leader had to be hobbled like an animal. None could hold Sir William's gaze.

'*Gamla vis Hruga uskit'r,*' the foreigners' leader snarled in Sir William's direction. The Dane had fallen onto his shoulder, his long red hair and beard sopping and dark. '*Brisfaidh mé do magairlí,*' he added in a different tongue.

'Help the Dane to his feet,' Sir William ordered two of his warriors. The foreigner cursed at the two men and attempted to bite. He was a vast man who exuded violence. He was as big in the chest as Raymond de Carew, and his bare arms bulged with muscle, but he was also easily the tallest man that Sir William had ever encountered. Before he could begin to curse at him again, the Lord of Abergavenny held up his hand.

'I have a proposition for you, Dane,' he said. 'It would

84

be in your interest to listen to it for, in ten minutes time, my warriors and I will ride away and that man,' he pointed towards Richard de Grenville, 'will sell you and your crew into slavery. If, that is, he doesn't hang you.' While the fury in the Dane's eyes did not depart, he did stop struggling. 'I heard you speak the French tongue, so I know you understand me,' Sir William coolly told him. 'What is your name and where did you come from?'

For many seconds the man said nothing, simply staring back at the knight through narrow, suspicious eyes. 'Release my bonds,' he finally demanded and spat onto the ground close to Sir William's feet. His hands were tied behind his back and that was where they remained as one of the Abergavenny warriors sliced apart the ropes on the Dane's legs to allow him to stand. As the man went to free the remaining bonds, Sir William stopped him.

'Your name?' he demanded again.

He bared his teeth angrily at the command. 'I am Sigtrygg Mac Ragnall Mac Giolla Mhuire, Jarl of Veðrarfjord. I am no Dane. Now, release me.'

In answer Sir William drew his own dagger from the base of his spine and dismissed his warrior back to his companions and their watch over the crew. 'My name is William de Braose, Lord of Abergavenny and Brecon,' he replied as he walked behind Sigtrygg.

'I don't care who you are, boy,' Jarl Sigtrygg replied as the first of his bonds at his elbows snapped apart. 'Just say your piece and I'll decide if I want to help you or not. Now,' he stressed his words, 'release my hands.'

The men from the nearby castle of Nedd were swarming over the ship and hunting through surrendered weapons for those better than their own armaments. One man had stripped a dead man of his chainmail and helmet and was testing his short sword to see if he liked the balance and weight.

85

'You say that you are from … Wether ford?' Sir William asked the jarl, struggling with the pronunciation of the strange word as his dagger danced upon the final piece of twine which fettered the captain's hands. 'Where is that?'

'Veðrarfjord is in Ireland,' Jarl Sigtrygg told him and tensed his arms to urge Sir William to grant freedom to his hands. With a moment's hesitation, he nicked the ropes binding him, allowing Jarl Sigtrygg to pull his hands free of the restraints. Sir William didn't immediately return the weapon to its sheath. Instead he watched the foreigner as intently as a shepherd would an unruly alaunt around his flock. Jarl Sigtrygg did not attack as he had feared. He simply nodded reassuringly towards his crewmen who returned the gesture.

'So, William de Braose of Abergavenny and Brecon, tell me what you would have of me?' Jarl Sigtrygg asked as he turned to face him.

'A private matter,' the knight replied. He hated that the giant man filled him with so much dread. He forced himself to return the dagger to its sheath and return Jarl Sigtrygg's unwavering gaze with as much composure as he could summon. 'It is an enterprise that will pay well and, more importantly, will save your hide from slavery or a hanging.'

'And that of my crew?' growled Jarl Sigtrygg.

'And that of your crew,' Sir William confirmed.

The foreigner sucked air through his teeth as he stared at the Norman. He didn't like the situation in which he found himself on the muddy riverbank in Wales. Defeat was not something that he was used to, and he hated the idea of being used like a servant by the haughty, pink-cheeked lord who commanded the warriors who had defeated him. He especially did not like that some of the locals were picking through his ship. His crew had been at sea for more than three months, circumnavigating Ireland during their spree of coastal violence before selling a number of slaves at Dubhlinn and making the crossing to Mann. There, Jarl Sigtrygg had been told of the rich pickings to be had in Dyfed, the disorder of the Norman lords and the incompetence of the Welsh chieftains. It was on the way home to Veðrarfjord, so the jarl had led his crew south and eastwards. However, all that he had found in Gwynedd were tumbledown settlements deserted by their inhabitants for the high hills and their summer grazing sites. Ceredigion had proven more fruitful with a greater number of monasteries and isolated seaside villages. This small success had emboldened Jarl Sigtrygg and rather than turn back towards Veðrarfjord, he had jibed and put the wind behind his ship, *River-Wolf*, setting her bows towards the Norman lands of Glamorgan. It was then that his troubles had started.

In St Bride's Bay the Bishop of St. David's warriors had tracked them on the shore, preventing them from making land. At Melrfjord they had been able to barter wine from a Gascon trader and honey-mead from a local Dane in return for some of the shaggy cow hides that he had taken in the lands of the Uí Néill, but there had been no chance of plunder and so they had pushed on down the coast, rounding the Gower Peninsula with a biting wind filling their sails, and made for the old Norseman's port of Sweynsey. One drunken night in the company of a talkative miller had given Jarl Sigtrygg his next target – the Abbey at Nedd.

Jarl Sigtrygg looked again at *River-Wolf* as two Normans in their grey chainmail argued over who would take a crate of the honey-mead. They had not yet found his secret store of silver coin wrapped in pieces of cloth and hidden in a hollowed-out kne beneath the steering oar, but

87

he knew that it would only be a matter of time. Then he and his crew would be utterly impoverished. He was relieved that he had decided to cut up the golden cross and cup stolen from the church on Kerlingfjord and store the pieces in the same strongbox rather than leave them intact with the other plunder of which the Normans were robbing him.

'The longer you tarry,' Sir William warned, 'the more you will lose.'

Jarl Sigtrygg growled in frustration. 'What would you have of us then?' he asked. The daybreak wind was cold as it wafted the braids in his hair and beard.

Sir William led the jarl away from the prying ears of Sir Richard de Grenville towards the muddy little tributary which wound its way back towards the monastery and the church which it served. 'I want you to kill someone for me,' he told the foreigner. 'Three people, actually. I'd like it to be done quietly without my name becoming attached to the act.'

'Killing is what we do,' Jarl Sigtrygg returned. 'It can be done secretly, but it will cost more.' He turned back towards *River-Wolf* where Richard de Grenville stood counting the captured foreigners. 'And how will you free my crew?'

'Silver is a powerfully persuasive friend. Are we agreed then?'

Jarl Sigtrygg clenched his teeth. 'Agreed, but I want paying up front.'

'You'll be paid when the deed is done and not before,' Sir William countered. 'And I will be keeping all your plunder and three of your men hostage to make sure that you keep to your task and do not disappear back to Ireland.'

Jarl Sigtrygg bristled in anger, partially at the affront to his trustworthiness, but mostly because he had indeed hoped to flee to his homeland at the earliest possible opportunity. He should never have come to the accursed land of Wales, he now realised. What should have been an easy theft had turned into a nightmare. All he wanted to do was to get back across the sea to Veðrarfjord with his plunder and pay back Konungr Ragnall what he owed once and for all. But the Normans had already killed four of his men and he was not willing to bring about the death of three more of his crew if he left them behind in Wales. The thought of parting Sir William de Braose from his heavy purse of silver also helped make up his mind.

'So,' Jarl Sigtrygg asked, 'who do you want dead and where do I find them?'

Chapter Four

Through a summery Dorset and Wiltshire, by Salisbury, Ludgershall and Reading they pursued him. Following the Thames Valley, they spent nights at Windsor, Wallingford, and Woodstock. They were always a day or two behind. It wasn't until they called at the great abbey of Ely that Strongbow and Raymond again caught word of his movements. The king, the monks said, was making for Westminster.

Everywhere Strongbow and Raymond had camped on their journey they found evidence that Henry's court had been there before them: trampled ground and abandoned barrels, the remains of cooking fires, horse faeces and fly-covered food waste. At each fortress people were pale-faced as they described the sudden and unanticipated appearance of the king and how they had been commanded to provide food, drink, entertainment and accommodation for his court as he had stayed in their region overnight. New justices had been appointed, they described. Landowners had been summoned, cases had been tried, and land disputes going back to Stephen's reign had been settled. Everything had been recorded by his army of clerks. Then, as abruptly as he had arrived, Henry was gone and his huge entourage with him, and the townspeople were able to breathe easily and count the cost his visit. The king's whirlwind progress through the kingdom was nothing new. It was said that Henry set a fast pace to his life in an effort to stave off weight gain. When he wasn't travelling with his court, he was hunting, hawking or riding in the countryside with his friends. The only time he stopped was to eat and even then he couldn't keep still and proudly walked around, reading aloud from books purchased at great price from Irish monasteries and the Muslim states of Spain on subjects as diverse as law and medicine. Even the business of his vast state was conducted from the saddle.

'I heard one ambassador dropped dead of exhaustion right into Queen Eleanor's warm lap when Henry toured Aquitaine last summer,' Raymond joked to his conrois. Alice of Abergavenny was the only one to laugh. Everyone else in Strongbow's retinue was too exhausted to join in their captain's merriment.

A frustrating week at sea had brought their company to the mouth of the Loire and three more days had taken them to the city of Tours. It was only as they prepared to make the overland journey to Poitiers that they heard that King Henry and his eldest son had already passed through Anjou into Normandy and thence onwards across the Narrow Sea to England. And so the weary men of Striguil had clambered back into their lord's ship, *Waverider*, and pursued the king northwards. By the time they had landed at Wareham in Dorset, Henry was already halfway to Westminster and they had been forced to give pursuit for another two weeks on horseback. Their efforts had left each of them angry, bored and exhausted. Everyone, that was, except Raymond. He was in his element. By day he teased, chivvied and babbled incessantly to his men, setting them tasks such as scouting ahead of their column as well as leading them out to hunt in the evening. Every day he had something new for his men to do, inspiring them to work hard despite their exhaustion and the summer heat which roasted their backs. He laughed at their jokes, took his turn on the picket line and none dared complain too loudly when their captain did more work than any two of them combined. While Strongbow feasted with the local lords and took rooms in their castles, Raymond spent time amongst the men of the conrois in the towns below, drinking long into the night with one and all, swapping news and rumours from around Henry's dominions.

Raymond was happy. He had Alice.

Despite Strongbow's protestations, Raymond had insisted that she join the conrois which had crossed Henry's lands and, dressed in a leather jerkin over her flowing blue gown, Alice had proven hardy enough to keep up with the men of the company. Since the first time that they had slept together in Striguil, Raymond had been caught in a web of lust which she made sure he enjoyed at every possible opportunity. For Raymond it was a new and fascinating experience. He had enjoyed the companionship of women when he could, but he had never had a long-standing mistress or a wife. He had always told himself that it was due to his lifestyle which he believed left little time for a marriage, that he had not the stable income to afford a wife, or support a family. In truth it had always been because of his pitiable and impossible love for Basilia de Quincy, daughter of the Earl Strongbow.

With Alice it was easy. Yet Raymond still felt a crumb of discomfort with their liaison for, despite not being married to Basilia or ever having any hope of making her his, he still felt shame that he had bedded Alice of Abergavenny, as though he had been unfaithful to Strongbow's daughter and that if she discovered his treachery, his dream of being with her would be over forever. That feeling of guilt had lessened the further that he had travelled from the March of Wales, and now, hundreds of miles from Striguil, while he sensibly did not flaunt it, he was becoming ever more used to their arrangement. In return for his protection and patronage for her brother, Raymond received something that he hadn't realised he had been missing for a long time: intimacy. That his relationship with Alice relied solely on his ability to promote Geoffrey's interests at Abergavenny with King Henry was not forgotten. Theirs was a relationship that would end whatever the outcome of their visit to the royal court. Success for their claim would mean that Alice would become a great lady and could no longer be associated with a landless warrior like he. Defeat meant that an alliance with Raymond was pointless, and he would be cast aside like an old sword that no longer kept its edge. Whatever happened he would lose Alice. Raymond hoped that they would never catch up with the royal court and that the happiness of the last month could continue further.

Now, heading towards the great Palace of Westminster, Raymond hummed a portion from the Song of Roland and watched the outline of Alice's backside, hidden below the stylish blue gown, as she perched on the saddle of her new palfrey just ahead of him. In the bright sunshine which poured through the alley of leafy trees, she looked stunning as she talked to her brother, schooling Geoffrey in what to say if and when he met King Henry.

'Beautiful, isn't it,' Strongbow said as he fell in beside his captain. Raymond blanched, but one glance at his lord told him that the earl was not admiring Alice's arse as he had been, but the Middlesex countryside, full of fields of wheat and locked by sunshine and flowering plants.

'Yes, Lord,' Raymond answered with a small smile. 'It certainly is that - soft and bountiful.'

Strongbow sighed. 'What are the chances that Henry has already left Westminster, this silly coronation done and dusted, and headed back to

France? Should we have waited in Normandy?'

'We have no choice but to press on, Lord,' Raymond replied and glanced at Alice, hoping that Henry had indeed continued onwards towards the south coast. It would mean another few days in her company. 'Unless you mean to abandon Diarmait, your marriage to Princess Aoife and the crown of Laighin?'

'Never,' Strongbow uttered, showing a resolve which Raymond had seen only rarely. 'We press on until we catch up with him, even if he leads us a merry dance all the way to the gates of Jerusalem.' The earl nodded his head as if he was still trying to convince himself of the truth of his proclamation.

Strongbow may have been exhausted from the long journey, but it was the stress which was hurting him most, Raymond determined. At every great fortress town of England Strongbow had mentally steeled himself for the momentous meeting with King Henry only for it to have been in vain as they found the king already departed. His lord had developed a cold and Raymond wondered how long he could keep up the punishing pace and the constant anxiety which the approaching royal meeting put upon him.

'Hold there,' a loud voice suddenly demanded ahead of the column which shuddered to a halt, 'in King Henry's name stop.' Two horsemen in the swaggering lion livery of the Angevin King of England stepped onto the road followed by a band of over twenty crossbowmen with their weapons trained on Strongbow's men. The warriors on foot were routiers, mercenaries from Spain, Flanders and Germany, loyal only to the English king's purse and damned to Hell by the Holy Father for their irreligious profession.

'Goodness gracious,' Strongbow expressed at the

unexpected appearance of the ragtag band of crossbowmen.

'Well, we've finally caught up with King Henry,' Raymond replied with a hint of reticence.

At his side Strongbow began to splutter.

Raymond deflected the sword thrust with his shield and brought his own weapon down on the helmeted head of the man wearing the colours of the Earl of Oxford. Dreigiau turned quickly, allowing his master to bounce a spear lunge from another enemy over his head and then punch the pommel of his sword into his new assailant's face. The man's great helm rang like a church bell and Raymond was sure that he heard the man encased in armour cry out his surrender as he fell from his saddle to the hard, dusty earth.

'Raymond de Carew,' called an excited voice from behind him. 'Get back into formation. Now!'

He considered ignoring the order. The Earl of Oxford's men were ready to break and run from the tourney field and Raymond wanted to take more of enemy knights captive and so quench his desperate need for money. Strongbow's bribes and Alice's upkeep in the inn in Westminster had left him in significant arrears and the arms, mail, trappings and mounts of captured knights could be sold to clear some of those debts. Their ransoms would make him rich for the first time in his life.

'Bollocks to you,' he said under his breath and kicked his courser forward to meet another of the Earl of Oxford's men. The knight's lance was only a few feet from striking his chest when Raymond nudged Dreigiau to his right and clear of the point. Once past that danger he stood in his long stirrups and struck the helpless knight twice in succession as their momentum took them passed each other. When Raymond turned sharply the rider was on the ground and his weapons loose of his grip.

'Damn you, you bloody fool! Come back here,' Roger de Clare, the Earl of Hertford, cried again as Raymond repelled two strokes from another rival. He brought his sword down on the knight's outstretched arm. The blow was not enough to break the skin, but the man dropped his weapon from his nerveless hand and tried to steer his horse away from the attack. Raymond forced Dreigiau in front of him, backhanding the knight with the rim of his shield in his steel-covered face. The man crumpled onto his back as Raymond circled around with his sword aloft.

'I offer you a pledge, I offer you a pledge,' the man shouted and held up his hands. Raymond smiled and pulled out of the downwards sword thrust.

'Get their names and oaths,' he ordered Geoffrey of Abergavenny. The Earl of Oxford's men were retreating at top speed from the mêlée and there would be no more ransoms from this encounter. Raymond spotted a small copse of trees in the distance which might offer them some respite and assumed that was where the Earl of Oxford would hide out and regroup.

'Raymond, you Welsh dullard, get back in line,' Lord Hertford, commanded sternly as he removed his great helm. Whether or not he was jealous at Raymond's three successes so early in the tourney was hard to say, but the earl was certainly annoyed that he had paid two shillings to have such a wayward lance like Raymond in his conrois.

The captain from Striguil cast a grin at Lord Hertford as he passed him and took his place in the crimson and gold line. The earl was one of the most valuable targets on the field and any fighter from the eight other competing teams in the tourney would love to claim the vast ransom by capturing him. Raymond reckoned that the nobleman was probably nervous and that was what made him so prickly. As Hertford shouted orders up and down the line, Raymond cast his eye over the meadows on either side of the London Road. Two miles to the west he could see Sir Robert Dagworth's men take on the conrois of the Lord de Ros while closer to Westminster, a Breton count took on a small conrois led by a Yorkshire knight in a white and blue surcoat. Raymond did not recognise him, but he was impressed by the way he directed his unit. Beyond that, Sir Nigel d'Evecque led his few warriors in a flanking attack on the rear of Lord de Ros's conrois in conjunction with Dagworth's men.

'Dagworth and d'Evecque have joined forces,' Raymond informed Hertford. His words were lost as a thundering charge from the west saw the entry of Prince Harry into the mêlée. A hundred or so knights followed their lord's command and plunged into the fray and from the crowds on the far side of the river a cheer went up. To a man they had gathered to watch the young prince's company compete.

'God for Anjou,' the prince shouted as he hoisted his lance in the air and pointed the way for his men. The audience echoed his call and applauded King Henry's eldest son as his knights attacked Dagworth's flank. From this distance, Raymond could make out little but it seemed that Prince Harry's huge conrois smashed right through Dagworth's men and into those of Lord de Ros and d'Evecque. He could not imagine how much it would have cost to put such a huge number of knights in the field. No less than fifty pounds, Raymond considered with a disbelieving shake of his head. It was as much as his father's estate at Carew Castle would make in a decade.

'We are going after Oxford,' the Earl of Hertford announced as he cantered up the line, ignoring the prince and the cheers of adulation. 'I want his armour to adorn my feasting hall! And you,' Hertford turned on Raymond, 'make sure and stay in the line this time.' The earl's voice was muffled and steely below the great helm which covered his head. 'My noble cousin Strongbow may think you a good fighter, but the mêlée is different to anything that you will have seen in Gwent. So stay in order,' he snarled. Hertford could not believe how a man mounted on such a small horse could possibly hope to survive the tourney, but Strongbow had insisted the stout warrior was worth the gamble. Certainly, he had shown a brute strength in taking three ransoms, but the tourney was about discipline, not the wild fighting he would've seen on the Welsh March. 'Must I explain the rules of the tourney for a third time?' the earl asked.

'No,' Raymond replied with a smile. The rules were simple: this was war on a small scale and in a defined area with identified participants. Rival teams fought it out while a large audience watched from the sidelines, baying for blood. Not that many competitors died during the mêlée, but every so often someone had his throat cut or bled to death from a particularly heavy blow from an enraged fighter. And then you were in real trouble because the Church would not allow any knight killed in the tournament to be buried in Holy ground. What would happen to a man if he was not to be buried amongst the flock of Christ when Judgement Day came? Raymond shuddered at the thought. A tourney also provided opportunity to capture and ransom a rich knight or nobleman and make a fortune. He had heard of the exploits of the best mêlée fighters, of their fame and great wealth. Raymond's jealousy pulsed in his chest. Even the most successful fighting seasons on the March could leave Raymond and his kin struggling to make ends meet – and each time they took to the field they risked their lives. There was not the same peril as a tourney knight. The most famous mêlées took place in Flanders, but this was Raymond's first experience of one. Every other kingdom in Christendom had banned the dangerous pursuit under pressure from the Church, but in celebration of his forthcoming coronation, Prince Harry had convinced his father, the Old King Henry, to allow him to host a tourney with some of the greatest knights from around Europe. It made this unique meeting on the London Road one of the most violent, desperate and exciting day's activity for both riders and their adoring fans.

'We need to watch out for William Marshal,' Raymond told the Earl of Hertford and lifted his arm to point in the direction of the danger. The earl followed his gesture to where, up on a hillock to the east, the greatest knight ever to set foot on the tournament field lurked: Sir William Marshal and his fifty-strong conrois. The man in the green and yellow surcoat had ruled the roost at every tournament in France and Flanders for a year and had become fabulously rich. It was said that he had never lost a tourney and that he had once singlehandedly taken on ten warriors and won. There was no more famous fighter in Christendom. Raymond wondered how much Prince Harry had been forced to hand over to get him and his company to leave the rich pickings on the continent for this scraggly English field. The potential takings from a prince, two earls, a foreign count, and a rich English baron may have been enough for Marshal to cross the sea to the backwater kingdom.

'What is he waiting for?' Hertford asked. 'I suppose he thinks he is too high and bloody mighty to take part?'

Raymond shook his head. 'He is waiting for us to exhaust ourselves by attacking each other. Once we are panting he will charge in and clean up the remaining ransoms.'

'That'll not please our little Harry,' the earl scoffed and nodded at the prince's conrois. 'He's not happy unless he is the centre of attention.' The audience had stopped singing 'God for Anjou' and were chanting Marshal's name, urging him to join the fight. 'His father will have his guts for garters if he gets involved in the fighting. It's not like Harry is a knight.' The earl continued to watch Marshal until he disappeared from view. 'We are taking old Oxford now,' he proclaimed and kicked his steed into action, leaving Raymond's concerns about Sir William Marshal behind. The rest of the conrois followed their lord, trotting over the London Road and uphill towards the copse of trees where the Earl of Oxford hid with his horsemen, licking his wounds. Raymond was the last to follow, chewing his lip as he eyed Marshal up on the hillock. The famous knight stood still, hidden beneath his great helm and barely moving as he stared across the wide London Road at the fight going on.

'Make sure you get their names,' Raymond told Geoffrey of Abergavenny and pointed at the three captured knights, 'and then give them my address at the inn. They will meet us there later to set the price of their ransom.' His new esquire nodded as Raymond, with one final glance towards Marshal, kicked his horse into a canter to catch up with the Earl of Hertford.

'What happens if you are captured?' Geoffrey shouted after his lord.

'Then their ransoms become the property of my victor,' he called back, not sure if his esquire would even hear his words. The knights' ransoms would give him the equivalent of several years' income and still allow him a bit of extra cash to bribe those court officials who Strongbow needed to support him when he finally met with King Henry. What he should do, Raymond knew, was to ride off the field immediately with his winnings safely pocketed. However, Hertford had paid him two shillings to fight with his company and he could not in all conscience abandon the priggish earl. Honour demanded that he remain at Hertford's side and so he clipped his heels to Dreigiau's flanks and urged him into a gallop.

Principle may have kept him there, but he was starting to enjoy his first mêlée. So why should he leave early? There were more ransoms to be taken and with that on his mind he charged after Hertford's men towards the spinney of trees where the Earl of Oxford had gone to ground.

The Earl of Oxford ran rather than be captured. He fled to the jeers of the distant crowd and the curses of Hertford's men who had again missed out on his rich ransom. The remainder of his conrois scattered across the London Road field leaving Hertford's troop alone in the copse of trees with their handful of captured knights.

'Damn it,' the Earl of Hertford spoke from beside Raymond. He pulled off his great helm and loosened the chainmail around his throat. 'Oxford will leave the tourney now. If I could have taken him prisoner...' He shook his head in disappointment at the missed opportunity for great wealth.

Behind the two men the prisoners stood awaiting their fate - loss of armour, horses and a ransom which could cripple their household for a number of years to come. 'Who commands the next biggest sum?' the earl asked the man nearest to him.

'The prince is worth most,' Raymond answered, 'then the Count of Rennes, I suspect.'

'Rennes then,' the earl said quickly. He, like Raymond, accepted that their forty-strong conrois would not be able to capture Prince Harry and nor would it have been politically sensible, though Hertford still could not shake his ambition to wrestle a hefty tribute from the king's son. 'Would it really be bad form to attack the snotty-faced little prick?' he asked. 'I know he paid for the tourney, but he is a pathological bore and it would wipe the smarmy smile off his face if he was forced to turn to his daddy to pay a ransom to me.'

'His coronation is tomorrow, Lord,' Raymond replied. His new chainmail, taken from Sir William de Braose, was tight around his chest and he had to flap his arms to get the links to sit correctly on his shoulders. 'It is probably best that he be in a good mood for that.'

Hertford sniffed in disappointment. 'His father would be rather angry.' The earl looked back towards the town of Westminster where a number of horsemen made towards a tight curl in the river's course. 'And there goes the Count,' he pointed his lance. 'Get our men ready to move out,' he ordered.

'We should wait,' Raymond told Hertford, placing a hand on the shoulder of the earl's mare. 'The prince has sent men to block his escape,' he pointed out a number of men riding to the north-west. 'Rennes will have to double back…'

'And that will lead him right past us,' Hertford finished his sentence with a look of complete joy. 'Oh well done, Young Harry!' he laughed, his head cocking back and forth much like Strongbow would have done. 'He might make a half-decent king after all.'

The Earl of Hertford was still laughing when Sir William Marshal's conrois launched their attack on the rear of his company.

Raymond clipped his heels to Dreigiau's flanks as a sword flashed down in his direction. His sudden movement took him away from the blow and almost unseated the rider who had thrown all his weight into the strike. The thunder of hooves and the cry of exultation surrounded Raymond as more of Marshal's riders poured through the trees to attack Hertford's conrois. Raymond forced his small courser to turn sharply to take another sword stroke on his shield. Beside him, the Earl of Hertford cursed and fumbled with his heavy helm as he attempted to slot it back upon his head.

'Geoffrey, with me!' Raymond shouted at his esquire as Dreigiau dodged another of Marshal's men who flew past, his mace and armour a blur of grey, green and gold as it swept in an arc well wide of his intended target. All around him there were warriors engaged in scuffles, but Raymond could instinctively tell that there was no hope for the Earl of Hertford's company. They had been caught flat-footed and unprepared. A knight, astride the biggest horse that Raymond had ever seen, yelled a challenge as he levelled his lance and roared towards him. Raymond glanced at the earl, still calling for his esquire to bring him a weapon so that he could defend himself, and kicked Dreigiau into a wide bend, keeping the knight on his left and drawing him away from Hertford. As the man matched his move, Raymond suddenly darted his speedy courser towards him, closing the gap before the knight could swing his unwieldy lance into position. In the blink of an eye he had turned his adversary's heavy lance aside with his shield and Raymond saw the man's eyes open in fear just before impact of sword on shield. Marshal's man disappeared over the side of the saddle as the captain from Striguil galloped past.

'Leave him be,' Raymond shouted at Geoffrey. To have taken the man hostage would've led to his own capture, he had no doubt, and as he looked left and right, Raymond saw that he had fought his way clear of Marshal's line of horsemen. He was free. All he had to do to claim the ransoms from his earlier victories was to keep riding to the safe area, leaving the Earl of Hertford's men to their fate. He turned to check on Geoffrey, riding close behind him, and in the distance he espied the earl through the dust cloud, surrounded by three of his esquires who were trying to fight off four of Marshal's combatants. It was then that a big man in an emerald and gold surcoat resplendent with a snarling, crimson lion leapt his horse over a large bushel and into the fight. It was Sir William Marshal himself and he was aiming straight for the Earl of Hertford's flank. Raymond looked through the trees and saw the open land beyond, the road back towards Westminster where Alice and three rich ransoms awaited him. He cursed as he realised that he couldn't abandon Hertford, and so he turned Dreigiau and charged to his defence.

'Beware right,' Raymond yelled at Hertford, who petulantly squealed for his men to rally to his side and defend him from Marshal. Raymond urged his courser to great speed but he could already see that he would be too late. Marshal did not even break stride as he passed between two of the earl's esquires and smashed his sword across the back of Hertford's great helm, breaking the leather strap under the earl's chin and spinning the steel pot around so that Hertford could not see. Raymond inhaled sharply through clenched teeth as Marshal prepared to bring his sword down again. The blow never fell. Instead, Marshal effortlessly juggled his sword into his left while simultaneously grabbing the reins from Hertford's hand and dragging the blinded earl away from the fight. A much practiced move, Raymond was wowed by the ease at which Marshal handled both weapons and steed. Nonetheless, he knew his duty and kicked Dreigiau forward to intercept the knight as they made their way back into the tight trees.

Immediately two men from Marshal's conrois came

forward to block his path and Raymond snarled, veering between them as they leaned forward in the saddle to swing their weapons at him. Both lunges missed their target by a hand's breadth, but beyond the duo were more yellow and green-surcoated warriors and Raymond darted through circling shields and flashing swords, searching the spinney of trees for a glimpse of the famous knight and the earl. He could sense the presence of the two warriors who had dodged seconds before and turned his horse suddenly to deflect one warrior's blow with his shield and another from the other side with his sword as the two horsemen swept past him. Another man on foot came at Raymond with his sword in the air and a deep gash in his cheek. Strongbow's captain didn't even bother using his shield, but removed his left leg from his stirrup and kicked the man full in the face with the sole of his foot.

Replacing his armoured leg, Raymond pulled Dreigiau around and searched the trees for any sign of the earl. There was no sight of him and he cursed. Around him, men in the arms of Hertford were being led away to give up their ransoms while those left at liberty were still fighting desperately to avoid the same fate. Hertford's part in the tourney was all but over.

'Let's get out of here,' Raymond told Geoffrey. As he pulled alongside his esquire he espied a look of sheer terror pass across his face. Sir William Marshal had arrived back on the tourney field and he came straight at Raymond de Carew.

As he had done with Hertford, Marshal approached Raymond from behind, aiming a sword blow at the Welshman's head and it was only the widening of Geoffrey's eyes in fear that warned Raymond to the danger. He tried to turn Dreigiau to meet him, but Marshal was not known as the greatest horseman in Europe for nothing and at the last second he let his steed drift to the left, sweeping his weapon down on his enemy's head. Any other man would have been knocked unconscious by the move, but somehow Raymond had the presence of mind to drop his reins and throw his sword across his back. Marshal's weapon clanged off the captain's blade – sending reverberations up both of Raymond's hands – though it proved enough to bounce Marshal's sword strike over his head. If Marshal was shocked that his trick had not worked he did not show it as he leant down and dragged Raymond's long reins from his lap and dragged Dreigiau forwards by his bridle.

'Marshal!' was all Raymond could muster to shout as he almost fell out of his saddle. Dreigiau was dragged forward by Marshal's bigger, stronger charger and Raymond, devoid of reins and balance, struggled to adjust his seat. 'Wait!' he exclaimed, but to no avail. The famous knight was not about to let another ransom go to waste. As he had Hertford, Raymond supposed, Marshal would drag him from the wood to where a group of men would be waiting to force him to surrender at spearpoint. Strongbow's captain could not afford to pay even the smallest ransom, never mind replace his saddle, sword and new armour. The thought of losing Dreigiau was unbearable and so he stayed in the saddle rather than cast himself onto the ground and escape on foot.

They had come out of the small copse and Raymond could see a small knot of men waiting down by the river for their leader to arrive. Some of those already captured by Marshal were unhorsed and watched by those warriors. Amongst them was the Earl of Hertford and Raymond knew he would soon join the nobleman if he did not act. Suddenly inspiration came to him. He desisted from pulling on Dreigiau's mane and instead squeezed the speedy steed's sides to increase his pace. Within a couple of strides Dreigiau had closed the gap on Marshal's charger and Raymond took aim and struck, not at his captor, but through his own reins, releasing himself from Marshal's grasp. He laughed as he softened his leg grip and leaned to his left, turning Dreigiau back towards the spinney and allowing Marshal to speed away from him. His amusement quickly turned to fear as Marshal realised that his captive had slipped the hook. If he wasn't so desperate to get away Raymond would have applauded Marshal's impressive horsemanship as he turned his horse on a sixpence to pursue him. He only had a split second to lift his shield as Marshal's mighty blow fell and knocked him backwards off his saddle, but as he tumbled the short distance from horseback into a prickly hedge, Raymond did consider that he had never been hit so hard. The branches scraped harshly on his armour as he tumbled through its grasp to meet the ground with a solid thump. He could hear the people on the other side of the river roaring Marshal's name, urging him to strike and take another ransom. They sought Raymond's defeat and good sport.

He rolled out of the bush as Marshal pulled his horse around to face him. Raymond still had his shield but his sword had disappeared in the long grass. Against a mounted man of Marshal's skill he knew he would not stand a chance in any event. He stole a glance to see if he could get to Dreigiau before his opponent attacked the short distance between them. However, the courser had trotted off to join the small group of knights awaiting Marshal's command.

'Oh, thanks a lot,' Raymond grumbled at his disloyal horse as he turned back to face Marshal. Sir William's steed snorted and stomped her feet, impatient to attack the unhorsed Raymond, but for many seconds the knight held her back and simply stared at the unhorsed warrior as if expecting another trick.

Strongbow's captain breathed out slowly as he attempted to come up with a ruse that would save him from utter penury.

'Think, think, think,' he kept repeating as he watched Marshal's slow, careful advance. The knight was not charging him like a madman, but trotting slowly in a wide arc, eying up his target calmly and professionally. Obviously Raymond's initial defence during the fight in the trees had made Marshal wary. For his part, Raymond wondered what sort of man was hidden below the great helm and chainmail when not one hint of human flesh was visible. With nowhere to run, he kept his back to the thorny hedge, denying Marshal the ability to get behind him. His opponent was only ten paces away and did not flinch when he saw Raymond turn his back on his advance and try to clamber through the hedgerow and into the next field.

But Raymond de Carew was not ready to run. Instead he hauled at a prickly branch with his hands and then tore away the few remaining tendrils that held it in place. He then darted towards Marshal with the rudimentary weapon held aloft. Raymond fancied that Marshal must have let a grin break across his face, hidden beneath the great helm, when he saw the seemingly panicked charge of the defeated man armed with a branch. However, his mare's reaction to the unexpected threat of the rustling bush was to suddenly scuttle sideways in fear.

Any other rider would have fallen from the saddle, but somehow Marshal hung on as his charger dropped her shoulder to get away from the prickles. Raymond was not about to let the chance go a-begging and he dragged the branch along the horse's flank, setting her scurrying the opposite direction with a frightened snort of horror. No man could have held onto the twisting and bucking horse, and Marshal finally slammed onto the ground as the crowd, and his knights, gasped in astonishment.

Raymond laughed as he watched Marshal sprawl on the ground. Many men would have stayed down, winded from the heavy fall but Marshal grunted only once on impact and then slowly pulled himself to his feet, seemingly unaffected by the fall.

'So you are human,' Raymond smiled as Marshal put his hand to his chest.

Raymond's opponent did not respond as he dragged his sword from the scabbard and stabbed it into the ground before him. He began dusting himself off as two of his knights galloped forward to aid their commander.

'Sir William,' one shouted and pointed at Raymond, 'shall we take him?' Marshal did not answer but held up his hand to wave them away. It was enough for the two knights who swapped nervous glances and then directed their horses back towards their companions and their captives.

'You know,' Raymond said loudly towards Marshal, 'I haven't two brass beans to rub together. Capturing me would be a waste of your time and effort.' The man clothed in metal pulled his sword out of the ground and in answer pointed it at Raymond's head. 'No, really,' he continued, 'I am Strongbow's captain! How much could a man working for him actually be worth? You must have heard the stories?' He held up the prickly branch. 'I can't even afford a proper sword,' he laughed.

'Here's one,' Marshal spoke for the first time, kneeling and picking up Raymond's sword and throwing the weapon in his direction.

Raymond nodded in gratitude of Marshal's chivalrous behaviour and cast the rudimentary, yet successful, branch aside in favour of steel. He took a deep breath as Marshal stalked forward and raised his sword aloft. Behind the famous knight, the nobles and townsfolk in the crowd cheered the greatest contest of arms they had yet seen on the prince's tourney field.

Chapter Five

'That's it!' Strongbow shouted as he stormed into the low roofed alehouse. Raymond leapt to his feet, almost upsetting the table as his lord entered. Candle flames and braziers whipped crazily on tabletops and walls brackets as a gust of wind swept through the drinking den. For a moment the earl's eyes lingered on Alice of Abergavenny from whose shoulders his captain had quickly removed his arm. His eyes narrowed judgementally at the woman before flicking back to his warlord.

'Collect our belongings, Raymond. We are leaving for Striguil immediately. Curse Henry! Who does he think he is dealing with, a backwater knight from the hills of Ceredigion with only sheep to command?' In the week since they had caught up with King Henry's court Strongbow had accomplished absolutely nothing. Frustratingly, the king had refused to allow the earl into his presence even after sending his herald to summon him to his Palace of Westminster before dawn each day. Strongbow had been hideously embarrassed as he waited outside the main hall in the scorching heat while the king judged ever lowlier legal cases inside. Lords, ladies, barons, local landowners and knights had been summoned into the king's presence while the disgraced Earl Strongbow stood outside waiting to be admitted.

Raymond did not have the heart to confess to the earl that on at least two of the days when he had dutifully remained at vigil outside Henry's door, the king had actually been hunting in the Middlesex countryside. In every tavern and alehouse Sir Richard de Clare was ridiculed and nothing Raymond could say or do would stop the iniquitous talk of courtiers and soldiers. To make matters worse, Strongbow had been forced to find lodgings with his men in the Thorney Inn while other less grand courtiers were entertained by the king in the palace or with the Hospitallers down river in London. And in the earl's noble opinion the Thorney Inn was populated solely by rats, drunkards and foul whores.

'That is unfair,' a drunken Borard had whispered to Raymond. 'The whores are by far the best available in Westminster.'

However, just that morning, Strongbow had been admitted into the king's presence. Finally a breakthrough! But of course it had been another of Henry's attempts to mock the earl and Strongbow had been forced to stand at the back of the hall amongst the lesser nobility while the king had taken a faux interest in a case about two local knights who felt that the other was encroaching on their hereditary rights to pasture lands. Strongbow had looked on helpless, unable to move from his embarrassing position or complain, as the arrogant king had laughed to his friends and pointed at the earl at the back of the hall. A head taller than everyone else around him, it was obvious who was the target of their scorn.

When finally his name had been formally read to the court it was only as *Sir Richard de Clare*, rather than as *Earl of Pembroke* or *Lord of Striguil*. In a move that could only have been choreographed to embarrass Strongbow further, seconds after his introduction Henry's tall steward strode ahead of the earl towards the dais and had whispered into the king's ear. Henry had shot Strongbow a victorious and malevolent glance as his steward had made a short announcement that the king would return the following morning, and had exited the main hall leaving the earl standing before an empty throne, the mocking whispers rattling around the stone walls. It had proved the breaking point.

'Well,' the earl continued, angrier than ever, 'I am no mere courtesan to be toyed with for Henry's entertainment. I am Strongbow,' he shouted the last statement so that everyone in the low ceiling alehouse stopped what they were doing and looked at the apoplectic man in the crimson and gold surcoat.

Raymond swapped a brief, apologetic glance with his companions, a broad-shouldered knight and a young priest with auburn hair whose eyes seem to record every word of the nobleman's outburst.

'Drinks for everyone on his lordship, the Earl Strongbow, in celebration of Prince Harry's coronation,' Raymond shouted and signalled to the owner of the inn. The men in the alehouse responded with a cheer and turned their backs on Raymond's table to resume their drinking.

'I hope you don't actually expect me to pay,' the earl growled as he cast his gaze over the motley group that accompanied his captain. He was sure that the surcoat which the knight wore was that of the Marshal family of Marlborough, but he could not place its wearer. The priest looked out of place, though Strongbow observed that he was not in the slightest bit uncomfortable despite being surrounded by coarse fighting men at their ale. Alongside the trio were Raymond's charges, the bastards of Abergavenny. The earl smiled thinly to Geoffrey and Alice before noticing that almost all of Raymond's milites were scattered around the wooden tables of the alehouse and had heard his flare-up.

'We must continue to be patient, my Lord. My friends,'

Raymond indicated towards the priest and the knight, 'know that King Henry is being...' he shook his head as he searched for the correct word, 'tiresome in his treatment of your lordship, but they think that he will meet with you after his son is crowned tomorrow.'

'It could be,' the auburn-headed priest butted in, 'that staying out of King Henry's way while he is in one of his moods,' he paused over the last word and raised an eyebrow towards the smirking knight, 'could be the best course of action for you right now. You do rather irritate him.'

Strongbow turned on the cleric angrily. 'What do you know of kings and earls, priest?'

It was Raymond's turn to intervene and he laid a hand on Strongbow's shoulder. 'This is Hubert Walter, Lord.' Raymond leant in close to whisper in Strongbow's ear. 'He hears many happenings that occur around the court, undertakings that could help your cause,' he stressed.

The earl stiffened at his captain's soft reprimand but he took his point and nodded towards the priest. 'I apologise, Father Hubert. I have been away from court too long.'

Hubert held up a hand. 'No apology is necessary. My advice remains the same. Keep your distance until Henry's business in England is done and pray that he comes through the coronation in better humour. You must remember that this whole occasion is about giving our errant Archbishop of Canterbury a bloody nose, politically speaking. I assure you that once done it will make our king enormously happy.' The priest held out a hand, inviting the nobleman to join them at their drinks. For a second it looked like the earl might refuse the invitation, as if sitting in a lowly alehouse with a priest, a mere knight, his lowborn captain and two bastards was another affront against his already delicate pride, but after a few seconds he acquiesced.

113

'It is all this sitting around which makes King Henry act irrationally,' the as-yet-nameless knight told Hubert. 'God, but I don't need to be on the receiving end of one of his tongue-lashings because he is fed up and bored. The sooner he gets back on campaign against King Louis, the better for us all.'

'This is William Marshal, Lord,' Raymond described. 'He won Prince Harry's tournament this morning.'

'I wouldn't know,' Strongbow grumbled, 'as I wasn't invited to attend.'

'Your captain did you proud fighting with the Earl of Hertford's men,' Sir William told the earl with a nervous laugh. 'Our bout on the London Road went on for longer than all the rest put together, until we decided to call it a day. It will take me many weeks to get over the effort.'

'It had better not,' Raymond laughed, 'for I want some revenge and tonight we will have another battle at my chosen battleground - the bar. Anyway, you put me on my arse first. I'll be pulling prickles from my backside for weeks to come!' Everyone laughed except Strongbow, who nodded and smiled politely before climbing to his feet.

'Good, good,' he said, though his tone was anything but that. 'We will keep the course upon which we have set and hope that King Henry will treat me as he would any other lord.' Strongbow sighed. 'I will see you tomorrow then. Goodnight.' He nodded to each of the men before turning on his heel and leaving the tavern for his rooms above.

'So that was Strongbow,' Hubert Walter said to Raymond as the earl vacated the room. 'He is not as impressive as his name would suggest. He wants to go to Ireland then?'

Raymond drank long from his mug of good Gascon wine before answering. 'He has little future in England,' he said finally. 'It may be that he can make something of himself across the sea.' He noticed Hubert's intrusive eyes exploring his face. Raymond wondered if he had done the right thing by approaching the sly cleric for help. Hubert was said to be a close adviser of King Henry, though he had attested no charters and was rarely seen in the king's company. 'It is probably too late for Strongbow anyway,' Raymond continued, adopting a flippant air. 'He is forty and my uncle, Robert FitzStephen, has this King Diarmait wrapped around his finger and his realm of Laighin won for himself. I even heard Diarmait has offered his daughter in marriage to Robert. Still, if Strongbow wants to waste his time rustling cattle in Ireland, I can't imagine why King Henry would be angry at letting him depart.' He leant back on the bench and shrugged his shoulders, taking another deep draught from his cup. Hubert mirrored his movement though Raymond was unsure if the priest was indeed relaxing or attempting to make him feel like he could be at ease when he should be concentrating. The priest's currency at court was information and Raymond did not want to sell his too cheaply.

'I had heard about Diarmait's offer also.' Hubert told him and paused to think, again studying Raymond with his suspicious green-grey eyes. 'I will do what I can to sway the king's opinion in Strongbow's favour. I can make no promises. Now,' he said glancing at Alice and Geoffrey, 'to what we were discussing before we were rudely interrupted by our friend the earl.'

'Abergavenny,' the young woman said.

'As I said, this will not be easy,' Hubert Walter told Raymond, 'and at this moment William de Braose and his father are completely unassailable. They are two of the king's most trusted nobles, and have promised many warriors for Henry's coming campaign in France. You, on the other hand, have nothing that the king wants or needs, but of course this may change in the future.' He gave a small smile of encouragement to Geoffrey and settled back into his chair with a mug of wine.

'What? That is all?' Alice snarled. 'Patience?' she spat the word out in Hubert's direction. 'For this we give you our money? We are the lawful heirs to Abergavenny!'

Hubert was on her in an instant. 'Lower your voice,' he snarled as his eyes darted around the room. 'Henry has spies everywhere and if you do not want my help, I assure you others will benefit from my time and advice. This king is not to be poked and prodded onto whatever path you choose. He will not care whether you have a document signed and sealed by the Lord above stating that your brother is the legitimate owner. If he has no reason to support your claim, and you offer no reason for him to support you, then you have no hope. To be successful you must wait and listen for your opportunity. It will take time,' he stressed with a contemptuous look which would have felled a courser. 'And it will take patience.'

Alice was not daunted. 'So much for the much vaunted influence of Hubert Walter,' she sneered as she whipped her headdress from her head to reveal a shower of golden locks. 'I knew this was a waste of my time,' she said scornfully to Raymond.

'Alice, lower your voice,' he responded as he grabbed her hand. 'This is the only way. We will keep at it until it is done,' he said supportively.

The young woman ripped her fingers from his grip and cast a livid glance in his direction. 'No, there are other ways to get what I want.'

'Sister,' Geoffrey murmured, urging her to be quiet and smiling at some men close by who had noted her outburst. Something in Geoffrey's body language piqued Raymond's curiosity, but his train of thought was disturbed

116

when Hubert Walter climbed to his feet and dusted off his dark brown robes.

'You are lucky that you have a friend in Raymond de Carew,' the priest told Alice, 'for otherwise your anger and quick tongue would land you in great peril. Of that I have little doubt.'

'Hubert...' Raymond started but was stopped when the priest raised his hand.

'We will talk again,' he said, 'but next time we shall do it alone.' With a seething look down upon the blond head of Alice of Abergavenny, he was gone. Seconds later Alice shot to her feet and would have run off if Raymond had not taken hold of her hand again.

'Alice, what is wrong?' he asked, confused at her flare-up of anger.

'You are not the only one who can make plans,' she snapped and tried to rip her hand out of his grasp, 'and how I do business costs nothing and makes more powerful friends than you could ever provide.'

'What are you saying?'

'That you can tell Hubert Walter that Geoffrey of Abergavenny does not need his help to have his lands returned to him.' She was alight with rage. 'And you can tell the same to your pathetic Strongbow. My brother and I will be gone by tomorrow evening.'

Raymond was confused. 'You are leaving? Where will you go? Has something happened?' He let go of her hand.

She held his gaze and licked her teeth inside her mouth as if considering whether or not to devour him. 'We are going with Prince Harry,' she said finally. Her eyes held a challenge.

'What?' he started to say, but a split second later Raymond understood what must have happened. While he had talked, begged and bribed behind the scenes on behalf of Strongbow and Alice, she had been making her own friends from the influential nobles who frequented the Thorney Inn looking for the companionship of whores. And who would have blamed them, Raymond thought? Walking into the alehouse they could not have missed the young beauty – dressed like a noblewoman thanks to Raymond's generosity – and surrounded by wenches. Already filled with lust they must have flocked to her table and whispered promises in her ear of great riches and even more powerful friends, if only she would give herself to them. Raymond wondered which knight in Prince Harry's retinue had promised enough to Alice for her to betray him. Anger filled his mind, thoughts of revenge, dark feelings fed by wine.

'Who is it?' he demanded. It wasn't as if he didn't know that this would eventually happen, but he never supposed that she would leave him so soon. 'Who?'

She shook her head and did not answer. 'Geoffrey, follow me,' she ordered instead. 'We leave tomorrow after the coronation.' She stomped across the alehouse towards the room which she had shared with Raymond. Behind her, Geoffrey slowly followed in her wake with a sympathetic shrug towards his erstwhile master.

'Who is it?' Raymond shouted at Alice's back, but she did not answer. Silence had over taken the Thorney Inn. It was Marshal's voice which broke the hush.

'I would rather go into a tourney without armour, helm or shield than have an argument with that young lady.'

'Agreed,' Raymond whispered as he watched his sometime mistress leave the inn for their rooms above. His anger receded slowly. He told himself that this had been their understanding all along, that she had never promised to stay with him and that he was better off alone anyway. Slapping a smile on his face he laughed

118

belatedly at Marshal's joke.

'Now, before you tell me the story of your first fight against the French,' Raymond said with a smile, 'what are you drinking?'

Strongbow had not been invited to the coronation of Prince Harry as joint King of England with his father. Nor had Raymond de Carew, of course, but during his all-night drinking session with Sir William Marshal, he had decided to sneak into the abbey to see the historic ceremony. To that end an unstable Marshal now smuggled him into the grounds of Westminster Abbey through the stone refectory.

'Ssh-ssh,' Marshal slurred. His breath was heavy with drink. 'There is an abbot around here somewhere and his voice would ring your ears like the bell calling monks to Lauds. So be silent.'

Together the pair rushed across the grassy cloister, heavy with dew, which clung to the side of the abbey. They wobbled drunkenly and laughed like two esquires up to no good. From there they skirted around the stone arcade which surrounded the cloister quietly. Checking every heavy oak door, Raymond finally found one unguarded and unlocked, and he pushed through only to find that he was faced with the rear of a tapestry. However, the tasselled edge of the wall-hanging was within his reach and he pulled it carefully aside so that he could peer into the south transept of the abbey. Beyond it was the nave where the greatest noblemen of England were beginning to assemble before the tomb of the King-Saint Edward the Confessor. He turned back to where Marshal waited just outside the door.

'I'll stay here,' he whispered, 'and watch the ceremony from behind the tapestry. You go inside to your seat and I'll meet you afterwards so you can sneak me into the great hall for the feast.'

'Alright,' Marshal replied as he rubbed the effect of ale from his tired eyes. 'How's your view?'

In answer Raymond pulled the tapestry aside again. 'Good God,' he whispered as he arched his back and stared up at the stone cathedral as if for the first time. Raymond gawped at the scene before him, dazzled by the colours, the sounds and the smells. He swayed under the effect of booze. Stretching his neck, he stared upwards at the huge dome at the western end of the nave. There, sixty feet high, was a gargantuan picture of Christ. His stern-featured and splendid head was wrapped in saintly gold leaf as he looked down upon king and commoner alike, his vestments of impressive blue and red. Raymond had to clutch at the collar at his throat to allow him more room to breathe as Christ's eyes bore down upon him from above. Light poured through a hundred tiny coloured windows, allowing God's presence to penetrate the dusty walls where brightly-coloured scenes from the story of Christ were adorned. The nave alone must have been two hundred paces in length and it was cold. He had seen the dome from the riverside, but it seemed even more gigantic as he stood directly under its majesty. He had to adjust his feet as the night's drinking unbalanced him again.

'You could fit the whole of Striguil inside the cloister,' he told Marshal, who was giggling at his friend's reaction to the great building. Raymond struggled to even comprehend how man created such a structure. Before he had arrived in England, he had thought the Cistercian Abbey of Tyndyrn impressive, but this dwarfed even that holy site. Surely God would see the church from Heaven and would heap rich rewards on the people who created and maintained the mighty building. Norman prayers would echo to the Heavens, though the distance was great, and

120

would be heard above all others, of that Raymond was sure.

'I will say a prayer for Lady Basilia before I leave this holy place,' he said and made a move to walk into the nave.

'No, stay hidden, you drunken fool,' warned the equally inebriated Marshal as he grabbed Raymond's arm and hauled him back under cover. 'I don't want you getting skewered by the royal guards who think you are here to assassinate the two King Henrys. Kings Henry?' he attempted before slapping Raymond hard on the shoulder. 'And you must forget about that hussy of Abergavenny,' Marshal continued. 'Women like her are better in other men's beds. Trouble, trouble, trouble,' he muttered as he left Raymond to his own devices and joined the growing assembly of people inside the great Benedictine abbey.

Raymond ducked back through the door and crouched beneath the cold stone archway. He was still covered by the dusty tapestry depicting St Thomas the Apostle, but beyond the drapery he could hear hundreds of people talking excitedly. He stole a look around the tapestry's edge to again admire Westminster Abbey. Massive columns of stone seemed to hold the whole interior of the structure up while coloured glass high in the building cast a thousand shapes across the smoky interior caused by braziers on the walls and the aroma of incense. Bright painted icons showing the lives of the saints adorned every inch of the walls whilst somewhere unseen a choir sung the most beautiful song that Raymond had ever heard. The murmur both lulled and excited the mind and it was all he could do not to be overcome by the size of greatest building in the Kingdom of England.

The music and the light, the smoky atmosphere from burning torches and the drink he had consumed the night before soon caught up with Raymond de Carew. He burped vomit suddenly, but somehow kept it down, and within a few minutes he had leaned back against the archway and fallen asleep.

It could only have been a short while later that Raymond woke up. A throng of colourfully robed people had crowded into the chairs beside him in the transept, seemingly unaware that a fully armed warlord from the Welsh March was hidden behind the tapestry feet away from them. All were staring towards the chancel, where Raymond could see a blond teenager in a fine red cloak lined with ermine kneeling before a cleric who extolled the Heavens in Latin. The youth, who could only have been Prince Harry, was sniggering despite the solemnity of the occasion and he received a jolly clout to his head from a ginger-headed man with a stubbly chin who towered over him. It was the Old King, Henry FitzEmpress. It was the first time that Raymond had seen him and he was thoroughly shocked at his appearance. Short, stocky and unkempt, the king looked more like a blacksmith than the almost mythical figure of whom he had heard. His arms appeared powerful and strong while his ginger hair was close-cropped yet dishevelled. The king was clothed in the gaudy robes of his office, a splendid Angevin surcoat and a golden crown rather than the unremarkable hunting attire Raymond had heard he usually wore, and he certainly looked incredibly uncomfortable in the rich clothes. He scratched his groin, uncaring, it seemed, that some of the greatest men in England watched his every move with inordinate interest. For some reason Raymond immediately found himself laughing along with the king, his good humour infectious even amongst the serious surroundings of the grand abbey. Even from a distance he was drawn in by the king's distinctive eyes – they were of the brightest blue and while now they sparkled with good humour, Raymond imagined that they could as easily repel an onlooker if Henry burst into one of his legendary fits of anger.

As Raymond watched, Henry returned his son's smile and rolled his eyes at the ludicrously lavish and dramatic ceremony. Above both men the feeble-looking Archbishop of York stumbled over his words, causing more mirth from the irreligious father and son. The archbishop looked disgusted with the two men but knew better than to complain. Behind him there were two thrones awaiting the kings of England.

Raymond could see many of the great churchmen of England in the transept on the far side of the cathedral, or at least those that had not followed Becket into exile. Bishop Gilbert Foliot of London looked nervous as he watched the service going ahead while beside him the Bishop of Salisbury, the brother of the Lord Constable of England, looking as daunting and severe as his famous sibling. On the other side of Foliot sat the elderly and venerable Bishop Walter of Rochester. Raymond was surprised to see the old man as he was said to be like a father to the rebel cleric, Becket. What must King Henry have threatened to have him at Westminster, he wondered? Plenty more bishops from England, Wales, Normandy, Maine and Anjou watched the ceremony. The rest of the men who populated the abbey were the lords of the land: earls, counts, barons, viscounts and knights, and their banners emblazoned the walls of the church like the billowing sails of a great colourful ship. Through the abbey walls, Raymond could hear the crowds from the small town and its hinterland who awaited the popular young prince's first parade as King of England. It would be they who would acclaim Henry the Younger as their rightful king, as had the English for each monarch for hundreds of years.

'Greetings, Raymond,' a voice like silk whispered

through the door which was ajar behind him.

'Bloody hell,' Raymond de Carew squeaked as he was lurched from his daydream. He quickly dragged himself to his feet and ducked out of the abbey lest the newcomer attract a guard to his hiding place. There he met a jovial Hubert Walter who stood in the arcade with a young and vaguely familiar teenager trailing in his wake. Raymond tried in vain to place the barrel-chested teenager but, unsuccessful in his attempts, he instead greeted his acquaintance, the priest.

'You scared me, Hubert. It's not like you to miss out on an event like this,' he said, squinting as the sun penetrated his drink addled eyes.

'Indeed, but young Geoffrey here,' he indicated towards the youngster and raised his voice, 'had to make a fool of himself with Rosamund de Clifford and so I suggested that we should get some air.' Beside him the young man looked angry and embarrassed and bowed his head to his chest.

Suddenly it clicked who the young man looked like. 'King Henry's boy?' asked Raymond.

'My apologies,' Hubert Walter exclaimed. 'I had forgotten that you haven't been at court because of Strongbow's circumstances. Yes, he is Henry's bastard,' he sighed. 'Geoffrey, the lay Archdeacon of Lincoln, and my reluctant charge.'

'I don't need to be looked after,' the acne-marked youngster complained. In his petulant features Raymond immediately saw how closely Geoffrey resembled King Henry, much more so than the youngster who would be crowned today. 'My brother Harry doesn't have a minder, Richard doesn't need to be watched, and I am older than either of them.'

'Geoffrey,' Hubert warned, 'if you persist in making improper suggestions to your father's mistress within earshot of her lord father and the Bishop of London, then I have to say that you do indeed require an escort.' The priest shook his head. 'And your brothers don't need chaperons because one is the Duke of Aquitaine and the other is about to be anointed King of the English.' Hubert shook his head and turned to speak to Raymond. 'Now be silent.'

Henry's bastard would not relent. 'It's not even a real coronation,' he grumbled, his jealousy evident upon his face. 'Without Archbishop Becket here it doesn't count. I won't bow to Harry anyway,' he sniffed and puffed out his substantial chest. 'I'm a prince too, Father told me so.'

Hubert rolled his eyes and spoke to Raymond. 'Apparently the Pope sent word that no one but his grace the Archbishop of Canterbury could perform the coronation. Honestly, Becket's scheming gives all the clergy a bad name.'

Raymond smiled, aware that Hubert was involved in every intrigue in England.

'Pope Alexander tried to send my uncle Bishop Roger to stop the ceremony, but Father closed all the ports to prevent him from crossing the sea,' Geoffrey gleefully described. 'Unfortunately it also meant that Eleanor and her children would not be able to get here,' he said, obviously happy at the absence of the queen, Eleanor of Aquitaine, and his younger half-siblings, 'except for Harry of course.'

'Geoffrey, go across the cloister to the kitchens and find us some food,' Hubert Walter said sternly. The young archdeacon tarried for a moment before catching the priest's imperious stare. That proved enough to make him think better of arguing and he slumped off down the stone arcade towards the kitchens. When he was gone, Hubert threw a despairing arm in the direction of the pantry. 'I do believe that he still thinks his father will disinherit Queen Eleanor's sons and he will become king thanks to some strange twist of fate.' Hubert shook his head. 'He refuses to be invested as a priest as his father desires, so he serves the See of Lincoln as a layman.' Disbelieving, Hubert held up his hands, unable to comprehend why anyone with King Henry's influential patronage would refuse to be placed in a position of power within the Church. 'He could be Archbishop of Canterbury if he just submitted to Henry's wishes.'

'And what would that make you?' Raymond asked.

'Busy, I would imagine,' Hubert replied. 'I have news for you, by the way,' he added, 'regarding both Strongbow and your issues with Abergavenny.'

'Do tell all,' Raymond said with a smile, 'starting with the earl's news, I suppose.' His heart fluttered momentarily as he thought about bringing Alice information that he had recovered her brother's lordship, but knew that his allegiance lay primarily with Strongbow.

Hubert sniffed deeply, leading Raymond to wonder if the priest was testing the air to see if he was drunk. He quickly realised that the priest was steeling himself. 'The king will meet with Strongbow today, during the coronation feast,' the priest said. 'Pray that nothing happens between then and now to annoy him. Honestly, I have no idea what he will say to him, but this at least is a chance for Strongbow to plead his case directly to King Henry.'

'That is all the earl wishes, Hubert, the opportunity to convince the King to release him or give him his lands at Pembroke back,' he said. 'What about the other news of Abergavenny?'

The priest chewed on his upper lip. 'Sir William de Braose is here in Westminster, Raymond, and is asking questions about the whereabouts of you and your two companions.'

That news worried him. He had guessed that his enemy,

126

like all the nobility of England, would come to Westminster but had hoped that his presence and that of Alice and Geoffrey of Abergavenny would have gone unnoticed. 'Where did you hear this?'

'That particular whisper came from within the king's household. I was also told that Sir William has hired a mercenary crew from Ireland to kill you. I tell you this for free because we are friends. My source is close to the sheriff. He told me that a Danish crew rowed past London Bridge yesterday, claiming to be traders. They anchored across the river at Lambeth, paid the harbour fee, but they didn't appear in the marketplace or make any purchases.'

'Danes?' Raymond's felt his pulse rise as he tried to comprehend the news which Hubert had given him. The king had mercenaries from Iberia and Gascony in his employ and they were considered the worst of all those damned souls who sold their swords for money. But a crew of Danes? He had never heard of anyone in Christendom foolish enough to hire a boatload of those bloodthirsty pirates to do their bidding. His father still told stories from his youth of when he fought against the crewmen of the dragon-headed ships who had crossed from Ireland to fight for the rebellious Welsh chieftains. Entire monasteries and whole Norman towns had disappeared, killed during a brutal campaign which had engulfed the Dyfed coast. His father had told him that there were none as pitiless or as savage as the Danes. Never had he mentioned them being used to garrison or protect – only to rampage and to kill.

'I ask this with fear in my heart,' Raymond began. 'Will Sir William send these Danes to take Alice and Geoffrey by force?'

Hubert considered the question, pressing his lips together and narrowing his eyes. 'Here in Westminster at the coronation, under the king's very nose? I find it hard to

127

believe that he will break the peace. But it is a long road back to Striguil with lots of places for an ambush, especially near the Thames. You had, I assume, intended to return home via Oxford?'

'Indeed,' Raymond said inattentively as he considered the advice. All trace of his night's drinking had disappeared though he felt a new sickness rise in his belly. 'Both William de Braose and his father are in the abbey with the king?'

'Yes, both were told to attend upon the king. I saw them both in the nave.' Hubert said and Raymond allowed himself to relax.

However, at that second, the king's bastard, Geoffrey, reappeared from the kitchen with several pears balanced on a bread trencher. 'I found some fruit,' he said absentmindedly, staring down at his load. 'I had more but I dropped three down some stairs when William de Braose surprised me coming out of the lay brothers' dormitory.'

While Hubert and Raymond swapped a surprised glance, Geoffrey examined one of the pears and then bit deeply into the fruit.

'William the Younger?' Hubert asked his charge.

'Um-hmnn,' Geoffrey hummed. 'It was strange, though. He didn't speak to me and had armour under his surcoat.' The king's bastard shrugged and took another bite of his pear. Juice squirted down his chin.

Hubert immediately understood what Geoffrey's words meant and he turned sharply towards Raymond, but Strongbow's captain was already gone, running through the stone arcade of Westminster Abbey. His sabatons slapped hard on the stone walkway as he sprinted in the direction of the river.

The Thorney Inn was one of the best known drinking dens

and whorehouses in Westminster. Some said that the alehouse had been there before the abbey, before the river had silted up to form the land on which the town was built. The first King Henry, who had been nicknamed Beauclerc, had frequented the establishment on so many occasions during his reign that it was rumoured that half of Westminster was populated by his baseborn offspring. He, and his liegemen, had made the owners of the inn rich and his presence had attracted many others who were assured that the wagging tongues of the court would not hear about what went on inside the low-roofed alehouse.

However, the Thorney whores' best pickings did not come from the infrequent visits of noblemen and lonely knights, but from pilgrims. They came in their droves to see the shrine in honour of the greatest of all English saints, the Saxon King Edward the Confessor. Westminster's memorial to St Edward was superior even to St Cuthbert's in Durham or that of St Edmund in deepest Norfolk. Hundreds made the journey from all over the kingdom and beyond. They wept and prayed before his tomb, appealing to their angelic king-saint to deliver their prayers to God and allow them peace and rich rewards in a hard world that gave them nothing but pain and destitution. And they were willing to pay for that privilege. They had only but to leave a small donation for the good of the humble Benedictine brothers who maintained the abbey and they would be assured of the noble saint's help for their interests. The Benedictines had become rich from the pilgrims' goodwill.

While the godly needs of the pilgrims were distributed by the brothers at the abbey, their earthly desires were seen to by the women who plied their trade in the Thorney Inn, and for far less than those religious men up the riverbank.

Inside, nothing but the best ales and the finest whores, depending upon your budget, were to be found at the famous alehouse - night time for pilgrims, and between prime and terce for religious brothers. Thanks to that steady flow of traffic, the Thorney was one of the most popular haunts in town and was normally stuffed to the rafters with people. Except, of course, on a day when England would see a second king crowned and paraded through the small town.

As he sprinted through the dung-strewn streets, Raymond de Carew knew that the inn would be deserted and cursed his stupidity for leaving his friends. Only a few of his conrois would have remained. He had dismissed the rest and told them to walk up into town for the festivities taking place in celebration of the coronation. It would mean that Alice and Geoffrey would be defenceless. He had no reason to believe that Sir William de Braose would have discovered where they were staying, but why else, he considered, would a man of his enemy's standing leave the coronation early and dressed in chainmail? Raymond prayed that he was wrong, that Sir William and his mercenary Danes had not already killed Alice and Geoffrey while he had dilly-dallied at the abbey and talked to Hubert Walter. There would be few witnesses, and who would really mourn the murder of two bastards in a whorehouse brawl?

'Oh Lord, please protect them,' he prayed as he ran. Smoke wafted through the air and stung Raymond's lungs as he dashed towards the river. Where it could be coming from he did not know. His legs burned with the effort and he promised that William de Braose would die if anything were to befall Alice or Geoffrey. His fear proved sobering. As he burst around the final corner, he stumbled over the arm of a dead man. He did not stop, though, for down the street the Thorney Inn was in flames.

Raymond raised his hand to shield his face from the blaze that had taken the alehouse. Somewhere inside a weight-bearing beam crumbled and the top floor crashed into the ground, taking the flaming roof with it. Everywhere Raymond looked he saw signs of a ferocious fight: chainmailed footprints in dried mud, pools of blood, and abandoned weaponry. Screams and shouts were all that penetrated the din of the flaming ruin and everywhere people ran with buckets of water to stop the flames from spreading to other buildings. The wind was blowing up the river like dragon breath, sweeping the fire towards the rest of the town of Westminster, the abbey and the palace. Raymond knew exactly what he had to do.

'You,' he shouted at a young man carrying buckets from the riverside, 'forget the water and grab that mule.' He indicated to a frightened beast standing with its feet in the muddy shallows of the Thames. 'And then get some ropes. Follow me to the flames.' Raymond didn't wait to see if the boy did as he was told and instead picked up a discarded axe and took off towards the building immediately to the north of the Thorney Inn. He could already see that the fire was smouldering in the thatch of the low house. Heat and smoke plumed out of a side door as he kicked it down with one well-placed foot.

'What the hell are you doing?' The owner stormed up to Raymond. 'That's my bloody house!' He was a big man and armed with a wooden bucket which Raymond adjudged capable of causing severe damage if he chose to lash out at him. He grabbed Raymond by the back of his surcoat and tried to pull him away from his home. The Norman resisted, hoping that the man would let go, but when he didn't Raymond swung his right arm backwards and clouted the man in the chin with his elbow. The man

131

crumpled to his knees immediately.

'I'm sorry,' he told the man as he stared into the smoke-filled building.

'Lord?' the young man from the waterfront said nervously from behind Raymond. 'What do you want me to do?' He was struggling to hold a terrified mule in its place and was equally alarmed by the closeness of the flames and the unconscious man on the ground. The youngster was obviously keen to get back to helping his neighbours put out the flames that threatened his town rather than help the stranger armed with an axe.

Raymond turned towards the boy. 'What is your name?' he asked and swiped sweat from his brow.

'Fulk.'

'Well, Fulk, we are going to save Westminster from this fire and make you a hero in the process. Are you ready to help me?' Raymond asked. The boy was blank-faced but nodded once. 'Good. First, drag that man out of the way and then give me one end of the rope. I am going inside to take out the supporting pillars and then we use the mule to pull the whole house down and make a fire-break. Understand? This is how we stop the fire from spreading. Not by throwing buckets of water at an inferno.'

Fulk nodded nervously and quickly hauled the insensible man away. Raymond took up the rope and, taking a deep breath, entered the smoky world of the house. With the rope between his teeth, he began hacking away at the wooden post nearest the front, all the while praying that the whole structure didn't come down on top of him before he had finished his work. The heat from above and the smoke that surrounded him were overpowering. Skittering chips of wood sprayed in his already teary eyes and several times he missed his target, slamming the axe into the wattle wall of the house. One such blow opened a small rent in the

132

wall and Raymond fell against it, sucking in the clean air from outside. A few more swings left the beam wobbling but in place and, abandoning the axe, he quickly tied the rope around the pillar.

It was desperately difficult to see as he coughed his way back through the building, feeling his way along the wall with his eyes closed. He exited, spluttering and wiping his stinging eyes.

'Get the mule moving,' he croaked at Fulk, who reacted immediately, slapping his hand down on the animal's hindquarters. 'Pull, damn you,' he coughed in Fulk's direction as he gasped for breath in the constricting confines between the burning buildings. Fulk did not let him down and pulled and cajoled the honking mule so that the thick rope went taut and groaned under the tension. Raymond watched the building and prayed that the rope would not catch fire before the braying mule could bring it down. He prayed the flames would not catch the next house, a smithy, before he could create the fire-break.

'Fall,' Raymond urged and coughed again. Shakily, he pulled himself to his feet and grabbed the rope behind the mule, adding his weight to the effort. Fulk too pulled for all he was worth at the bridle of the mule. Nothing seemed to work.

'Damn you,' Raymond shouted, his teeth gritted with supreme effort. 'Break!'

Suddenly, as his hoarse voice echoed around the burning walls, something gave way and the thatched roof tumbled towards the two men and their mule with a violent crash. All three darted away from the danger, the mule breaking free of Fulk's grip and indignantly kicking his hind legs out at his master before cantering towards the river. Raymond and his companion watched from a safe distance as the rest of the building collapsed into a fiery mound on top of the remnants of the Thorney Inn.

'Well done, Fulk,' he said to his new companion. 'Well done indeed. If you ever find yourself in Wales and in need of work, come and find me. My name is Raymond de Carew and I always need good men like you.' The boy nodded timidly and, as Raymond again broke down into a fit of coughing, he disappeared back towards the riverbank.

'Raymond,' a weak voice called from beyond the burning buildings. It was Strongbow. He was battered, bruised and covered in ash and sweat, but he was alive. 'We were attacked, Raymond,' he said with a startled look in his eyes. 'Attacked!'

To Raymond it looked like the earl had awoken from a swoon. He coughed loudly because of the smoke in his chest, but he dutifully climbed to his feet to greet his lord. 'I am glad to see you,' he took the earl by his shoulders to steady him, feeling the prominent bones under Strongbow's mail. The earl was shaking but in his hand was a bloodied sword.

'They were Danes,' Strongbow replied, 'I am sure of it. It was like something out of a nightmare, Raymond: savages with axes and circular shields coming through the smoke. It was like the old tales.' He began panting and shaking his head. 'They were after your charges, Geoffrey and Alice of Abergavenny. I don't think they were expecting to find my warriors here.' The earl began blinking vociferously and Raymond wasn't sure if it was due to the acrid smoke or the high emotion of the situation.

'They must have been watching us and attacked when they saw the men go up to watch the coronation,' Raymond said and bowed his head as the guilt and enormity of his short sojourn hit him. Here and there he spotted men wearing or carrying Strongbow's colours, at least five of them, walking amongst the site of the fight.

'Don't worry, Raymond,' Walter de Bloet said as he approached. 'You weren't here but we showed them. Lord Richard showed them.' He nodded respectively towards the earl. Strongbow quickly returned his nephew's curt nod.

'What about our people,' Raymond asked Walter, 'are any hurt?' The growing blaze meant that he had to shout over the roar issuing from the wreckage of the Thorney Inn. Before his miles could answer, a wail echoed through the smoke. It was Alice. She was sitting only a few metres from him beside the river with tears pouring down her face and her blue gown covered in ash and mud. Geoffrey was at her side, a long gash across his head and blood on his face. Raymond was by her side in an instant, lifting her to her feet. He took her face in his hands. 'Are you alright, Alice? Are you hurt?'

'Geoffrey is injured,' she replied, rubbing away her tears with her fist. 'You promised that you would protect us,' she accused and pulled her face from his hands. 'But you were not here when we needed you. You are a liar,' she told him.

Raymond looked at his erstwhile mistress and shook his head. 'I am sorry...' he began and knelt down onto one knee beside Geoffrey. The boy had a head wound but Raymond could see that it looked a lot worse than he'd first assumed. As he reached forward to help the youngster Alice slapped his hand away.

'I don't need your help,' she spat. 'Prince Harry is already sending his private physician to help Geoffrey.'

Raymond stepped away from her. 'Why would the Young King help you?' he asked.

Alice tossed her hair to block her face from Raymond and spoke quietly to her brother, ignoring her former lover. 'He won't come himself,' she finally snarled. 'He's being crowned, but his knights are on their way. They will protect me,' she said with a defiant nod of her head, 'and they will take us to the palace tonight. He says that he will make sure I get back Abergavenny.'

'The prince will help you?' Raymond attempted to comprehend Alice's statement. 'Harry?' he asked again. A laugh built in strength as he slowly began to understand. He, a mere warrior from Wales, had been cuckolded by the heir to the greatest royal dominion in Europe. 'The snivelling little bastard who I saw acting like a child at the abbey?' he asked. Alice said nothing, pursing her lips angrily. 'He's fifteen, a wet behind the ears daddy's boy.' Raymond laughed again when he received no response. Alice's angry countenance confirmed that the prince had indeed taken his place in her affections. Raymond dragged his hands over his face and head, as if uncovering himself from under a hood. He wasn't angry, and that surprised him. In fact, the more that Raymond thought about the development, the more relieved he was; relieved that Alice had found a powerful protector who could see her dream of capturing Abergavenny come true. And for himself? He was relieved that he could return to Striguil to continue his worship of Basilia without the guilt of having a mistress sharing his bed. In any case, how could he be jealous of a prince? Raymond might as well have been envious of God's power or angry at the sun for rising. He could never hope to rival the boy who had just been crowned King of England in the great abbey of Westminster. Alice of Abergavenny had opened her legs to a powerful and impressionable youth, and was now in a position to take on the power of William de Braose. And that meant she no longer needed Raymond de Carew.

'I never thought that I would say this, Alice, but I wish you well with him, and that he returns what you deserve.' He smiled at her.

'That is all that you have to say to me?'

'What else can I say?' He lifted his chin and nodded over her head to where a small group of horsemen raced towards the burning alehouse. All the men were young and wore their own arms above their highly polished armour. They came to a halt beside Raymond and Alice.

'Lady,' their leader said without so much as a glance at the burning buildings. He leapt nimbly from his horse's back to lift Alice to her feet. 'I am Sir Bertran de Born, and I come with King Henry's greetings. I am to escort you and your noble brother to the palace.' He swept into a dramatic bow before the Abergavenny siblings, pointedly ignoring Raymond, who, covered in mud and ash, was hardly recognisable as a man of any note. 'I have alerted the sheriff that a fire has broken out. King Harry wishes that he could have come to help you and assures me that he will not rest until he discovers who perpetrated this dreadful crime.'

'My Lord Harry is a great king,' Alice replied, casting an angry and victorious glance at Raymond. Despite the dreadful condition of her clothes Strongbow's captain reckoned that she would still dazzle the royal court. 'I know who is behind the attack, but that can wait until later. I am afraid all our belongings have been taken by the fire.' She nodded at the burning building.

'Do not worry, Lady Alice,' Sir Bertran said. 'King Harry will provide everything that you require. Do you have a palfrey?' he asked.

Raymond held up his hand. 'Don't worry, Sir Bertran. I will get her a mount.'

The French knight looked at Raymond for the first time and nodded. 'Well go and get it then, man,' he demanded. A coin spun through the air to land at Raymond's feet.

'Fulk,' Raymond shouted down the river, 'bring your

steed for Lady Alice.' Turning back, he addressed Geoffrey, who had regained consciousness and had clambered to his feet. 'Are you sure you would not rather stay with me and learn to be a proper warrior?'

The youngster glanced at his sister before answering. 'The prince has agreed to take me on as his esquire,' Geoffrey shrugged his shoulders. 'I only want to get my inheritance. I am sorry.' He bowed his head.

'Well then, there can be nothing else to say,' Raymond began, locking his eyes on Alice. 'But remember this: if you ever need my help, know that you will have it.' With that he turned around and walked away, pausing only to give Sir Bertran's coin to Fulk.

'What the hell is that?' he heard Bertran de Born shout as Fulk approached with the angry mule in tow. Raymond laughed as he imagined Alice's anger at having to ride through Westminster to the palace, covered in ash and mud, on such a poor mount. Without turning he walked past the raging fire that had been the Thorney Inn.

He found Strongbow sitting on a table top outside a house a little downriver from the remnants of the inn. Around the earl sat their milites, who had forced the occupants to scarper so that they could have the house to themselves.

'We killed a few of the Danes in the alehouse and then blockaded ourselves inside,' the earl recapped the tale for the benefit of his warlord. 'They were led by a beast with a red beard tied in two braids. His shield showed a black boar mask and it was he who set the inn on fire, but we fought our way free. That's when young Geoffrey was hurt. He saw William de Braose and attacked him by himself. I sent Nicholas de Lyvet to help him. The rest is a bit of a blur.' Strongbow looked like he would continue, but bit back his words and instead nodded across the road to where four bodies lay. One was wearing Strongbow's crimson and gold. It was Nicholas. The other three bore no devices. Leather tunics, chainmail, circular shields, axes and heavy beards beneath the distinctive conical helmets – they were Danes.

'What do we do now?' Strongbow asked Raymond. 'Go after them? Or do we go back to Striguil?'

'I think that our troubles with William de Braose may be over now that Alice and Geoffrey have left our company,' he said before telling his lord about how the siblings had been taken under the protection of Prince Harry.

'This goes way beyond those two,' the earl replied. 'The Danes attacked me and my household, and that cannot be allowed to stand. So what should we do about it?'

The captain considered his lord's question. He desired nothing more than to give chase through the streets as his enemy retreated towards their ship, harboured at Lambeth if Hubert Walter was to be believed. They had killed one of his men and that was a score that demanded to be settled. But Westminster was no battlefield, he knew, and the streets were crawling with King Henry's troops. Raymond was sure that the king would not deal kindly with armed bands of men fighting in when the coronation was happening at the abbey. That was to bring disrespect on a solemn occasion. To attack was to invite certain defeat.

'We should not pursue them. We came here for one reason and that was to ask King Henry to grant you a licence to go to Ireland, Lord. I think we should stick to that task.'

'My saints,' Strongbow whimpered as he turned to look northwards at the great Palace of Westminster as it loomed above the thatched rooftops. 'I think I'd rather go after the Danes.'

Sir William de Braose's father shoved him into the wall of the cold anteroom and held him there. The back of his skull cracked painfully on the stone wall of Westminster Palace.

'Danes?' Lord Bramber hissed. 'You bring those damned marauders to Westminster during the Young King's coronation? Do you wish to see us both thrown into Henry's oubliette?' He stole a glance over his shoulder as if he was sure that some of the king's routiers would already be searching him out for questioning.

'Get off me,' the younger man growled as his father's gnarled hand closed around the edge of his leather coif. With his other hand Lord Bramber cuffed the chape from his son's head. Sir William's forehead took most of the force of the blow. 'Please, Father!'

'You think a hood will keep your secret safe?' the older man whispered. 'Do you think for a second that the king's spies will not have heard that it was you who broke the peace? Why did you tell me?' he asked with a sad shake of his head. 'Now I will share in your fate.'

Sir William's red cheeks pinched at his father's words. 'I had to do something. Abergavenny would have already been lost if I had not acted,' he said indignantly and swept his father's hand from his tunic. 'Though fear not, dear father, if it comes to it I will allow the wolves to dine on my flesh and let you scamper to safety.'

His father's eyes narrowed at his son's insult. 'I allowed you to take control of Abergavenny and Brecon. How can I trust you to rule those lands, not to mention mine in England after me, if you can't even despatch two children and a priest —'

'I killed the priest,' Sir William interrupted.

'Without almost causing a war on the March,' Lord Bramber ignored his son's words. 'Your actions have brought unnecessary attention to our family and worse, they give credence to the claims of this boy Geoffrey.'

'I killed the priest as you told me,' his son snarled. 'No-one else knows that the boy's parents were married. No-one will believe them.'

'Strongbow obviously does, and so might the king. Do you think Henry wants our family to have more power than he or his brute of a son? If he hears of this episode he will investigate the reasons and claims. He will seek to curtail our power. That bastard Ranulph de Glanville will make sure he knows, and if not you know his nephew, Hubert Walter, will certainly find out. At best we will be in hoc to the king for *granting* us our Welsh lands. At worst, he will come down on the side of that Geoffrey, and Abergavenny will be lost to us for ever. And all because you couldn't execute a simple task I would expect an esquire to accomplish,' he added, his voice dripping with scorn.

Sir William cursed loudly and thumped his fist into the wall. 'It's not like you've done anything...'

'Keep your voice down, boy,' his father hissed and looked over his shoulder into the hallway where the oak doors or the great hall lay open. The feast to celebrate the new king's ascension had not yet begun, but everywhere there were servants going to and fro. There were enemies and allies with ears open for news to use to their advantage. He walked across the cold little room, used to store benches in preparation for the feast, and slowly closed the door. He didn't say anything when he turned back. Instead he locked his eyes on his son, staring at him as a physician would a badly injured limb. 'So where did you find your Danes?' he finally asked, his voice even. 'I don't imagine you travelled all the way to Ireland or the Scottish lands to hire them?'

'In Wales,' his son told him. 'Jarl Sigtrygg attacked Nedd Abbey while I was there. Instead of fighting him over a few trinkets, I offered him some silver to do the job.' He did not add that he had spent a small fortune buying their freedom from Richard de Grenville. 'Danes are cheaper than Gascons.'

'At least Gascons are discreet,' Lord Bramber replied. 'At least Gascons don't try to burn down half of Westminster. At least Gascons don't try to murder Richard de Clare of Striguil in full view of the king and his court.' He turned his back on his son and walked towards a small table where his cupbearer had left a jug of wine. Without offering any to his son, Lord Bramber filled a mug and drank long and slowly, running the day's events over in his mind. The stupid boy had acted without thinking when he had hired the Danes to do his dirty work, and that was not in keeping with the position and power of the Lord of Radnor, Bramber, Builth, Barnstaple and Totnes, and a hundred other minor manors strewn across the kingdom. A great baron of England did not use a hammer when a dagger was the obvious tool for the job.

'Strongbow will go back to Wales,' he told his heir. 'He will fear another attack.'

Sir William smiled. 'Perfect, I'll leave immediately. I can intercept him at…'

'Be quiet,' Lord Bramber interjected. 'You and your Danes have caused enough problems. I will fix this situation and you will watch and learn and do everything that I tell you to do as soon as I say it. We are in greater peril than you seem to realise.'

His son looked at him with a mixture of anger, impatience and disbelief. 'All I want is my mother's estates.'

'We shall see. You have coin with you?'

Sir William nodded slowly and suspiciously.

'Fetch it,' his father replied, 'and let us see how much King Henry values his most amiable subjects.' His son looked at him in confusion. 'First lesson: a king can be bribed like any other man.' With that he turned on his heel and marched from the empty room towards the great hall of Westminster.

His son tarried longer, watching as his father faded into the stream of servants in the corridors outside the hall. He hated the thought of buying the king's support, especially as it meant that he had failed for the second time to kill his cousins. He allowed his anger to get the best of him.

'Thomas!' he shouted.

'Lord?' his page skidded to a halt at his master's heel. Sir William did not turn to look at the boy.

'Sir Anthony de Sherley is in the stables. Find him and tell him to go to Jarl Sigtrygg – he will know where he is. Sir Anthony will tell the Dane that I will require his services for more time than I initially believed. He is to tell Jarl Sigtrygg that he will only receive payment when he completes the task.'

'Yes, Sir William.'

'And, Thomas…'

'Yes, Sir William?'

'Do not let my father know what you are up to or I will have the skin off your back.'

'Yes, my Lord,' the page answered as he scampered off.

Sir William scowled and followed his father towards the hullabaloo stemming from the great hall. Two men in the lion surcoat of Anjou guarded the entrance, but they barely moved as he passed through the vast oak doors and down the stairs into the colossal room. An army of fawning followers, certainly over a thousand, paraded their wealth and importance in the belly of the hall. They ate and drank. They swapped stories, made pacts, and negotiated marriages while, to Sir William's right, the King and his son shared the dais with the bishops and great lords of the

143

realm. Flowers, tapestries and candles added to the colour and each nobleman sought to outdo his peers with ever more gaudy clothes and arms, showing off more followers and giving grander gifts in celebration of the crowning. Steaming food and fires mingled with body heat to create a stale, humid atmosphere in the hall. Here, every man was a rival or a vassal, blood and marriage ties were currency and knights' fees gave authority. Sir William de Braose could almost taste ambition and the threat of violence issuing from the great men and women in the hall of Westminster. He could taste the power.

'First, we must make our introductions,' his father said as he appeared at his shoulder. Sir William felt a hand on his back and took a step forwards, Lord Bramber at his heels. He was being herded towards the dais where King Henry sat enjoying a joke with a knight in a green surcoat. Behind the warrior was a long line of men in a hundred different motifs and badges of nobility, all awaiting a private audience with Henry. The greatest men of the kingdom had come to Westminster to show their loyalty to the crown of England and Sir William was suddenly nervous. He had met the king several times before, but had never spoken to him. On every previous occasion he had deferred to his father's lead and he suddenly felt ill prepared for the task at hand. He cursed Lord Bramber for forcing him to face the king and tried to remember the lessons of his youth; how one greets a king, court procedure and practice. He was so preoccupied, his eyes taking in his suzerain lord, that he did not see a long hand slide across his chest to prevent him from reaching his target.

'Where do you think you are going, young man?' a haughty voice asked. 'Not to greet the king, I would suggest; not without my say-so.' The tall man who had spoken did not so much as look up from a long, curling piece of vellum which he scrutinised closely.

'Sir Theobald,' Lord Bramber chirped from behind his son, 'my son wishes to congratulate the king...'

'Kings, I think you mean,' the man said as he allowed the parchment to wind up in his fingers. With his other hand he called a monk to his side, issuing swift and silent orders before finally turning to look at the father and son before they were able to circumnavigate his reach. 'Kings,' he repeated and nodded to Lord Bramber. 'What a peculiar world we live in. Don't you think?'

'We wish to talk with the Old King,' Sir William stated confidently.

'I wouldn't call him that if you want to find favour, young man,' Sir Theobald retorted with a twitch of a grin. 'But I do understand your eagerness to approach him. My brother was telling me only this morning that you are having rotten luck maintaining your late mother's estates in Wales. Is it on this subject that you wish to converse with our noble lord?'

'I have never heard of Hubert Walter being wrong about anything,' Lord Bramber said with some annoyance, 'but on this count your brother is indeed misinformed. Of that I assure you, Sir Theobald. My son and I simply wish to congratulate King Henry on a splendid occasion which will live long in the memory.'

Theobald nodded and smiled, never taking his eyes off the younger man. 'It is proper to approach the King's Steward if you require access to either of our kings.'

'You seemed busy...' started Sir William.

'I was, have been and still am, but I can always find time for men of your standing.' It did not escape either father or son's attention that Theobald stressed the word *can*.

'I'm in a hurry, Sir Theobald,' Lord Bramber whispered.

A huge smile broke across the steward's face. 'As am I,' he exclaimed loudly. 'There are many, many people who wish to meet the king today,' he waved a hand at a long line of supplicants, 'and there is so little time to allow everyone to do so. For instance, do you know that there was an incident down by the river earlier today? The Sheriff of London says he wants to investigate, and of course that meant that the Lord Constable was equally as interested, even if it was only to discover why the sheriff was so concerned about a fire in a whorehouse. So everything has been moved forward to allow them to talk to our kings,' he shook his head in mock disappointment. 'So little time.' The tall knight tapped Sir William on the chest with the rolled-up piece of parchment. The red-cheeked youth looked as if he would strike out at the steward, but his father stepped between the two men.

'We have been friends for a long time,' the elder man laughed and leant forward to embrace the steward. As he drew back, Sir William saw Theobald expertly conceal a small purse amongst his robes.

'Not only are you a close friend of my own family, but of King Henry,' Sir Theobald said, 'and I am sure that he would want to see you as soon as possible.' With that he spun on his heel and walked towards the dais. 'Follow me,' the tall man instructed. Every eye in the long line of lords and knights watched Lord Bramber and his son as they followed the steward towards the front of the great hall. Was it jealousy that Sir William saw in their eyes? He smirked at one fat baron from Somerset and enjoyed his angry, impotent glare. William liked having the attention of the lords of England on him despite the presence of two kings.

A single long digit indicated where Theobald wanted the two men to stand. 'Be ready to attend upon the king,'

146

he added as he walked away.

'Kings, you mean,' Sir William sniggered, but Theobald seemed not to hear as he disappeared amongst the flamboyantly clothed knights who encircled Henry FitzEmpress awaiting a moment to attend upon the powerful monarch. 'How much did you give him?' he asked his father.

'A pittance in comparison to what the king may demand of you,' the elder man said through pursed lips. 'You should have killed Alice and Geoffrey in the wilderness when you had the chance. Which reminds me; we must talk about your infatuation with your pretty cousin, boy.'

Sir William inhaled sharply, ready to respond, but the incongruous sound of hooves clashing on stone stopped him. All the men waiting to speak to the king went quiet and turned to see what had made the sound. At the far end of the hall a knight in full battle dress allowed his stallion to stomp angrily, scattering dried reeds. The man's helm was huge and ornate, crowned with a long flowing ribbon of blue and white squares which matched his surcoat.

'What is he doing?' Sir William asked.

'Sir Robert de Marmion, the king's champion,' his father told him, 'is a nobody from Lincolnshire, but his wife is a niece of Melisende of Jerusalem.' He shook his head. 'The two with him are the Lord Marshal and Humphrey de Bohun, the Lord Constable.' Everyone in the hall had now turned to look at the fully armed men who threw an ornate armoured glove onto the ground before the open doors of the great hall.

'Who here denies my Lord Henry's right to the crown,' Marmion called timidly. 'Who here denies his right to rule?' Hidden below a great helm, Marmion's voice sounded tiny. 'Who?' he screeched as he attempted to make himself heard through his metal hood. To make matters worse his attempts to draw his sword from his side failed when his right elbow became entangled in his blue and white cloak. Muffled laughter began from the people in the great hall of Westminster, Sir William among them.

Up on the dais the newly crowned Young King Harry climbed to his feet with a face like thunder. 'God's teeth, Marmion. You are supposed to be intimidating,' he exclaimed. 'I'll send you back to Scrivelsby on a mule and play champion myself if you can't perform your duty.'

'My- my Lord,' the knight on horseback stuttered as he kicked his horse into action, trotting the stocky mare in two swift circles around the hall. Suddenly Marmion's voice seemed twice as loud, brash and full of vigour as he called for any man brave enough to take his sword in hand and fight him. Most realised that it was the barrel-chested Lord Constable − on foot and leading Marmion's horse − that was shouting the champion's challenge at the assembled Lords of England. To complete the farce, on his last circuit of the hall Marmion's mare lifted her tail and defecated before the dais.

The Young King threw his hands in the air in exasperation and whispered loudly that the whole occasion had been ruined by Sir Robert de Marmion. 'Come forward, then,' he added lifting his gold goblet in mock salute to his champion's bravery as was expected of him. He took a long drink and held the cup out for the mounted man to accept.

Robert de Marmion nervously removed his helm, revealing a mousy-looking man, and took the king's cup. With a deep breath he swallowed the remainder of wine within and then held the cup aloft. 'Long live Harry, our king, and his father, Good King Henry,' he shouted. He had been expecting a loud acclamation but instead he received an embarrassing silence.

'Come on, you cretin,' Sir Humphrey de Bohun said as he led Marmion's horse from the hall. The hubbub of talk and laughter resumed with Old King Henry's bombastic roar of mirth loudest of all.

'He will see you now,' Theobald's hand dropped onto Sir William's shoulder. 'You are in luck - he is in a good mood after that farce.'

The steward led the two men through the throng of people towards the dais where the king slugged from a carved wooden mug, disdaining the ornate gold and silver goblet before him on the table. Sir William felt the apprehension rise in his chest again. He could feel his father's presence at his back and noted that he continued to hide behind him. Steeling himself, he promised to not let his father's fears overtake his own ambitions for his estates in Wales.

'Well, well, well,' the Old King said as the trio stopped before the dais. 'What do we have here? Lord Bramber, you old scoundrel, and your son...' His voice drifted as Theobald took one stride forward and leant across the table to whisper in the king's ear. As he did so, Sir William studied Henry FitzEmpress, King of England and Suzerain Lord of everything between the Pyrenees and the land of the Scots. He was scruffy, though dressed in the finest clothes that money could buy, and in his hand was an open leather book, in what language he could not tell, for he could not read a word. Sir William greedily eyed the six gold rings inlaid with rich stones which, he assumed, the king had removed from his fingers and laid out in a straight line on the table before him. Two were especially lavish; the first bore a large ruby and was tessellated with golden lions while the other was emerald and bore the papal seal. The king himself was less memorable than his affectations. Of average height and cursed with limp red hair, he could have been mistaken for the son of a tanner or a smith. But there was strength in his arms and bawdy, hoarse voice.

'My steward tells me that you wish to discuss a delicate subject,' the king said to Sir William. 'So,' he added, his eyes shining malevolently, 'please, do tell all.'

'Bollocks,' said Marshal as he dropped onto the bench beside Raymond de Carew at the back of the great hall of Westminster. It was the first time that the Raymond had heard the knight use bad language of any kind.

'What did the King tell you?' Raymond had to shout despite his friend sitting close by his shoulder. The great hall was awash with noise from the hundreds who crowded in to feast and celebrate the ascension of the Young King Harry. All the great men of England, as well as many from the continent, had come to commemorate the coronation of his heir. There was no-one from the Welsh March other than Strongbow and Raymond; the men from the frontier were considered too rowdy by the Angevin court, too set in the dangerous old ways of the Norman marauder.

'…but I wanted my arms on every wall, not yours.' The Young King's petulant cry penetrated the din, 'and two tourney days, not one.' Whatever was his father's response, Raymond could not hear. Marshal had heard the arguments between the two before and so he ignored the exchange, breaking a leg of lamb away from the rest of the carcass and tearing at the flesh with his teeth.

'King Henry wants me to take Prince Harry on as my apprentice,' he said as he chewed. 'It is a great honour, I suppose, to join his mesnie household,' he grimaced, 'but I can already imagine the youngster parading me around at every tournament in Flanders like his own personal trophy.'

'He could make you a lot of money,' Raymond replied.

150

Marshal shook his head. 'Only the desperate will give his company a fight at a tourney. Who in their right mind wants to be on a vengeful king's hit list if they succeed in capturing some of his knights? At any rate the arms and horses of desperate men will hardly be worth the effort of fighting them off.'

'But the Young King is a good fighter?'

'He could be,' Marshal considered, 'but from what I have seen he little more than a wastrel and layabout.' He turned to Strongbow who sat quietly by, picking at the mutton in his bread trencher. He greeted the earl who, having been admitted by Raymond's friend, Hubert Walter, had been relegated to sit amongst the lowly and bawdy hearth knights at the furthest point of the hall from the dais. 'I heard about the attack,' Marshal said and turned to point a greasy finger at Lord Bramber and his son as they joked and laughed with the Old King. 'It was an ill-done thing.'

'Sir William must have come straight here after the attack on the inn,' Raymond replied. 'He may be worried that we will attack him now that his Danes have gone.' Following the departure of Alice and Geoffrey, Raymond and Borard had made their way down to the riverside and stared across the river towards Lambeth where a single ship under oar had been making its way upriver against the current. At the steering oar had been a giant man with a red beard in two braids, as Strongbow had described. Raymond had watched impotently as their enemy had fled the scene of the crime.

'I can't believe that they are so brazen as to come to court,' Strongbow replied. The earl still had the vestiges of smoke from the fire on his face and clothes. 'If I did not think that King Henry would declare me outlaw, I would go straight back to Wales and burn Abergavenny and Brecon to the ground.' He looked around at Raymond as though he wished to know if that had been the correct response.

'Who is that with King Henry now?' Raymond asked Marshal, giving Strongbow a tight-lipped, though supportive, smile.

'Ranulph de Glanville, the Justiciar's man,' Marshal said of the bearded man at the Old King's shoulder. 'He all but runs Henry's court now that Becket is gone and nobody gets to meet the king without the say-so of Ranulph's nephew Theobald.' He nodded in the direction of the king's tall steward who roamed in front of the dais like a great alaunt guarding a castle bailey. 'They will both be friendly to your cause, however. Hubert Walter is Theobald's younger brother and our priestly colleague,' he coughed to stress his uncertainty at the term, 'has already cleared the way for you.'

Raymond raised his eyebrows. 'I'll expect a large bill in due course from Hubert.' He turned towards Strongbow. 'Are you ready to meet King Henry?'

'Right now?' The earl looked distraught. 'With those two fiends whispering malice against me?' He eyed Lord Bramber and his son. 'God's peace, Raymond, but why did you ever bring those two bastards of Abergavenny to my hall? They have caused me nothing but trouble.' Strongbow blinked as if his eyes were beginning to water.

Raymond pictured Alice's beautiful face, but said nothing.

'It is now or never,' Marshal announced and climbed to his feet, lifting his chin in signal to the steward. 'Remember that King Henry likes nothing better than a man who agrees with him,' he told the earl as he too stood up. 'He hates defiance and would rather have a broken man serve him through fear than a brave one in loyalty. I urge you not to show any fight even if he antagonises you…'

'Which he probably will,' Raymond added. 'Marshal has agreed to introduce you to the king, Lord, and has been advising him in your favour since the day we met on the tourney field. I pray that the king is playing Sir William for a fool, teasing out their secrets as they hope to earn his good favour.'

'He probably means to do the same to me.' Strongbow was sweating terribly, his sparse hair caked to his head and his armpits uncomfortable. Nevertheless he nodded to Marshal who gave him a last sympathetic grin before walking away towards the dais to prepare his approach. This was the moment that Strongbow had been dreading, the moment which had haunted him as he had crossed the sea and the lands of France and England; his meeting with Henry FitzEmpress. Suddenly the earl felt compelled to talk to his famous father and he cast his eyes heavenwards, through the arched roof of Westminster Palace. The words failed him and instead he bowed his head and said a short prayer to St Benedict, appealing for his aid and advice.

'Let's go,' said Raymond from beside the earl. Strongbow opened his eyes to see Marshal waving for them to join him and the king on the dais. The earl experienced acute alarm as he approached the dais. Henry FitzEmpress laughed bombastically with his court cronies, pointing in Strongbow's direction and whispering jokes, he was sure, at his expense. Thankfully, behind him he could sense the encouraging presence of Raymond de Carew. He tried to remember the advice which Marshal had provided and prayed that nothing would upset the king before he had that for which he had come: an unambiguous and definitive licence to journey to Ireland. He thought of his mother in Heaven and prayed that he would not let her down again.

'Sir Richard de Clare of Striguil, Lord,' a voice woke Strongbow from his daze. It belonged to the king's steward, the tall man with an icy stare who wore the same blue and yellow arms as Ranulph de Glanville. The steward cast his daunting gaze down upon the earl as if he did not consider him worthy to talk to his king.

'Hubert Walter's brother,' Raymond whispered behind Strongbow. 'Keep going, Lord. Remember, he is on our side - though he hides it well.'

'Strongbow,' a derisive voice echoed throughout the great hall. 'Really? Who invited *him* to attend my son's big day?' It was Henry FitzEmpress who had spoken. 'Well, let the traitorous churl come forward and I will hear what he has to say.' He did not blink nor avert his gaze as the earl tottered towards him and swept into a deep bow. The stout ginger king's shining eyes bored into Strongbow while upon his face Henry wore the barest hint of a smile. He was enjoying the discomfort that his unwavering gaze had on his subject.

'You look like you have been through the wars, Strongbow. The stories of your friendship with beggars are not false after all? I, for one, never doubted them for a second.' The king giggled and took a long drink from his mug of wine.

'I was attacked at my lodgings,' Strongbow described and indicated to the blood on his surcoat, 'this very afternoon, Lord King.'

'Who would attack you?' Henry said scornfully as he wiped his mouth on his sleeve. 'And what the hell would they steal from you? Cheap bliauts and dirty braies? Oh for God's sake stop shaking, man,' he ordered, recognising Strongbow's fear. 'I am not going to kill you, *yet*.' He let the silence stretch as Ranulph de Glanville tapped the king on the arm and for many minutes they conversed secretly. No-one in the great hall was brave enough to interrupt. 'So,' he asked as he turned back to Strongbow, waving

154

Ranulph away, 'now that you have piqued my interest, who molested you?' His voice easily penetrated the din from the revellers in the body of Westminster's hall. Strongbow's eyes flicked to Sir William, who squirmed angrily beside the king's seat. Henry missed nothing and laughed at the youngster's uneasiness. 'Do you want to accuse someone? Well, I would think extremely carefully about what you think you saw or I may see fit to rethink my decision on letting a traitor like you keep his fortress at Striguil.'

'My family won those lands by their strength of arms, not by the grant of any king,' Strongbow replied and wrung his hands together behind his back. 'They are not yours to bequeath or deny.'

'Easy, Lord,' Raymond whispered to Strongbow but Henry seemed not to mind the earl's rebuke, issuing a snort of laughter at his small act of defiance. Raymond's eye drifted towards William de Braose and his father. The younger man stared balefully at the earl while the elder, Lord Bramber, chewed nervously on his lower lip. Raymond suddenly realised that they were as scared of Strongbow as he was of them. Both parties were caught in Henry's trap and neither party truly knew if they were in peril or protected by the king's favour.

'What say you?' the Old King waved a hand in Sir William de Braose's direction. 'Inheritance is a tricky and complicated matter, is it not? Your experiences in Wales must've given you a new and fascinating point of view on the subject.'

The younger man looked to his father, who offered no assistance before shaking his head and pathetically shrugging his shoulders. Henry coughed a laugh.

'The men who attacked Lord Strongbow were mere outlaws, Lord King,' Raymond interjected brightly. 'They launched a pitiable attack on a simple household at rest.

Even a peacock troubadour like Sir Bertran de Born could have bested them and sooner, rather than later, I will catch up to them and I will teach them the king's justice; nothing for you to worry about, Lord.'

Henry turned on Raymond immediately with his stern grey-eyed stare. Such was the power of his eyes that Strongbow's captain immediately wondered if he had made a serious mistake in speaking up. However, Henry's anger quickly turned to mirth and his barking laughter made every man on the dais visibly relax.

'You hear that boy,' the king leant over towards his son Harry. 'He called your friend a prize peacock!' He laughed again and turned back towards Raymond. His finger shot out to point at the Marcher warrior. 'What's your name, lad?'

'His name is Raymond de Carew,' said the petulant voice of the Young King before Raymond could answer. 'Not content with offending my comrade,' he put a hand on the shoulder of a furious Bertran de Born, 'he almost ruined the dignity of my tourney yesterday by playing the fool with Sir William Marshal.'

'Good,' the Old King replied and turned back to look at Raymond. 'Next time make sure and knock my son's block off while you are at it so I don't have to keep on funding this ludicrous hobby.' Without waiting for Raymond to respond, the king turned to Ranulph de Glanville who circled behind him like a great dog waiting for scraps at a kitchen door. 'How much was it this time?'

'Two hundred pounds.'

'That's my income from the Rutland estate for a year!' the Old King laughed long and hard before turning on Strongbow once more. His smile dropped away immediately. 'So tell me, Sir Richard, why have you expended so much effort trying to attend my court? Could

156

it be that you have adopted some of Henry de Hereford's bastards? Young William de Braose says you are trying to steal Abergavenny out from under him.'

'Of course not, Lord,' Strongbow began nervously. 'I merely offered them a roof over their head while you decided upon the veracity of their claim.' The earl breathed in deeply and looked the king directly in the eye. 'My reason to come before you, Lord King, was because I have a request to make of you...'

'A request?' King Henry cut him off instantly and leapt forward in his seat and smashing his fist down on a table. Every cup and plate rattled and every conversation that had been going on in the great hall stopped. Henry did not seem to notice. 'Why would I help you, who hurt me worse than death by supporting that bastard usurper Stephen de Blois? What I should do is throw you from the nearest castle wall with a long bowstring around your neck and another short one tied to your balls. I owe you nothing but a long, painful death. So tell me, Strongbow, what request would you have of me?'

The sudden venom of Henry's words seemed to act like a strike of a mace on the earl who stepped back, bumping into Raymond who, for his part, realised that what he was seeing was King Henry in a good mood.

'The earl wishes to obtain your permission to depart your lands, Lord,' Raymond told the king. 'As you have stated your dislike of his presence at Westminster, I wonder if it would be to the benefit of both Earl Richard and your own royal person to see him gone.'

The king laughed. 'Do you fear to speak for yourself, Strongbow?'

'I do not, Lord,' squeaked the earl. 'I seek your permission to go to Ireland with King Diarmait Mac Murchada as your licence directs. I have nothing left to give you in my present standing. In Ireland I hope to be able to find some small fortune,' he dropped his eyes to the floor, 'to better serve you.'

'I see,' King Henry mumbled as he dropped back into his chair. He picked up an emerald ring from the table before him and looked deep into the green jewel, rolling it around in his fingers. '"*To better serve me*", you say. If I grant you leave to go to Ireland, your estates in Wales will be left without a lord?'

Strongbow nodded. 'My son-in-law, Sir Roger de Quincy, will act as deputy in my stead.'

Without answer Henry leant back in his large wooden chair and waved a finger in the direction of Lord Bramber. For several minutes they whispered secretly as Ranulph de Glanville listened in. Raymond licked his lips with concern, wondering what Henry could be saying to Strongbow's enemy.

'My Lord Richard,' the Young King Harry spoke to Strongbow while his father communicated with Lord Bramber. 'I wanted to thank you for helping to save my dearest Alice and her brother from those ruffians earlier today. Doubtless they were some of my father's routiers who attacked you...' He cast an eye in his father's direction to see if he was listening. '...but if you offend Holy Mother Church by purchasing the services of such irreligious mercenaries that is the kind of behaviour you should expect.' He again glanced in his father's direction, but it was clear that the Old King was not listening to his son's words. King Harry looked irritated.

'Your thanks are not needed, Lord King,' Strongbow replied. 'The girl was under my protection, but I am thankful that you have now taken an interest in her wellbeing on this day of all days.'

'A lovely creature,' Harry mused. 'I have asked Sir Bertran to compose a song about her. I am sure that he alone can do her beauty justice.' He was speaking to Strongbow, but his words struck home with Raymond de Carew. He ground his teeth as he watched the newest King of England accept the earl's obsequious words as if *he* had waded through the blood of an army of Danes to save the damsel in distress. The thought of being cuckolded by this fallow youth was galling, but Raymond calmed down and reminded himself that he had never actually had claim to the beauty from Abergavenny.

'I must add my heartfelt congratulations on your coronation, Lord,' Strongbow added with a bow to the Young King of England.

'Yes, yes,' Harry said absent-mindedly, his eyes flicking to his father who was still deep in conversation. 'I think it is sensible to make good and lasting friendships with those that one means to rule one day,' the Young King paused, 'and I obviously think that there is a great deal of credence to young Geoffrey of Abergavenny's claims in Wales.'

Raymond froze as he listened to the words come from the King Harry's mouth. His eyes flicked to Sir William de Braose and his father. They too had heard the declaration and were angrily staring at the Young King.

'You should concentrate on your food, young pup,' King Henry told his son and heir, 'and leave the real work to the big dog.' The king punched a fist to his wide chest and turned back to his advisors.

'No, Father,' Prince Harry grumbled, 'I should be included – I am a king after all.'

Henry's laugh was somewhere between a caustic bellow and jolly giggle. 'You sit there and watch how it is done, boy.' The king turned towards Lord Bramber. 'That pup is too much like his mother,' he told them loudly. 'She is always sticking her nose in my business too. Proud bitch,'

159

he added with a smile.

'You will not speak of my mother like that,' Harry cried as he landed a punch on the table top.

The murmur from the feasting nobles diminished to listen in to the growing argument between the Old and Young Kings of England.

'My court, my law,' Henry announced without turning to look at his son.

'I should have my own court, like King Louis had after he was crowned by his father.' He pulled off his golden circlet as he slumped into his chair and contented himself with staring broodingly at the back of his father's head.

'What do you think that they are talking about?' Strongbow whispered in Raymond's direction with a nod towards the Old King.

'Nothing that we can influence now,' his captain replied. 'We must trust that Hubert Walter has won Ranulph de Glanville to our side.' Strongbow turned and looked at him as if a particularly bad smell had wafted through the great hall of Westminster.

'Well, Strongbow,' Henry said quietly as he turned back towards the two men from Striguil, 'it seems like I was overly angry with you.' The earl smarted in shock at that statement but said nothing to interrupt. 'Your request is one that interests me,' the Old King continued, 'and Sir Ranulph has advised that I should...' Henry stopped talking suddenly as a servant approached the dais holding a gold gilt wine bowl in two hands. It was half-filled with red wine which sloshed around. Henry smiled broadly and waved his page forward, forgetting whatever he was about to say to Strongbow. The king climbed to his feet and accepted the wine from the boy. Two trumpets sounded behind him.

'My lords and ladies,' the king raised his voice causing

160

the rumpus to slowly subside. 'We are here in my Palace of Westminster to celebrate the coronation of my son Harry as King of England.' He swept his hand towards his son who still slumped in his seat, still annoyed it seemed. 'It is not often a man can see his son crowned king,' Henry said with an infectious smile, 'but it sends a message to France,' he paused to allow boos to echo around the hall, 'and to that bastard Becket, that no King of England will cower before them ever again.' The king bounced on his toes as he spoke, enjoying the attention of the noblemen as he raised the bowl towards the heavy oak beams which soared above them all. 'The King of the English is strong. His son is strong, and his family is strong. His empire is strong and his dynasty is strong!'

The noblemen of England and Normandy cheered their overlord, thumping tabletops and raising their cups in salute. For so long, civil war between the heirs of William the Conqueror had troubled the land, almost leading to the fracture of England. Now, the kingdom's succession was assured and they would have peace and prosperity.

'And what of Louis of France?' the king asked the crowd, sensing their goodwill. 'He trembles in his bed in Paris wondering if he will ever be man enough to beget a son!' Laughter accompanied the Old King's words. 'We must never forget that we have enemies, my friends. That twice-damned devil Becket plots, prays and fumbles his beads at Louis' feet, whispering to the pitiful Frank that he should raise an army to crush poor England. I am here to say, no, not while I am alive!' he shouted, his voice echoing around the heavy beams and stone floor. 'And not while my son sits on the throne by my side.'

The noblemen in the room roared agreement but Raymond noticed that many of the churchmen in the great hall bowed their heads when Henry abused Becket's name.

161

'All of you get on your knees while I serve the new King of England his first cup of wine,' Henry commanded. The shuffling noise from the people climbing to their knees was loud but Raymond had eyes only for King Henry, who turned to his son and bowed, though his eyes never dipped or deferred authority. With a smile the Old King handed him the golden bowl filled with wine to the new.

'Beat that speech, pup,' Raymond heard the Old King whisper.

The younger man scowled deeply and momentarily looked like he would not accept the wine from his father. But as quickly as the defiance appeared on his face it was gone and the blond teen smiled swiftly and climbed to his feet, raising his hands to the cheers that accompanied his opportunity to speak.

'Thank you, Father, for your words, though perhaps they should have mentioned more of my accomplishments, not simply those of your friends King Louis and Archbishop Becket,' he smiled at his father and raised the bowl of wine so that everyone could see it. Henry returned his son's leer with a warning in his shining eyes. Harry did not heed it.

'I thank you for serving me my customary first cup of wine, my loving father,' the Young King said as he took a long draught. 'I think everyone would agree that it is only fitting that the son of a mere count serves the son of a king.' The newly crowned Harry smiled and drank deeply from the golden bowl a second time. The silence of Westminster Hall was followed by murmurs which blossomed into shocked chitchat at the Young King's words.

'What did you say?' King Henry asked. He was almost quivering with rage, his good mood gone in an instant. 'What did you say?'

Harry smirked as he sat in his seat. 'I was merely

162

pointing out that I am a king's son, while you are no more than the whelp of a count.'

The Old King let fly a bellow of maddened Angevin gall and swept plates of food from the tabletop before him. Raymond smiled as a pigeon pie scattered all over Sir William de Braose before he was forced to dodge out of the way of a wayward steamed lamprey.

'You scurrilous hound, you bastard pup, you chirping chick!' the king roared. 'How dare you speak to me like that? Do you think I give a fig for your opinion?' He cast his seat aside and grabbed his son by his shirt, pulling him so close that the Young King seemed to struggle under the stench of his breath. 'I have more sons than you that could sit on this throne beside me, you little shit,' he continued, launching the Young King backwards. Luckily Bertran de Born was on hand to catch King Harry before he fell from the dais and cracked his head open on the stone floor. 'At least your brother Richard is not in the pay of France!'

'If I was in the pay of England I would be above these accusations,' the Young King called back, without actually denying receipt of a pension from the Frankish monarch. 'If you had given me Anjou or Normandy to rule with my own court, then –'

'You will get nothing of mine while I live,' the king snarled and pointed a large finger at his son.

'Then we can have nothing more to say to each other,' his son stated and made to leave. 'Sir William,' the Young King called to Marshal, 'we are for Normandy on the morrow. Please make the arrangements for my household...' he paused and corrected himself, 'for my court to travel.'

'Yes, Lord,' Marshal said to his new lord with a look of apology to the Old King.

'You little bastard,' Henry shouted at his son, 'you

ungrateful little whoremonger. I will get you back for this insult. I will hear of it if you go to Louis and Becket in Paris!'

The Young King did not even turn as he strode from the dais accompanied by a large number of followers and left the hall by a heavy door in the west wall. As the door thumped closed behind them, Henry FitzEmpress turned back to the shocked men in the body of the great hall of Westminster with a face like thunder. It was as if he was noticing for the first time that the nobles were in his presence and had seen his shame.

'Get them out of here,' he whispered in the direction of Sir Theobald. 'The feast is over.' The King of England was quivering. 'Over!' he screamed suddenly. 'Get out of my hall,' he shrieked as his face turned red. 'Out!'

Shambling feet began the exodus of men. Tables rumbled and benches screeched as they were pushed aside. Complaints echoed on the stone walls as great men shuffled towards the doors.

'Wait, you, stay where you are,' the king called. Every lord that had been leaving the hall suddenly stopped and turned to face the dais, believing perhaps that the king had retracted his command. 'You,' the king's voice wavered, barely under control, and Raymond de Carew turned around to see the king's finger settle on Strongbow's chest. The heavily bejewelled embroidery at the king's neck shook violently. 'The Earl Strongbow,' he said disdainfully. 'Get you gone from me as far as your feet can carry you,' he cried, his lip turning in disgust at the earl's presence. With that the king turned on his heel and strode through a door behind the dais, Ranulph de Glanville and Theobald in his wake. The great hall of Westminster was left awash with conversation, a tumult of gossip and chatter.

Strongbow did not turn but stood stock still before King

Henry's table staring at the crimson lion banner which decorated the walls. It was only when the oak door which led to the solar crashed shut, wafting the tapestry and making the lion rampant dance upon the flag, that he moved.

On the far side of the dais Sir William de Braose eyed Raymond angrily. 'I've not forgotten your insults,' he hissed. His father's hand landed on his shoulder for a moment before he shrugged it off. 'I want my armour back. You were lucky at the Thorney Inn, but back on the March,' he shook his head, 'you have no hope.' With that Raymond's enemy disappeared with his father into the depths of the palace.

'Lord, we should go,' Raymond whispered to Strongbow, delicately placing his hands on his lord's arm and guiding him towards the door.

'We are done, Raymond,' the earl whimpered, 'done before we even set off. My dreams, my ambitions are in tatters. I dare not defy King Henry again.' His shoulders slumped and he began coughing again.

Raymond patted him on the back as he ushered him through the mass of men and tables towards the main door. They had sought the king's permission to leave his lands, but they were no better off now than they had been when they last saw Striguil.

Henry's words still rang in his ears: *Get you gone from me as far as your feet can carry you.*

They had failed and the earl's dream for conquest was over. Not only the earl's ambitions, Raymond thought with dismay. He was returning to Striguil where he was nothing but a simple hearth knight in the employ of a baron with few prospects. And he was alone. Gone was the adventure that he had shared with the earl, gone were the sea journeys. Finished was his affair with Alice of Abergavenny. What waited for him back in Striguil? Nothing more than patrolling the border regions, debt collection from his lord's subjects, and his futile worship of sweet Basilia, who he loved but could never possess.

An image of Basilia overtook his thoughts. To be worthy of an earl's daughter he knew that he would have to perform a deed which would astound all Christendom. For, despite her father's fall from grace and her own bastard birth, Basilia was of a rank so far above his own that he could have no hope of ever having her. He was a man without fortune or property while she was the wife of one of the most high-born men in the kingdom and heir to Striguil. To win her hand he would have to earn a reputation and he knew of no way to accomplish this other than by his strength of arms. Excitement stirred in Raymond as King Henry's words came to him again: *Get you gone from me as far as your feet can carry you.* He put a hand out to stop Strongbow and looked into his master's face.

'I don't think we are done yet,' Raymond told him. 'The king did say that you were to get as far away from him as possible. Ireland is a terrible long way to go, Lord. So you could say that by going to King Diarmait's side you were indeed following his orders,' he said. 'I say you have the king's permission to cross the sea. I say we go to Ireland as he told us to do.'

Strongbow exhaled deeply and ran his smoke-stained hands through his fading hair. 'You think so, Raymond?'

The warlord smiled. 'The king will not stay in England for long. Across the sea he has the King of France, our errant archbishop and, it would seem, his wayward son, to keep him busy. He will need all his resources to subdue them. Would he even notice that we are gone from these shores?'

Strongbow looked doubtful, cowed as he was by the Old

166

King's vitriolic outburst, but Raymond was not going to allow his lord's delicate nature get the better of the opportunity.

'We should leave Westminster tomorrow, Lord,' he said as they stepped out into the sunlight. In the distance smoke tumbled skywards from the smouldering ruin of the Thorney Inn, 'and the next time you see Henry FitzEmpress you too will be a king,' Raymond told his lord. 'Give me an army and I will give you a crown, Strongbow. Find me ships to cross the sea and I will win you a kingdom.'

As the earl lifted his head, Raymond saw the defiance and determination return to his grey eyes. Together they would journey to the edge of the world where Raymond's skill and Strongbow's name would win a throne. That would show the King of England, Raymond decided; to be forced to meet his former subject Strongbow on equal terms. Alice of Abergavenny could have her King, he thought jealously, for he would create a better one across the sea in untamed Ireland.

Chapter Six

Raymond's optimism continued into the next morning. He and Strongbow had talked long into the night about their plans and how they could bring them about. Ireland was all but unknown to either man, but what Strongbow had learned from his uncle Hervey de Montmorency led both men to agree that an army of no less than a thousand men would be needed, and that would take time to bring about.

He had risen before daybreak to begin organising the earl's household to leave Westminster, but even that had not been early enough to see the departure of King Henry from the town. The only thing left to indicate the presence of the royal court was a large dust cloud to the east, kicked up by the transit of the huge number of servants, warriors, councillors and other hangers-on, as they made their way towards London Bridge. With King Henry gone, Strongbow's folk, like everyone gathered at Westminster, could relax and make their own preparations to depart.

The earl's horses and carts collected in the street, still warming in the summer sunshine, while pages and esquires ran to and fro to with their masters' possessions. Westminster awoke while they worked and soon all the noises and smells of urban trade surrounded Strongbow's men. Stalls selling all manner of wares had arrived; a honking flock of geese, a fruit stand manned by oblates from the nearby monastery, and a long avenue of fishmongers already rivalling the geese in the noise they made to advertise the freshness of their produce. English and French tongues battled for supremacy in the ears of potential clientele.

'This fellow said he wanted to talk to you,' Borard announced as he approached Raymond. The captain was sat on the stone step of the burnt-down inn cleaning his tack. He followed the direction of Borard's dirty thumb as it indicated towards a young man at his side.

'Fulk?' Raymond recognised the boy who had helped him bring down the house during the fire the day before.

'Sir,' Fulk replied as he retreated from an awkward bow.

'How can I help?'

'Well, sir, I was out early this morning, before first light, making deliveries to the royal court for my master the butcher, and I saw a ship under oar making for the sea.' He flapped an arm towards the Thames which sparkled in the morning sunshine.

'And?'

'It was a Danish vessel, sir. Irish-built or so it looked to my eye.'

'Go on,' he told Fulk.

'Everyone in town has been saying that it was Danes who attacked the inn, sir. They are angry that someone would attack our town, so I made my delivery and then followed on foot up the London Road. Up at the Dane's Street,' he pointed downriver, 'I got to talking with a shopkeeper. The captain of the ship had stopped and bought some supplies before making for the bridge at London. The man was able to tell me the name of the captain and their destination.' Fulk looked expectantly at Raymond.

The Norman fumbled at a pocket for a coin, placing it in Fulk's hand. 'Tell me.'

'Their leader is called Sigtrygg, a Dane from Ireland, sir. He was raiding in Wales when he was hired

169

find your master, the archer...'

'Strongbow.'

'Yes sir. One of the crewmen told the shopkeeper that Jarl Sigtrygg was making for Bramber Castle to get his payment, but that they had also sent a company overland, I don't know why, sir. They bought three goats and a sheep...' He counted upon his fingers as he listed by foreigners' purchases.

Raymond dropped a hand onto the boy's shoulder. He now had a name for the man who had killed Nicholas de Lyvet during the attack on Strongbow at the Thorney Inn. He promised that should the opportunity present itself, he would kill Jarl Sigtrygg, the sword-Dane from Ireland with the red-braided beard and the charging boar standard.

'You've done well, Fulk,' he told the boy.

'Lord, I would like to go with you to Wales,' Fulk told him, an eager look on his face. 'I can cut meat and did a lot of droving for the master butcher. You could use me in your country.'

'Would your master not miss you?'

'He has five sons, sir, and all will learn the trade. I won't get rich being a butcher in another man's business.'

Raymond smiled at the ambition of the young freeman of Westminster. 'Alright, lad, go and say goodbye to your family and then you can start by helping Borard get the earl's belongings onto those packhorses.' He pointed at several animals, tied to the side the house that Raymond had appropriated for Strongbow.

Fulk nodded quickly and excitedly at the ease of Raymond's agreement. 'Can I tell my father that I am in the pay of the Lord Strongbow?'

'No, no. You work for Raymond de Carew,' he told Fulk, who looked less impressed. 'And that means a lot of hard work. So be back soon.' His new servant ran off towards the white wattle-walled houses leaving Raymond to ponder Fulk's words. Why, he wondered, would William de Braose's mercenary Danes be travelling to Bramber to collect payment when, as far as he knew, they had failed in their mission: to kill Alice and Geoffrey of Abergavenny. Before he could consider the question fully he was interrupted by a shout from amidst Strongbow's noisy horse train.

'That boy has just told me that he is your servant now,' Borard demanded. 'Exactly how are you going to pay for him? You said that you are poorer than King Henry on Maundy Thursday afternoon.'

'Sir James FitzJames came through last night with half his ransom,' Raymond told him. 'He bought back his armour and horse. That, and the other ransoms I took during the tourney, will allow me to have a hundred servants!'

'And what about your poor warriors?' asked Borard. 'How will they fare from your sudden windfall?'

Raymond laughed, producing a purse from his jacket and tossing it to his friend. 'Make sure everyone gets their share and buy them a drink on top of it from me.'

Borard caught the money and tested its weight. 'A small cup each might do no harm,' he replied, secreting the purse amongst his clothes. 'I will not partake, of course.'

Raymond nodded at his lieutenant, but he still could not shake the feeling of unease brought on by Fulk's words. 'Any news from William Marshal?' he asked.

'None,' Borard replied, realising instantly that Raymond actually wished for news of Alice of Abergavenny. 'I am sure that is because Little King Harry kept him up late with his drinking and gambling.'

'The Young King gambles?'

'According to one of his household cooks,' he said with

171

a wink. 'She told me that he owes half of Maine to Sir Bertran de Born. Could you convince him to give me a game of dice?' he asked as he tapped his pocket. The purse of coin clinked cheerfully.

Raymond de Carew did not laugh; the wound caused by Alice's departure with the Young King was still too raw for merriment.

'Oh look, our brave new recruit is back,' Borard said and nodded in Fulk's direction. 'I will make sure he has something to do. The sooner we get the horses ready the sooner we can get out of this stinking rat hole.' Borard had made it clear that he and the rest of the conrois were keen to get back to Wales. While their captain had plotted with Hubert Walter, played war with William Marshal, and conducted his romance with Alice of Abergavenny, they had become bored and idle in Westminster, missing their families and the routine of the Welsh frontier. The summer was upon them and whereas in fat, lazy England it was a time for peace before the harvest, on the March it was a time when men went raiding. The Striguil warriors were desperate to get back to their homeland before all the best plunder was taken and the best treasures hidden. Raymond understood their desire, but his aim was a land beyond the frontier. For many minutes he stared north towards where the river turned back in the direction of London. That was the route that the Young King would travel on his way to Normandy. That was the road that would take Alice from his life for ever.

'Raymond!' Sir William Marshal's animated voice pierced his daydream and the noise of the bustling marketplace. The captain smiled cheerily as his friend trotted his horse between the little tented shop fronts, but immediately he could see that the green and yellow surcoated knight was bearing bad news and he braced himself to receive it.

'What is it?' he asked as he grabbed Marshal's bridle.

'Geoffrey of Abergavenny and his sister - they have been taken by William de Braose.'

Raymond struggled to comprehend the news he had received and shook his head. 'They were under the protection of the Young King. Sir William would not dare attack them!'

'You are right,' Marshal replied. 'But King Henry had no such qualms. He sent a message late last night demanding his son hand the pair over to him. Henry must have realised that the prince was enamoured with Alice and, to get him back for his remarks at the feast, promised Alice and Geoffrey to Lord Bramber. The Prince refused, even when the Old King threatened to cut off his income, so, while Harry was gambling with Bertran de Born in the early hours, Henry had them kidnapped by his routiers. I am sorry Raymond, but I could not do anything to stop it. They were gone before I knew what was happening.'

'The Old King still has them?'

Marshal shook his head. 'Lord Bramber bought them from the king and gave them over to his son.'

'They will make for Abergavenny?' Raymond asked as he began belting his sword to his side, his eyes dark and his brow creased in concentration. He knew what would befall Geoffrey and Alice if Sir William de Braose had his way. He would not repeat his mistake of keeping them alive as he had when Raymond had caught up with him in Wentland.

'Unlikely,' Marshal answered. 'I gather that Sir William and six knights left Westminster under cover of darkness with the two siblings. They were going east, making for London Bridge. Bramber Castle is their destination.'

Raymond cursed. For all he knew, Sir William could be

173

across the Thames already. With King Henry's court already between him and London Bridge, there was little hope that he would be able to catch up. And even if he could, how could he be certain that Alice and Geoffrey had not been transferred into the Danish chieftain Sigtrygg's ship? Thanks to Fulk's discoveries, he knew that the longship had been headed in the same direction. He dismissed the idea almost immediately. Sir William wouldn't risk having his captives in anyone else's custody, not after all he had gone through to again have them in his hands.

'I have to go after them. Will you ride with me?' he asked Marshal.

'The Young King wants to be in Kingston by this evening. His ship awaits us at Wareham,' he replied with pursed lips and a slight shake of his head. 'I think you should consider what you are about to do, Raymond. If King Henry discovers that you have attacked his court favourite, you will be declared outlaw…'

'And Strongbow can say goodbye to Striguil,' Raymond finished the sentence and shook his head. 'Damn it! Though she abandoned me, I cannot do the same to her. I must go after her.'

'She is lucky to have you,' replied Marshal. 'May fortune smile upon you, my friend,' he said as he leant down to grip his friend's forearm.

'God be with you. I hope we shall meet again. Borard!' he yelled. 'Forget those packhorses and get our coursers saddled. We have a mission.'

'A mission?' Borard replied. 'What about Striguil?'

'Twelve riders will come with me, the rest to stay with Earl Richard and Walter de Bloet.' Raymond stated as he secured a mace to his belt and began searching for his shield amongst the contents of the nearest wagon.

174

'So where are we going?'

'To save a damsel in distress,' Raymond grimaced as he hoisted his chainmail coif onto his head. 'We ride to defeat a tyrant and do deeds worth singing about. We ride to –'

Borard held up a hand to stop Raymond from saying anything further. 'Save your breath. You listen to the troubadours far too much,' he finished with a despairing roll of his eyes. 'God, but I do detest chivalry. What is the plan then, Sir Lancelot? Charge up the road and kill King Henry?'

Raymond smiled at Borard's remark and called Fulk of Westminster to his side. 'Do you know where the ferryman lands on the southern shore?' he asked the younger man.

'At Lambeth,' Fulk replied and pointed an outstretched hand towards the distant bank opposite Westminster. Raymond had to shield his eyes because of the sunshine pouring over England from the east. He could see a small wharf amongst the rushes, and a few thatched rooftops. Several sheep roamed around the fields above the dancing marshland and there were villeins in the fields.

'Are you sure they have a horse ferry?' Raymond asked his new servant.

'Of course, Lord,' Fulk exclaimed, shocked that he would ask such a thing. 'My uncle is one of the ferrymen for the archbishop.'

'Signal him then. We need to get to across the river as soon as possible.' Already a plan was enfolding in his mind, one of daring and mischief. 'Borard, take the money we received from Sir James FitzJames and go with Fulk. Pay the ferryman for shipping men and horses across. Give him whatever he wants.'

Borard stared down at the pouch of money in his hand like it was a kitten he was being forced to drown. 'You want me to give it away again?'

'Fulk, show him the way,' Raymond told the boy as Borard gave his captain one last despairing look. Both turned and walked towards the water's edge. Raymond turned to find Strongbow at his side.

'Is there a problem with the baggage?' the earl asked.

'I have a pressing matter that requires my attention across the river, Lord,' he told his master as he checked the length of his stirrups on Dreigiau. He put them up three notches. In battle he liked them to be longer to provide extra balance, but the ride ahead would be tough and the saddle all the comfier for the change.

'A pressing matter across the river?' asked a confused Strongbow. 'But we are bound for Oxford, Raymond, and then on to Striguil.'

'I am sorry, Lord, but for your own sake please do not ask any more questions.'

'Oh dear,' Strongbow shook his head and studied Raymond de Carew. 'Another adventure,' he sighed. 'Would this involve a certain girl from Abergavenny?'

'Yes, Lord,' Raymond admitted.

'You are not going to attack the Young King, are you?' Strongbow seemed genuinely concerned that his liegeman would take on the might of the Angevin monarchy.

'No, but my enemy is no less well protected.' Strongbow did not answer and Raymond sighed as he unbuckled his sword and pulled off his surcoat emblazoned with the crimson and gold Clare arms in one swift movement. He held out the colourful garment to Strongbow. 'I will not let your name be attached to this act, Earl Richard. So I ask that you release me from my oath. Your nephew, Walter de Bloet, will see you safely back to Striguil.' He shook the surcoat and urged Strongbow to take it, but the old Earl simply stared at the colourful folds. 'You know that he has always wished to

176

command your conrois, Lord.'

'I will keep this for you, Raymond,' the earl said as he accepted the surcoat. 'Do you understand?'

'Yes, Lord.'

'You are still my captain, Raymond de Carew, even though I do release you from my service. I have need of you and all these men. So accomplish this deed, whatever it is, quietly if you can, and then hurry home to Striguil. We have bigger prizes to claim than petty revenge in England.'

Raymond smiled and pulled on a tatty green surcoat with no heraldic device. 'I will race you back to Striguil, Lord Strongbow.'

The earl grimaced. Turning his back on his captain, he signalled towards Walter de Bloet. 'I want us ready to leave Westminster in the hour, nephew.'

Raymond felt a sudden surge of pity and affection for the earl, so desperate to claim the esteem of kingship across the sea, yet trusting enough to let his warlord dash off on the eve of that feat.

'Raymond,' Borard interrupted his thoughts. 'The conrois is ready to move out.'

He nodded in answer and leapt into his saddle with a single bound. His riders looked at him expectantly.

'So what is going on, Raymond?' asked William de Vale, the esquire.

'Yeah, what's the plan?' enquired Denis d'Auton. 'I thought we were for home?'

'I am going after Geoffrey of Abergavenny and his sister Alice,' Raymond replied, loud enough for all his companions to hear. 'They have been taken prisoner and will not survive long. I won't order you to come with me. Our enemy rides at the head of a strong force of horsemen supported by those Danish devils who attacked us at the Thorney Inn.' A number of the milites growled angrily,

177

swearing vengeance against the men who had killed their friend, Lyvet. 'But also because William de Braose has the ear of the king and should we fail to get away without being recognised, then we run the risk of being declared outlaw.'

'Lady Alice saved our horses,' Bertram d'Alton's voice barked from amongst his men, 'so I say we owe her our help.'

'What difference would it make if I was to be made outlaw?' asked William de Vale.

Borard climbed into the saddle beside him. 'Where you go, Raymond, we go,' he stated. 'Who knows, there may even be a bit of profit in it?'

Raymond smiled and turned his horse southwards so that his men would not see him blush.

'Well then,' he said with determination, 'let's ride.'

The forested glade was the perfect place for a murder. Steep wooded sides sloped away from the path on both sides; one uphill and the other down into the heavily forested valley where the River Mole wound its way towards Buckland, and piping birdsong of redshanks echoed.

'Perfect,' Sir William de Braose hummed happily. He was not talking about the beautiful surroundings, where yellow kingcups mixed with ivy-laden trees in the soft summer sunshine. He and his small company had passed Mickleham earlier in the day but had left Stane Street below Boxhill to follow a tiny path along the Mole Valley rather than continuing on the same path towards the big town of Dorchester. For the first time since leaving London they found themselves free of fellow travellers.

'You men,' Sir William flapped a hand at the twenty hired Danes. 'Go forward and scout those trees,' he ordered with no idea if the vicious-looking warriors understood a single word that he spoken. 'Forward,' he insisted at the leader of his mercenaries, pointing ahead and downhill.

The foreigner slowly nodded and shouted something in his coarse language which made his crewmen laugh. As the foreign mercenaries walked forward, Sir William felt his lip sneer. He had been forced to accept twenty of Sigtrygg's men into his company as they travelled back to Bramber Castle. The jarl had sought him out as he and his knights had attempted to flee Westminster with the two bastards of Abergavenny. Jarl Sigtrygg had demanded his payment or threatened that he would inform the sheriff of Sir William's part in the fire and the murder of one of Strongbow's mesnie household. Penniless after bribing the king, William could not pay but he had convinced Jarl Sigtrygg that he had silver at Bramber. The jarl had been suspicious and had ordered his men to remain with the Norman knight until the debt was paid. Sigtrygg and the remaining members of his crew had taken the sea route with the warning that he would be waiting for Sir William in Sussex. That had forced the young knight to make all haste on the road southwards ere the jarl thought to take his payment from within Bramber's walls while both Sir William and his father were absent. He knew that he had to be rid of the Danes' company before they did any lasting damage to his reputation, but for now he could not free himself of their presence.

The foreigners had, however, proven a welcome security against attack. He had no real reason to fear ambush on the road south, of course - no band of outlaws or highwaymen was likely to mistake the troop of horsemen and infantry for the pilgrims and merchants who frequented the road, but he still felt jittery. Even with the Old King's help in the kidnapping of Geoffrey and Alice, he could not shake the worry that Prince Harry would pursue him and take back his new mistress.

William called to the most senior knight in his conrois. As he watched the Danes disappear around a corner ahead, grizzled old Guy Wiston joined him from the back of the column.

'Is it time?' Wiston asked.

Sir William did not turn around to look at him. 'This is as good a place as any.'

'Yes,' Wiston said absentmindedly. He took a dagger from his belt and examined its edge.

'Make it quick,' Sir William said as his eyes flicked around to look at Geoffrey and Alice of Abergavenny, tied at the knees and hands, in the cart. 'Take one man with you to dig their graves. I'll lead the rest of the company back up the road a bit to make sure no one is coming this way. Understand?'

'Whatever you think,' Wiston replied. 'Abergavenny is your inheritance, not mine.'

The younger man turned his horse towards the cart which carried Alice and Geoffrey. Against his will, Sir William felt the pang of desire as he looked at his beautiful cousin. She had given herself to him in the wilderness of Wentwood and an image of her body in the firelight leapt into his mind. She had thought to save her brother after the priest had died by Wiston's hand. Sir William consoled himself that it had been a sin and Alice's death was justice. The thought sat comfortably on his ambitious shoulders.

'Cousins,' Sir William greeted them. Geoffrey wilted under his words.

Alice was undaunted. 'Where are you taking us?'

'To Bramber, of course,' William lied. 'There you will be kept safe and secure. Geoffrey will go to the monks of Battle Abbey and you, cousin, to a nunnery.'

'The Young King will come for me,' Alice replied, 'and he will make you cower before him.'

Geoffrey looked up, expecting violence, but William de Braose smiled sweetly at the siblings. 'No, he will not come, Alice. He is enamoured with the sound of his own voice, that one. I wager that he had already forgotten you.'

'You worm,' whimpered the girl as tears began to show.

Sir William laughed, stopping only when shouting erupted in the distance. His eyes narrowed and his pupils danced in their sockets as he listened for more tell-tale signs of combat in the valley where the Danes had disappeared. There! The distant clash of weaponry emanated from the depth of the glade and was followed by the briefest shouts of alarm.

'Harry!' Alice of Abergavenny exclaimed breathlessly, a smile of victory beaming from beneath her tear-stained face as she turned back to stare at her captor.

'Be quiet,' Sir William snapped as he considered the situation. Certainly the sounds indicated that the foreigners down in the valley were under attack, but what did he care if they died? They cost nothing if they were dead. More important was finding out who was attacking them. Before he could react, three Danes burst from the tree line and, spotting Sir William, sprinted towards him.

'Lord,' their leader panted. 'We have come upon bandits in the forest.' The foreigner kept his head bowed in subservience to the powerful young knight.

'Are they the Young King's men?' asked Sir William, momentarily shocked at the Dane's grasp of the French tongue. Then he remembered that Jarl Sigtrygg had been able to speak the language.

'They are not mounted, Lord,' the foreigner answered in his strange lilting accent.

'How many?' he demanded.

'Ten at most, armed with bows. We should send cavalry, Lord, to help chase them off.'

181

Sir William ignored him and considered the situation. An idea quickly began to take form in his mind. He turned his back on the Danes.

'Guy!' he shouted in Wiston's direction. 'Get my conrois ready. We are going to drive away those bandits.' The man nodded his helmeted head in assent and began issuing orders to the other warriors.

'You are from Ireland?' he asked of the mercenary leader.

'Yes, Lord,' the Dane answered, keeping his head bowed in deference to the noble heir to Bramber. 'My name is Ulf.'

Sir William noticed that the foreigner had a Norman horn at his side. Probably plunder from some poor murdered soul, William decided. 'I have another job for you, Ulf.' He urged his horse away from the cart. 'Follow me.'

'Yes, my Lord,' the man answered and walked away from where the Abergavenny siblings were chained.

Sir William searched among his clothes and produced two coins. 'That,' he said as he threw the first of the coins into Ulf's hands, 'is for the boy's soul. And that,' he flicked another in the Dane's direction, 'is for that of the girl.' The second coin shimmered in the air before falling into Ulf's hands. 'And this,' Sir William continued, shaking the little money remaining in the worn leather purse, 'is for your silence.' He held the purse by the ties at the top, swinging it gently between his thumb and forefinger. Ulf's face was shadowed by the wide nasal guard, and his chin covered in chainmail, but his eyes shone at the sound of the money. 'Do you understand what I am asking of you? I do not wish for you to pray for them.'

'Yes, Lord,' the man replied in his strange accent. 'We will take them somewhere secluded and make it look like

182

the bandits killed them?'

William de Braose smiled and tossed the purse on the ground beside the man's feet. 'Exactly,' he said. 'Keep this to yourself and you will have my favour and more silver than you could ever imagine. Open your mouth to anyone, including your jarl, and it will be the last thing you do.'

'Yes, Lord,' the man replied as he gathered the coins into his pockets.

'Good. Get it done then,' Sir William said as he trotted back towards Geoffrey and Alice. His horse barely broke stride as he passed the bastard cousins whose deaths he had bought.

'These goodly Danes will take you somewhere safe while I chase off these outlaws,' he said with a sly smile. 'Goodbye.'

'King Harry will come for me,' Alice spat at him but Sir William merely laughed and kicked his horse into a canter which took him past the group of cavalry awaiting his orders.

'Follow me,' he shouted. 'Let's get rid of these scum,' he ordered. He pulled his chainmail coif up onto his head and drew his sword from his red scabbard. Sir William could not help but let a smile spread across his face. Finally, after so many weeks of fretting, his cousins would be gone and his rich Welsh inheritance secure. First he had to deal with the outlaws who had unwittingly provided him with the perfect cover for Geoffrey and Alice's murder. Their heads would be presented to the Sheriff of Surrey, as would their blame for his cousins' deaths. His troop of horsemen trotted over the brow of a hill and down into the belly of the valley where the ambush had occurred. As he slid his war helm onto his head, William de Braose noted that it was strangely silent in the glade, but for the rustle of leaves, the tinkle of running water and the clip of horses' hooves.

'Fan out,' he told the men who followed him. Locked inside his great helm, William could see almost nothing except that which came from directly ahead. The stillness in the valley worried him and he gripped and re-gripped his sword hilt nervously.

Then he saw the Danes. Each had at least four or five arrow shafts protruding from his chest or face. They were all dead.

'Where are the outlaws?' he shouted at his men who, like he, searched the trees on either side of the road for any sign of the bandits. 'Fan out!'

Why woodsmen would think to attack heavily armed warriors, Sir William did not know. Normally they relied on hunting down travellers, tradesmen and pilgrims. This attack was not in keeping with what he knew of outlaws and Sir William's eye drifted back over the bodies. For the first time noticed that some of the Danes were missing armour and weapons. Often the dead were stripped of their arms by their enemy, but Sir William wondered why only a few of the mercenaries had been foraged for equipment. Closer investigation showed that the stripped men, alone of the dead Danes, had not been killed by arrows. Instead they had been brought down by shots to their legs, and then their throats had been cut. Sir William shook his head in confusion.

'No sign of the bowmen,' Guy Wiston shouted from further up the road. 'They must have scarpered as soon as they saw us coming.'

'No,' he replied, his eyes screwed up in concentration, 'there is something else going on.' Sir William dismounted and knelt at the side of one of the Danes who had been stripped of his leather armour and weaponry. There were two arrow wounds in the man's legs - one in the ankle and a second in his left thigh. 'They were trying to capture these ones without killing them,' he said quietly.

'Looks like they killed him anyway,' Wiston said as he dropped down beside his lord. A pool of blood gathered from a gaping wound on the dead man's throat.

'But why bother?' Sir William asked. 'They took him down with arrows as he ran away, stripped him and then cut his throat. Why?' he asked.

'They liked his armour too much to ruin it,' Wiston answered with a smile. 'I wonder why they didn't take the same from these other fashionable wretches? Twenty coats of good armour would fetch a pretty price at market.'

William froze as a thought entered his head. 'How many bodies are there?'

'Twenty in total,' Wiston answered, sweeping a hand over the dead and counting them one at a time. 'This fellow and nineteen others. Why do you ask?'

'If there are twenty bodies here, and we only had twenty in our company, then who were the three that came back to the top of the glade?' Sir William quizzically swept around and looked back through the trees to where he had last seen Geoffrey and Alice of Abergavenny. 'Who the hell was that Dane I spoke to?'

Without another word he threw his leg over his horse's back and thundered back up the hill.

The Dane untied Alice's hands delicately. He did not speak and nor did he raise his helmeted head to look at those who he had been paid to murder. His five crewmen gathered around him.

'Where are you taking us?' the girl asked as she watched her hated cousin and his conrois disappear through the trees to flush out his enemy. She had watched Sir William's conversation with the Dane intently, and prayed that she had misread what had gone between the men. Her wrists

185

were raw where she had clawed at the ropes in an attempt to free herself and her brother. 'Why are you taking us away?' she demanded.

The foreign mercenary said nothing in reply to the girl but, keeping a hold on Alice's hand, slashed the ropes which bound Geoffrey of Abergavenny to the cart. A shadow cast by the mercenary's tall helmet kept his face and any human emotion hidden from Alice.

'Why did he give you money?' Alice questioned the foreigner again. When he didn't answer she tried a different tack. 'The Young King would pay a fine ransom for the lives of my brother and me,' she said as sweetly as possible. 'He will be here presently, and will reward those who protect his loved ones.'

'No,' was all that the Dane replied.

'Do not do this to us,' Alice screamed and attempted to loosen the Dane's grip on her arm. The warrior's hold was immovable as he hauled both to their feet and dragged them up hill away from William de Braose remaining column of servants and soldiers.

'Come,' the Dane mumbled as he hauled Alice up hill and into the trees. Geoffrey's arm was taken by one of his cohorts. Both siblings fought against the mercenaries' great strength, but loose soil provided no foothold and though they passed many trees, neither sibling could grab any hold to stop the march that inevitably took them towards a shallow grave in the woods.

'I have a friend with money!' Alice squealed as she fought.

'The Young King?' the Dane asked, his voice laden with scorn.

'No, Raymond de Carew,' she pleaded. 'You have heard of him? He won the tourney at Westminster...'

'Bloody typical,' the Dane replied and angrily hauled

the girl upwards with a sudden jolt and a scathing laugh. Moments later they reached the tree-lined ridge and they picked up pace as they hurried over the hollow roots which punctuated the ground beneath them. As they reached a small hollow, the Dane stopped and looked around him. He dropped Alice's arms and put his fingers to his mouth, blowing a short, sharp whistle which reverberated around the trees. Alice of Abergavenny, despite her exhaustion, charged the Dane in a last effort to free her brother.

'Wait,' the man managed to say before Alice leapt on his back and began wrestling with him. She screamed and scrabbled at the armour wrapped around her would-be murderer's face until she, the Dane and Geoffrey fell into a writhing pile in the belly of the hollow. The rest tried to pull the girl off their crewman until laughter pealed from their left.

'How is it, Lady Alice, that every time we deliver you from death you thank us by threatening or attacking one of my warriors?' asked Raymond de Carew calmly from a few paces away. He was surrounded on all sides by fighting men, all armed lightly with bows in hand and arrows nocked and ready to fly. 'How about you two stop fighting and we all get out of here?' he added with a laugh. All his men were amused at the sight of the girl straddling her captor, attempting to throttle him.

'Raymond?' the girl asked without removing her hands from the face of the man below her.

'Get off me,' the Dane commanded, rolling onto his back and launching Alice off him and onto the ground. Getting to his feet, he threw away the Danish helm and pulled the chainmail hood from his chin and head, revealing his face. She recognised him immediately as Borard, though his beard and most of his hair had been hacked off to disguise him. The other Danes began

187

stripping away armour to reveal more of Raymond's men: Asclettin FitzEustaceand Thurstin Hore.

'Well, that was easier than I thought it would be,' Borard told Raymond as he brushed twigs from his shirt. 'Are we ready?'

Raymond nodded and turned towards Alice, still sitting on the forest floor, disgruntled and untidy. 'Yes, back to the horses,' he said. 'We have what we came for.'

Chapter Seven

'What did you think you were doing?' Basilia de Quincy shouted at Raymond and cuffed him around the head. The noise of his chainmail hood rattling on his shoulders echoed around the stone walls of Striguil Castle.

'My Lady, wait.' Raymond raised his arms to defend himself from another of meek Basilia's stinging blows. Her gown was blue and he hated that he would get it dirty or, worse, cause Basilia to hurt herself as she continued her attempts to strike him.

'You left my father to cross England alone to go off to … I don't know what.' She wrinkled her nose in anger. 'He could have been set upon by thieves or brigands, and you don't even care.'

Raymond had never seen Strongbow's daughter so furious and he was not sure what he had done to prompt it. A week had passed since his men had attacked Sir William de Braose and his Danes in Surrey, and Raymond and his conrois had returned through the gates of Striguil that very hour to find an angry Basilia, a distant Strongbow, and a strange buzz around the walls of the castle. What had happened in his absence, he did not know.

'Basilia...' he began before being cut off.

'You will call me *Lady* Basilia. We are not children playing games any longer, Raymond de Carew. I am the lady of this castle and you will treat me with the dignity of that position or you will be driven from Striguil like the lowly cur that you are.'

'Yes, Lady Basilia,' Raymond said and bowed his head. 'I am sorry for whatever I did to offend you.' Strongbow's daughter was already gone back towards her rooms with a prickly whip of her heavy linen wimple. Already feeling guilty over his whirlwind affair with Alice of Abergavenny, Raymond was compelled to follow the woman who he had loved from a distance for so long. He wanted to explain himself, to tell her how embarrassed he was at having taken a lover, at abandoning her father. He could see no other reason for Basilia's anger. He watched her disappear onto a staircase and Raymond was after her in a second, his chainmail coif rattling on his hauberk as he ran.

'Lady Basilia, please wait,' he shouted, aware that several pages had observed his contretemps with their lord's daughter. He hit the first step and could hear Basilia's dainty footfall upon the winding stair ahead of him.

'Go away,' she called over her shoulder as she climbed. 'I want nothing more to do with you.'

However, Raymond was faster and quickly caught up with Basilia. He grabbed her elbow as she flew upwards into the tower. She stopped in her tracks beside a tall window looking out over the steep cliffs to Afon Gwy. As she turned Raymond saw tears in her eyes.

'Lady Basilia, what has happened?'

'Nothing, I caught my foot.'

'Is it your father? Sir Roger?' Basilia turned her face aside at mention of her husband. 'Sir Roger, then,' he said with a slow nod of his head. 'What has he done?'

'I am sorry,' she mumbled, breaking free of Raymond's grasp and dashing up the steps away from the captain. Raymond tarried for a few moments before his feet again took him upwards.

190

'Lady Basilia, wait,' he called. He rounded the curling corner as she opened the door to her rooms.

Inside, in full view of his wife, was Sir Roger de Quincy's bare backside. Below him was one of the Welsh serving maids, her heavy skirts strewn across her face as the knight had his way with her. The girl's feet tugged at the small of his back and she moaned in delight. Strongbow's daughter froze in the doorway, unsure what to do as she saw her husband in bed with another woman. Raymond quickly reached forward and pulled the door shut to block her sight of his betrayal.

'What the hell?' he heard Sir Roger shout within the room as the door slammed shut. His cry was accompanied by a muffled squeal of ecstasy from his conquest.

Basilia slid down the wall and slumped onto the stone step, burying her head in her hands as she wept. Seconds later, a red-faced serving girl appeared through the door and disappeared down the stairs. She had left the ancient oak door ajar and Raymond caught a glimpse of Sir Roger pacing around the low table in the bedroom, stuffing his loose bliaut into his hose and wringing the hair above his forehead. For the first time that Raymond could remember the ever-immaculate knight was ruffled and untidy. The door again swung shut, hiding the colourful bed curtains and wall hangings, and closing Raymond and Basilia in the cold grey confines of the staircase.

'My Lady, let me help you,' Raymond said softly and reached out his hand towards the weeping woman. As he leant downwards the door gulped open, allowing daylight to flood onto the stairs.

'What the hell do you think you are doing?' Roger de Quincy demanded as he poked his head through. He stopped when he recognised Raymond, but did not seem to notice Basilia in the darkness of the step. 'Oh, it's you.' Sir

Roger seemed surprised to find him outside his room. 'What are you doing here? Are you a peeping tom now?'

Raymond was seething and a single look from his livid brow silenced Roger. 'How could you do this?' Raymond whispered. Every word was soaked in anger. He could not understand how someone who possessed Basilia could do anything other than worship and love her. 'Why would you betray her?' His fist gripped the hilt of his sword at his hip.

'A little fun, Raymond,' Roger replied. 'You understand. I have seen how you act with that lass from Abergavenny...'

'You and Alice?' Basilia whimpered from the step. 'You and ... that *puterelle*?' She shook her head and began sobbing harder than she had before.

'Basilia, I am sorry...' Raymond began but was interrupted.

'Oh my God, you let my wife see me in there?' Sir Roger accused, a finger pointed at Raymond's chest. 'You hedge-born miscreant, I knew that you were in love with my wife, but I didn't think that even you could stoop so low as to tell tales like a jealous child and then lead her to find me here. I shouldn't wonder that you paid that serving wench to seduce me. Yes, I wager that is what happened!' Sir Roger's eyes flicked about in his head and it seemed that he was already concocting a lie that he could tell Strongbow.

'That's not what occurred,' Raymond told Basilia. 'It isn't true.'

Sir Roger ignored Raymond's words. 'Oh do stop blubbing, Basilia,' he ordered. 'If you had been able to do more in bed than lie there like a side of ham then I wouldn't have to find my pleasure some other way.'

Without thinking Raymond reacted. He roared incoherently and drove a huge punch into Sir Roger de

Quincy's stomach before his under-cut lifted Strongbow's son-in-law off his feet and back through the oak door of his bedroom. He would have done more had not Basilia screamed and laid a hand on Raymond's leg to stop him.

'No!' she squealed.

Sir Roger scrambled away from Raymond, holding his chest. 'Are you mad? I am Strongbow's heir! I will have you hanged for this, Raymond,' he shouted triumphantly as he saw the blood drip from the cut on his chin and collect on his fingers. 'You two must be having an affair!' he suddenly accused as he clambered unsteadily to his feet. 'Why else would you be up here? You wrote her a love song before you left for France! My wife has been deceiving me! I have been betrayed. Let me past,' he ordered as he approached the door.

'Not until you apologise to your wife.' Raymond stood immobile on the top step. 'And admit your guilt to the earl.'

'Step aside, you whoreson, I am going to tell Strongbow who his daughter has been bedding,' he replied just as forcefully, holding a hand to his bleeding chin. In spite of himself, Sir Roger de Quincy was beginning to panic. He was unsure about how Strongbow would receive an allegation of infidelity against his daughter, especially when both Basilia and Raymond would immediately launch their counter-accusation. A short conversation with the serving woman would quickly discern the truth. That Raymond had punched him would work in his favour, Sir Roger was sure, but how Strongbow would react, he did not know. Would he protect his family name by hiding his son-in-law's misdemeanour? All Sir Roger knew was that he first had to get away from the violent dullard, Raymond de Carew, and his whining wife.

'Step aside,' he yelled.

Gritting his teeth and with a final glance towards

Basilia, Raymond moved away, allowing Sir Roger to flee down the stairs, his feet fading as they slapped on the stone steps.

'My Lady,' Raymond began, 'I am so sorry that you saw what he was doing in there.'

'It is not the first time that I have come across him with another woman,' Basilia said, her head still wrapped in her arms. 'While my father was away with you in Poitou, he was brazen. He flaunted his affairs in front of everyone.' She shook her head and her sobs echoed around the dusty corridor. 'It was humiliating.'

Raymond reached out and touched his lord's daughter on the arm, stroking the embroidered linen sleeve tenderly. 'He is a fool and you deserve better,' he told her and steeled himself. He could hide it no longer and her tears, if anything, made his desire for Basilia even stronger. 'I would love you as you deserve to be loved,' he blurted out. 'I have always loved you. Since I arrived at Striguil as a page to your mother, and you were a girl. I've worshipped only you all my life.'

For a long time Basilia said nothing but kept her head down and Raymond held his breath, not daring to disturb the silence of the corridor. Only the flickering flames from candles made noise and they wheezed and gasped and lit up the white-washed walls.

'You tell me this now?' Basilia looked up at Raymond with tears and anger in her eyes. 'My husband has shamed me and accused me of betraying him and you think it is an appropriate time to tell me that you love me?' She climbed to her feet and looked Raymond directly in the eye.

The captain was a brave man and one of the greatest fighters on the March of Wales, but in that second he was a small boy again, frightened and unsure of what to do next.

So he kissed her.

'Get off me, Raymond,' she appealed, pulling away from his lips and punching him on the shoulder.

'I love you,' he exclaimed.

She took three steps downwards, away from Raymond with tears forming again in her eyes. 'You are no different to my husband,' she accused. 'You would make me your whore?'

'Never, my Lady,' Raymond appealed. 'I love you.'

Basilia laughed and it was cold, reminding Raymond immediately of Sir Roger de Quincy's caustic manner. 'Is that why you have been shacked up with Alice of Abergavenny; because you love me, another man's wife?' She let the silence drag as she stared expectedly at him. He had no answer to her allegations. 'You are no different to any man,' she told him. 'My only value, the only value that any woman possesses, is what land and prestige she can bring to your bed. I thought you valued me in a different way, that you sought my friendship and my judgement. I can see now that I was wrong.'

'I wished to admit it sooner,' he started, 'and to tell you that I have loved you for longer than I can remember. And Alice...' He bowed his head and let his arms fall to his sides. 'I was lonely.'

Basilia was not even listening any longer. She swiped tears from her face and raised herself up to her tallest extent. 'I could never love one born so low as you, Raymond de Carew. You are but a poor warrior at my father's hearth, not even a knight. You are not worthy to wash the mud from my palfrey's hooves,' she said loftily and angrily. 'I am the daughter of the Earl of Pembroke and no son of a Welsh spearman will ever have claim upon me.'

Raymond was shocked at Basilia's anger, but he had pride and before he knew what he was saying, his own ire found the form of words and spilled from his mouth. 'I will not forget myself again,' he told her. 'I want no measly earl's girl for my wife. I will have no one other than a king's daughter. You should remember that, *Lady* Basilia, for I mean to put your father on a throne and for accomplishing that great task I will demand land and then, as a lord in my own right, I will ask for your hand again. I hope at that time to be considered worthy of your love.'

Basilia held his gaze for a moment, her brown eyes flickering between anger and agony. Then she turned on her heel and hurried down the stairs. Raymond did not follow. He was devastated, confused and embarrassed at his behaviour, fearful that he had ruined that which he had dreamed about for so long. He had lost Alice of Abergavenny to the Young King and now Basilia hated him because of his own stupidity and impatience. Raymond urged righteous anger to rise against Sir Roger de Quincy, but it would not intensify in his chest. Instead he slowly descended the stairs and made his way back towards the bailey where he promised that he would drink ale until he forgot everything that had occurred in the keep. The steps which took him from the top of the donjon to the gatehouse were a blur and Raymond had to shield his eyes from the strong sunlight as he exited into the bailey. It was because of the light that he did not see Milo de Cogan slink up behind him and grab his elbow, pulling him down the steps towards the marshalsea where several esquires cleaned their masters' coursers.

'What have you done?' Milo asked across the back of one horse. He pretended to fiddle with the length of its stirrups as he spoke. He seemed genuinely concerned, a characteristic which Raymond had rarely seen his cousin display.

'I did nothing,' Raymond protested. 'Basilia has found out about Alice...'

'What?' Milo interrupted. 'The earl's daughter? What on earth are you talking about? It is William de Braose that you need to be worried about.'

'William de Braose is in Sussex,' Raymond replied with a careless wave of his hand, 'probably still shouting and squealing like a child who has had his favourite toy taken away.'

Milo shook his head. 'He is here in Wales. They say he has hired three hundred Gascon routiers and has sent them to Brecon and Abergavenny,' Milo tugged down twice on the leather straps attached to his saddle to make sure they were secure. 'I saw, with my own eyes, a ship stuffed with Danes make land at Nedd.'

Raymond felt his body bristle with anxiety. Gascon mercenaries to the north? Danes to the west? What was William de Braose planning, he wondered. 'Is he considering a raid on Strongbow's lands?'

Milo laughed long and sarcastically but did not look up from his tack. 'Really, cousin, you are so naïve. It isn't a raid that he is planning. Sir William is preparing to go to war.' He flicked his eyes up to meet Raymond's wide-eyed stare. 'Did you truly believe your little escapade in Surrey would remain a secret? Tut-tut, Raymond.'

'A war?' He was aghast at his cousin's news. He thought that his ambush had been executed without anyone recognising him. Obviously Sir William had realised that only Raymond or the Young King would have gone after Geoffrey and Alice of Abergavenny.

'A war against Strongbow,' Milo confirmed as he tucked the excess leather from his stirrup under the flap of his saddle. He and his war band were bound for Goodrich Castle now that Raymond had returned to take command of the conrois of Striguil. Behind Milo his rag-tag band of hobiler-archers collected in the bailey ready

197

to depart for the north.

'Was there a big man with a boar on his shield amongst the Danish crewmen? He had a braided red beard.'

Milo shook his head. 'I didn't see anyone like that, but I did not dare to get that close.'

'What were you doing as far west as Nedd?' asked Raymond. 'You were supposed to be keeping an eye on Roger de Quincy here in Striguil.'

'A small pecuniary enterprise,' the archer explained with an evil grin which he quickly shook from his face. 'It turned out to be a waste of time and I was back before Sir Roger even knew that I had gone. It was lucky that I did go considering the important information I gathered for Strongbow.'

'I cannot believe that Sir Richard de Grenville would support William de Braose,' Raymond mumbled.

'Not only him,' Milo told him. 'At least three other Lords of Glamorgan have agreed to help him. We could find ourselves in peril of invasion from two sides.'

'What does Strongbow want to do?'

'He dawdles as usual,' Milo sniffed. 'He knows he cannot afford a fight with Abergavenny, let alone one with the knights of Glamorgan. He cannot survive a war on two fronts, Raymond. I heard Sir Roger in there with him.' He nodded his head towards the great hall. 'That sot told him to sell you to Moorish slavers and then send Alice and Geoffrey back to William de Braose for a hefty ransom. He was blathering something about you having had an affair with Lady Basilia too...'

'An affair? Is he out of his mind?'

'Possibly, but I don't think the earl will give it too much heed. The threat of war worries him more.'

Raymond nodded. 'We should send an envoy to the Earl of Gloucester in Cardiff and ask him to stop the knights of

Glamorgan from crossing his lands to attack us from the west.'

'Gloucester is the king's cousin, Raymond. He will support Henry's lapdog.'

'King Henry and Gloucester are not friends,' Raymond told his cousin. 'A small bribe would buy his support.' He thought of his tourney winnings and of how for less than a week he had been a rich man. 'We should also send word to Humphrey de Bohun and Baderon of Monmouth.'

'Bohun is Sir William's cousin, and do you really think Baderon will have forgiven Strongbow for taking Goodrich from him? You'd have better luck with Seisyll ap Dyfnwal.'

'Baderon is married to Strongbow's aunt. He will surely help his family.' Raymond was more hopeful than confident and Milo's incredulity increased his pessimism. Why, he considered, would the lords of the March risk war to defend two bastards and an out of favour baron? Why would they risk the displeasure of King Henry when there was nothing in it for them?

'I need to speak with Strongbow,' Raymond said. Milo was obviously thinking the same thing, for he nodded fiercely.

Before he could move another voice echoed around the noisy bailey: 'Raymond le Gros, I should take you out and flay the skin from your bones.' It was Sir Roger de Quincy who had spoken from the entrance to the stone fore-building. 'Your perverse devotion to that whore of Abergavenny has brought war to Striguil and I demand to know why we shouldn't throw you, the bitch and her pup brother to the wolves who threaten us and so sate their murderous desires?' Behind Sir Roger, Strongbow loitered in the darkness of the fore-building.

Before answering the charge levelled against him,

Raymond glanced across to the thatched building where Alice and Geoffrey had been staying. Both the siblings were standing in the doorway of the hut watching Sir Roger's very public declarations.

'My Lord Strongbow,' Raymond spoke directly to his master, ignoring the heir to Striguil, 'I would not have you conduct a war for me, Lord Strongbow, for I can fight for myself, but I know that you would never consider abandoning two children to such a horrible fate unless you were being advised to such a strategy by the council of evil-hearted men.' He cast a vicious glare at Sir Roger de Quincy.

'You insolent Welsh bastard,' Sir Roger replied before Strongbow's hand fell on his son-in-law's shoulder.

'This is getting out of hand, Raymond,' Strongbow said as he came into the daylight. 'Sir William is only after the girl and her brother. If they attack, I will be forced to appeal to the king to step in, and you know that King Henry will be ... displeased with that. God knows I am not in his favour as it is. I must send them back to their cousin.' Strongbow looked genuinely distraught at the judgement.

'You are, of course, correct, Lord,' Sir Roger continued, sending a victorious glimpse in Raymond's direction. 'You men,' he signalled to two of his own warriors, 'take those two bastards into your custody,' he pointed an outstretched finger at Alice and Geoffrey.

'Wait,' Raymond shouted, forcing the warriors to look towards Sir Roger for direction, 'there is another way, my Lord,' he told Strongbow, 'one that is to all our benefit.'

Sir Roger laughed scornfully and ordered the men to carry out their orders. 'Don't be silly, my Lord. He will get us all killed.' Behind them Alice screamed as she was grabbed around the wrist. Geoffrey scrambled away, but tripped over a gander which honked angrily as Sir Roger's

200

man took hold of the boy by his throat.

'Wait, Lord,' Raymond appealed again, 'I can make you richer than you have ever been before and prevent a feud with Abergavenny at the same time. You have to trust me.'

Strongbow looked from his son-in-law's face to that of Raymond de Carew and held up his hand to prevent Sir Roger's men from hauling Alice and Geoffrey into captivity.

'This had better be good, Raymond.'

Sir John de Stafford sighed as he listened to Strongbow's tale. He nodded and spoke at the appropriate moments, but he didn't believe a word of the convoluted tale which the Lord of Striguil spun. Despite being perfectly credible, one look at Strongbow's angry son-in-law told King Henry's messenger everything he needed to know about the accuracy of his story. Sullen, shifting his weight from foot to foot and unable to hold Stafford's stern stare, it was clear that Sir Roger de Quincy knew what Strongbow was saying was false. The fact that Sir Roger seemed unable to keep his temper also revealed much to the astute warrior from the Scottish March.

'I don't need to hear about every detail of your visit to London, Sir Richard,' Stafford interrupted Strongbow again, raising a rueful hand in the air. 'The justiciar merely wants to know where I can find your man, Raymond de Carew, so that I can arrest him. He is accused of brigandry and I must take him to the Sheriff of Surrey for judgement.'

The earl's steward had invited Sir John into the main hall of Striguil Castle two hours before and had claimed that his master would join him soon. He had proceeded to liberally pour wine for him, but Sir John was on business too serious and, as ever, he was too wily to fall into the trap. He had stayed sober and sharp for he was on a mission to stop a war on the March of Wales. That required a clear head. Then, when he had become convinced that he would never be allowed to see the earl, he had been shown up the winding stairs to the solar where he had found the nervous lord of the castle.

'Raymond, you say,' Strongbow replied, fiddling with a strand of frayed wool at his cuff. 'He is not here.'

'He is not here,' Sir John repeated and nodded his head. A man who was above suspicion would have asked about the charge levelled against his liegeman, of that he was sure. 'I was reliably informed by the brothers at Llanthony Secunda that he and his conrois had been headed this way no more than twelve days ago. Do you deny that he made it this far?'

Sir John sighed when Strongbow simply shrugged. He turned to study Roger de Quincy. The young knight could not hold Stafford's gaze.

'What are you looking at?' he asked petulantly before turning his back to stare into the depths of the hearth.

'Nothing at all, Sir Roger, you have told me more than enough,' Sir John told him and turned back towards Strongbow. 'So you are telling me that Raymond is not here in Striguil?'

'He is not,' the earl confirmed. 'We argued in Westminster, Sir John, and parted with harsh words. He arrived in Striguil almost a week ago demanding money and release from my service.'

'This you gave him?'

'Grudgingly,' Strongbow admitted. 'He leaves me shorthanded, but I have my best men searching out more warriors to defend my lands.'

The knight nodded. 'I had heard rumours that you were looking for soldiers as I came west.'

'In any event, no sooner had I released him than he

202

insulted my daughter and my family.'

'How?'

For a moment, Strongbow looked offended by Stafford's abrupt question. 'He declared his love to my daughter and asked her to run away with him,' Strongbow adjusted in his ornate chair. 'Naturally she refused. On your honour I would ask that you keep that information to yourself.' The Lord of Striguil waited until the knight nodded before continuing with his tale. 'Raymond and his friends fled, but not before they assaulted Sir Roger. Two days later they stole a ship, *Waverider*, from my harbour at Suðbury.'

'Why did you have a ship ready to sail?' Stafford asked. 'Where were you headed?'

'My daughter and I were planning a visit Walsingham.'

Stafford frowned. 'That is a long journey, but common, I suppose, at this time of year. Do you have any idea where de Carew was headed?'

Strongbow turned to Sir Roger and swapped a swift glance with him. 'When he was here, Raymond claimed that he was headed to Ireland to join his uncle, Sir Robert FitzStephen.'

'That twice-damned rebel,' snarled Sir Roger de Quincy.

John de Stafford ignored the younger man. 'Raymond had no plans to launch an attack on Abergavenny or Brecon?'

'None,' Strongbow replied sternly. 'What possible reason would Raymond have to attack Sir William de Braose?'

Sir John ignored the question. 'And you can swear that you have no aims in that direction?'

'Of course not!' Strongbow declared and half clambered out of his chair. 'What man of my age wishes to spend what little remains of his life in the saddle on campaign?' The earl sighed and lowered himself slowly back into his squeaking chair.

Sir John scratched the end of his nose with his forefinger as he studied Strongbow, whom he guessed was only in his forties, though the man's shabby garb and demeanour did make him seem much older. 'What of William de Braose's bastard cousins?' the king's messenger asked. 'Raymond de Carew is accused of kidnapping them from his household. Sir William claims that Raymond was acting on your orders.'

'I have heard nothing of them since Westminster when they left my care for the court of Young King Harry.'

Sir John de Stafford shook his head, realising that he would probably never get to the bottom of what had happened. He had his ideas, but he had run into so many lies in Abergavenny, when he had interviewed William de Braose, as well as in Striguil, that it made the truth impossible to determine. Indictments had been met by counter-accusations while sworn oaths had been backed up by the offer of bribes and even, from Sir William, threats of violence. The justiciar had stated that the primary aim of his mission was to broker a peace between the vying Marcher lords. Sir William had been angry at that. Yet Sir John believed that he could still accomplish that goal. Strongbow, obviously a fading power, sensibly did not have the heart for war and William de Braose was a fool if he believed his father's friendship with the king would grant him dispensation to ravage a neighbouring lord for the sake of misbegotten revenge.

'I have your word that you will keep the peace on the March?' Stafford asked Strongbow.

'I will not lift a sword against any of the King's subjects,' the earl told him, 'unless it is in defence.'

'Then I will return to Abergavenny and persuade Sir William that his current conduct will not meet with King Henry's favour,' said Sir John as he climbed to his feet. 'I thank you for your hospitality Sir Richard. I will inform the justiciar that Raymond de Carew has escaped our jurisdiction. If you should cross paths with him again you would do well to warn him that King Henry does not forget and rarely forgives.'

'Thank you, Sir John,' Strongbow replied. 'I pray that you pass on my best regards to my neighbour in Abergavenny, and inform him of my continued friendship,' he allowed himself a small, shallow smile, 'despite this serious mistake on his behalf.'

Sir John smiled at the defiance of the old man. 'I will give him your greetings, Sir Richard.'

'Thank you. Now, Sir John, I am afraid I must retire as I am suddenly feeling weary.' The earl climbed to his feet and waited for the king's agent to bow and make his way out of the solar. Sir John was tracked by Roger de Quincy as he retreated down the stone steps, but Strongbow's heir did not speak as they joined the few remaining hearth knights in the great hall below.

Four milites in the service of the justiciar ate loudly and laughed at a shared joke in the body of the room. Sir John did not feel like joining the men who had accompanied him in his journey and instead walked over to where Sir Roger de Quincy stood.

'Sir Roger,' Stafford greeted him, 'I am sorry to see that you are unwell. I saw Raymond de Carew fight William Marshal at the tourney in Westminster and it is no disgrace to have been roughed up by a man like him.'

'I am fine. I was caught unawares by the rogue. That is all.'

'This is my first time in Chepstow,' Stafford told his fellow knight, using the English name for the town. 'It is beautiful countryside. Is the hunting good?'

'No.'

'Oh, I see.' The young heir to Striguil was agitated, that much was obvious to Sir John. He searched his mind for anything else to talk about. 'This is delicious wine...'

'It is terrible,' Sir Roger replied. 'It is from a vinery in Lincolnshire. The Cistercians make it cheaply and therefore poorly. It is exactly to Strongbow's tastes; cheap and poor.'

'He has money problems, then?'

'Hah!' Sir Roger de Quincy laughed, sinking what remained from his cup. 'I am married to the heiress of a dying patrimony. Each year Strongbow sells off more and more land to pay his debts, leaving less for me to inherit. You rode through Tidesham on your way to Striguil?'

'I did. Good timber.'

'I know for a fact that Strongbow intends to sell off the whole manor to Bishop Roger of Worcester. And all to pay off a stinking Jew,' he shook his head. 'If he is not handing over money to him, then he is dispensing estates to the Church and what does he get for that?' Sir Roger rubbed the ends of his fingers together as if he was sprinkling sand onto the wooden floor. 'Nothing. I am to inherit a lordship with no land and of no distinction.'

'These are tough times for us all,' Sir John said. 'Do you have any news from Ireland?'

Sir Roger scornfully spat on the floor. 'There is no future in that land, no more so than there is in the land of the Scots. Strongbow should forget his throne,' he said as he poured another mug full of wine. He did not offer any to Sir John.

'So Strongbow still has designs on Ireland?' Suddenly Sir John had stumbled upon a new lead in his investigation. He had seen with his own eye's the earl's embarrassing performance of homage at the coronation feast in Westminster, and had heard from several sources about why it had occurred.

Sir Roger choked momentarily on his wine and began shaking a finger at Sir John. 'No, no. I spoke out of turn,' he quickly claimed. 'I am not supposed to say anything about...'

'About?'

'About Raymond the Fat and Strongbow's plans,' Sir Roger admitted. 'Sir John, if you can promise me that I will not lose Striguil, I will tell you what you need to know. But I want assurances that I will keep this castle if Strongbow is outlawed.'

'Outlawed?' Sir John was now confused. 'Why would your father-in-law be outlawed?'

'Because you have been lied to,' the dark-haired knight claimed. 'Raymond didn't steal the ship; he was given her by Strongbow in order to go to Ireland. My wife's great-uncle, Sir Hervey de Montmorency, is in on it too,' he added quickly. 'He cannot be trusted either,' he licked his lips, 'not like I can.'

'To what purpose has Raymond de Carew been sent to Ireland?'

'Conquest,' Sir Roger described. 'Strongbow has been promised a throne if he invades on behalf of a local chieftain, or some such nonsense,' he said. 'The earl has sent Raymond ahead secretly to prepare a bridgehead while he arranges an army of invasion. Raymond was able to employ over fifty bandits from Seisyll ap Dyfnwal's lands – outlaws, each and every one. You see, King Henry gave no assurance that he would release Strongbow from his service. He has no licence so he wants to invade in secret. I tell you this only because I trust you, Sir John, to tell the King that I will be a trusted friend to him amongst his many

207

enemies on the March. If, that is, he allows me to keep Striguil, Goodrich and Usk.'

Sir John said nothing but had a long drink from his goblet as he mulled over this news. 'What do you think I should do exactly? Arrest Strongbow?'

'If you think it necessary, I would not dream of...' Sir Roger dropped his voice as a page passed close by, yawning and holding a load of clean bed linens. 'I would make a far better friend to King Henry than my father-in-law,' he whispered.

Stafford could not believe Sir Roger de Quincy's brazen betrayal of Strongbow. However, he felt sure that Sir Roger would indeed be better equipped than Strongbow to function in the dark world of the Plantagenet court where King Henry's plotting and politicking was to the fore. He felt a sudden sympathy for the old warrior Strongbow, who like Sir John himself, had spent most of his life struggling to earn a piece of land to call his own. And yet the life of a nobleman was never easy when a king like Henry FitzEmpress sat on the throne enacting edicts, publishing proclamations and issuing writs to strangle the independence from the lords of England.

'I will tell the king of your offer, Sir Roger,' he lied. 'I recommend that you keep this information to yourself in the meantime. We would not want to raise your father-in-law's suspicions prematurely. To that end I would suggest being the most committed and goodly son-in-law that you can possibly be until I can get this information to King Henry in France.'

'Of course,' Sir Roger said, suddenly keen.

Sir John looked at the treacherous Sir Roger and forced himself to smile. 'Striguil would be lucky to have a man of your calibre at its head.' He bowed. 'You,' he commanded the justiciar's men, 'we are departing now.' Moans echoed as the warriors realised they would have to climb back into the saddle and spend the night in the open countryside rather than the comfort of Strongbow's hall. Sir John de Stafford did not stop to listen to their dissatisfaction. Out on steps to the bailey, he stopped and stretched his back, staring over the bailey walls at the wide Afon Gwy. The river wound its way southwards to where it met the mighty Severn. Freshwater met salt and river met sea, and beyond that the mysterious land of Ireland lay. Sir John snorted a small laugh and pulled his cloak closer around his shoulders, thinking of his wife and daughters at home safe in their small manor house. What ambition stirred in a man of Strongbow's standing, he did not know or share but it seemed like he was surrounded enemies both within and outside his own castle.

'Good luck,' John de Stafford, a man who had known ambition and disappointment, whispered upwards to where Strongbow slept alone in the solar of Striguil.

Part Two

The Bridgehead

Chapter Eight

Crashing waves woke Raymond de Carew from sleep. The wooden belly of Strongbow's ship squeaked beneath his cold and damp woollen clothes as he rolled onto his shoulder. He stared through the darkness. Down the length of the vomit-strewn ship his company of warriors shivered and prayed that they were having nightmares and would soon awaken in their warm beds far away from the cold beach. It was summer everywhere, it seemed, except Ireland.

A hundred and ten men, sixty horses, a priest and one woman had made the crossing from Striguil the day before. Lurching across the sun-soaked waves, Strongbow's ship, *Waverider*, had come across none of the dangers that downed so many other vessels in the Western Sea. Raymond knew that his small ship might have encountered waterspouts, whirlpools, and any number of sea monsters, not to mention pirates, evil spirits and storms. But his luck had held out.

'Thank you, St Nicholas,' he said towards the dark purple sky. He prayed that his gratitude found the ears of the sailors' saint. 'Thank you for bringing us safely to this,' he paused as more rain sprayed across the sheer-strake, 'lovely place.'

The headland was called Dun Domhnall and Raymond had beached the ship in a small cove below the cliffs to the east. During the night the rain had swept in, ever heavier, shaking the rigging, whipping ropes and scattering water

213

across his small fighting force. Everywhere men huddled together attempting to find any nook that would protect them from the creeping cold which seeped over the rail. One of the young remounts had spotted that Raymond was awake. He tried to stamp his feet to attract his attention and Raymond reached out to silently soothe the cob, hoping that his calming valerian concoction would keep the animals under control for a little bit longer.

'Holy Trinity,' he exclaimed as another blast of drizzle tumbled over the starboard quarter of *Waverider* and froze his face. He pulled himself up to a sitting position. Only a hangover could have made the dark morning worse, but thankfully Raymond had abstained during the crossing - unlike many of his new allies. The seventy Welsh archers had come at a high price, but he knew that with Seisyll ap Dyfnwal's men by his side his plan, and by extension Strongbow's invasion, had a real chance of success. If, that was, the Welshmen survived the after-effects of so much drinking.

It was a grim start to the campaign. A howling gale swept off the ocean and froze every exposed piece of skin. His knuckles somehow managed to find a way to knock themselves off every hard surface, causing an excruciating if momentary pain to erupt in his otherwise nerveless digits. The snot dripped from his upper lip to mingle with the freezing salt spray from the ocean. Wet, coarse sand found its way into every soft ripple of skin, and the ripping winds pierced his woollen clothes to Raymond's bones. *Waverider* was hidden on the less exposed beach, surrounded on three sides by the headland of Dun Domhnall, but it remained a damp, cold misery. From above, dripping water scattered from the half-stowed and noisy rigging to land squarely on Raymond's shoulders. Under his vast cloak he had a skin full of wine and a quick slug of the liquid warmed against his chest proved enough to lessen the wonderful wretchedness of the south coast of Ireland. He hefted himself to his feet and walked over to his nearest comrade.

'Are we in hell?' William de Vale asked groggily as Raymond shook him by the shoulder. The esquire had been another to overindulge during the crossing and was paying the price for that excess.

'No chance,' Raymond replied with a laugh, handing over his own wine skin. 'Hell, I am sure, would be much warmer than this.' He looked out over the side of *Waverider*. 'I can tell you that we are definitely not in heaven either.' Another wave from the retreating tide smashed into the stern of the Norman vessel and made the wooden planks strain and twist loudly. The sail above them cracked like a whip. William groaned and hung onto the wretched wooden pallet that was his bed. Raymond slapped his young esquire on the shoulder sympathetically and shouted down the ship to rouse Borard and Amaury de Lyvet. Several Welshmen growled and swore at the captain in their own tongue, perhaps demanding that he be silent and let them sleep. He ignored them and moved further down *Waverider*.

'Amaury,' Raymond called again, 'get your section awake and start moving the coursers onto the beach. It will be daylight soon enough.'

He nodded obediently in Raymond's direction and began calling the names of men under his direct command. He had taken the place of his elder brother, Nicholas, who had been killed by Jarl Sigtrygg in Westminster, and had proven a steady and trusted subordinate. His order was met with more groans from men who pretended to be asleep even when Amaury poked and jostled them. Borard echoed Amaury's calls and soon the whole company was awake

215

and getting ready to work.

Bracing himself for the impact, Raymond leapt down onto the beach, happy that both would carry out his orders. He felt vulnerable without his armour and he wrapped his cloak tightly around him as if to make up for the absence of chainmail. To have gone to sea without his coat of steel would have been to invite rust, not to mention the obvious dangers if he had fallen overboard wearing his hauberk and coif. He missed its weight as he made his first steps on Irish soil.

It had already been getting late when they ran the ship up on the beach and Raymond could not imagine why any Gael would have had his eyes on the sea in this Godforsaken part of the world. Still, his nerves jangled and he searched the horizon for any hint of danger. He prayed that the steep cliffs which rose above the beach had protected them from prying eyes during their night-time landing. Daylight was beginning to threaten the eastern sky as Raymond walked the few steps to the shore and doused his face with salty water.

'Holy Lord, that would wake the dead,' he said as another gust howled off the sea. Their landing site was on a long peninsula which poked out from the south coast into the western ocean and was surrounded on three sides by high black sea cliffs covered in vegetation. It was the perfect place for a landing, as Strongbow's uncle had described. Sir Hervey de Montmorency had also informed them that there was a small and ancient fort up on the headland above the beach which would serve as an effective rally point if the small contingent of Normans were discovered by the natives.

Raymond watched as weak sunlight spilled drearily over the watery scene before him, unveiling for the first time the black rocks which punctured the surface of the

216

bay. He had not realised how fortunate his crew had been to navigate the landing without sinking Strongbow's ship in the shallows. Further out to sea, Raymond could make out several low grey blurs on the horizon which gave away the position of the tiny islands which the ship had rounded in the fading light of the day before.

The last words of a prayer drifted over the rumble of the ocean to where Raymond stood. Lying prostrate on the low-lying black rocks was a man. Raymond had thought him one of the jagged boulders in the bay and he jumped in surprise as his words reached him.

'Captain,' William Ferrand greeted Raymond. His voice was hoarse and his head was still bowed on his wringing hands as they rested upon the rocks. 'How are you finding your first day in Ireland?'

'Cold,' Raymond answered. He tried to dismiss the discomfort that Ferrand's presence inspired. Six years before, the warrior had been one of several hundred refugees who arrived in Striguil under the command of Sir Roger de Quincy. Raymond had listened as the leader of the fugitives had told a tale about the gallant defence of the frontier castle of Aberteifi following the death of the constable, Robert FitzStephen, Raymond's uncle. Sir Roger had spoken about how, with their last vestiges of strength depleted and FitzStephen dead, the small garrison had sued for peace with the besieging Welsh rebels. Strongbow had broken down in tears as he had listened to the tale and had urged the brave escapees to remain in Striguil as his guests, showering Sir Roger with glory and praise. It was only later that dark rumours about the fall of Aberteifi had begun to circulate, whispers that not only said that Robert FitzStephen was still alive and imprisoned, but that he had been betrayed by Sir Roger de Quincy and his lieutenants, of whom Ferrand was principal. In the six years since their arrival at Striguil, Raymond had had little to do with any of the men in Sir Roger's retinue. Yet somehow William Ferrand had managed to find out about his plan to flee to Ireland and had stowed away aboard Strongbow's ship at port in Suðbury.

'How are you feeling?' Raymond asked.

'I am here in Ireland as penance for my sins,' said Ferrand as he climbed to his feet, his face still turned towards the sea. 'I am not here for my comfort, but to make clean my soul.' He slowly turned around to face the captain. Immediately Raymond felt the automatic and unwelcome feeling of disgust as he looked into the face of a leper. Ferrand's granulated and pale skin looked dead. Knuckles of skin clumped hard upon his face, sending a shudder through Raymond's body as it had when he had found him on the ship. He had been assured by Dafydd FitzHywel - whose brother and grandfather had both perished from the disease - that the gravel-voiced warrior would not inflict the horrible condition on anyone else, but Raymond still felt himself take an involuntary step away as Ferrand looked at him. His left nostril was missing, as was part of his upper lip.

'Surely a pilgrimage to St David's or Our Lady's in Walsingham would have been a better place to do penance for a man in your condition? You would have done well to have stayed in the leper house in Tyndyrn, surely a good place to get back on your feet.'

'It was a good place to die, nothing more. It is not from Holy Mother Church that I seek atonement,' Ferrand replied with a grimace and turned his back.

Raymond knew of what he spoke. After they discovered the stowaway on board, the other milites had told him that Ferrand had spent much time at Tyndyrn Abbey praying for forgiveness for his part in the betrayal of Robert

218

FitzStephen at Aberteifi. They said that he had performed any task that had been asked of him as contrition and that he had picked up the disease from the sufferers who often went for help from the Benedictines. They also said that when he had begun to show signs of the disease, Sir Roger de Quincy had ejected him from his retinue and it was only the kindness of Lady Basilia that had saved his life, finding a position for him at the port of Suðbury where, no doubt, he had been perfectly placed to find a way onto *Waverider*.

'Do you think this is the edge of the world?' Ferrand asked suddenly as he stared out on the grey, rolling sea.

Raymond shrugged, wondering why the leper had asked him such a question. 'Could the edge of the world really only be four days' sailing west of Striguil?'

Ferrand seemed not to like Raymond's response. 'Jesus and his disciples sought the solitude of the desert when they needed to contemplate the condition of their souls. We don't have a desert so this vacant and desolate place will have to do for me. This is the edge of the world,' he asserted, 'the end of this world and thus closer to Christ's kingdom.'

'Despite it being the edge of the world, we have enemies all around us,' Raymond replied, 'so if you are going to eat our food you had better be willing to pull your weight. Are you capable of work?'

Ferrand bowed his head and turned around to face Raymond. 'What do you want me to do?' His sunken eyes could not hide the challenge. He did not want pity.

'When the time comes, I shall need a warrior who will stand his ground,' he said, remembering Ferrand's history. 'Until then, report to Borard and tell him that I am going up onto the headland to investigate the fort. Tell him that we need to have everything out of the ship and inside the walls by nightfall. After that you can get out on the promontory and start fishing for my supper. You will find everything you need on board *Waverider*.'

Ferrand nodded sternly as he pulled a thin piece of cloth around his face to mask his affliction. 'I won't let you down, Raymond. I am here to fight with you whatever the odds. You will never stand alone in battle while I live. That is my pledge and, with God as my witness, I hope to die having accomplished this oath.'

Raymond nodded suspiciously at the leper. 'With any luck our presence here will remain secret until Lord Strongbow arrives. Only then will the real fighting will begin. Geoffrey!' he shouted suddenly back towards the ship. A head popped up from amongst the ship's stores. 'Come here and bring William de Vale with you.' He watched as Geoffrey of Abergavenny disappeared only to re-emerge on the beach with the other young man at his side. Raymond's esquire trotted towards him, leaving William trailing behind.

'Sir,' Geoffrey greeted his captain eagerly as he came to attention. William de Vale was less enthusiastic as he dawdled up the beach huddled in his cloak.

'Your sister is happy?' Raymond asked Geoffrey as they waited. William gave Ferrand a wide berth as the leper walked in the opposite direction towards the ship.

'She did not enjoy the crossing, and...'

'And?'

'And she is still angry,' Geoffrey said but did not elaborate as William de Vale finally sauntered up to the pair.

'Lovely morning,' he said sarcastically, grabbing Geoffrey around the neck, playfully wrestling with him.

'Let's get moving,' Raymond said as he pointed towards the small path which led from the beach steeply up onto the headland. Why was Alice angry, he wondered? He wagered that the hero Roland, or any of his paladins, did not have his problems. Not for the first time, he cursed his awkward ways with the fairer gender.

The twenty-foot climb up the face of the cliff was not as gruelling as Raymond had thought it would be. Opportunely, the three men discovered a path well-worn into the hillside and they quickly scaled the sand and clay cliff face. The wind buffeted Raymond's face as he approached the top, almost blowing him back down the path to the beach below.

'Careful,' William de Vale warned as he pushed his captain back into the wind as it tumbled across the peninsula. 'Oh my, what a place to call home,' he added with a cynical look plastered across his face. They stood at the neck of the small headland. Two hundred paces away over a flat and grassy expanse, another cliff face fell away into the sea. Sea sprayed over the high cliffs as the stiff morning gale rocked the small daisies which grew there. Few trees punctured the landscape as he looked south towards the sea. Raymond could barely tell the difference between land, sea and cloud.

'So where is this fort?' asked William.

Raymond turned around and, looking over the cove where their ship was beached, indicated to the promontory which pointed eastwards like an arrowhead.

'Sir Hervey told Strongbow that it was out there. Let's walk that direction and take a look at it. Keep your eyes open for the freshwater spring too. It's on the north side close to the beach.' It was a hard haul as they stomped half a mile into the wind through the long grass, bushes and brambles which covered the sand and shale ground, but they eventually came across the curling defensive stone wall partially hidden by vegetation.

'It's well made, though a bit low.' Geoffrey had to shout

to Raymond over the roar of the waves and wind as he laid his hand on the piled stones.

Raymond looked at the heavy blocks and nodded in approval of the craftsmanship. 'The walls are old but they are solid. They must have been part of a bigger, circular fort that used to stand here. The rest must have fallen into the sea a long time ago.'

'Who the hell would want to live out here?' William shouted back as another wave sprayed another white cloud of water over the cliff.

'Sir Hervey said it was called Domhnall's fort.'

'Domhnall must have been a proper dullard,' William added, though low enough that Raymond could not hear.

The Norman captain leapt up onto the wall. The youngsters clambered after him to investigate within the elliptical fort defences. They quickly identified the overgrown remains of several stone buildings in the middle of the old village which Raymond suggested could be made comfortable with minimal effort.

'We could knock down this part of the wall to make a gate, and use the blocks to reinforce the wall,' Geoffrey shouted. He turned and waved down to the men unloading the ship on the beach below.

'There are loose blocks on either side too,' William de Vale said as he knelt on the inside of the fortifications. 'The wind has scattered them, but we can make the wall higher than it is now - should make us pretty secure.'

'What about the coursers?' Geoffrey asked his captain.

Raymond stared northwards and did not answer. It was only in the distance that he could see woods, vast and dark which stretched in all directions. A sheet of rain blurred his sight.

William de Vale answered the question for his lord. 'The horses can remain outside the walls under guard for one night, but then we will have to make them stables to protect them from this wind.' William's eyes flicked up towards Raymond to make sure that he had answered correctly, but his captain still stared inland and remained silent. 'Makes you wish that we had a castle here,' William grumbled and shuddered as the wind and rain whistled through the settlement again.

'Don't you see?' Raymond shouted down to William from his place on the low wall. 'It is a castle! This,' he stamped his foot on the ancient fortifications, 'will be our citadel, the sea cliffs which surround us, our impregnable motte. A castle needs a bailey,' he swept his hands across the headland to the north and west, 'and here it is.'

William jumped to his feet and crawled up beside Raymond. He considered his warlord's words for a few minutes and soon saw their sense. 'We are missing an outer wall to our new castle,' he said, nodding at the open grassland before him which Raymond had identified as the bailey.

'Well,' his captain replied with a grin, 'I brought my shovel, I hope you brought yours.'

Mud plastered Raymond's face as he dumped another spade full of earth from the belly of the ditch onto the heavy woollen blanket. Sunlight sparkled on his sweating brow as it did on the distant ocean beyond the wall.

'Haul away,' he shouted up to the Welsh archers with whom he had been paired. He and Geoffrey of Abergavenny paused and panted as they watched the two men tug on the ropes attached to the blanket. Both archers grunted audibly as they dragged the heavy soil up to the top of the ten-foot-high earthwork.

'I bet you wish you had stayed an oblate now,' Raymond joked to Geoffrey, who raised an eyebrow rather than waste any energy answering. Perspiration poured from the boy's brow and his thin, sunburnt arms shook with the effort of the work. Up and down the length of the peninsula men toiled in fours to create a second wall inside the first rampart, which they had completed five days before. The stone, mud and wattle double enclosure would form the outer defences to their fortifications, stretching two hundred paces across the narrowest point in the headland to give Raymond's army extra space outside the stone walls of the tiny Gaelic fort. Work was already complete on the wooden stockade which crowned the outer earthworks and Raymond listened to the drumming of metal on wood as more of the tall trunks were trimmed and forced deep into the soil on top of the inner palisade.

'Have they remembered to seed the outer earthworks with grass?' Raymond called up to the archers' commander, a tall, dark man called Caradog ap Tomos. The Welshman stopped his work and shouted inaudibly across the wall at someone on the far side of the defences.

'They say that the grass seed is going in now,' Caradog called down to the Norman captain in his sing-song French. 'A sprinkling of rain and the grass will pop up in no time.'

Raymond grunted at the response and began to shovel more soil onto the blanket. He made a mental note to check the work on the outside embankment for he knew that if his men did not plant foliage on the muddy banks then the first heavy rain could destroy their building work in minutes. Roots from vegetation would hold together the mud foundations better than any mortar.

'Check to see if we are high enough,' Raymond shouted up at Caradog after the Welshman and his partner hauled the next blanket of mud upwards. The archer finished his exertions before disappearing from view. He returned with a long stick, which he laid across the ditch from the top of the embankment upon which he stood to the finished outer wall. Two bowstrings dangled from the middle of the stave and brushed the bottom of the ditch next to Raymond and Geoffrey.

'Looks high enough to me,' Caradog shouted down to his captain. At Raymond's side Geoffrey whooped in relief that his toil was over.

'Not so quick,' Raymond cheerfully told him. 'You still have to help with the timber palisade while I see if the others need help completing the digging.' Caradog and Geoffrey groaned like petulant novice monks, but did not argue.

Raymond knew that the wooden wall which crowned the battlements would take no time to construct in comparison to the earthworks which would hold the heavy posts in place. However, getting their hands on timber to use in the building works had proven problematic. Because the land on the isthmus was sparsely populated by little other than limp trees and coarse bushes, Raymond had despatched Amaury de Lyvet into Banneew Bay in *Waverider*. There the warrior had discovered the remnants of the fort which Raymond's uncle, Robert FitzStephen, had used during his invasion of the year before. Amaury had scavenged all the serviceable timber from FitzStephen's wall and transported it across the bay to use on Dun Domhnall's much grander defences. It had not been enough, and Amaury had been forced to journey further into the interior of the island where the forests grew to cut down the many heavy trunks required for the wall.

'At least the sun has come out,' Raymond joked to the exhausted Geoffrey as he slugged away at a skin of spring water. The weather had indeed improved from the dreadful conditions of their first night in Ireland. Though cloudy, it was incredibly warm and the men sweated profusely as they worked. However, Raymond found the digging of the fortifications most rewarding, the pleasant summer heat toasting the sweat from his bare back. Exercise, as always, was a welcome distraction from the calculations and assessments that accompanied command. Geoffrey was not enjoying it quite so much, and was suffering greatly from blisters on his hands. The esquire grimaced as he poured water on the open wounds.

'My father always told me that manual labour makes a warrior great,' Raymond told his esquire. 'It builds up strength better than swinging swords –'

'Bertran de Born did that,' Geoffrey interjected.

'And it gives you stamina,' Raymond looked meaningfully at Geoffrey's blistered palms. 'You should go back to the fort and get your hands bathed and bound. I've heard that vinegar can help harden them.' He paused. 'Get your sister to help you.'

'I'll be fine,' Geoffrey replied gruffly and spat on his flayed palms.

Raymond nodded, appreciative of his esquire's show of hardiness. 'Good lad, but I also want you to rustle up lunch for the workers.' He threw his shirt over his head and began walking towards the inner gate. 'I am heading to the other end of the wall to see how the work is going there. You are welcome to come with me and lend a hand to inspect the new defences?'

Geoffrey thought about the long, dark walk to the far end of the fortifications by the outer gate. Over two hundred paces on a cold, muddy path of little more than a carpet of brambles and hay, and enclosed on both sides by the new walls – a walk which did not appeal to the youngster.

'Lunch,' he repeated, listening to the sound of chopping wood, spades digging into earth. 'I suppose that I could head back up to the citadel and see to that,' he chanced. 'Is fish alright?' he shouted at Raymond.

'Like we have anything else,' the captain joked. 'Give my regards to your sister,' he added quietly as he reached out to test the strength of the timber frame on the inner gate. It felt smooth beneath his hand but for the knots where his men had sawn off stray branches. He gave it a shake but the structure did not budge.

'I will,' Geoffrey replied as Raymond pushed into the dark and windy tunnel between the battlements.

It was noticeably colder in the tight five-yard gap where the wind howled up from the sea cliffs. The mud underfoot did not make it any easier and his toes froze as his sabatons partially disappeared into the cold sludge. Raymond made a mental note to have more woodchips and loose stones put on the pathway to make walking in the cramped confines less arduous. If a fight did occur he did not want his warriors bogged down moving between the battlements rather than fighting atop them. The mixed mud and gravel walls on either side of Raymond were cloaked in heavy wattle sheets, pegged in place by long wooden hooks to give extra stability to the structure. He ducked under the wooden allure which crowned the outer rampart and gave the sheets a quick tug to make sure that the construction was secure. It was and, reaching up above his head, he hoisted himself up onto the raised platform from where his archers would fight. Immediately he felt the sun warm his face, despite the increased breeze. The wooden planks beneath his feet creaked and he jumped twice to test the allure's strength. It withstood his weight easily and he smiled at the good work his men had performed in so short a time. Next, Raymond placed his hands on the heavy timber trunks which defended his army's temporary home. He gave them a brief shake but they too were immovable.

Before him lay shimmering flat land that stretched into the distance where the hills began. Heat from the blazing sun made the air next to the ground flicker and blur, making the land to the north of the Dun Domhnall peninsula look like a gently rolling green sea. It was beautiful, he decided, as well as the perfect bridgehead. However, his army could not stay in the castle by the sea forever.

'You absolute bastard,' a Welsh voice interrupted his pleasant daydream. Someone had struck their fingers with a hammer as they laboured on the fortifications. Raymond laughed as he saw one archer hopping around in front of the walls holding his hand. Inevitably, grumbles had emerged from the Welshmen left behind to construct the walls. They were angry that the horsemen, who had been sent out on scouting missions, were not pulling their weight and taking their turn at the shovel. Raymond had silenced their complaints when he had stripped off his crimson and gold surcoat to get stuck into the earth-moving alongside them.

His men worked both outside and inside the fortifications as he walked towards the barbican above the cliffs on the western side of the headland. As the captain strolled, he signalled to those who still laboured on the inner wall and joked with those men outside the defences. Some sprinkled grass seed onto the earthen bank while others drove short, thin, sharpened stakes into the soft earth in front of the wall, to aid structural strength and slow up anyone who made it far enough to attack the walls. Raymond had observed first-hand the damage that a stake could do if a man impacted with one of the savage spikes.

The walk to the western end of the battlements took only a few minutes along the allure, and it was there that he found Borard directing the workers putting the finishing touches to the outer barbican. Raymond was about to

228

congratulate his men on a job well done when a war horn sounded in the distance. He looked up at the horizon where four ragged horsemen approached the fort. Behind them, and wrapped in a cloud of dust were more men and animals of a number unknown.

'Is it our men?' one archer outside the fort shouted up to his captain on the vantage point.

'Difficult to tell from this distance,' Raymond replied. 'Nevertheless, I think this would be a good time to test that the gates close properly.'

With one final glance at the distant warriors he issued his orders: 'Everyone get inside the fort and make ready to repel ladders,' he shouted. 'To arms!'

Raymond wished it had indeed been an enemy who had approached Dun Domhnall, but, rather than an opponent that he could meet across a shield wall, his visitor was an ally with whom he would rather not have met at all.

'Those *women* you brought with you will be nothing but trouble, Sir Hervey,' Raymond told his guest. He had to raise his voice so that he could be heard above the echoing sound of the waves on the cliffs below his quarters.

Sir Hervey de Montmorency ignored Raymond's statement and instead poked him in the middle of his chest with a gnarled finger. 'You will have the men build sheds for the cattle outside the fort's outer walls. I cannot stand their stink so I want them out. Then I want each of your lieutenants to give me their reports. You will see to the sentinels tonight,' he said as he picked at the fish and bread meal which Geoffrey of Abergavenny had provided. Raymond frowned as Hervey forced a section of bread between his decaying teeth, sliding it around in his mouth until he was able to swallow. For all his time spent with warriors, Raymond had never grown accustomed to the sort of table manners which Hervey was displaying. It infuriated him enough to speak his mind to his earl's uncle.

'My men report to me and the cattle will be housed inside the bailey wall. I will of course see to the picket line, for what sort of commander would I be if I did otherwise?'

Hervey did not miss Raymond's jibe. 'You will do as I tell you,' he replied, his mouth and lips plastered with half-chewed bread and fish meat.

'My men, my fort, my command,' retorted Raymond.

Hervey's eyes narrowed. 'Siol Bhroin is mine and Dun Domhnall is in Siol Bhroin. Therefore this fort, and every soldier in it, is mine.'

'King Diarmait granted this land to Lord Strongbow, as well you know. You and I are equals, Sir Hervey. If you wish, you can take command of the fort across the bay at Banabh while I command here.'

In Striguil, Raymond would never have been so bold to question Sir Hervey's right to lead the army, but they were beyond the frontier now, perched out on a cliff in a fort built by his own hands. This was his chance to prove himself and he was not about to allow the earl's uncle to usurp his authority. Sir Hervey had returned to Ireland with the earl's answer for King Diarmait and had waited until news of Raymond's landing had reached his ears. Then he, three mercenaries and four sullen prostitutes from the Waesfjord slave market had crossed the estuary to the Siol Bhroin peninsula and walked south to the gates of Dun Domhnall.

'I am the earl's uncle,' Sir Hervey rasped and climbed to his feet, sodden food spraying from his mouth in Raymond's direction. 'Do not forget your place, boy. You are no more than a hearth knight and I command you to get the men ready to march at dawn.'

Raymond watched Hervey closely, angry at his insult

but thrown off by his demand. 'You wish to take the men outside the walls? All of them?'

'All of them,' Hervey repeated, his eyes shining. 'We march on Veðrarfjord at dawn.' He ran his dirty fingers though the remaining strands of his greasy long hair which were plastered across his balding dome.

'Veðrarfjord?' Raymond choked such was his surprise at Hervey's declaration. The city was second only to Dubhlinn in size and power, and Raymond had done everything he could to conceal his small army's presence from the Ostman colony town. Not for a moment did Raymond think to take his warriors outside those walls looking for a fight.

'Veðrarfjord,' Hervey repeated.

Raymond put his hand to his forehead. 'Forgetting for a second that we have a responsibility to maintain this bridgehead for Strongbow, what do you possibly think a hundred men could accomplish against the walls of Veðrarfjord,' Raymond asked.

'We claim it,' Sir Hervey said calmly, his eyes flicking up to meet Raymond's gaze, 'in my nephew's name, of course.' His countenance changed suddenly. 'If Robert FitzStephen can take Waesfjord with but a few more warriors, we can storm Veðrarfjord's walls.'

Raymond knew Hervey to be ambitious and desperate, but he had never thought him fool enough to take on the impossible task of assaulting that stronghold. The city was said to be twice as large as Waesfjord and twice as wealthy in warriors. FitzStephen had led an army of a thousand spears to capture the walls of Waesfjord and even then it had been a close-run thing, he had been told. Veðrarfjord, Raymond knew, could not be taken by anything less than that force, but rather than fight with the earl's uncle, which he knew would be pointless, Raymond climbed to his feet

231

and walked to the door of his billet. He pushed open the door and beckoned for Sir Hervey to follow. With a victorious look on his ancient face, his rival consented and shadowed him. It was already late, but most of the men sat around enjoying the warm weather as the daylight faded into the western ocean. They played dice and chatted of times past as they gathered around fires which dotted the headland. They gambled and chewed on the steaks from a bullock which their captain's servant, Fulk, had slaughtered earlier that day. He was particularly glad to see that some of the longhaired Welshmen were intermingling with the Normans of Striguil.

'Men, listen up,' Raymond shouted as he forced an axe from its place buried in a chopping block. He nimbly leapt onto the rudimentary platform so that he could see all his warriors. A few started to get to their feet, but he signalled for them to remain where they were seated. 'Sir Hervey here, who you know, wishes to talk to you.' Raymond jumped down, the axe slung across his soldier, and bowed briefly to the nobleman.

Sir Hervey looked angrily at the captain, realising that he could not evade addressing the warriors. His first attempt at clambering onto the low block of wood was unsuccessful and rather than try it again the spider-limbed knight stood beside it and cleared his throat to speak. 'Your Earl Strongbow, my nephew, has given to me the task of leading this venture.' He had to pause as the warriors' disconcerting murmurs echoed through the camp. 'And as such I have decided that the time is right to cross to Veðrarfjord and launch an assault on their walls. There will be riches for all!'

Silence followed Sir Hervey's declaration and Strongbow's uncle cast an angry eye at his own ragged band of warriors who, sitting separately, began halfheartedly clapping their master's words.

'Bloody crazy idea,' Asclettin FitzEustace shouted.

'There are not enough of us to assault Tyndyrn Abbey, never mind a city. We must wait for the earl to come,' called Thurstin Hore, firelight bouncing off his bald head as he spoke.

'What does Raymond say?' Caradog's heavily accented question was taken up by five other men: 'Yes, what does Raymond say we should do?'

'I command here! I make the decisions,' Sir Hervey shouted back at them, his bony finger pressed into his own chest. Boos emanated from around the camp and drowned out Sir Hervey's shrieks for silence. In the end the French nobleman threw a hand in the air and walked away from the crowd and back towards a small house that he had commandeered for himself. He stopped in his tracks when the din subsided. He turned to find Raymond de Carew had once again leapt atop the chopping block.

'Men,' Raymond called and held his hands in the air. 'Sir Hervey has every right to put forward his claim to command our army,' he said. More jeering followed but it diminished as he smiled at them. 'No, no - he has the connections, the status, the experience, the trust of the Earl Strongbow, and a knighthood which, as you know, proves that he can fight better than any man.' Sarcastic laughter rattled around the ancient Gaelic fort. 'I have no knighthood and few connections to the nobility,' Raymond continued. 'My family is less esteemed than your average gaggle of geese, but you know me and I imagine that you will have recognised that I wish to keep building the wall to protect Dun Domhnall. If the time comes when the Ostmen want to make a fight of it, I want us to be ready to protect our bridgehead.' Grunts of agreement echoed from the veterans at Raymond's words. 'So who do you want to lead you?' he asked. Only one name rang out from the army and with a smile Raymond hopped down from the chopping block and, one-handed, buried the axe back where he had found it. He then walked past Sir Hervey towards his billet.

'You think that asking the opinion of the men you are meant to command gives you any right to lead them?' Sir Hervey called after Raymond. 'The opinion of these men matters not a pinch. They are sworn to my family.' He flapped an arm in the direction of the army. 'I lead and they will follow.'

Raymond did not turn. 'I will enjoy your attempts to get those men to move out without my say-so, Sir Hervey.'

'You are neither of blood nor birth worthy of command. Captains are not chosen by acclaim, but by birth and by blood!'

That stopped Raymond in his tracks. He turned around to look at Sir Hervey. 'Yet kings in England are chosen by acclaim. I heard it myself at the Young King Henry's coronation in Westminster.' He gestured towards the warriors. 'And our people have spoken!'

As he spoke one of the soldiers, his head covered by a hood, detached from the rest and came forward.

'May I speak to you, Lord,' the hooded man said to Sir Hervey. He nodded his assent. 'I can promise you this,' the man rasped, 'if you give me the kiss of friendship before the army's eyes,' he said as he drew down his chape, 'then they will trust and follow you Veðrarfjord.'

Hervey offered Raymond a victorious look as he turned to meet the fawning supplicant who offered him leadership. 'Of course,' he said as he looked William Ferrand dropped his hood so that Sir Hervey could look full in his leprous face. The knight immediately recoiled in disgust and hopped away in horror at its decaying appearance.

234

Laughter rolled around the camp.

'Come on, give me a kiss!' Ferrand appealed again causing even more mirth to issue from the assembled army.

Sir Hervey recovered quickly from the shock of being face to face with a leper. 'You will stay away from me,' he told Ferrand. 'And you,' he turned to Raymond, 'I will have command of this army, one way or another, and I will have Veðrarfjord.' With a last sneer at the two men, he turned on his heel and walked towards his tattered troop of warriors.

Raymond watched him go, keeping his eyes on him as he disappeared into the building followed by one of his threadbare prostitutes. Sir Hervey's warriors had set up bivouacs at each corner of the low-roofed house, almost as if they expected to be attacked by Raymond's men from any direction at any time. He was about to suggest that Ferrand double the guard on his own billet when the leper interposed.

'So that is Strongbow's uncle?' Ferrand wheezed. 'I must tell you that I don't like the look of that man,' he said as he wrapped a scarf around his leprous face.

Sir Hervey was not the only addition to the garrison at Dun Domhnall that day. Late in the night Raymond was rustled from his sleep by a hand on his shoulder. Predicting mischief from Strongbow's uncle, he swept a dagger from amongst his clothes and placed it against Borard's windpipe.

'Don't bloody move,' Raymond snarled before realising that it was his friend.

Borard smiled as Raymond withdrew his dagger. 'You have broken that oath you made to Lady Basilia at Strongbow's feast,' he said. 'You cursed.'

'Damn it,' Raymond whispered, genuinely displeased at

235

his misdemeanour. 'What is going on?' he croaked as his eye's adjusted to the light from Borard's torch.

'We have a visitor waiting outside the gates. He says he wants to talk. He knew your name.'

'You didn't let him in?'

'He is a Gael.'

Raymond hummed neutrally as he righted his heavy cloak on his shoulders. 'My sword?' he asked and Borard grabbed it from where it hung on the wall of the little thatched house which the two men shared.

'You have no need worry about being killed in your sleep, by the way,' Borard told him as they made for the door. 'I just discovered that you have a guardian angel.' As they passed outside, Ferrand's disfigured face caught the light of Borard's flaming torch. He was sitting upright and staring into the heart of a small fire. A frightening sentinel if ever there was one, Raymond thought.

'Captain?' Ferrand asked, his eyes flicking suspiciously towards Borard, as the two men emerged from the building.

'It is fine,' Raymond replied, heartened somewhat by the efforts of the stowaway warrior. 'Get some rest and I will wake you when I return from the gate.'

Ferrand nodded, again glancing at Borard, before curling up against the stone wall of the house. 'Be sure that you do,' he said.

Borard and Raymond giggled silently as they walked away from the leper through the old Gaelic fort. Everywhere men had repaired the tumbledown houses, or constructed their own using slabs of turf. Raymond nodded to the two men who guarded the gates to the fort before following the cliff face towards the distant main wall where torches burned brightly in the darkness.

'Do you think our visitor is an emissary from King Ragnall of Veðrarfjord?' asked Borard.

Raymond had wondered the same, but had abandoned the idea. 'Kings do not usually send one man to talk,' he replied. 'It may be different in this land, but they usually send an army of priests and warriors to put the fear of God in you.'

'I suppose you are right,' his friend considered as they climbed up onto the allure on the outer wall. 'Do you think the Ostmen even know we are here at Dun Domhnall?'

'I would imagine that it's a certainty.'

Cattle called to each other in the distance from the small pen that Raymond had built out on the southern cliffs. As they walked the length of the fortifications the two men chatted about the cow which had fallen over the edge two nights before. Raymond wanted to move their pens away from the cliffs, but Borard was concerned about putting them near too the well and inviting disease into their camp.

'So where is our visitor?' Raymond asked as they arrived at the barbican, their talk of cattle put on hold. Walter de Bloet was whittling a long stick and simply lifted his chin to indicate over the top of the gate.

Raymond took Borard's torch and leant over the wooden defences. 'Is anyone there?'

The sound of someone spitting cchocd from the darkness. A figure shrouded in shadow clambered to his feet from where he sat with his back to the gate and moved out into the light cast by Raymond's torch.

'About bloody time,' the man said as he stabbed his spear into the ground and dusted earth from his hands.

'Who are you?' Raymond said, thankful that the man, dressed in the Irish fashion of a long cloak, woollen trousers and leather armour over a linen shirt, could speak French.

'Fionntán Ua Donnchaidh,' the man said curtly, 'and I come with a message for the Earl Strongbow.' He had short

237

curly hair and no beard, but otherwise his countenance was like the natives of the island whom he had seen during their cattle raids. His face was lined – with age or experience, Raymond could not readily tell – and he had a permanent smirk across his face, his eyes closed to mere slits beneath his heavy eyebrows.

'You may give your message to me,' Raymond told Fionntán, unwilling to let the Gael know that Strongbow was not yet at the Norman bridgehead. 'I am his captain, Raymond de Carew. Would you like to come inside the fort and speak properly?' The Gael studied Raymond for a moment before slowly and suspiciously nodding his assent.

'So,' Raymond asked as he met Fionntán between the walls of the fort, 'for whom do you speak and what has he to say?'

In the light from the torches, the Gael's heavy brow threw shadows over his eyes and although he was a thin man, Raymond knew instinctively that he was a tough one. He held out a hand which Fionntán took. It felt like an old rope made strong from holding down dancing ship sails.

'I speak for Sir Robert FitzStephen. His messages are that you are welcome to Laighin and that you should keep your eyes open. Trouble surrounds you.'

'You know Robert?' asked Raymond keeping a cheerful smile on his face. 'He is my uncle. How is he keeping?'

'He is adventuring in Tuadhmumhain.'

Raymond didn't recognise the name. 'And how is his brother, Maurice? Still barking out orders like a mare in heat?'

'Maurice FitzGerald barking out orders?' replied Fionntán. 'That does not sound like him at all. He is quieter than a church mouse ...'

Raymond held up his hands. 'I apologise. I know Maurice's true nature, but I had to make sure that you are

238

who you say you are.'

Fionntán grunted irritably at the small ruse.

'Come,' Raymond continued, indicating back towards the citadel on the point of the headland. 'We will talk more and get you some food.' He nodded towards Geoffrey of Abergavenny and pointed at the camp. The youngster understood him immediately and made to run ahead of the two men to arrange food for them both. However, Fionntán's hand shot out and grabbed him by the shoulder to prevent Raymond's esquire from leaving.

'I would prefer to keep my presence secret from Hervey de Montmorency for now,' he said with barely contained contempt. 'He and Robert have a history...'

Raymond nodded. 'Most people have a history with Robert, but fear not — brave Sir Hervey has already let it be known that he wishes to lead a cattle raid tomorrow. He will be gone for several days.'

'I will stay by the gate,' Fionntán replied gruffly, 'until he has departed and then I can find out who I can and who I cannot trust.'

'Whatever you think best, but any friend of Robert's is a friend of mine. You say he is at war?'

'In the west, on King Diarmait's son-in-law's behalf,' Fionntán replied. 'Sir Maurice FitzGerald holds Waesfjord safe. Nevertheless both promise that they will give you help if and when the need arises, and if they are able.'

'At present they are not able to send aid?'

Fionntán smirked and held his hands out from his sides. 'I am all the help that you require, Norman.'

Raymond smiled, already enjoying the company of the self-opinionated Gael. 'That's good,' he said looking back at the ancient fort, 'for I do believe that I need all the assistance that I can muster.'

239

* * *

Raymond and Fionntán watched from the allure as Sir Hervey and his ragged troop left Don Domhnall in the early morning sunshine. A weight seemed to have been lifted from Raymond's shoulders as he watched his lord's uncle push north through the grassy expanse towards the deep ford and the forests of the north.

A number of goats, sheep and geese roamed freely outside the bailey under the supervision of the workers, and as Raymond watched, one of his milites, Dafydd FitzHywel, chased Hervey's warriors away from the flock rather than let the unkempt soldier steal one.

'That is a dangerous man,' Fionntán said, flicking a hand at the departing horsemen. 'Hervey will make trouble for you wherever he goes.'

Raymond laughed. 'If I told him not to attack Veðrarfjord he would go directly there with his poxy prostitutes and lay siege to the city.'

'In that case you should tell him to stay away from the edge of the cliffs at night time.'

'I only hope that his good sense can successfully combat his greed,' Raymond raised his eyebrows. 'While he is gone I was thinking that you and I might take a little diplomatic trip upriver.'

'To the Ostmen of Cluainmín?' guessed Fionntán, referring to the small market town ten miles to the north.

Raymond bobbed his head. 'They control the estuary and I need an escape route if Dun Domhnall falls to attack. The old fort at Banabh would seem the best rally point,' he waved a hand towards the small island partially visible as the sun rose above Banneew Bay. 'It would be easier if we were not set upon by longships while we ferried across. Have you had dealings with Cluainmín before?'

The Gael nodded but kept the details of that association

240

silent. 'Ship,' he said instead as, in the bay, *Waverider* appeared.

'Ours,' Raymond replied quickly. 'I sent them upriver for timber and to pilfer a few more cattle. We will need to be ready with provisions when Strongbow arrives – whenever that will be.'

Fionntán nodded approvingly. After Sir Hervey's departure, Raymond had given him a short tour of Dun Domhnall and the Gael had been mightily impressed by the strong defences and preparations that Raymond had made. Not, of course, that he told him that, preferring instead to concentrate on a few minor defects before giving his suggestions about how the fort could be improved.

'I'll go up to Cluainmín with you in your ship,' Fionntán told Raymond. 'All Trygve, their king, cares about is his silver mines, so if you can convince him that you have no knowledge of them, he will not interfere with you in your fort,' he assured.

'My interest is only in Veðrarfjord.'

'He won't be opposed to that. They are trading rivals after all.' Fionntán's eyes were dark hollows. 'A word of warning: the King of Veðrarfjord, Ragnall, is no fool,' he said. 'And if he has heard of your little castle on the cliffs he will come for you with many men. He may even guess that you will send envoys to Trygve of Cluainmín. I heard about your landing in the corn market in Waesfjord and my guess is that those same traders will have wagged their tongues in Veðrarfjord as well,' he turned back to Raymond, suddenly serious, and poked a finger into his chest. 'Konungr Ragnall hears all.'

'Which make it all the more important that we come to an agreement with Cluainmín and that they stay out of our business here,' Raymond insisted. He had indeed spotted a great number of sailors eying up the fort as they crawled their way along the coast in their merchant vessels towards Corcach, Hlymrik, Veðrarfjord to the west, as well as Waesfjord and Dubhlinn in the east. 'We must leave before the tide turns,' Raymond informed his new ally.

Fionntán grunted in response as he watched *Waverider* head towards the beach at Dun Domhnall. 'My last experience of Norman seamanship was less than perfect. At least this time we will not be sailing at sea.' Fionntán stopped suddenly and his lined face contorted into shock as he turned and stared over Raymond's shoulder. 'Who is that?' he muttered.

Raymond turned around to follow his new friend's gaze and spotted Alice of Abergavenny in the sunny distance. She had come out of the lodging which she shared with her brother. In her arms, Alice had some fish for Raymond's supper, though as usual she would give it to her brother Geoffrey to serve. The captain immediately dropped his eyes and turned back towards Fionntán. He had still not spoken to Alice since coming to Dun Domhnall and only Geoffrey's insistence had led his former lover to agreeing to act as his cook.

'Who is that?' Fionntán again gasped as he shaded his face from the bright sunshine. He raised his hand further to wave as Alice turned around to look at them. Raymond was surprised to see her return the gesture before scampering off towards her small hut.

Raymond paused, unsure how to answer. 'She is my ...' he shook his head. 'My cook, my ward. Her name is Alice of Abergavenny.' A sudden surge of anger emanated from deep within Raymond as he watched the effect of Alice's beauty on the obviously entranced Fionntán. 'So we leave for Cluainmín in the hour?' he added.

'We will leave once your ship has broken bulk, yes.'

Raymond nodded, annoyed by Fionntán's interest in the

woman he loved, *had* loved; the woman he had saved from William de Braose; the woman who still refused to speak to him. Fionntán noticed the change in Raymond's manner and raised a heavy eyebrow in his direction.

'I must oversee the work at the new cattle pen,' Raymond stated and walked away rather than have to answer any more of Fionntán's questions about Alice.

'I will come and get you,' Fionntán shouted after him with a knowing smile on his face. He watched Raymond march towards the main wall of the fort before turning back to observe *Waverider*'s slow progress down the estuary.

'How goes it with you?' Raymond greeted the group of labourers who were on their backs enjoying the glorious sunshine rather than completing the work which he had set them.

'Fine, fine,' William de Vale exclaimed as he jumped to his feet, urging his two companions to follow his example. 'I was giving the guys a little break,' he lied.

'Your rest is over,' Raymond said as he pulled his surcoat over his head. 'Fulk,' he spoke to the butcher's apprentice from Westminster, 'get me nails and a hammer.'

William groaned.

'Or would you rather take an extra shift mucking out the coursers?' Raymond asked. 'You could do with going on a ‧ hack - you look like you could do with the exercise,' he said and poked him in the stomach with the end of his mallet.

'No, no,' William apologised, 'let's make a start,' he said, picking up a pile of hazel and ash rods. He began twisting the withies into the shape of a wattle fence. Raymond crouched on the other side, nails in his mouth, and tacked the flimsy rods to the sturdy upright posts which had been driven deep into the ground beside the inner gate. Despite his talk with Borard the night before, Raymond had

243

decided to move the cattle pen to just inside the new double embattlements beside the thatched stables. A heifer had pushed through the old enclosure fence and had tumbled to its death during the early hours. The dying screams of the poor animal had woken the entire army until Caradog had hung over the edge and shot the animal. Although his milites had stolen over fifty of the small black cows, as well as a handful of bulls, he could little afford to lose any more to the sea. He knew that Strongbow could follow him across the sea at any time and he had to be ready to feed the army that came with him.

'Why aren't we building the new cattle pen outside the walls of the fort?' Fulk asked. 'They have already eaten almost every blade of grass inside.'

'Yeah, and I ... I mean we,' William de Vale corrected himself, 'are getting tired of having to drive the animals out of the fort and into the countryside every day.'

'It's necessary if the cattle are to remain healthy,' Raymond replied and continued to knock nails into the fence.

'Are you afraid of someone attacking us? Why else build a pen inside the bailey?' asked Fulk.

'I'm more worried about the amount of cow dung that they produce,' William laughed as he twisted another rod into the fence.

'I'm not afraid of being attacked,' Raymond replied. 'I am wary of it though. Now, no more questions, let's get the pen finished.' For many minutes they did not speak and Raymond was so engrossed in the labour that he did not realise that Alice of Abergavenny had made her way down from the old fort and was standing behind him. William de Vale's wolf-whistle was out of his lips before he could stop himself and he quickly buried his head in the work as Raymond leapt to his feet, a snarl of anger issuing from between his teeth.

'Alice,' he greeted her as nonchalantly as he could. 'You are well?' His heart raced. 'You are snug?' He internally castigated himself for using the ridiculous word and he could feel his ears going red.

'I am fine,' she said, her discomfort apparent. 'My brother says that you are going north. Are we to remain here?'

Raymond hoped for a long-sought apology, thanks even for saving her life and that of her brother. He wanted her to admit that she had been stupid to have betrayed him when she had chosen the Young King over him. She was neither contrite nor apologetic.

'Well?' she insisted when he did not answer instantly.

'I am going north. There is a town called Cluainmín,' he waved a hand upriver, 'but you will be staying here for your safety.'

'Who was that man you were talking too?'

Raymond did not answer and studied Alice. There was no hint of friendship in her eyes, only anger. 'Have I offended you in some way, Alice of Abergavenny?'

She gritted her teeth and turned to leave, but Raymond caught her arm. With a swish of hair she twisted back and slapped him across the face. Her eyes shone with fury.

'Touch me again, and I will kill you.' Her eyes narrowed to slits. 'I don't need you to take care of me,' she said.

'You could have told me that before my men and I chased halfway across Surrey to rescue you from William de Braose.'

'The Young King…Harry, he would have come for me. You ruined everything! And now we are here in the last place on earth anyone would want to find themselves. I will never have Abergavenny,' she raged, 'and it is your fault.' With that she stormed off towards the citadel. Raymond called after her, but she did not even break stride.

William de Vale whistled slowly and swapped a glance with Fulk. 'If she is typical of a damsel in distress I think the troubadours have been lying to us.'

'Quiet, and get back to work,' Raymond commanded as he watched Alice of Abergavenny scamper towards the old fort. He was confused, utterly, by her anger, but he knew now that he would never find happiness with her. However, a lingering guilt remained and he knew that sentiment would never diminish. He had taken over a hundred warriors across the sea into a strange land where they could be assaulted at any time without hope of flight or support. He had defied lords and kings, he had almost started a war, and he had been named outlaw. And he had done it all because he thought it the only way to keep Alice safe from danger.

'Well, no more,' he rumbled.

'Raymond,' Fionntán's shout interrupted his thoughts. 'The ship is ready. Let's go talk to the Ostmen.'

With one final glance at Alice's blonde hair, he turned on his heel and made for waterside.

Chapter Nine

Danger lay upriver. That, Raymond could feel in his bones as *Waverider* glided up the brown waterway where vegetation circled slowly and sank beneath her plunging wooden oars. On each side of the ship trees hung limply, the longest branches dipping into the river from the bank and blanketing the land beyond from the Norman's view. The sails had been robbed of wind by the tangle of trees and the summery conditions, and so the men rowed, their dipping oars the loudest sound on the slowly swirling river. It was stifling, this country, and the sensation was not helped by the heavy armour which clad each warrior who journeyed north.

'See anything?' Fionntán asked. William de Vale hissed at him to quieten down. Everyone aboard, except the smirking Gael, conversed in hushed tones as they floated towards Cluainmín. Those who had been on ship during Amaury de Lyvet's foraging trips told tales of darts, arrows and stones arcing suddenly from the shore from assailants unknown and striking down men as they toiled. Oddly Raymond had yet to meet anyone who had been wounded whilst sailing on the River Banneew despite the oft-told tales.

'I can see nothing out there,' Raymond squawked back at the Gael. His turn rowing was over and so he had taken up a position in the bows of *Waverider*, keeping watch on the shoreline for dangers unseen in the shallow riverway. Bright sunshine turned still pools of water on deck into vapour and more steam hung from dripping green leaves on shore. Beads of sweat ran down Raymond's brow and he could feel more beneath his mail. The strong summer sunshine danced off shimmering surfaces and dazzled his eyes. As they rounded another bend in the Banneew, he espied a small homestead and farm carved from the forest. Two shirtless fishermen with long beards paddled coracles in the river, sweeping sculls in small circles to propel the ungainly craft forward. Both men gawped as *Waverider* swept past and began paddling with all their might for the riverbank. Raymond laughed at the men's effort, their unwieldy vessels providing no speed for their getaway. The little coracles rocked as the wake from *Waverider* struck them and the fishermen clung onto the animal hide sheer-strakes as they span towards the reedy shallows.

'How are we for depth?' Amaury de Lyvet called from the starboard quarter. The steersman's question was echoed up the boat by several men at the oars to the warlord's earshot.

Raymond looked over the side into the brown, sandy river and began swinging the sounding line around his head. The hollowed out lead weight spun as it flew, dragging the thin knotted rope from his hand and forward over the bows of *Waverider*. As the lead hit the water, Raymond began doubling the line between his outstretched arms. He felt the weight impact with the riverbed and, as the line ran alongside the boat, he began counting the fathoms. He did not get far.

'Less than three fathoms,' he shouted back at Amaury, earning another appeal from William de Vale to keep his voice down.

'Slow oars,' the steersman shouted to the crew of *Waverider*. Happy to stop the work, the men complied immediately and sat back on their benches, swiping sweat from their faces.

'What is her draught?' Raymond asked Amaury as he walked down the length of the ship.

'Two yards and a bit,' the sailor replied. 'Enough, I hope.'

'But you have been further up river than here,' Raymond said. 'Haven't you?'

Amaury raised his eyebrows, but did not answer.

'No time like the present for a bit of exploring,' Fionntán interjected. 'The Ostmen can get up the river, so we can too. What is the bottom like?' he asked.

Raymond swung the wet sounding line and caught the lead weight so that he could study a thick wad of tallow which he had pushed into the space where the rope was tied. As it had been dragged along the bottom the sticky material had picked up debris.

'Nothing but sand,' Raymond said as Amaury and Fionntán swapped concerned glances. Raymond had learned that the Gael was also a sailor and knew the waters of Ireland's south coast as well as any man. The two launched into a conversation about whether or not they should continue upriver on foot or by ship. After a few minutes of discussion between the two, Fionntán sat down at his bench and Lyvet gave the order to continue rowing.

'And you,' Amaury added with a finger pointed at Raymond. 'Keep your bloody eyes open. I don't want to ground her on this damned sand.' The journey continued as slowly as before with the noise from the sounding line falling in the water the only thing interrupting the squeak of wooden oars on the rails of the ship. The men continued to toil as the sun shone above them.

'Two fathoms,' Raymond shouted as the river began to narrow and sweep westwards. Amaury pulled the tiller into his stomach sending *Waverider* into deeper water closer to the eastern bank.

'Keep bloody casting,' he shouted at Raymond, but the warlord was no longer listening for, over a vast expanse of rushes and mud flats, were the masts of many ships. And beyond that, the Ostman longfort of Cluainmín came into view.

Raymond inhaled sharply as *Waverider* slid into enemy territory.

The Ostmen of Cluainmín looked on suspiciously as Raymond led four of his warriors through their town. Ahead of the small party was the hustle-bustle of commerce but by the time they passed the noise had lessened to only whispers. Fionntán, William de Vale, Amaury de Lyvet and Geoffrey of Abergavenny all wished they had weapons at their sides when they saw the animosity of the bearded men and guarded women who watched them from shadowed doorways.

'I don't like this,' Geoffrey whispered as they marched behind the three warriors who had met them at the shoreline. The trio had mail shirts and carried brightly painted circular shields by their sides. All had spears which they rolled around in their fingers.

'I don't like this at all,' repeated Geoffrey.

Amaury growled his agreement. 'Why did they disarm us?'

'It is fine,' Raymond replied. 'They are nervous of outsiders and jumpy, so keep your mouths closed,' he raised his voice so that all his men could hear, 'and if they offer us hospitality leave your cups full. We don't need any drunken arguments today.'

Raymond's sabatons clattered on the street made of split timber which wound its way between the little cottages. More roads peeled off between the little plots and gardens where the townspeople grew their vegetables and kept their pigs and goats. Cluainmín was built on flat land cleared of trees on a large curl in the river. The town had a long, tall wall of earth and heavy wooden posts which was surrounded on three sides by a deep fosse. Beyond the walls were more low thatched cottages of those people not important enough to possess a home within the longfort defences. Everywhere he looked were shops and moorings, fishermen and merchants, inns, tradesmen and clients of every kind. The townsfolk milled, traded and talked, and bartered, and swapped news within those moss-covered walls. That the inhabitants were Ostmen surprised Raymond, for the people seemed to dress no differently to Fionntán. However, as they passed he could identify both the Gaelic tongue and Danish being spoken.

'Is it true that they mine silver here?' William de Vale asked his captain. 'Where do you think they have it?'

Raymond stopped and turned on the youngster. 'What was the one thing I told you not to talk about when we entered the town?'

William looked sheepishly at his feet.

'I don't want to hear it,' Raymond said when the esquire began to apologise. 'Get back to the ship. You aren't going any further,' he said.

William smiled, but quickly saw that Raymond was serious, and moved away, grumbling about missing the possibility of a feast. The three Ostman warriors watched the exchange suspiciously, but a cheerful shake of the head from Raymond seemed to allay their fears and they directed the remaining guests onward.

'Are we going up to your king's house?' Raymond asked, but the nearest warrior simply shook his bearded head to indicate that he did not understand the French tongue.

251

'*þræll*,' the guard shouted to one of the small crowd who followed the Normans through the town. A small, bald man in a dirty woollen shift tied with a length of rope scampered between the warriors and began babbling in the Danish tongue to the leader, his head bowed towards the ground in submission. He then turned around to face Raymond.

'He says that Konungr Trygve is concluding some business in the town marketplace and that he is taking you there to meet with him,' the bald man said in good French. He caressed his hands as he spoke, rolling them around like seaweed in the tumbling in the surf. His eyes and body language were fawning and Raymond could detect no hint of foreign accent in the man.

'You are Norman?'

'Frankish, Lord,' he said, his eyes alight, 'from Limoges.'

'A slave?'

'They would call me a thrall,' the man said as the group rounded a long corner into an open space where a large group of traders haggled and shouted. 'Like them,' the man added as he nodded over the heads towards a low stage where two men stood with bowed heads and their hands bound.

It was a slave market.

Raymond grimaced at the sight of Ostmen bartering for the possession of their fellow man. There were slaves in England of course, and no better treated than those wretches on view in Cluainmín. However, the Church often preached about the evil and repugnance of slavery and dissuaded noblemen from buying human chattel. Evidently the Church's objection to the practice was not preached amongst the Gael and Ostmen, Raymond considered. He spied another ten slaves bound to a fence to the right of the raised platform. Two were teenagers, another three were women and one had skin as dark as the heartwood on a yew hunting bow.

'Konungr Trygve, our king,' the translator tugged on Raymond's sleeve and pointing a finger towards an enormously fat man cloaked in fur and lounging on a litter on the far side of the marketplace. To Raymond he looked like one of the fat seals that sunned themselves on the rocks on the Welsh coastline. Trygve's arms were covered in bright tattoos while his blond beard was heavy and hung with many trinkets. The konungr barked a hoarse laugh in the direction of the slave dealer on the raised dais, before holding up a fat hand to indicate a higher bid for the two unfortunate slaves on show.

'You have to wait here,' the translator told Raymond as the lead guard babbled unintelligibly in his direction. 'After the slaves are auctioned you will be able to talk to Trygve.'

Raymond saw that the konungr had settled on a price for his new acquisitions with the other men unable to match his opening bid. As the two slaves were taken from the platform by Trygve's men and the next three females were forced onto the stage in their place, Raymond questioned the translator about the Konungr of Cluainmín and his relations with the other towns on the south coast.

'It has been many years since the men of Cluainmín went pillaging,' the slave said. 'Vestmen, the Gaelic natives, trade in corn and animals, slaves and butter. There is one who brings bird skins and tame hawks...'

'I wonder what name we *Vestmen*,' Fionntán shot a scathing look at the translator, 'will give you Normans? Perhaps *Ramhargall*? The fat foreigners,' he said poking a long finger into Raymond's gut. 'I remember Trygve's uncle, the one who founded this town,' he said, taking a bite from a pear. 'Trygve was only a steersman on one of his ships out of Veðrarfjord.'

'Trygve comes from Veðrarfjord?' asked Raymond.

Fionntán nodded. 'Konungr Ragnall was not pleased when Trygve pissed off with a ship and its whole crew to join his uncle here,' he remembered with a half-smile. 'The only reason he didn't wipe them off the face of the earth back then was because Cluainmín wasn't big enough to trouble Veðrarfjord's trade.'

'And the difficulty with navigating the river means they are bloody hard to attack,' added Raymond.

'Indeed.'

'There does seem to have been a great deal of resentment between the two towns,' the translator added, still keen to impress the French-speaking guests.

'Good,' Raymond replied. 'What about Waesfjord?' he asked of the town to the east which Robert FitzStephen had captured the summer before from its Ostmen occupants.

'Trygve trades with them…' The Frankish slave would have continued but, from the other side of the marketplace, a new voice pierced the hubbub of the slave auction and drew the attention away from the platform. Raymond turned and looked at the new man who had spoken so loudly in the sloshing Danish language.

Immediately, Raymond was glad that he had hidden a dagger from the warriors of Cluainmín during their weapons search at the harbour moorings. The man who had spoken exuded violence and strength, and swept his gaze over the marketplace as if he would gladly have killed every single person without a second thought. He was a giant, taller even than the Earl Strongbow, who towered over most men, and he strode slowly onto the platform as he spoke. His arms were bare and defined with muscle and as he strode along the wooden dais, he flicked the garments from one of the paraded slaves' shoulders as he passed by so that he could see her breasts. He then shoved the slave master from his path as the man protested the interruption to his auction. Three people in the crowd were knocked to the floor as the slave master crashed from the platform.

Raymond only had eyes for the newcomer. On his back, he espied a circular shield painted with the snarling face of a charging boar. If anything, the bearer of the armament better resembled the vicious animal than the colourful reproduction, his red beard knotted and braided so that it looked like two tusks coming from each side of his mouth. Raymond had no doubt of the newcomer's identity. It was Jarl Sigtrygg, the man who had attacked Strongbow at the Thorney Inn in Westminster.

'What is he saying?' Raymond asked the translator.

'He says that the thralls in this market are of poor worth and that if Konungr Trygve agrees to help his friend, Ragnall of Veðrarfjord, there will be many slaves of a better value…' the translator paused, his eyes flicking towards Raymond.

'When the fort of the foreigners falls,' Fionntán finished his sentence as all eyes in the marketplace swung around to stare at the small group headed by Raymond de Carew. They knew that the giant newcomer meant Dun Domhnall and that the slaves would be Raymond and his warriors.

Fionntán threw his pear core to the ground and leant back against the building behind him, waiting to see what Raymond would do as Jarl Sigtrygg of Veðrarfjord slowly raised a hand to point at Raymond and shouted another challenge in his direction. The crowd gasped at the words, but as Fionntán began to translate Raymond held up a hand to stop him.

'I can guess exactly what he said,' he told his friend while keeping his eyes on his challenger. 'He wants to kill us all. The pig-faced bastard and I have a bit of history. I killed

255

twenty of his warriors in England less than a month ago.'

'My name is Jarl Sigtrygg,' the warrior replied in heavily accented French. 'And you are my enemy. You killed my crewmen. I kill my enemies and piss on their bones,' he told him. 'You are my enemy,' he repeated.

Raymond simply began to chuckle as, on the other side of the marketplace, the Konungr of Cluainmín shouted a question.

'Trygve asks why you are laughing,' the translator told him, one eye on Jarl Sigtrygg who visibly fumed at Raymond's reaction to his threat.

'I am laughing because this is not the first time I have had my life threatened,' Raymond laughed again. 'It's not even the first time this day!' As the slave shouted his answer towards the Konungr of Cluainmín the people began laughing. 'And of the two women to threaten my life this day, this one I will fear least.' He waved a hand at the jarl before making an apologetic nod towards Geoffrey of Abergavenny for making a joke about his sister.

'It may not be the first time that you have been threatened with death,' the jarl snarled, 'but it will be the last.' He jumped down from the raised platform and made for Raymond, producing a long dagger from beneath his shield as he ranged forward.

Raymond had his own knife in his hand in moments and crouched ready to meet Sigtrygg. The people of Cluainmín divided as the giant jarl pushed a path towards Raymond and swept his circular shield onto his left arm. The Ostman stabbed his weapon forward angrily with a roar, but Raymond was ready for the move, deflecting the blade with his right while simultaneously landing an uppercut to Jarl Sigtrygg's nose with his left hand as the Ostman attempted to raise his shield.

As blood burst brightly from his deformed, upturned

nose, Jarl Sigtrygg looked shocked at the speed of Raymond's reaction. He screamed in anger as his weight took him past his adversary and crashed into the Frankish translator. The two of them fell to the floor in a tangle of legs and weaponry.

'Now you have a pig-nose to match your tusks,' laughed Raymond as Jarl Sigtrygg rolled onto the slave, bleeding profusely from his misshapen snout.

'What do we do?' Geoffrey asked as he danced on the spot like an excited puppy.

Blood streamed from Jarl Sigtrygg's nose as he climbed back to his feet. Raymond could see that the Ostman's nose poked unnaturally upwards as would that of a boar. He roared in pain and shook his head, scattering blood widely.

Amaury de Lyvet had come to Raymond's side, producing a hand axe from somewhere on his person while Geoffrey held up his fists like a page ready to defend his honour against his peers. Fionntán still lounged against the wall, apparently unafraid of Sigtrygg's menace. The jarl wiped blood away from his mouth with his bare forearm and began speaking angrily in Raymond's direction.

'He says that he is going to pull your innards out through your ears,' Fionntán translated. 'I don't think that it is possible, but I admit to wondering if a man of his size could do it,' he winked at Geoffrey of Abergavenny.

As Geoffrey sent a concerned look towards Raymond, Fionntán redirected his words towards the Konungr of Cluainmín who watched the agitators with great interest. Fionntán spoke in the Danish tongue, whipping his hand in Raymond's direction at various times.

'What are you saying?' Raymond whispered to his friend.

'I reminded Trygve of some lines from the *Hávamál*,' said Fionntán. 'A list of good manners,' he described, 'and the proper way for a true king to treat his guests,' he raised his voice as he added some further indictment against Trygve's hospitality. The fat konungr listened to Fionntán's words and grimaced, waving his arm towards more of his warriors who ran to Sigtrygg's side and pointed their spears at the warlord. The jarl from Veðrarfjord spat on the nearest soldier, but did not continue his attack.

'Help me,' a whimper came from the ground nearby. As Raymond turned he could see that the Frankish translator-slave was bleeding profusely onto the timber street. He had been stabbed when the jarl had collided with him and his arm hung limply at his side. The Norman could see a large wound on his elbow and dark blood poured down his forearm. The rotund Konungr of Cluainmín hauled himself to his feet and climbed down from his litter as his warriors chivvied Jarl Sigtrygg to one side. Trygve waddled across the marketplace followed by yet more warriors and two priests, casting a venomous look at Jarl Sigtrygg as he knelt beside the wounded translator and delicately extended his arm to look at the wound. The slave screamed in pain.

'The tendon is severed,' Fionntán told Raymond. 'He'll never have full use of it again.'

The konungr spoke softly to one of his attendants and then began patting the slave on his head with a sad look on his face. Below him the translator began desperately shaking his head and pleading with his master, clinging to Trygve's sleeve by his good arm with tears running down his face. The konungr delicately quieted the slave and patted him on his head as he would do a terrified dog.

Confused, Raymond turned to Fionntán for an explanation of the unusual behaviour. The Gael didn't answer, but nodded back towards Trygve. As Raymond turned his head back, the konungr stabbed the wounded slave in the neck and slit his throat.

'Stop!' Raymond shouted as the translator gurgled on his own blood. 'Why did you do that?' he demanded of Trygve who, for his part, looked genuinely sad as he wiped his dagger on the dead slave's dirty shift.

'The slave was badly injured and in terrible pain,' Fionntán told Raymond with a shrug of his shoulders. 'No point keeping and feeding him if he can't work. He can't pay his way by simply translating for Franks.'

Raymond shook his head and swapped a disgusted look with Geoffrey and Amaury. They did not understand what had occurred either. However, Raymond did not want to offend Trygve and asked Fionntán to deliver his formal greeting to the konungr.

'Please tell him that I have come to Cluainmín in friendship,' Raymond said, 'and that I also come with more than empty promises like the men of Veðrarfjord,' he looked at the giant Jarl Sigtrygg who, having been shepherded away at spear point, brooded close to the raised platform, examining his wounded face with his fingers. 'I bring generous gifts rather than trouble and bloodshed.'

That caught the attention of Trygve and, ignoring the overtures of Jarl Sigtrygg, he beckoned Raymond to follow him back towards his litter. With one final glance at the Jarl of Veðrarfjord, the captain pushed through the quickly diminishing crowd. Trygve collapsed back into his chair, wiping the sweat from his brow as he did so. The fur-lined seat squeaked and strained under Trygve's massive weight and, as he rearranged his clothes, the konungr began questioning Fionntán.

'He asks what generous gifts you bring,' the Gael translated Trygve's words. 'And why you bring them.'

'I bring the best wines that Christendom can provide, and more besides,' Raymond said as his friend interpreted. 'As to why, I suspect he already knows my purpose here.'

259

Trygve nodded his head.

'The konungr says that he enjoys your Frankish wines and that he hopes you brought a lot of it,' Fionntán said with a small smile. 'He says that you are welcome to Cluainmín since you have not attacked any of his ships or prevented any traders from entering the Banneew as he feared that you would. However, he warns that while he has no argument with you, he doesn't want one with Veðrarfjord either.' Fionntán paused as he listened to Trygve speak. 'He says that Jarl Sigtrygg has been sent to Cluainmín by Konungr Ragnall to demand that he help them attack Dun Domhnall, should Veðrarfjord feel the need to eject you. Trygve says that he has been put in a difficult situation and that it will take a lot of Frankish wine to allay his fears.'

'Thank the konungr for his honesty,' Raymond replied and bowed to the portly chieftain, 'and tell him that I would not wish to bring any trouble to Cluainmín. All I want is to be left alone at Dun Domhnall. I have no interest in any town unless they are under the thrall of Veðrarfjord. Then we will have a problem.'

Fionntán cringed but interpreted Raymond's words. Trygve smiled knowingly, his hands in the air in mock surprise.

'He says that he is too old to want to fight a war with his friends and neighbours,' Fionntán interpreted, 'and too experienced to not realise what you are up to, perched out on Dun Domhnall like a bunch of gannets. He guesses that if one was so minded they could house a thousand men behind the new walls?' Both the Gael and the Ostman king smiled as Raymond stumbled over his response. 'He says he will make no decision until he gets a sufficient wergild from Jarl Sigtrygg for the slave he damaged. He doesn't want the jarl disappearing without first paying for his little indiscretion.' Fionntán pointed at the dead translator whose body still lay in the marketplace.

'I will send a cask of my best wine to help him through the negotiations,' Raymond told Fionntán. 'And I will have another six ready to toast his decision if he decides upon an alliance with the men of Dun Domhnall.'

'Ha!' the konungr spat a sudden burst of laughter and slapped his thigh with his hand. Raymond smiled and, as the konungr repeated the joke to his warriors, he studied Trygve. The Ostman was richly clothed in bright linen and fur, but it was the ornate trinkets at his wrists and neck that drew the Norman's attention. All were made of rich silver and embellished with precious stones. The seven or eight warriors behind the konungr were equally well adorned in the precious metal and before he could stop himself, Raymond pictured himself wearing the jewellery and rewarding his own milites with the intricate, swirling bracelets and torques. He licked his lips.

'Tell him that I would be interested in trading wine for silver,' he told Fionntán. The Gael looked as if Raymond had slapped him in the face.

'What did I tell you?' Fionntán snarled, grabbing Raymond's shoulder and pulling him away from Trygve's litter. 'We do not mention the silver. These Ostmen protect their mines like a vixen guards her fox cubs. No outsider even knows where the mines are! If you mention the silver they will become suspicious and guarded.' Behind the pair, Trygve began talking again, directed at the Norman party.

'He wants to know what we are arguing about,' Fionntán told him and, with a last forceful look at Raymond, he began talking to Trygve in his own language. 'I told him that I was promised some of the wine you are giving him,' Fionntán said angrily. 'And I asked if Jarl Sigtrygg and his men were staying in his hall,' he waved a

261

hand to the north where the largest building in the town stood. 'He replied that they were, though the konungr is not happy about it. Jarl Sigtrygg has been making a name for himself among the Ostmen. He has been going raiding,' he told Raymond. 'They have heard that he killed a Norse chieftain called Magnus on Strangrfjorðr, and then sacked a monastery on Kerlingfjorðr. The konungr warns that Jarl Sigtrygg is not the type of man to let an insult pass.'

Raymond nodded in agreement. 'He came by land?' he asked and Trygve confirmed it. 'Then we shall stay on board *Waverider* tonight and anchor close to the eastern bank.'

As Fionntán interpreted his words, Trygve shifted uncomfortably, but did not object to Raymond's statement. Instead he called over one of his warriors and whispered in his ear. The man nodded and cast a look in Raymond's direction before walking into town trailed by more bearded fighters. Raymond stared at their backs suspiciously as Trygve began babbling in his direction again.

'The konungr says that he will expect the cask of wine before sundown,' Fionntán said. 'He bids us good day.'

Dismissed, Raymond bowed to the Konungr of Cluainmín and turned back towards the harbour, trailed by Geoffrey, Amaury and Fionntán. He walked past the patch of blood where the slave had been killed by Jarl Sigtrygg and frowned. 'We are staying on *Waverider* tonight,' he announced. 'Every man sleeps in his armour with his weapons at the ready. If Jarl Sigtrygg decides to make a fight of it, I want us to be ready.'

'We will have nowhere to run if he wants trouble,' said Fionntán as he scratched at a louse beneath his long orange cloak. 'The channel to the main river is so narrow that two bowmen could kill us all from the shore.' He stuck his thumb in his mouth before holding it up to test the wind.

'And worse, we will not be able to rely on the sails.'

Amaury nodded his head in agreement. 'Sitting ducks on a still pond.'

'We will be ready,' Raymond insisted and, with one final look into the marketplace where Jarl Sigtrygg's men plotted their revenge, he began walking back towards the harbour trailed by Amaury and Fionntán. 'A man who believes in the blood feud can always be relied upon to act before he should.'

'A blood feud?' Geoffrey of Abergavenny asked as he eyed the patch of bright blood on the ground of the slave market. 'I don't like this at all,' he added before scampering after his comrades.

Music and the smell of turf fires drifted across the shimmering river to where *Waverider* lay under anchor. Water lapped and gulped at her wooden hull as men snored on her creaking benches. The day had been hot and cloudless so the night was cold, and Raymond watched his breath mist before his eyes, catching the light of the bright moon and the flickering yellow glow of whale-fat lamps from the town walls. The eastern bank was a gaming board as firelight cast by the revellers' torches passed through the masts and stowed rigging of longships in the harbour.

Loud laughter from the town made Raymond turn and examine the western bank where Cluainmín stood. His eyes easily identified Trygve's large feasting hall over the riverside palisade. The dancing firelight emanating from within told the Norman that many men had attended the konungr's feast and he felt a pang of disappointment that he had been not able to join them. Another peal of drunken delight lanced across the night-time scene. A number of men sang a hearty seafaring tune which ended in a bawdy splatter of laughter and ovation upon table tops. Raymond turned his back on the merrymaking and grabbed a water skin from where it hung by the steering oar. He drained a mouthful as he walked across *Waverider*'s deck towards the darkness of the eastern riverbank. He could see little amongst the pouring vegetation, and he urged his eyes to focus. Nocturnal animals were making a racket in the gloom, not as much as the men on the far bank, but certainly sufficient to mask any careful assault on the crew of *Waverider*. Not even the light from the full moon could penetrate the depth of trees on that riverbank. Above him he could hear a bat flying around the rigging, but he only had eyes for the shrouded shore to the east. Something out there drew his attention. Yet he could neither see nor hear anything in the heavy foliage.

Unheralded, Basilia de Quincy entered his mind. Usually, her image stirred feelings of guilt and desire in equal measure, but now he felt only regret. Soon, Basilia was replaced by the memory of Alice's angry outburst at the cattle pens and he exhaled loudly, wiping his hand over his face as the frustration and confusion returned. As he turned to walk back to the steering oar, a noise from the dark shore caught his attention and he turned on his heel and stared out over the still water of the river to where he thought that he had heard the delicate scrape of metal upon metal. Nothing moved and no more sounds echoed from the gloom.

Raymond held his breath.

'There are people in the trees,' Fionntán whispered as he appeared silently at Raymond's side. 'I've been watching for many minutes.'

If Raymond was spooked by Fionntán's sudden appearance, he did not show it. 'Warriors?'

'I can't see who they are, but they are armed. I only count two of them,' the Gael said and Raymond did not doubt that he was correct.

'Dubhgall,' Raymond murmured. *The Dark Foreigners*.

'Indeed.' Fionntán nodded. 'But which ones – Veðrarfjord or Cluainmín?'

Raymond's eyes narrowed. 'Why would Trygve's men guard the eastern bank rather than the town harbour?'

'It would seem pointless,' Fionntán whispered. 'Unless he means to get rid of us. Should I raise the crew?'

'No. Whoever it is, I doubt that they will attack us with only two men. They are watching us.'

Fionntán sniffed. 'And if it is Jarl Sigtrygg?'

'He has no vessel so his only option is to hit us with arrows from the bank. If it were me I would wait until a little before daybreak when we are at our most vulnerable.'

'We could sail away.'

Raymond shook his head. 'It makes no sense for Trygve to guard the eastern shore – it must be Jarl Sigtrygg. But if Trygve hears us under oar he will become suspicious and you are correct, he will send a handful of bowmen out onto the point,' he indicated downriver to where the river, unseen in the darkness, narrowed. 'He could spray *Waverider* with arrows as she tries to pass. With this small wind we would have to take to the oars and we would have no cover. It would be a massacre.' Raymond blew a lungful of hot air through his hands to warm them up. 'No,' he decided, 'we stay put.'

'What about the Ostmen?'

'It is troubling,' Raymond replied. 'Jarl Sigtrygg would be mad to attack. He'll be hard pressed to hurt us and it will accomplish nothing other than driving Trygve to our side, or at least away from his. He might believe that Veðrarfjord can defeat us without Trygve's help?'

'You did call him a hog-faced prick. Some men cannot let an insult like that lie. It plays on their mind and until they see the blood on their swords they will carry it with them.' He cleared his throat and shook his head perhaps, Raymond thought, to eliminate a memory from his own background.

'Anyway,' the Gael continued, 'the Ostmen love a good feud and you may have started one with the worst brigand these islands have seen in fifty years.'

'"*May have*" started a feud,' Raymond repeated and rubbed his face as he considered his situation. 'There is nothing for it, I'll have to find out who they are,' he said. 'Get the men awake and tell them to make a bit of noise like we are drinking and getting rowdy.'

'What exactly is your plan?' Fionntán asked as Raymond swept off his cloak and began unbuckling his sword-belt.

The captain smiled as he took off his surcoat, decorated with Strongbow's arms, and draped it over the edge of the ship. 'I'll have a quick and quiet look around. Whoever is over there,' he nodded towards the riverbank, 'they are up to something and I want to know what it is.' He pulled his long red bliaut over his head and threw it on top of his surcoat leaving him in only his hose. He then kicked off his sabatons and tucked them into the front of his breeches. Picking up his sword-belt, he buckled it over his right shoulder. The heavy leather scabbard was cold on his spine. Around him, his milites growled as they were shaken awake by Fionntán.

'Go away,' Geoffrey of Abergavenny told the Gael and rolled over, wrapped in his cloak. A swift kick to the esquire's backside had the boy to his feet as well as providing a warning to several other sleeping warriors not to mess with Fionntán.

Raymond waited until the Gael had everyone on their feet and his milites had started to growl in anger at being woken. He then crossed to the steering oar and, with a deep breath, hoisted himself over the wale and down the wooden clinkered hull. He gasped as his bare feet struck cold water and used his arms to lower himself downwards into the river.

'Holy St Nicholas' beard,' he whimpered as his shoulders went under and his breath scattered the surface as he panted and paddled. With one hand on the hull, he waited for several minutes while his body adjusted to the temperature, sweeping his feet in circles as his father had taught him during their lessons of his youth. Soon, his breathing became less shallow and, covered by the ongoing noise from his men aboard *Waverider,* he pushed away and began silently swimming upstream, helped part of the way by the rope which tugged on the anchor.

The light from the town flickered on the surface of the water and mixed with the constant white of the moon. A fish popped to the surface a few feet in front of him, preying on flies which buzzed around. After only a few seconds the anchor rope went deeper than he could reach and Raymond continued the slow progress for many minutes, paddling northwards against the flow of water. He was almost blind as he swam into the blackness, but in his mind's eye he pictured the shoreline that he had studied during daylight hours. When he adjudged that he had swum far enough, Raymond turned to his right as quietly as he could and made for the shore. He knew that any noise could draw the Ostmen to the waterside and a single arrow could end his involvement in Strongbow's great adventure. Raymond swept the thought from his mind and, almost immediately, he felt mud beneath his toes and tough stalks of rushes strike his face. Now wading, he paused as water flowed from his bare shoulders to drip noisily into the Banneew. His eyes adjusted to the darkness. He could now make out the sandy shoreline and the trees beyond, but could see no sign of the warriors that Fionntán had spotted. He started forward through the deep rushes and buzzing bugs until the water came up to his knees and soon the mud became stone and shingle, making it more difficult for him to move quietly. Shivering, he slowed his progress but, before long, his feet hit a tangle of grass and bramble. Above his head a bent tree bough arced downwards to touch the river. He had entered the forest.

Nothing moved ahead of him and Raymond turned to look across the bay at *Waverider*, outlined in front of the lamp-lit town. Despite his efforts in the water, he had only ended up about twenty paces upriver of the ship and that realisation made him pause. He could still hear the noise from his men and he prayed that it had been enough to mask the clamour he had made while swimming. A splash from the river made him jump and was followed by a shout of derision and a bout of laughter. Someone, probably Fionntán, had hurled something heavy overboard to conceal his movements. Raymond smiled at the Gael's ruse and turned back towards the darkness of the trees, hoisting himself over a huge tree root where he quickly rammed his sabatons back on his feet. Reaching down to the ground he found some soft mud and scrawled markings across his face, chest and arms to aid his concealment.

No man could stay silent in the heavy vegetation, but Raymond was more nimble than most his size and he carefully and patiently made his way through the forest with barely more than a sound. He could only have been walking for a few minutes when a voice in front of him, more a whisper, spoke a few words in the Danish tongue. Had the man not spoken Raymond would have bumbled right into him where he stood with his back to a tree. The Norman froze and silently sank to his knees, his eyes searching the darkness for threats and a path to retreat if one came about. A second man, with a deeper voice, replied to the first Ostman's question in hushed tones. A gap in the trees allowed the moon to shine through and Raymond caught a glimpse of the second warrior as moonlight reflected off his shimmering fish scale armour. He was seated and had a long blonde beard, a gold clasp at his shoulder and was emptying a skin into his mouth. The sound of sloshing wine emanated around the trees. At the seated man's shoulder, Raymond could see a shield bearing a snarling boar mask. They were Jarl Sigtrygg's men.

Raymond slowly reached over his shoulder and gripped the sword at his back and waited, his eyes unblinking as they locked on the nearest Ostman. That Sigtrygg was planning to attack *Waverider* he did not now doubt. Raymond had never responded well to intimidation and promised that the two men would die as a warning to their jarl to back off.

He waited, barely breathing and watching. He waited, fingering his sword pommel. He waited until the noises emanating from *Waverider* increased and then he sprang at the nearest of the two men, cleaving his head in two with a vicious downward cut as he dragged the weapon over his shoulder. The second Ostman, seated on the ground, yelped at the sudden appearance of an enemy amongst the trees and rolled away towards a spear propped against a fallen bough. Raymond was on him in a second, crying a shout of venom as he swung his sword one-handed at the man's head. Somehow the blond warrior hoisted the boar-faced shield and deflected the thrust away from his body. Raymond stumbled after the clumsy lunge, taking the shield with him, but the Ostman did not take advantage and attack the Norman. Instead he took his opportunity to flee and sprinted away from the river and into the depths of the forest.

Raymond cursed and picked up the man's abandoned shield. He feared what would occur should the warrior report back to Sigtrygg, likely drunk at the feast in town. The jarl from Veðrarfjord would be furious and would seek revenge. Worse, Trygve would be infuriated that Raymond had broken the peace and any hope for a deal with Cluainmín would be finished. With the noise of the fleeing Ostman still echoing around the trees, Raymond took off after him.

Jarl Sigtrygg's warrior was panicking, he quickly realised as he tracked his path. Rather than make his way back towards safety and his jarl's side, the man was running inland into the forest. Perhaps he believed that he could lose his pursuer in the dark depths, but it did not take much effort for Raymond to shadow his quarry as he noisily smashed through bush and briar. The terrain suddenly sloped uphill and the Norman captain's thighs burned as he forced himself onwards. He considered stopping his pursuit and doubling-back to the river for surely, he thought, the two had taken a boat across from Cluainmín and the remaining man would return to the vessel. He was neither gaining nor losing any ground on the noisy Ostman. And something else was perturbing Raymond - a faint glow of firelight above the trees. He slowed to a stop, confused at the sight coming from the depths of what he thought was the uninhabited eastern shore. Ahead he could hear the Ostman using his weapons to cut his way through the tangle. Raymond followed more methodically, his ears alert and suspicious, as he moved ever eastwards and uphill. He suspected that he and Jarl Sigtrygg's warrior must have come at least half a mile into the forest when, up ahead, the shouting began.

Raymond froze and gripped the straps on the back of the circular shield. Creeping forward, he heard the crash of steel weapons and the thump of many feet. A man bellowed in fear and was silenced. Raymond again went still and urged his eyes to penetrate the dimness. Curiosity pushed him further in spite of the danger. Ahead angry voices spoke and orders were shouted at warriors unseen. Heavy feet stomped on hard earth. Why were there warriors this deep in the forest, he wondered and slowly began sneaking forwards. As he approached the pinnacle of the hill he espied torches between the trees and again slowed, crouching and making sure that he made as little noise as possible. Ahead was a vast area of hewn stumps and rough bracken-roofed hovels. The whole expanse was arrayed in firelight from a hundred torches which ringed a mass of Ostman warriors, oxen, carts and filth-covered slaves.

'Oh no,' Raymond said quietly as he stared around floodlit expanse, 'Fionntán is going to kill me.' For he had stumbled upon the secret which the Gael had warned him to avoid at all costs - it was Trygve's silver mine. If he was discovered by the men of Cluainmín, all his hopes for a treaty with Trygve would certainly be finished, he knew. From his hiding place, Raymond watched as oxen teams carted iron ore from the mouth of the mine, fifty paces away, to where chain-bound slaves toiled with shovels and picks at debris from deep in the earth. Dung and burning wood tickled his nostrils. Above everything was a fort, simple in construction though Raymond did not doubt that it would allow the warriors to protect their new found treasure-trove from any attack.

But Trygve would trust to secrecy first. Raymond could see that Jarl Sigtrygg's warrior had already died to protect the knowledge of the silver mine's location and he did not want to join the Ostman on that particular journey. The man's body was lying prone on the ground with three men surrounding him and more gathering with weapons at the

271

ready. One man, who Raymond remembered from the slave market that morning, was issuing loud orders and pointing into the trees.

'Time to go,' the captain said quietly and began to slide back into the forest. He cursed as his foot strayed into a dry, rustling bushel a few steps into his flight.

The shout echoed clear through the still forest and Raymond knew immediately that he was in trouble. Abandoning any attempt to remain unseen, he began running through the forest in the general direction of *Waverider*. He cried out as he ran headlong into a low branch which whipped across his face, but he was on his feet in a second, treading more carefully as his eyes adjusted from the flickering firelight at the silver mines to the dank darkness of the forest. Behind him, he could hear the heavy stomp of warriors, their jangling chainmail and the clash of steel weaponry on leather, leaf and wood. Many men were chasing him.

He did not doubt that he could outpace the armour-clad warriors, but he worried about what would happen if he led them straight to *Waverider*. If Trygve thought that one of the Normans had discovered his mines, not one of his small crew would leave the settlement alive, of that he was sure. Raymond looked back over his shoulder where he could see a number of torches amongst the trees. Despite their weaponry, the Ostmen were making fast progress through the forest which they understandably knew better than he. Clambering over a tree root, his eyes espied the glow from Cluainmín and he redoubled his efforts to race in that direction.

Movement and a yell came from his left and it took all of Raymond's speed to get the boar-faced shield up to deflect a spear thrust by a young beardless youth coming from the other direction. The Ostman squealed as he struck,

272

the war cry of a novice, young in battle but keen to mark this night with his first kill. Raymond didn't give his adversary the chance. He twisted his shield to throw the boy off balance and drew his sword, all impulse and reaction. He deflected the beardless boy's next lunge away to his left and for a second the two warriors circled each other like fighting cats. The young man had lost the element of surprise and now was faced with an enemy ready to meet his attack. He hesitated.

Raymond did not know if his opponent was Trygve or Jarl Sigtrygg's man, only that he could not let him live. Even in the moonlight the boy would recognise the Norman captain and betray his presence to his chieftain.

The youngster shouted words – in which language Raymond could not tell – as his eyes flicked over the Norman's shoulder. Raymond caught a glimpse of torches, close by, reflected in the boy's eyes and threw himself into an attack with two swift downward cuts wide to his left and then his right. As the youth moved his shield across his body to intercept the second blow, Raymond turned his cut straight across the boy's body and sliced his sword deep into his skull. The boy sighed once as he crumpled to the floor. He turned to see several torches in the near distance and exhaled heavily. Raymond took a few backward steps and made to flee, but instead tripped and fell across the outstretched feet of Jarl Sigtrygg's man, the spy who he had killed as he had climbed out of the river. He would have taken off into the trees but as he scrambled to his feet a plan began to unfold in his mind.

With one eye on the approaching torches, he threw the Ostman's shield onto the ground close to the dead youth and then hoisted Jarl Sigtrygg's man upwards so that he sat on the ground with his back to a tree. Raymond snatched a hand axe from the boy's belt and, with a moment's pause to compose himself, buried it in Jarl Sigtrygg's spy's brains. Blood splattered across his face and he used a sweaty forearm to wipe his eyes and mouth. He then pulled the man's sword from its sheath and jammed it into his hand. Happy that his small ruse would convince his pursuers that the youngster had killed their prey, Raymond quietly and quickly slinked the last few metres to the water's edge. *Waverider* was still noisy and easily identifiable in the corona of whale fat lamps blazing beyond her in the longfort. He pulled off his sabatons and stuffed them back in his hose, slipping into the freezing water with a small yelp and some furious panting. As he began swimming, he was dimly aware of angry shouting in the forest behind him.

'What have you done?' whispered Fionntán as he offered Raymond a hand over the side of *Waverider* and hoisted him upwards so that the Norman could get his hands onto the sheer-strake. The Gael then reached over the side and grabbed Raymond by his leg and dragged him into the ship.

'What have you done?' Fionntán asked again. Behind him, many torches buzzed like fireflies in the forest. All his men were on her port side staring at the excitement on the eastern shore.

'Hopefully I've sorted out a couple of our problems in one swoop,' Raymond replied as he shivered and wiped snot from his nose. He propped his sword against the mast, threw his cloak around his shoulders and joined his men as they watched the disturbance which continued in the trees. Branches shook and scattered leaves in the river as the Ostmen of Cluainmín moved around beyond the sight of the Norman crew but for the glow of their torches. It was obvious that they had discovered the body of the young warrior and that of Jarl Sigtrygg's man and were angrily

274

discussing what they should do with the information.

'Are they going to attack us?' Geoffrey of Abergavenny asked. All of *Waverider's* crew turned to look at their captain in anticipation of an answer.

Raymond shook water from his hair like a dog. 'I don't know. But for now we wait and we watch.'

The herald appeared at the harbour wall at first light, shouting across the river to *Waverider*, waving his hands and pointing back towards Trygve's hall.

'He says that the konungr wants to talk to you,' Fionntán translated. Like Raymond, he had seen out the night on watch, always alert and ready to react to any attack that might befall them. Daylight had brought hope to the crew of *Waverider*, hope that the worst was over, and they could finish their business and return to the relative safety of Dun Domhnall with an alliance to guard their eastern flank.

'He says that you must come immediately,' Fionntán continued as the messenger shouted from the distant shore. Unusually for a herald, he was clothed in armour and had an axe cradled in his arm. 'They have called the Þing together.'

'Meaning?' asked Raymond.

'Meaning that someone has started an argument,' Fionntán replied, 'and someone is to blame. Can you guess how the Ostmen sort out disputes of this sort?'

Raymond grunted an affirmative, picturing crossed swords and a circle of rage-filled faces urging on desperate blood-drenched combatants. 'Why would they want me there?'

Fionntán shrugged. 'We can still make a break for it.' He looked up at the sky and spat over the side of the ship. 'The wind is fine, and I say we can shoot the shallow channel.' He held out an arm and pointed at an almost invisible waterway between the eastern bank and the sand which blocked the centre of the channel a hundred paces downriver from the town. Raymond would not have seen the route had not Fionntán pointed it out, though he doubted that any vessel of *Waverider's* size could possibly traverse the stream without becoming grounded.

'We run and we admit complicity in whatever the hell they may or may not accuse us of,' Raymond replied with a shake of his head. 'No, tell Amaury to prepare the oars and take us back across to the town. You and I will go and talk to Trygve and this…*Þing*,' he said.

Fifteen minutes later, Raymond and Fionntán were walking through the slave market, following the Ostman herald towards Trygve's hall on a slight bluff to the north.

'What should I expect when we get there?' whispered Raymond, his feet clattering hollowly on the wooden beams below his feet.

'No idea.'

It was the first time that Raymond had heard anything but assurance from Fionntán, and the change in his demeanour worried him greatly. The Gael had begun talking to their guide in the Danish tongue.

'He says we are going out of the longfort to a great oak where the Þing is in session,' Fionntán translated.

'Not at Trygve's hall?' Raymond replied, looking up at the great building crowned with a vast thatched roof.

'No,' Fionntán said nervously and followed the herald who turned to his left and made down a side street towards the town walls. As they moved away from the river Raymond made a conscious effort to remember some of the landmarks: a cage of cats for skinning, a house with brown roof needing new thatch, a pigeon coop with a red cloth roof to protect the birds from the sun. Should he and

Fionntán need to get out quickly, he did not want to get lost in the tiny streets which sprang from each other like branches on a beech tree. They passed through the gates of Cluainmín where several visiting traders eyed Raymond and shared a joke at his expense. He had abandoned his chainmail, but his crimson and gold surcoat was alien to the eye of the Ostmen. It was vivid, effeminate even, amongst the dull earthy colours of the town. The sword at his side and the coif at his shoulders should have been enough to warn the men that Raymond was a warrior, but he did not mind if every man in Cluainmín thought him soft. If they underestimated his skills they gave him the advantage should it come to a fight.

Little farms dotted the fields outside the town walls. Swaying crops danced in the little wind while cattle crowded into small-holdings and stared dumbly at the group as they passed. Slaves dilly-dallied outside the homesteads in the sunshine only to leap to their feet when they saw the herald approach. Raymond knew that the poor wretches would never have been so indolent if their masters were nearby and concluded that it would not only be the great men of Cluainmín at the Þing; every freeman with a patch of land to farm would have their say. Lords led and freemen followed: that was the order of life in Henry's kingdom, but here in Ireland everything seemed to be different. He was unsure whether he liked or loathed that ideal. The slaves, like the few folk left in town, stood up and stared at Raymond's colourful presence as he and his two companions passed by on the road. A long straight field, brimming with wheat not yet ready for harvest, bounded the street while the smell of animals drifted from pens not far away. In the distance Raymond could see the top of a great oak standing alone on the side of a small meadow already cut for hay. He could see several white tents, open fronted and crowded with little benches and many Ostmen milling around. It was in that direction that their guide took the Norman and his Gaelic companion, babbling in his own tongue to Fionntán as they walked.

'Yes, yes,' Fionntán smiled sarcastically, 'the Þing is the best entertainment you can have with your hose on,' he repeated, turning to Raymond and rolling his eyes. 'It's up ahead. They started without us. Apparently we are going to enjoy this.' As they came upon the tents, another warrior stepped towards Raymond and pointed at his sword and Fionntán's spear, wagging a finger in their faces.

'He wants us to disarm. Have you another blade hidden inside your clothes?' Raymond asked his ally.

'Two,' Fionntán replied with a sniff.

'Good,' Raymond smiled and unbuckled his sword, pulling a mace from the small of his back and lobbing it to the guard. He didn't wait for the Ostman to search him for the large dagger sheathed at his spine, and instead walked through the tents towards the big oak hidden behind the small hill. A hundred faces, men and women, turned to stare at him as he stood on the ridge of a grassy gully and looked down on the Þing of Cluainmín. Any talk that had been taking place had stopped as Raymond appeared.

'They probably think you are the entertainment in those gaudy clothes of yours,' Fionntán joked at Raymond's shoulder. The captain was too nervous to retort and instead bowed to the people of the town.

'Thank you for inviting me to your gathering,' he said fluttering a hand in welcome to those in the gully. Fionntán lazily translated and the people of the town giggled at his words, the suspicious atmosphere broken, as they talked amongst themselves.

'What did you tell them?' Raymond asked.

'That though you dress like a mad, dancing girl, you are

278

indeed able to testify like any sane man.'

'Thanks for that,' Raymond said and bowed again, this time smiling. 'It is very helpful. What is happening now?' he asked as an old man with a short white beard began talking, his hand gripping a piece of bark on the old oak tree halfway up the gully. The man read from no parchment yet did not pause for thought as he half-shouted, half-sang the words to the gathered throng. All the people were silent and listened intently to the old man's words.

'*Our fathers have handed down to us the laws of our people,*' Fionntán translated. '*The law binds us together, the law separates men from beasts…*' he paused and turned towards his Norman companion. 'You get the idea – the old man is the lawspeaker and he will recite all the laws of Cluainmín so that anyone who is brought forth is fully aware of their beliefs and therefore cannot fall back on lack of knowledge as a defence.'

'Am I to be tried for a crime?' Raymond asked and received nothing more comforting than a shrug of his shoulders from Fionntán.

'I'd better listen in so that I can advise you … should it come to that,' the Gael added and turned back to the lawspeaker who continued to deliver what could only be an extensive set of rules which governed the Ostman judicial system. Below the white-bearded man sat Trygve. The fat konungr was the only man who had a chair, his litter from the day before, and he listened seriously to the lawspeaker. It was many minutes before the old man finished speaking and sat down on an exposed root to observe the court proceedings.

'The gist is this,' Fionntán told Raymond as the hubbub from the crowd gathered pace. 'One man, one vote on the guilt of the defendant, but it is Trygve who sits in final judgement and hands out punishments and fines. The lawspeaker will make sure he acts within the law. If you are discovered to have perjured yourself,' he raised his eyebrows, 'the penalty is death. Remember that should you be questioned.'

Raymond did not have a chance to answer before Trygve struggled to his feet and began an angry soliloquy, his finger outstretched in the direction of a small group on the far side of the gully. Up on the hill, an irate Jarl Sigtrygg spat counter-accusations back at Trygve backed up by loud shouts of support from his crewmen.

'It isn't me on trial,' Raymond realised with a smile, 'it is Jarl Sigtrygg.' Relief flowed through his chest as he watched Sigtrygg shake his head angrily and scream curses across the gully towards the Konungr of Cluainmín.

Fionntán also breathed a sigh of relief. 'Thank the saints. It sounds to me like the konungr himself has brought this case before the Þing. Not only does he want compensation for the slave that was killed, he accuses Jarl Sigtrygg of murder and attempted theft.' He paused for several seconds to listen in on the discourse between the two parties. 'He says he has evidence and witnesses that back up his allegations.' As Fionntán spoke Trygve's fat finger swept across the gully to settle on Raymond.

'I am one of his witnesses,' the captain realised.

After a split second of shocked silence, Jarl Sigtrygg's warriors burst into voice, mocking and laughing, and pointedly dismissing Trygve's claims and the evidence of a fat foreigner in a fancy tunic. Despite not understanding their words, Raymond felt his face flush with colour as they taunted him, but his embarrassment was overtaken by more laughter, this time aimed at the konungr's attempts to hoist his great weight from his litter. Trygve was not bashful and called forward two warriors to help him to his feet. Once upright, the old bear threw curses and criticism at the men of Veðrarfjord, too confusing for Fionntán to translate. In the end it was only when the lawspeaker called for silence that the lengthy confrontation subsided.

'This is madness,' Raymond said. 'I have no idea what is going on. Have they started taking evidence?'

'No, they are still swapping insults ... oh wait. Now Trygve is demanding ten pounds of silver to settle the case immediately. All Jarl Sigtrygg has to do is admit guilt about what happened in the woods last night. I think it may be a trick.'

The jarl did not explode in fury as Raymond had expected and instead calmly turned towards the foreigner on the far side of the gully. 'Trygve says you have evidence against me,' Sigtrygg shouted at Raymond in French. 'If you tell him any lies I will kill you. Understand?'

Raymond did not answer and instead whispered in Fionntán's ear. The Gael cleared his throat and switched back into the Danish tongue. 'The captain is ready to give his testimony about the night in question. He wonders if he must take some sort of oath?'

Raymond turned to look at Sigtrygg's reaction as Fionntán spoke. The jarl was furious and had the same look on his face as when Raymond broke his nose at the slave market. The only reason he did not react in the same fashion and charge the Norman was because he was distracted by the shield thrown from the gully edge by Trygve. The painted device was a blur as the disc spun towards the grass below the men of Veðrarfjord. It bounced once and settled at Jarl Sigtrygg's feet for all to see. It bore the jarl's boar mask and a splash of crimson. The Þing went quiet as Trygve shouted a few short phrases in his native tongue.

Fionntán inhaled deeply. 'He says the shield is Jarl Sigtrygg's, but the blood belongs to Trygve's youngest son.'

Thankfully no one was watching Raymond. Unlike Jarl Sigtrygg, who looked confused at Trygve's declaration, Raymond went still, his eyes wide with shock. The boy he had killed in the woods had been the konungr's son! Guilt and remorse was followed by relief, for there could be no alliance between Veðrarfjord and Cluainmín if Trygve thought Jarl Sigtrygg had killed his boy.

The argument had started again – Trygve's anger and Jarl Sigtrygg's protestations of innocence. Two of the konungr's men had broken from the main group and become embroiled in a wrestling match with two of the jarl's warriors. More went to the aid of their compatriots and soon a full blown fist fight was taking place on the far side of the gully. Trygve and Jarl Sigtrygg did not move to intervene. Instead their eyes were locked together in a battle of wills across the heads of their fighting bannermen. After the initial coming together, the two factions were slowly pulled apart from the fighting by older heads, and the lawspeaker's call for calm finally ended the unrest and permitted the proceedings to continue.

'He is asking if Jarl Sigtrygg denies that it was his man who killed Ivarr Trygvesson,' Fionntán interpreted the lawspeaker's words, 'and that his aim was to steal some of the konungr's possessions.' In response the jarl laughed and spat haughtily his answer at the konungr. 'Sigtrygg says that it will take more than a shield with some blood on it to prove his complicity in murder,' Fionntán translated, 'and as to the theft charge, he says that he has not even heard what he is accused of trying to steal.'

Trygve lurched to his feet in answer to that and launched a tirade of shouting in his guest's direction.

'The konungr knows a lot of swear words,' Fionntán joked to his Norman companion as the outburst continued, 'but he is reluctant to mention that he has a mining operation hidden in the forest. I suspect that few of the townsfolk even know where it is. He claims that Jarl Sigtrygg knows of what he is accused and is being obtuse.'

The jarl and his crew were laughing now, making a mockery of Trygve's court and shaking their heads in disgust at the absurdity of the charges. Jarl Sigtrygg raised his voice above the hullabaloo and addressed the lawspeaker directly.

'He says that unless Trygve brings forward some real evidence against him, or tells him what he is accused of stealing, the charges should be dropped.' Fionntán told Raymond.

A grim smile had spread across Trygve's face and a snap of the konungr's fingers brought two of his retainers from behind the oak tree carrying two bodies. Raymond recognised each one. The first was Trygve's son, his face a mess of blood and eviscerated flesh. The second was the man that Raymond had chased into the woods and had been killed by the guards at the mines. The body was stretched out on the bank below Trygve so that all could see it. A bearded man stepped forward as this was done and began talking.

'That witness claims he recognises the dead man for he saw him twice yesterday,' Fionntán translated. 'The first time was in the slave market with Jarl Sigtrygg while the second was when he was caught in the woods attempting to steal the konungr's belongings and was summarily sent to meet his maker.'

Jarl Sigtrygg sneered and again demanded to know what he was accused of stealing, but Raymond could tell that the production of the bodies had him rattled. Trygve ignored his rival as a last body was brought forward. It was the man who had been spying on *Waverider*, still with an axe buried in his head and his dead eyes staring at the heavens. As the dead man was draped on the edge of the gully alongside the first two, the lawspeaker turned to Raymond and asked him a question.

'Do you swear to tell the truth on pain of death?' Fionntán asked on the old man's behalf. Raymond nodded and the Gael delivered his answer in the Danish tongue. 'What did you see last night?' he asked.

Raymond looked at Trygve and then at Jarl Sigtrygg. Both were listening intently to his answer, one encouragingly the other with barely concealed contempt.

'I will kill you and skin your children alive if you speak lies against me, Englishman,' Jarl Sigtrygg shouted across at him. 'I will sail down to your little fort and kill every man, woman and child I find there. I will...'

'I anchored in the river close to the eastern shore,' Raymond interrupted. 'Having been attacked at the slave market I thought it best that we remain in the river's midst and so keep the peace in Cluainmín.' Beside him, Fionntán interpreted his words for the benefit of the people of gathered. 'One of my men heard a clash of arms in the forest close to the riverbank and we saw that man,' Raymond paused to point at Jarl Sigtrygg's spy who was laid out to his left, 'fighting with a brave young warrior.' The captain grimaced as he indicated towards Trygve's son. 'Despite the darkness, my men and I watched as the two taunted and shouted at each other. Then they charged and with their last blows they each felled the other. It was only later that my friend,' he put a hand on Fionntán's shoulder, 'told me what they had said before they had died.' Raymond paused and bowed his head. When he said nothing for a few seconds Trygve barked a question in his direction.

'What did *I* say?' Fionntán asked nervously.

Raymond levelled a finger at Sigtrygg's crewman. 'He said that when his jarl came back a-viking there would be silver for all who helped him.'

The Þing erupted with noise as Fionntán reluctantly translated Raymond's words. He then closed his eyes and began murmuring a prayer, but Raymond's words had the desired effect – Trygve leapt to his feet and began issuing orders for his men to kill the men of Veðrarfjord while Jarl Sigtrygg's men produced weapons of their own in an effort to defend themselves. The townsfolk to Raymond's right squeaked in worry and began running away from the fighting, immediately swarming around the Norman and the Gael as they fought their way out of the gully.

'Raymond!' Jarl Sigtrygg screamed as his men fell back from the blades of Trygve's men. For a second their eyes locked over the fighting and fleeing people as they were swept in opposite directions. 'Raymond, you whoreson,' the jarl yelled. 'You are a liar. I know nothing of any silver and you damn well know it.' In his fury, Jarl Sigtrygg was all but oblivious to the fighting that took place an arm's breadth from him. His crewmen had to drag him away from the gully, along the ridge as they defended themselves from Trygve's warriors. 'We shall meet again soon, Englishman,' Jarl Sigtrygg shouted. 'I will bring the whole host of Veðrarfjord and burn you out of your little fort. I'll let my axe do its work then,' he bellowed as he brought his short sword down on the arm of one of the warriors who threatened him. 'And all who stand beside you will die or burn.' He pointed his weapon at the captain before fleeing down the far side of the gully and out of Raymond's sight.

'Are you out of your mind?' Fionntán whispered at his side.

'Come on,' Raymond said and pulled the Gael back towards the tents where they had left their weapons. They had to dodge through the agitated crowd and by the time Raymond had his sword and mace back at his side all but a few of the people were left in the area and were on the street back towards the town.

'What now?' asked Fionntán. 'Back to *Waverider*?'

Raymond shook his head and raised his chin as Trygve appeared at the top of the hill above them. He waddled towards them with a smile on his face and embraced Raymond, squashing his rich adornments against the captain's chest. He then babbled at Fionntán.

'Jarl Sigtrygg and his men have fled. The konungr claims that if that is not the sign of his guilt then he does not know what is. The jarl had horses waiting in a copse a little way to the north and was able to fight his way there and make good his escape. He thanks you for your evidence and says it made all the difference.'

Raymond smiled as Trygve slapped him on the arm. 'Tell him I don't fully understand what I said that was so controversial, but that I am glad that the truth was of benefit to Cluainmín. Give him my condolences for the death of his son.'

Konungr Trygve began laughing.

'He says that he has plenty more sons and that none of them will be taking part in any attack on Dun Domhnall,' said Fionntán. 'He also says that he will make our trip home quicker than that which brought us to Cluainmín.' The Gael looked confused as he translated Trygve's words.

'How?' Raymond asked. 'Is there some river system that we do not know about?'

Trygve grinned at that and shook his head as he replied.

'He says that we will be faster because he will see us on our way lighter by those six casks of the beautiful French wine which you promised him,' Fionntán interpreted.

Raymond nodded appreciatively at the jest. 'First the wine and then we are for home.'

Chapter Ten

Alice of Abergavenny watched as the crew of *Waverider* pulled one last time at the oar to build up speed. The hiss of the wooden keel as it slid up the sand could even be heard high up on the headland of Dun Domhnall where she stood. Laughter rose from the ship and Alice gasped as she watched her brother leap over the side of the ship with a rope in hand and land in the shallows, water reaching his middle and a smile upon his face. A month ago he would not have been so audacious. Raymond's influence had rubbed off on her brother. She grimaced with sudden jealousy.

'Good, they are back,' said Borard from Alice's side. Bare-chested and sweating, he was nursing his right arm where a large purple bruise was beginning to appear. 'You see that?' he said showing his injury to Alice. 'Hell of a bang I've got there.'

Alice said nothing and kept her gaze directly ahead. She had felt too many eyes stealing glances at she moved around the fort while Raymond was absent. She knew what they wanted. Her gaze drifted away from her brother, who anchored the ship to a tree on the cliff face, and towards Raymond de Carew. Infuriatingly, he was smiling. Even overseeing the unloading of goods from a ship, he was still having a good time. What, she wondered, was so funny about fruit, leather shoes, skins and barrels of live mullet, plaice and crab?

'Of course,' Borard continued, inching closer to Alice

with his arm held out, 'when you play *our game* you are lucky to come out of it with your head intact,' he laughed. The game of which he spoke involved two teams of mounted men throwing a dog pelt stuffed with wool around outside the bailey. There were rules of course, but they were rarely enforced and usually the Norman game ended with a fistfight when competitiveness made way for anger.

'So, you and Raymond, eh?' Borard said through pursed lips. 'Or are you...?' he allowed his words to stretch hopefully.

'How dare you,' Alice gasped and stepped away with a look of sheer fury on her face, recognising immediately what the warrior was implying.

'No, no. You misunderstand...' Borard began to say as she stormed away from him, downhill towards the double embattlements; anywhere to get away from the warriors of Dun Domhnall. Wolf-whistles screeched around her as Alice dashed past the two guards on the gate.

'How are you, lovely lady?' another man said as she scampered through the bailey, dry mud crumbling under foot as she increased her speed. 'Come on back here and give me a smooch. You could pretend that I was the Young King,' he laughed and made a kissing sound.

Alice was blushing now and tried to walk towards Raymond's new cattle pens with as much dignity as she could muster. The cows stirred in their enclosure, looking for food, but Alice scuttled past towards the main gate where a lone warrior sat beside the inner gate. When he turned to look at her, Alice was horrified to see that it was the leper, Ferrand.

'Where are you going?' he croaked, letting her get close before speaking. There was no warmth in his voice and Alice shied away from him rather than breathe the air which Ferrand exhaled.

'I'm going for a walk, to greet my brother.'

Ferrand watched her, his eyes sunken beneath the gnarled and granulated folds of diseased skin which gave him such a suspicious look. 'Captain Raymond will want some dinner.'

'He can get it himself.'

'Yes, he could,' he said, reaching out to take her blue sleeve. 'But I would rather you made the effort.'

'Why?' she stormed, tearing her arm from his hand.

'Because you owe him a great deal and you getting him a few meals will be a great comfort to him.' Ferrand said calmly. 'He made himself an outlaw for you.'

'I didn't ask him to save me,' Alice replied, feeling her anger rise. 'I didn't need his help.'

Ferrand's hand shot out again and grabbed Alice by the cheeks, twirling her so that she faced the same direction as him, his chest against her shoulder blades. 'Look,' he said, shaking her face painfully.

Alice was shocked and sore, and disgusted that the leper was touching her skin. 'Let me go,' she exclaimed through her pinched cheeks.

'Look,' he stressed and shook her again. 'Up on the hill, who do you see?'

Alice adjusted her gaze and saw that Borard had followed her out of the ancient fort and was standing watching the sea. 'Him. Borard.'

'Did he have to ask Raymond to save him? Borard disappeared from Striguil one day, right out of the blue, and Raymond spent a week hunting him down. He finally found him, penniless and drunk out of his mind, in a Gloucester gutter. The captain convinced Strongbow to take him back into his service and now Raymond keeps his pay safe so that he can't kill himself with booze and can buy himself a farm when he gets too old to keep up with the conrois.'

Ferrand flipped her around so that she saw William de Vale, the esquire, as he tended to his armour and shared a joke with Dafydd FitzHywel. She could feel his breath hot on her neck.

'William's father sold his sword to Maredudd ap Gruffydd and helped him take Llansteffan Castle from Maurice FitzGerald of Pembroke. No noble knight would take his son on as his apprentice because they feared to offend Sir Maurice, but Raymond was willing to upset his own uncle in order to give the boy a chance at making a future for himself.' His voice hissed in her ear. 'And Dafydd? He is a mongrel son of a Welshman and a lowborn Norman lady – who else but Raymond would've had him in his service?' With that he let Alice go, allowing her to spin around to face him. 'And then there is the poor leper who had been dismissed from every door in Gwent, but Raymond gave him back his sword and gave him the chance to find a noble death in battle rather than a shameful end as a pauper in the streets. Everyone in Dun Domhnall owes Raymond loyalty, girl, in one manner or another. And we all have our ways of paying him back.'

Alice did not answer, but backed away from Ferrand before fleeing through the gate and into the darkness between the battlements. She could not accept that she owed Raymond anything; he had taken what he wanted from her when he had the chance and in return had provided nothing – no meeting with the king and no route to regaining Abergavenny. Anger infused Alice's chest as she skirted the deeper patches of mud which appeared amongst the carpet of woodchips. Her fury took her past the four archers who lounged on the wood barbican and out into the grasslands beyond the walls of Dun Domhnall. Yelps and whoops and thundering hooves immediately surrounded Alice as she was presented with a game of charging horsemen. The trampled grass led a path across the peninsula, and then a full mile inland before the game had brought the Normans back towards the gates of the fort. As well as the noise from the men in the free-for-all, there was more from those on horseback who circled outside the main fracas, shouting encouragement and tactics.

Alice frowned and turned to her right, skirting along the wall to escape the danger of the horses. Though she had said she had wanted to greet her brother, she turned northwards to avoid the beach where *Waverider* was landed. She knew of a little copse which hid a small, private cove. The steep sides meant that horses could not venture down into its belly and she knew that the little inlet would provide her with the solitude she so craved, away from Borard, Ferrand and Raymond de Carew. She had only arrived at the top of the small bay when she heard more hooves, thumping into sand and coming in her direction.

'Oh, what now?' she asked and climbed over a root so that she could hide. In the shadow of the rowan tree she was well hidden and was able to see over the slope of the hill and down to the beach where a beautiful black horse without a rider thundered towards her. Foam was at the gelding's mouth and Alice could tell that he was terrified. Without thinking she began to clamber out from behind the tree with the aim of scaling the cliff and soothing the wayward horse. Before she could move Alice saw Raymond in the distance as he detached himself from the crew of *Waverider* and began jogging down the beach towards her. She ducked back amongst the shadows to watch him. The skirts of his bright surcoat splayed out as Raymond trotted up the beach and Alice could see that he was scaring the horse even further.

'Idiot,' she whispered. Alice could see that the gelding felt trapped, swinging his head and circling nervously

291

below the cliff face as he searched for a way to flee from Raymond. The horse must have been bought in the Ostman town to the north, Alice thought, and had broken free of Raymond's men when brought to shore.

Raymond, she saw, had slowed down and now walked slowly towards the gelding with his hands in the air, singing a tune which she recognised as one her mother had sung when trying to get her brother to go to sleep in their youth. He had a long length of rope over his shoulder and shoved a long stick into the sand close to the surf, tying the rope to the top and then slowly pulled the length taut as it stretched to the cliff face. The horse watched him nervously, twenty metres away at the furthest point from the sea and the Norman where the rocks formed an impassable barrier. Raymond next unbuckled his sword belt and threw his colourful surcoat across the centre of the makeshift fence. This only made the gelding toss his mane and stamp his hooves more furiously.

Alice watched intently. She had seen many warriors attempt to tame young horses when her father had ruled Abergavenny. They had always preferred to intimidate the animals with whips until they were too terrified to flee any further and finally relented to whatever their new masters required. Raymond had no whip as he ducked under the rope fence. Instead, Alice watched him do something particularly strange: he sat down on the sand with his back to the gelding and placed an apple on top of his head.

The gelding shifted uneasily in the furthest corner from Raymond, the constantly shifting sea and the terrifying fence, eying the strange behaviour of the warrior with suspicion. Alice was equally puzzled by his peculiar inactivity and for many minutes reflected on what he was doing. The gelding soon provided her with an answer as his curiosity won over his fear and, making sure to keep an eye on the Norman, he slowly circled closer. The red apple was a huge inducement while the waves tumbling onto the shore and the fence draped with his surcoat remained a major concern. However, the gelding slowly neared Raymond and then, after another long pause and flickering of ears, he reached out with grasping lips to peck the apple from his head. Retreating a few steps for fear of a trap, the gelding stopped suddenly to chew the tasty treat and continue to observe the human who acted so differently to those who had hurt him and imprisoned him on the terrifying ship. A burst of noise from *Waverider*, a little down the beach, sent the horse's ears into crazed twitches, but another apple appeared immediately on Raymond's head and without thinking the horse plodded forward to take the tasty fruit. This time, rather than bouncing away, he stood over the sitting man to eat the apple.

Alice watched as Raymond placed another apple on his head, letting his hand linger so that when the gelding inevitably reached for the fruit he was able to pat the side of the horse's face and soothe him with a few words. It was only when he started to get to his feet that the gelding spooked and shied away from him. Raymond didn't stop smiling as he quickly walked towards the horse, away from the beach to the point furthest from the sea and fence. Once there he placed another apple on his head and began waiting while the gelding began to trot anxiously around the centre of the enclosure. For many minutes the horse pondered the twin terrors of ocean and fence before moving tentatively towards the Norman warlord.

As soon as the gelding was within three paces Raymond walked away, holding the apple on his head. From her hiding place, Alice giggled as the gelding trotted after Raymond and for the next ten minutes Strongbow's captain led the horse in a merry dance around the small enclosure.

Even when Raymond walked into the surf, kicking a shower of water high in the air as he ploughed through, the horse followed behind him and, when the Norman kicked over the fence, the horse followed, stepping over the surcoat that had scared him so badly moments before. Alice watched Raymond give the horse a fourth apple, amazed at the change in the gelding's demeanour after such a short space of time. Raymond was even able to slip a leather bridle over the young horse's muzzle and then give him a large hug around the neck.

'That's okay,' Raymond spoke soothingly. 'You are a big dope, aren't you? You've made yourself all red in the face for nothing. We'll have to come up with an appropriate name for you, won't we?'

'Rufus,' said Alice before she could stop. As soon as the words left her mouth she ducked back behind the tree root for fear that down below on the beach, Raymond would have heard her.

'That's right,' Raymond continued to talk to the horse as he wound up the rope fence. 'You didn't like being stowed in a ship, did you … Rufus.'

As he said the gelding's name Alice cringed and realised that her former paramour knew that she was watching. She steeled herself and rose to her feet.

'Hello, Raymond.'

'Lady,' he replied. 'I did not see you there. Would you like to walk back to Dun Domhnall with Rufus and me?'

Her first impulse was to shake her head, offer scorn, and return to the privacy of the small cove, but Raymond did not even bother to wait for an answer and started walking away with the gelding close upon his heels.

'Hey!' Alice exclaimed and jumped out of her hiding place to follow, her coldness forgotten as she climbed down the cliff face. It was only difficult due to her skirts, but she

294

did not give up even when her feet went from beneath her fleetingly, leaving her grasping the toothed black rocks by only her fingertips. 'Raymond,' she shouted crossly as her feet touched the sand. He was some way up the beach and turned to look at her, tossing her an apple as he abruptly leapt up onto the gelding's back. Alice was shocked, not at Raymond's actions but at the speed at which the gelding calmed down and allowed the Norman captain to walk him towards her.

'He's a good horse,' he said as he rolled off Rufus's black back and to the sand, 'a big softy. Would you like a ride?' He held out his hand to her and she nodded slowly.

The horse was nervous and looked towards Raymond for direction as Alice slowly made her way to his side. The apple in her hand sealed the deal, however, and as Rufus chewed she hoisted herself onto his back. They didn't speak as they walked back, but Alice felt herself relax as Raymond led her past *Waverider* and, with some difficulty, up the steep slope to where the Norman fortifications rose out of the headland like a whale breaching green waves.

'I'm sorry I was so angry with you,' Alice told him suddenly when they were almost at the outer gate, but Raymond did not turn. 'And I wanted to thank you for saving Geoffrey and I. My cousin would have killed us, and Harry … he was not coming to save us.'

Raymond brought Rufus to a stop and turned to look at Alice of Abergavenny, a serious frown upon his face. 'You never need to thank me. You are my friend.' With that he clicked his tongue twice and led the gelding into the shadow under the wooden barbican. Alice felt the horse's skin crawl at the sight of the darkness, but without missing a step he ploughed into the depths between the fences behind his new master. It was an environment that he would never have experienced before, but Raymond's hand instinctively soothed Rufus' flank and the horse took comfort from the contact.

Alice's stare shifted from the horse to the back of Raymond's head, his short blonde lock curling slightly as if touched by heat. Like Rufus, everyone in Dun Domhnall followed him, not because they had to and not because they were being forced. They trusted him. In all the time she had been with the Young King she had never seen him inspire anyone with anything other than money and, though she had immediately been dazzled by it, she now saw in Raymond all that was missing from King Harry's character. With him she would be safe and respected. He would probably never be able to provide her brother with an army to capture Abergavenny but, if he would have her, she would try everything to make him happy until he could. However, that would have to wait for, as they passed through the inner gate and made their way past the cattle pens and into the bailey of the fort, a much-agitated Sir Hervey de Montmorency ran up to them looking even more bedraggled than ever.

'Ostmen, Raymond,' he stated, the fear obvious on his lined face, 'thousands and thousands of them.'

The Uí Dubhgain woman below him had finally stopped screaming, but Jarl Sigtrygg slapped her one last time to make sure her struggles were over. Instead she attempted to cover her breasts with what remained of her cheap woollen clothes. That annoyed Jarl Sigtrygg and the warrior wrested both her arms away from her chest and forced them above her head so that he could see her naked body. The woman whimpered and pressed her tear-soaked face into the shards of her clothing which gathered on her shoulder, but the jarl did not allow that and, with his free hand, forced her to look at him before planting a kiss on her mouth.

296

Around him his warriors killed or subdued the men who remained in the small fishing homestead at Dun Conán. Screams of anger and fear surrounded the jarl, but he did not let that interrupt his grunting efforts. A number of sheep, two goats and a slave were chivvied past him by two of his crewmen and one greedily eyed the woman under Jarl Sigtrygg before grabbing the slave and forcing her behind the empty cattle pen on her knees. The jarl laughed as he watched three small children who huddled together in the doorway of the wattle house and watched him assault their naked mother.

'Those three,' he shouted as he stood up and hoisted his hose back around his middle, fixing them in place with his long leather belt. 'And this one,' he said as he placed his big foot on their naked mother's stomach. The woman whimpered and flinched as he touched her. 'They'll fetch a pretty price in Dubhlinn despite her being *an ugly whore*.' He said the last three words in harsh Irish so that the woman could understand, a huge smile beaming from behind his braided red beard. The woman sobbed again and rolled onto her shoulder, flapping her hand in the direction of her dead husband. Jarl Sigtrygg laughed at her anguish and grabbed his battle-axe which was buried in the man's belly. The husband's spilled innards were almost dry as they lay beside him, but more blood escaped from the fissure as the weapon was pulled free.

'Is there time for all of us to have a go?' Amlaith, his ship-master, asked the jarl as he pulled the part-naked and bruised mother to her feet and shook her into silence.

'We'll see,' Jarl Sigtrygg replied as he stuck his head inside the door, his large hand gripping the wooden lintel, and looked around the tumbledown building. 'Ragnall will be here by nightfall. Then we cross the river and make for the foreigner's fort.' He flapped a hand southwards over the muddy estuary which flowed across the wooded landscape like a battle scar rent by a giant of old. Twenty ships had left Veðrarfjord on the morning before under Jarl Sigtrygg's command. It had been a long haul at the oar, with the summer sun blazing down upon the necks of his crew, but his army had arrived safely and their vessels now filled the sandy inlet on the western side of the peninsula. Six hundred seaborne warriors stared across the stream at the edge of the forest beyond which stood the den of their enemy.

By the end of the day another two and a half thousand would join them under Ragnall's white raven standard though, of those warriors, Jarl Sigtrygg only valued the few from Veðrarfjord who accompanied the konungr. The remainder were savage Gaels under Donnchadh Ua Riagháin and Máel Sechlainn Ua Fhaolain, useless in the jarl's opinion. But what did that matter? Ragnall's information said that there could be as few as three hundred warriors at the promontory fort at Dun Domhnall, defended by a measly earth and timber wall.

'Four more miles,' Jarl Sigtrygg told his ship-master, 'and then we'll have them all in chains.' His eyes flashed and he bared his porcine teeth. 'Except for Raymond de Carew,' he added, his left hand massaging the bridge of his broken nose. He had set the bone himself and it remained misshapen and bent upwards like a snout. 'Him, I will rip and burn.' The jarl looked down at his longship, *River-Wolf*, which nestled amongst the sand and reeds at the riverside, and towards which the living inhabitants of Dun Conán would be herded like cattle. 'Make sure those slaves are not damaged,' he ordered Amlaith. 'We'll make for Dubhlinn straight after we get our share of the slaves from the fort and get them sold there.'

'Not Veðrarfjord?'

'The other jarls will all head straight home with their takings. They'll flood the market and lower the asking price. We'll head north and make a killing from the foreigners.'

Amlaith's response was interrupted by the Uí Dubhgain mother who made one last, desperate appeal to Jarl Sigtrygg on the behalf of her children. 'Please, great lord,' she cried in her native tongue, still clutching her tattered clothes to her chest to hide her nakedness, 'do not rob my children of their lives.'

The jarl shook his head in disbelief at the stupidity of the woman. 'I'm not going to kill them,' he told her. 'I'm going to sell them.' He couldn't understand her grumbles. The children's lives as slaves would hardly be any different to those they would have had on the miserable farm. With another shake of his head he turned away from her screams and walked back towards the wattle and mud-built hovel. The walls stank in the heat, but Jarl Sigtrygg reckoned that it would serve as a shelter for one night while he prepared for battle. Inside, the straw bedding seemed fresh and a small dung fire already burned in the middle of the circular room. Closer investigation revealed a thin stew of vegetables and roots in a pot, bubbling away. He rubbed his hands together, thanking his ship's black cat for good fortune. Crouching down beside the pot, Jarl Sigtrygg pulled his cache of weapons from his belt and propped them against the wooden bed area which took up one wall. His chainmail he kept wrapped around his body. Too often he had heard tales of his kinsmen stabbed in their sleep when they believed themselves safe from the vengeful knives of the Gael. He found a heel of baked oatcake in his robes and plunged it into the heart of the stew.

'It'll do,' he said as he gobbled down as much as he could soak up. His hunger somewhat sated, Jarl Sigtrygg investigated what little remained of the woman's hovel. He cast aside a large wattle panel which would have hidden the sleeping pallet of the parents from the children, but there was little of value other than a pair of leather sabatons and some cheap woollen clothes. To make sure there was nothing of worth hidden, Jarl Sigtrygg kicked the loose straw away from the corner of the room and used his long dagger to scrape away a few inches of earth, snorting with the effort of shifting the dry dirt.

'Hunting for truffles, pig?' asked a voice behind him.

Jarl Sigtrygg turned angrily with his dagger ready to stab whoever had spoken. Only a man sick of life insulted Sigtrygg, jarl and captain of *River-Wolf*. Fear stayed his hand and the death strike did not fall. The man who had spoken was the one man who truly terrified him: Ragnall Mac Giolla Mhuire, Konungr of Veðrarfjord. His father.

'Lord?' he stumbled and lowered his knife. 'I wasn't expecting you to arrive until nightfall.' As usual the Konungr of Veðrarfjord's presence made an uneasy feeling rise in Jarl Sigtrygg's chest. His father was old and thin, bald and weak of arm, but he did not blink as he gazed at his son. Ragnall's mouth, behind a wispy grey beard, was like that of a frog, stretched and reedy, and his voice was high pitched. He was demon-born, Jarl Sigtrygg was sure, and he knew secrets about him that no man could know. Half the time, he felt his body urging him to cut Ragnall's throat; he didn't know why he wanted to do it to his father, or why his mind was so scared to see it through, but again he felt the murderous pull of the dagger in his right hand.

'We left the Gael to make their own way through the forests,' Ragnall told him as he plunged a large wooden spoon into the depths of the stew and withdrew it, 'so we made good time.' He sniffed the food without taking his eyes from Jarl Sigtrygg and dropped the spoon on the floor of the shelter when the aroma disappointed. 'Everything is as it should be with the fleet?'

Jarl Sigtrygg nodded. 'I was going to send out scouts –'

A gnarled hand silenced him. 'The Ui Fhaolain will send some men south. They are better suited to the work. If they spring a trap they can be easily replaced. You killed all the inhabitants of Dun Conán?'

'No,' Jarl Sigtrygg replied. 'We took them for slaves?' He cursed himself for squeaking a question.

The konungr did not speak for many seconds, instead warming his long, thin hands by the fire. It was summer and it was hot, yet Ragnall seemed cold.

'You will release your slaves,' his father stated. 'There will be plenty when we take Dun Domhnall and the ones you took here will only slow you down.'

'There will be no women or children in the foreigner's fortress,' Jarl Sigtrygg grumbled as two men entered the house, longhaired Gaels wrapped in saffron robes with gold at their wrists and neck. Both were kings of a sort, Jarl Sigtrygg knew; Donnchadh Ua Riagháin ruled the Uí Drona, far to the north, while Máel Sechlainn Ua Fhaolain was chief of the Déisi, a powerful tribe from the lands beyond Veðrarfjord. Both were moustachioed and wrapped in the mustard-yellow robes which the Gaelic princelings preferred.

'My friends,' Ragnall greeted the two men with a lift of his chin. 'Your scouts have returned?'

'My tánaiste led them through the forest and crossed three streams before they came to the walls of Dun Domhnall,' the younger man, who Jarl Sigtrygg recognised as the Uí Fhaolain chieftain, confirmed. 'You were correct about the wall, though the foreigner's ship has gone from the beach.'

'Then they are trapped,' Jarl Sigtrygg interrupted. 'We

should take our ships and land them on the beach, then assault the walls. We will be victorious by nightfall tomorrow!' *And with my need for slaves and vengeance sated*, he thought.

'Two of my people were killed by their archers,' the grey-haired Donnchadh Ua Riagháin warned Ragnall as he too investigated the pot in the middle of the room. 'They were two hundred paces from those who shot them. More would've died had they not retreated.'

Jarl Sigtrygg snorted and struck himself in the middle of his chainmailed chest. 'We men of Veðrarfjord are harder to kill than you Vestmen. Armour and a good shield will keep you alive from archers if you Gael had the sense to carry them.'

Ragnall of Veðrarfjord swapped a knowing glance with Donnchadh and Máel Sechlainn before slowly turning to stare at his son. He watched him until Jarl Sigtrygg's smile disappeared. 'If we land our ships on the shore they will have us at their mercy until we get our warriors off the beach,' he told him, his voice full of scorn. 'Armour or no, they will perish under the arrow storm. *My* ships will remain here at Dun Conán. The army will march to Dun Domhnall.'

Jarl Sigtrygg scowled. He hated the thought of going to war without his beloved *River-Wolf*. She, rather than the city of Veðrarfjord, was his real home; she was safety, his rallying point when all else had failed him. That Ragnall wanted him to leave his ship at Dun Conán infuriated him, but he knew better than to put up a fight. 'And what of Trygve of Cluainmín?' he asked instead. 'He helped our enemy. He helps them still.'

The konungr nodded his head. 'First, we shall deal with Dun Domhnall and then we will march on Trygve.' Ragnall sat down on the floor next to the fire, studying Jarl

302

Sigtrygg. 'You make enemies too easily, boy,' he said. 'My friends,' he raised an eyebrow towards the two Gaelic kings, 'would like nothing better than to string you up. Máel Sechlainn says that you raided his lands over the last two summers, stole women and cattle.'

'I...'

Ragnall held up his hand. 'Save it. As long as you serve me well, you are safe from his retribution.' The konungr took a long slug of water from a skin and studied his son. 'As long as you are truthful to me. So where is it?'

Jarl Sigtrygg shook his head in confusion at the sudden question. 'Where is what?'

'Don't play me for a fool, boy. You will tell me where Trygve has his silver mine.'

'What silver mine?'

Ragnall bit his lip and produced a long dagger from the scabbard at his side. 'I won't be toyed with, Sigtrygg.' He began whittling a stick into a point. 'I know that two of your crewmen were killed, that you were thrown out of Cluainmín, and that you were accused of theft -'

'And murdering his son,' Jarl Sigtrygg shook his head. 'And I didn't do that either. The Norman lied -'

'You whoreson,' exclaimed Ragnall, casting the wooden stick aside and climbing to his feet. 'You are a liar,' he accused, the whites of his eyes huge as he started forwards at Jarl Sigtrygg. 'You want the mine for yourself! I know your secrets, boy. Do you remember that? And do you think I would hesitate to give you to Trygve? Or let Máel Sechlainn have you to kill?' He pointed a finger at the moustachioed Gael. 'I want that silver mine.'

The jarl felt the anger rise in his chest. 'I know of no mine, silver or otherwise. All I know is that two of my men were killed in the forest and that Raymond de Carew spoke against me.' He had never reacted well to accusations and

303

he took a step forward, hoping to dominate his father with his size.

The Konungr of Veðrarfjord, though old, was not daunted by anyone. 'You won't tell me where it is?'

'I don't know where it is.'

Ragnall snorted in repugnance. 'After everything I have done for you? Well, you can think about your future while you are watching over our ships, boy.'

'What do you mean?' the jarl asked suspiciously.

'My army will march to Dun Domhnall tomorrow at first light, but you will remain here at Dun Conán.' Ragnall stared at Jarl Sigtrygg, daring him to argue. Behind him, the jarl watched the door of the hovel open. A number of warriors entered led by Jarls Gufraid and Sigtrygg Fionn, his father's closest cronies.

'There will be no slaves and no booty at Dun Conán for you. Your name will be remembered in no songs,' Ragnall told him. 'For you, there shall be no glory. So are you still sure you don't want to tell me where Trygve has his mine?'

Jarl Sigtrygg looked over his shoulder to where his weapons still lay. He then glanced at his father's bodyguard, men loyal only to the Konungr of Veðrarfjord. 'I have told you that I don't know anything about any mine. I did not know it even existed until you spoke of it.'

The konungr grimaced. 'Then why don't you go and check on your ships, harbour-master,' Ragnall told him, waving a hand in the direction of the door, leaving Jarl Sigtrygg in no doubt that he was to exit the hovel. He turned his back on his son and began conversing with the two Gaelic chieftains. 'And Sigtrygg,' Ragnall added as the jarl forced his way past the three bodyguards, 'send in my slave with some food. There's a good lad.'

Furious, Jarl Sigtrygg stormed from the room. His anger raged as he walked away, the laughter of the three kings following in his wake. He ground his teeth as he thought of ever more fanciful and violent ways to kill his father. Dun Conán was now filled with Ragnall's army and little fires sent lines of smoke towards the darkening sky as the army set camp between the coast and the forests of Siol Bhroin. Below the army, on the beach, twenty longships and their crews milled around, distributing food, testing weapons and readying armour for battle. The stench of so many humans in such a confined area annoyed the jarl's nostrils and he turned away from his countrymen and their allies, heading south towards the river which guarded the settlement's back. There, he had beached *River-Wolf*, and he would find his crew and his few meagre takings from Dun Conán.

The thought of being left behind to guard the ships disgusted him. He had a higher calling at Dun Domhnall and nothing could stop him from seeking vengeance on the man who had insulted him in the Cluainmín slave market; the fat fool who had spoken lies against him at Trygve's Þing. The blood-feud could not be set aside, could not be forgotten, not by a man such as he. A warrior was nothing without reputation and Jarl Sigtrygg would not let Raymond de Carew's slurs affect his standing amongst his people.

'Amlaith!' he shouted for his ship-master as he neared his beautiful, sleek ship. The experienced sailor appeared from beneath her old sail which was strung from the rail to make a rudimentary shelter.

'My jarl?' the seafarer asked as he struggled out from beneath the sail, a mug of cloudy beer in his hand.

'We are leaving on the next tide. Get everything ready.'

'The next tide?' Amlaith asked. 'But it is almost nightfall.'

'We are leaving,' Jarl Sigtrygg insisted.

'What about the battle?'

305

Jarl Sigtrygg spat on the beach in answer. 'Get us ready to sail – do it quietly and quickly,' he asserted, turning away from Amlaith to look up at the army, perched above the dunes. Ragnall was the only man who Jarl Sigtrygg feared, and he could feel the apprehension seep into his chest again. He swallowed it down like a shard of tough meat. Ragnall could find another man to look after his fleet while he went to war.

For his son was a jarl, not a harbour-master.

Sigtrygg was a Vikingr.

Chapter Eleven

With one charge they killed twelve men. Asclettin FitzEustace led them, his huge frame terrifying as the Normans burst around the shoulder of the wooded hillock to fall upon the few Gaels who had already alighted upon the riverbank. They were only ten in number, but the line of horsemen was unstoppable as they followed Asclettin into the brawl. His billowing crimson and gold surcoat snapped like a whip as he carved his way through the small company, stabbing left and right with a heavy lance. At his back came squat Thurstin Hore, punching downwards with his spear, and following him was steady Bertram d'Alton, Denis d'Auton with his famously long reach, and the rest of the conrois. Raymond came last, standing tall in his stirrups, to pierce the shoulder of his target.

Those Gaels still in the midst of the river, or those on the far bank, could only watch impotently as the whooping Normans flashed past, all colour and size and steel, and disappeared into the blinding morning sun. One man quickly stooped into the water and found a smooth rock, but by the time he had armed his sling the foreigners had vanished into the foliage with only the thunder of their horses and the peal of victorious acclaim remaining to mock them. First blood had been drawn by the invaders.

'What are you waiting for?' King Máel Sechlainn shouted at the men in the stream. 'Get moving forward and find out if there are more of them out there! Slingers,' he then demanded of another group, 'get ready to batter them if they come back.' Behind him, his whole army had stalled and he knew from experience that those in the rear would have no idea of what was happening at the front of the column. If they tarried for too long the kern would sit down, fall asleep or begin eating, and it would be hours before the army would be on the move again.

'Get bloody moving, you lot,' he ordered again with a finger settled on the scouts in the water.

The infantry swapped nervous glances at their king's command, but edged forward again as they stole uneasy glances at the riverbank and raised their javelins above their shoulders. The re-emergence of drumming horse hooves and breaking foliage stopped the men dead in their tracks.

'They are coming back,' one exclaimed and began backtracking into the deepest part of the stream where he fell over, losing his grip on his wicker and hide shield as he plunged into the knee-high water. As the sound from the horsemen grew louder, more warriors began to flee back to the safety of the shore and into the line of slingers, disrupting them as they swung their weapons around their heads.

The ten Normans did not press home another attack. Instead they trotted past in formation, their banners unfurled and whipping like fishes' tails above their grey armour and bright surcoats. They merely looked down on the enemy with a haughty disregard as they passed by.

'Get throwing!' Máel Sechlainn shouted at his slingers, but their bombardment started only as the last man disappeared out of range and the thump of rocks striking sodden earth proved to be a meek echo underneath the rumble of the warhorses' hooves.

It wasn't his army that was supposed to be under attack, Máel Sechlainn thought grimly. He was supposed to be facing a beaten enemy, puny in number and hidden behind little more than a turf and timber wall. What the foreigners' commander believed he could achieve by sending so few men against them, he did not know. All his enemy had accomplished was to delay their inevitable defeat. He turned to look at the vast army behind him. Some at the front had kept their feet and weapons ready, but most, further back from the small action, had sat down to talk and rest as he had feared. His army had stopped and he knew that behind them so would the forces of the Uí Drona and the Ostmen of Veðrarfjord.

'What now?' Máel Sechlainn's tánaiste demanded as he joined his king at the riverbank. 'The tide will turn soon and this stream will be impassable. We need to get across this one and the one after that as soon as possible.'

Máel Sechlainn had little love for his late cousin's son, Toirdelbach, but the younger man had been able to raise a band of warriors almost as big as his own and so had the right to air his opinions.

'What do you suggest?' Máel Sechlainn asked of the taoiseach from the high hills above his own tribal territory.

'Send two hundred across as one,' Toirdelbach advised, 'and then get the slingers and javelin men in the water. If the foreigners come back they'll be ready for them.'

Máel Sechlainn nodded in agreement. 'You can lead them,' he told Toirdelbach, 'since you obviously know what to do.' He couldn't keep his voice free of derision, but his tánaiste seemed not to notice as he began issuing orders to the army and then plunged into the small stream with his warriors at his back. Máel Sechlainn held his breath as Toirdelbach began climbing the bank on the far side. He was sure that the horsemen would again appear to press home their advantage, and he urged them to come for ten

309

horsemen could not defeat a force of two hundred! That, he was sure, was impossible.

Fifty slingers, up to their waists in water, formed the path between which the detachment of spearmen forded the river and they began to slowly swing their weapons around in an arc as Toirdelbach and his derb-fine prowled around on the riverbank. The slingers were ready to unleash a barrage of fist-sized rocks should the enemy reappear. However, there was no pulse of hooves and soon all two hundred of Toirdelbach's force was on the bank, their javelins poised to strike and their shields held high.

'It is all clear,' Toirdelbach soon shouted back across the stream to his cousin. 'The foreigners have gone. You can bring the rest across.'

Máel Sechlainn frowned as he wrapped his colourful cloak around his arm and stepped off the bank and into the stream. The water reached to his knees to soak his long mustard shirt and he grimaced at the cold. He wondered why the foreigners had given up so easily. With a hundred warriors he might have held the ford for many days against almost any foe. Máel Sechlainn wanted to believe that it was rank amateurism of his enemy, but something told him that he should be careful to not underestimate the foreigners from across the sea.

'Get the army moving again,' King Máel Sechlainn instructed his derb-fine who, as was their station, were at his heels. As they disappeared to affect his orders, their king began wading towards the opposite bank, the cold sandy water splashing up to his middle. Toirdelbach was waiting for him at the riverbank but offered no assistance to help his king from the stream.

'Which way did they go?' the king demanded of his tánaiste.

'South,' the younger man stated, flapping a hand towards where the sun hung high in the sky.

'Then that is our way too.'

'I thought you said we would be fighting Danes!' Asclettin called to his captain as the Norman conrois trotted southwards through the trees. It was hot and underneath their chainmail all the men felt beads of sweat flow beneath their gambesons, trickling down their spines even after a short period of fighting. 'Not that I'm complaining. These Irish are easier to kill than Ostmen.'

Raymond did not share in Asclettin's mirth. Instead he laid his hand on Dreigiau's sweaty shoulder and patted him fondly. The courser was aware of every shift of his rider's weight and his ears buzzed with activity as Raymond whispered his appreciation for the animal's work that day. He snorted excitedly. After his conrois had attacked the enemy, Raymond had led them down the length of the river as it cut a deep, winding rent inland across the Siol Bhroin peninsula. It was only then, as he had counted the warriors in the enemy column on the opposite bank that he had understood the predicament in which his small army found themselves. He had tallied at least two thousand in the enemy host, but he knew that they could easily have the same again hidden from his eyes. Sir Hervey had been correct. Thousands opposed them.

The Norman captain leant forward and, with a click of the tongue, urged Dreigiau into another canter. He was mindful of the conrois mirroring his movement as he led the way to the next stream which blocked the enemy's path south to Dun Domhnall. The trees, bluebells and nettles were a blur, not because of the speed at which Raymond passed, but due to the thoughts that swept through his head and dulled his mind to his

311

surroundings. His army was outnumbered by at least twenty to one! The enormity of that figure took some time to settle in Raymond's mind. Only at his most pessimistic had he ever believed that he would face such a force, and already he wondered if he could possibly defend Dun Domhnall against them. His mind pictured the horde of savage, half-naked Irish climbing the fort's walls, an Ostman shieldwall coming up behind, and Alice of Abergavenny with tears upon her face.

It was little over a mile to the next creek and his conrois covered the distance in minutes, emerging from the wood with the sound of the sea to their left. The little village had been deserted since Borard and Dafydd FitzHywel had raided it for cattle a few days after his army's arrival in Ireland. The Normans and Welshmen had killed only those who had put up a fight, but the locals had decided to take their remaining possessions and head north to another settlement further up the coast. Raymond had left a small force of ten archers to take up residence in the abandoned homestead and guard the crossing. The Welshmen had started to build a small palisade around the biggest house, knocking down the others for timber, but it was as yet incomplete and in truth was little more than protection against the wolves which roamed the peninsula by night. As they rode downhill towards the nameless creek, Raymond and his conrois were greeted by Fionntán and the archers' commander.

'Captain,' Caradog hailed him as he drew near. The tall archer had his bow strung and a knapsack at his hip containing everything he owned. Raymond guessed that all the men on the picquet line were ready to retreat at the first provocation.

'What news?' Fionntán asked without offering a welcome.

312

Raymond leapt down from Dreigiau's back. 'We gave them a bloody nose at the crossing, but at best we only slowed them down.'

'And what else did you think you would accomplish?' he asked with an air of annoyance. 'So how many do they have?'

'At least two thousand, probably twice that,' Raymond admitted. 'From what I saw, they were mostly Gael, but I saw a large body of armoured Ostmen in the column across the river.'

Caradog clenched his jaw determinedly. 'They'll be here soon?'

'By midday, if not before.' His hand still on Dreigiau's bridle, Raymond switched his gaze towards the wide creek, a good bow shot in breadth, which streaked between the village and Dun Domhnall which was a mile distant and hidden behind a low ridge. He had to shield his eyes from the sun, but the causeway of blackened wooden trunks was clearly visible now as it had been when Raymond and his conrois had crossed a little after sunrise that morning. The ancient laneway of logs was sturdy enough in the squelching mud, and allowed two men abreast to cross the creek when the tide was at its lowest.

'How long until high tide?' the captain asked.

Fionntán looked at the height of the sun and then at the concourse where muddy puddles peppered the creek either side of the wooden causeway. 'Six hours,' he answered with certainty.

'It will be impassable then,' Caradog, who had been stationed at the village for many days, confirmed.

'Here at least it will be,' Fionntán corrected. 'But it narrows to barely a stream two miles behind that hill.' His hand fluttered towards the west where an assembly of seagulls silently spun in the air above a group of trees, taller

313

than those around them.

Raymond nodded his head. 'So the question remains: do we hold our ground and hope that Dun Domhnall's walls will keep them back, or do we evacuate across the bay in *Waverider*?'

Caradog looked at his feet rather than answer while Fionntán shrugged. 'We can fight them here or we will face them there at Banabh. It makes little difference …'

A warning shout from the other side of the village made all three men turn and interrupted Fionntán's considerations. Up the road an archer appeared and gesticulated wildly towards the woods to the north. The man was too distance for his words to reach the trio, but all three understood his meaning for, over the brow of the knoll, the rumble of cow-skin drums overcame the call of gulls.

The enemy were almost upon them.

'Get across the causeway,' Raymond ordered, 'and get ready to defend the crossing.'

Alice of Abergavenny stood on the stone battlements of the ancient Celtic fort and listened as the noise of livestock arose in the north. Below her the animals in the Normans' cattle pens stirred and twitched and moaned as they heard the distant baying of their kind in the distance. Their calls peppered the constant din of war drums and horns as the enemy approached the Norman bridgehead.

She had been awoken before dawn by the sound of horsemen leaving the fort and had made it up onto the higher ground above the beach in time to see Raymond leading his small conrois out of Dun Domhnall and northwards. Their torches had produced only enough light for her to identify their bearers. It was from the north that Sir Hervey had reported seeing the army of Ostmen, though

314

Alice could not imagine what Raymond thought ten could do against an army as large as that which Hervey had testified was approaching. She prayed that nothing had befallen her protector and hugged her shoulders against the morning breeze which gusted and hauled at her clothes from the south-west.

'Sister,' Geoffrey greeted her nervously as he clambered onto the allure. 'William de Vale told me that there are ten thousand warriors coming for us.' He giggled nervously. 'That can't be true. Can it? If it was, Raymond would get everyone back in *Waverider* and take us back to Wales.' He flapped at hand at the ship which had returned from Banabh an hour before and had again been beached below the cliffs. 'Wouldn't he, Alice? Of course he would,' he replied to his own question, even if his answer lacked conviction. Alice said nothing as she watched the horizon and listened to the sounds of their approaching drums.

'He must think that he can negotiate with them,' chanced Geoffrey.

Alice shook her head slowly. 'I don't know what he plans to do. I'm simply glad he didn't take you with him today.'

'I'm his esquire,' Geoffrey told her gruffly. 'I should be at his side when he goes into battle. Did you ask him to leave me behind?'

'Of course not,' Alice snapped. 'Of course not,' she repeated in a friendlier tone. 'He left before I had risen and I had not spoken to him since Sir Hervey brought news of the enemy. He was too busy with preparations.'

Geoffrey grunted disbelievingly. 'Well, he won't leave me behind again.'

She shook her head at his obstinacy and worried for her brother's safety. Geoffrey did not seem to care about his claim to Abergavenny any longer – it had been some time

315

since he had even mentioned the Welsh castle, or his enmity towards those who had taken their inheritance. He had replaced it with talk of horses and swords, armour and lances, Raymond, castles and battle splendour. Her brother did not seem to understand that by allying himself to Raymond he was not fighting for his own benefit, but for Strongbow's cause, and that none of his efforts on that earl's behalf would garner any influence with King Henry. Strongbow was out of favour with the king and Raymond was little better than a brigand, which meant that Alice was as far from getting back her home as ever. Despite her renewed friendship towards Raymond, she cursed the luck that had led to Prince Harry abandoning her, the unfairness of the world, and her brother for not sharing her vision to take back Abergavenny.

'I want you to promise me that you will not put yourself in danger, Geoffrey.' Alice turned away from the sparkling inlet to look at her brother. 'I know you wish to prove yourself, but it would be foolish to throw your life away trying to show your valour to Raymond.'

Geoffrey looked angrily at his sister. 'He has taught me to fight well,' he replied, 'and everyone will be needed to do their part if the enemy has the numbers that William de Vale says they do.'

Alice was no longer looking at her brother. Her hand was outstretched and her eyes wide as they looked out to sea. To the south-west a sail had appeared around the end of the peninsula.

'Ship,' she told her brother. 'Ship!' she repeated with greater urgency, jabbing her finger towards the sea. Geoffrey spun on his heel and, shading his eyes from the midday sun, he followed the direction given by his sister's hand where he soon spotted the dark hull going southwards under oar.

316

'Is it a warship?' Alice asked.

The esquire nodded his head. 'It's too long to be a merchantman, too low in the water,' he told her, though how he could tell at this distance, Alice could not comprehend. She could barely see the dark hull and the dipping oars as they rhythmically drew the ship southwards. In fact to her eyes it looked like the warship could not possibly be afloat, so low was she in the water.

'If you were going to attack Dun Domhnall and you had a fleet of ships,' she chanced, 'surely you wouldn't only send an army to attack from the north.' She looked her brother deep in the eye. 'You'd also send warriors by sea and surround the fort from all sides?' She knew from her fireside conversations with Fionntán that the fortress-city of Veðrarfjord was up a river to the west, much like Cluainmín which was found at the top of the estuary to the east, and so she assumed that any war vessel coming around the western cape would be an enemy.

Geoffrey bit his lip nervously. 'Do you think...' he stopped to gather his thoughts. 'Do you think that they could be the first ship in an enemy fleet?'

Alice nodded her head, deliberately slowly.

'Then we better tell someone?'

'We should.'

Geoffrey offered his hand to his sister and, with another glance at the ship in the distance, she hitched her maroon skirts in her left and took it in her right. Together they ran through the citadel's gate towards the main wall. Her linen headscarf dropped across her shoulders as they sprinted, but Alice did not stop to fix it. She was suddenly reminded of their flight from the Benedictine Priory at Abergavenny a few short months before. Back then, her heart had fluttered with excitement as she had led Geoffrey through the priory's cloister garth. As they dashed towards the

317

unlocked door by the buttery, she had attempted to convince him of her plans to take back Abergavenny from their cousin. The priest had been waiting for them outside the priory's walls and on horseback they had fled along the course of the River Wysg and into Wentwood. That was where William de Braose had discovered them. Had Raymond not stumbled upon them and set their captor to flight, she wondered what would have happened. Would they already be dead? Or would they have been forced back into their respective Holy Orders? All that she knew was that she would never have found herself on the strange shores of Ireland with an enemy host bearing down upon them.

Unlike their flight from Abergavenny, it was Geoffrey who now led the way through the broiling bailey of Dun Domhnall. Panic was palpable amongst Raymond's tiny army and it was understandable, Alice thought, considering the rumours that abounded. All had heard the call of cattle and the bang of drums. Everyone knew what it meant.

'Sir Hervey?' Geoffrey shouted as they arrived at the inner gates. Warriors ran hither and thither to prepare the fort for warfare. 'Sir Hervey?' he tried again, dropping Alice's hand to cup the sides of his mouth. Everyone ignored the youngster. Two men carrying bundles of arrows argued with a Welsh archer about the best place to store them. Another stepped between the warring trio to stop them from coming to blows. On the outer walls, pages and esquires distributed heavy rocks in preparation for an assault. They worked quickly with little care and each impact of stone on wooden walkway earned a whinny, squawk or mew from the animals that milled around the crowded pen and nearby in the bailey.

'Where could he be?' Geoffrey asked his sister as he dashed away from her to search along the fighting step

318

upon the inner wall. 'Sir Hervey?' he called again, scaring some chickens to flight.

'He has probably high-tailed it to Banabh,' Alice chanced, though her brother was too far away to hear. It was then that she spotted the knight in the distance upon the outer wall. His profile was unmistakable with his stooped back, grizzled chin, and the long, lank hair which grew from his balding head. 'There he is,' Alice shouted to her brother. 'I see him on the barbican.'

His search of the inner wall complete, Geoffrey ran back to where his sister stood, a little inside the gate, and stared between the double embattlements to where Alice had indicated.

'You're right!' He took off down the dark tunnel between the walls, nimbly dodging warriors and obstructions while scattering wood chips from the pathway beneath his feet. Alice followed more slowly, aware again of the eyes of men upon her. By the time she arrived at the barbican, Sir Hervey and his two ragged liegemen were engrossed in an argument with Geoffrey which she could hear as she climbed the ladder.

'What about the men who rode out this morning with Raymond?' Geoffrey demanded of Sir Hervey. Alice had never seen him so forceful and was momentarily unsure if she had heard correctly. Gone, it seemed, was the boy who had not wanted to leave the priory at Abergavenny, the boy reluctant to press his claim as lord and landowner. Gone was the nervous teenager who had quaked before Strongbow in the hall of Striguil. Instead there was Raymond's esquire, determined, defiant and protective of his master. She reached the top of the wooden structure, but was disregarded by the four quarrelling men.

'How do we know if they are still alive,' Sir Hervey wheezed indignantly. 'That idiot Raymond took ten men to

319

fight ten thousand!' The knight turned away from Geoffrey to look back over the sea at the Ostman vessel. 'And now you tell me that there is a fleet on the way to attack us? You think that I will simply sit here and allow us to be wiped out?'

Geoffrey scowled and snorted indignantly. 'We should wait for Raymond to return. The tide is against anyone coming from the west,' he said. 'We still have time.'

Alice wondered what had gone between her brother and Sir Hervey, and what the Frenchman had said to so anger Geoffrey.

'She has the wind behind her,' one of Hervey's ragged companions told his master without acknowledging Geoffrey's comment. 'Once they get the sail up it'll only take them an hour to make land.' He nodded towards the beach to the west of the Norman fort and closer to the Ostman ship.

'We could make a shield wall at the top of the path from the beach,' Geoffrey intervened desperately. 'We could hold them until Raymond gets back.'

'Shut your mouth, boy,' Sir Hervey hissed and shook his head. 'God alone knows where Raymond is, or if he will even return.' For his part, Sir Hervey looked distressed by the sight of the ship and he continued to stare at her, his lined face screwed up as the sun beat down upon him. 'We cannot hold Dun Domhnall,' he said quietly.

Geoffrey took a deep breath as if he was again about to argue, but Alice took him by the shoulder and pulled him away towards the ladder. Her brother continued complaining as they descended to the ground from the raised wooden platform.

'What did he say?' Alice demanded.

Geoffrey shook his head grouchily. 'That a boy like me knows nothing of tactics…'

320

'No!' Alice snapped. 'What does he plan to do before Raymond returns?'

'He wants to take *Waverider* and evacuate to Banabh Island.' Geoffrey nodded his chin towards the east, beyond the wall and across the estuary.

Alice was taken aback. 'He wants to leave Raymond behind?'

'He wants to leave all our supplies – the horses, the cattle – everything!' Geoffrey threw his hands out from his sides in exasperation. 'He's going to abandon all of it,' he exclaimed.

The siblings had reached the inner gate and Alice took in the view of the bailey as she emerged from the shadows between the walls: to her left was the cattle pens and marshalsea with its roof thatched with dried reeds from the nearby estuary, and behind that was the ancient fort on the headland where she could see their quarters. She swivelled to her right to where, over the tents and rudimentary huts, she could again see the Ostman vessel. She had cleared the western cape and as Alice watched, the captain turned his stern into the wind and ordered his men to begin raising the square, yellow linen sail.

'There will be at least sixty warriors on that ship,' Geoffrey stepped past his sister and looked out to sea. 'That is nearly as many as are left in Dun Domhnall. If even one more ship follows the first, the fort will be in grave peril.'

Geoffrey sucked air between his teeth and turned to tell his sister to go up to their quarters and gather anything of value to take with her on *Waverider*. For, he considered, there was no stopping Sir Hervey's plan, and at the very least his sister would be safe from the army to the north if they crossed the estuary. However, Alice was no longer at his side. Geoffrey frantically turned in a circle to discover where his sister had gone, but she was nowhere to be seen.

'Alice?' he called and skipped back towards the battlements. He was halfway up one of the ladders when a sudden stamp of hooves made him turn.

'Out of my way,' squealed Alice as, mounted on a sorrel horse from the marshalsea, she cantered past Geoffrey and towards the inner gate. 'On, Rufus!' she exclaimed encouragingly as the horse bought in Cluainmín hesitated before the high and looming walls. 'On, Rufus,' she called again, and the horse responded, barging into the darkness.

'Alice, wait!' her brother called, but she did not turn as warriors jumped aside rather than be trampled below Rufus' hooves. Geoffrey ran after her, ignoring the insults from the men who had been forced from her path. 'Alice!' he shouted again. However, his sister was already through the outer gates and, rather than follow futilely, he quickly clambered onto the allure through the rough-hewn struts. There he watched his sister urge her horse to greater speed, his mane flapping as they headed northwards through the grassland before Dun Domhnall's walls.

'Alice!' he appealed one last time though he knew that his voice would not carry over the grassland to her ears. Yet he knew where she was headed.

She was riding to warn Raymond. She was riding north to save him.

'Loose!' Raymond shouted again as he watched the single file of armoured men finally turn and flee back towards the nameless creek's northern bank. Of the final flight of arrows only one struck home, burying itself in the thigh of an Ostman as he backtracked towards the far side. The remaining arrows splashed into the fast-deepening muddy water or clattered into the causeway, sending shivers up the wooden walkway behind the escaping warriors. Raymond's ears still rang from the sound of one arrowhead colliding with an Ostman's shield boss. The Norman captain momentarily marvelled at how such a slender object as an arrow could hit home with such great force. At his side, the ten archers had nocked the next flight, but he gave no order to shoot.

'That should do it,' he said instead and as one the archers relaxed their arms, letting the weighty draw of the bowstring gradually release. Sweat poured from the men's brows as they let the breath finally escape their lungs, and returned their arrows to the pouches by their hips. Raymond congratulated them for their efforts but the Welshmen ignored him, sharing a joke of their own, spoken so quickly that the Norman could not understand. They all laughed.

'Catch your breath and get some water into your bellies, but stay ready. If they come back you will be needed to do the same again,' Raymond told the Welshmen as he waved his dismounted milites forward into the heat of the early afternoon sun. As they passed the archers, some of Raymond's conrois nodded respectfully and joined their captain on the bank of the creek where the causeway met the southern shore.

'Get ready to link shields here,' Raymond told his warriors. 'If they come across the walkway, they will be two abreast at most, so we will be able to stop them. I'll take the right end, Bertram the left,' he ordered before calling for Dafydd to run forward onto the causeway and collect as many arrows as he could. 'We'll need every one, but don't forget that they have slingers,' he warned, 'so don't go any further than halfway across.'

Young Dafydd nodded once before scampering onto the willow and board causeway which stretched across the muddy riverbed between the two banks. Under his weight the walkway bent and squeaked and sank into the deep

323

mire. It was, Raymond guessed, already two hours past midday and he could see that, as Dafydd ran across the boards, water squirted in every direction. The tide was slowly starting to turn and he once more allowed himself to hope that he could hold the enemy army here at the causeway. Another day would allow him time to decide what he was going to do. Could Dun Domhnall's walls hold back an attack by so many foes? Or would he have to admit his failure and flee back to Wales before the might of Veðrarfjord?

He raised his eyes from the sparkling pools which peppered the muddy creek to the low, green ridge which faced him. There, the enemy waited for their chance to flood across the last barrier keeping them from attacking Dun Domhnall. Cattle calls, stomping feet and hide drums had heralded the arrival of the allied army of Gael and Ostman, but now the only thing that Raymond could hear was the rumble of many voices as they carried over the riverbed to where his small force prepared to meet them. He could see the enemy amongst the trees as they sat down in ringed groups, talking and making last minute adjustments to weaponry and armour. Those on the hillside were the men of Veðrarfjord. Even from more than a bowshot away he could identify them as Ostmen. Unlike the Gaelic tribesmen, nearly all wore helmets and most had painted circular shields. Those that had chainmail shone when the sun struck their steel rings, as did the blades of sword, spear and axe as they were sharpened by communal whetstones. Most had hardened leather coats over their clothes and in their hands were knives and axes more used to domestic chores than to war. They were many, he reasoned, but they would be unproven. Where the Irish were camping he could not discern, but from the sound of the cattle mewing, he knew that they too could be not too far away.

'Raymond!' an uneasy voice called from below him and his gaze switched swiftly from the treeline above to the riverbed. Dafydd, laden with an arm-full of arrows, was racing towards him, his feet clattering over the thin boards. Splashing water gave the miles the appearance of great speed. Beyond Dafydd, Raymond spied movement on the much-trampled bank opposite. Enemy warriors had again ventured out onto the causeway.

'Shieldwall,' Raymond exclaimed and leapt down from his vantage point upon a large stone. Seconds later Asclettin and Thurstin had joined him on the mud and pebble bank, and had linked their shields with his. The jangle of chainmail and snarls of anger from his left told him the remainder of his small company had taken their position alongside their fellows. Raymond stole a glance down the line of locked willow boards, and counted nine lances protruding from his small conrois.

'Ready,' Bertram shouted to his captain from the far end of the shield wall, indicating that he was on the extreme left of the position.

'Stay sharp,' Raymond called back and settled his eyes on the far shore. The enemy warriors had stopped to rescue the bodies of those killed during the first assault, their feet clattering on the walkway as they were dragged away. Raymond quickly counted seven dead, but it was the party standing behind them that interested him more. The glint of gold at their necks and wrists marked them out as members of the nobility.

'Archers!' Raymond shouted over his shoulder to the ten men lounging in the shade of the trees. As they gathered behind the shield wall, he momentarily considered unleashing a volley of arrows on the enemy as they worked, but quickly dismissed the deceitful notion.

Fionntán leapt up onto the rock which Raymond had vacated. His shadow stretched all the way to the river as he raised his hand to his brow to block the reflected sunlight from dazzling him.

'They want to talk,' he stated, nodding a head in the direction of the nobles. 'There are three of them ... and one is Ragnall Mac Giolla Mhuire.' He spat on the muddy bank. 'The King of bloody Veðrarfjord.'

Raymond allowed his teardrop-shaped shield to dip, and he stared over the rim along the line of the causeway to where a small group tarried by the far bank.

'They are scared of your archers and are awaiting your permission to come forward,' Fionntán told the captain. 'What do you want to do?'

'We lose nothing by being mannerly,' Raymond said and removed his spangenhelm from his head. Fionntán scowled and the Norman countered with a wide smile, tossing his lance to one of the archers before strapping his crimson and gold shield across his back.

'I don't like it,' Fionntán told him. 'They don't even have a priest with them to assure your safety.'

'*Our* safety,' Raymond corrected, and chuckled as Fionntán gave him a horrified look. 'You don't think I'm going out there by myself? It could be dangerous, and I need you to translate.'

Fionntán looked disturbed despite Raymond's grin. 'Ragnall speaks French,' he replied, his lined face giving away a hint of worry. Nevertheless, the exile from the lands of the Osraighe followed the captain onto the rickety causeway with little more than a barely audible curse.

Water and mud sloshed between the boards of the causeway as Raymond walked forward to meet the foreigners. He had not noticed the salty stink as he had led Dreigiau and his conrois across the causeway earlier in the day, but now it annoyed his nostrils like the first step into a castle marshalsea in the morning. Glancing to his right he hoped to see signs of the tide rising, but the estuary was too distant for him to discern. The landscape was filled with squawking waders and gulls which hunted amongst the slimy grasses and bare rocks for insects and molluscs. That those birds remained told Raymond that the water was frustratingly slow in rising. He stopped halfway along the causeway and drew his sword.

'What are you doing?' hissed Fionntán.

Raymond did not answer and instead, in full view of the enemy, stabbed his sword downwards into the mud and water alongside the causeway. It slid easily into the mire halfway to the cross guard.

'I'm at the bottom,' he told the Irishman and gave the sword two more pushes. 'There is no way they can cross unless it is by this path.'

'And now they know that too?' Fionntán chanced.

Raymond flexed his eyebrows and stood up, feigning study of the wet blade before wiping it on the skirts of his crimson and gold surcoat. 'And they already know that if they come in single file our archers will fill this waterway with their dead.' He stooped to recover an arrow which Dafydd had missed, tucking it in his belt by his hip. 'So they will have to go westwards, or waste another day sitting on the far side of the inlet staring at us. That will give us time to decide if we are going to stay or if we flee from Dun Domhnall.' He sheathed his sword in his scabbard, waiting for his enemy to join him in the middle of the riverbed. They were led by a thin, unpleasant-looking man whose sharp, angular features stretched his mouth across his face and gave him the look of someone who had come across something foul. The green shirt beneath his chainmail was embroidered with black crosses and, though he wore some

327

ornaments, they were not gaudy like those of his companions. The Ostman did not take his black eyes from Raymond's face as he came forward.

'It is Ragnall,' Fionntán whispered.

Behind the Konungr of Veðrarfjord were two Gaels. The younger man had the front of his head shaved closely from his brow to his ears, though his hair hung down his back almost to his leather belt. The other rattled like he was wearing mail though Raymond could see no armour amongst his thick woollen attire. He realised that the noise came from the man's wrists, neck and fingers, loaded with gold and silver rings and armlets.

'Do you recognise the other two?' he asked Fionntán.

'Neither, though the younger one has the look of the Uí Fhaolain about him,' the Irishman replied with a sniff. 'I fought with them against the Uí Meic Caille, must be fifteen years back,' he said with a hint of wistfulness. 'Good people, fond of the mead though.'

Raymond bowed deeply as the men stopped before him. 'Greetings, Lord King,' he said. 'I am –'

'We know who you are Raymond de Carew,' Ragnall of Veðrarfjord interrupted in perfect, if accented, French, 'as I know that you are aware of our names.' He looked pointedly at Fionntán over Raymond's shoulder. 'Don't think that I don't remember you, ship-master,' he told the Gael with the hint of a threat. 'I remember you very well.'

Raymond felt Fionntán's discomfort and rather than allow the Konungr of Veðrarfjord to unsettle his ally he took a different tack, mirroring Ragnall by looking around his shoulder towards the two men by his side. 'I'm afraid you have me at a disadvantage,' he said, 'for I do not know your names.' He smiled and nodded to each. The elder seemed shocked at being addressed in the overly familiar fashion, but the younger man returned his welcome.

328

Ragnall, however, turned his toady face on Raymond immediately and searched his eyes for deceit. Finding none, his strained features settled somewhat.

'He is Donnchadh Ua Riagháin of the Uí Drona,' he flashed a thumb at the older man, 'and Máel Sechlainn Ua Fhaolain of the Déisi. Now,' Ragnall stated without waiting for any further pleasantries to be forced upon him, 'we will talk of your people and what is going to become of you.'

Raymond ignored the bluster of the Ostman and turned to Fionntán. 'Day-sha?' he asked. 'O-drone-a?' The wood beneath his feet squeaked as he half-turned towards his companion.

The Irishman nodded. 'The Déisi are from the mountains west of Veðrarfjord. They pay tribute to Ragnall. The Uí Drona are from lands a long way to the north. I don't know what brings them here, but it cannot be anything good.'

'They are here because of your friend, Diarmait Mac Murchada,' Ragnall stated bluntly. 'The Uí Drona lands are between those of Diarmait and the Osraighe so no matter to which Donnchadh allies himself he will make an enemy of the other.'

'So he chooses to pay tribute to you?' Raymond chanced.

Ragnall scowled. 'My ships can be up the river to support him in less than a day. How long will it be before your master can join you from Striguil?'

That statement shocked Raymond and he felt the icy grip of fear grapple at his heart. How, he wondered, did the Konungr of Veðrarfjord know about Strongbow?

Ragnall laughed at Raymond's disquiet. 'Perhaps you thought us all witless savages? Or just ill-informed to your master's reasons for sending you to Ireland?' He sneered widely as Raymond remained mute. 'You are his cowhand,

329

yes? His chief drover, sent here to steal cattle so that when his actual army arrives it will be well provisioned before his proper warriors attempt to claim my city by siege?' Ragnall smirked as he delivered his insult.

The captain had been called many names in his life, but to have his position belittled to that usually held by a serf infuriated him. He was no cowhand. His face flushed with anger.

'I have known about Strongbow's plans for almost a year, you fool!' mocked Ragnall. 'I knew that he had met with Diarmait Mac Murchada, and what that Uí Ceinnselaig bastard offered him for his help. Should I be offended that you are all Strongbow sent to fight me?' His sneer flashed across his face again as he sniggered. 'Well, here is what I know of you, since you obviously know nothing of my people: you are done, finished,' he said bluntly. 'You have no hope of help...'

'My uncle, Robert FitzStephen...' Raymond spluttered.

'Is in the far west fighting beside the Uí Briain,' Ragnall countered quickly. 'So he will be of no help to you.' He let the implication of his statement hit home, watching Raymond squirm for several seconds, before speaking again. 'You are alone, without hope of support – not from north, south, east or west – with, what, little more than three hundred men out on your headland?' Raymond didn't correct Ragnall's inflated assessment of his army's strength. 'I have over five thousand warriors at my side – five thousand,' the konungr lied. 'Do you actually believe that your little cattle pen can withstand us?'

Again the Norman captain did not offer an answer.

'No,' the Ostman continued, his eyes narrowing in concentration. 'For you know as well as I that there can be only one outcome of this campaign. So you will abandon your little fort and scamper away in your ship.' He smirked knowingly as Raymond shifted his weight nervously between his feet. At his back the usually composed Fionntán cleared his throat and licked his dry lips, equally taken aback by the konungr's words.

'But where will you go?' Ragnall asked. 'Not back to Wales in disgrace? No, you are a cowhand with ambition. I can see it in your eyes. You wish to prove yourself. So you must be considering merely crossing the estuary?' The Ostman studied his enemy through narrowed eyes. 'At Banabh will you be in a better situation than at Dun Domhnall? No, of course not, for you know that I will be only a few days behind you.' Ragnall jabbed his gnarled finger at Raymond's heart as he made the declaration. Behind the Konungr of Veðrarfjord, the two Irishmen shared a silent joke which Raymond was sure was at his expense. Ragnall did not join in their laughter.

'Thus, you will make for Waesfjord,' he continued. 'But you will find no friends amongst my folk, only people who hate you and wish to throw off the new Norman yoke imposed by your uncle last summer. Consequently, you will be forced to go north to FitzStephen's new castle at the crossing of the River Sláine.' He paused and for the first time a smile spilled across his face, his hands stretched out as if in prayer. 'And that is where my army will find you in a week's time.' His eyes narrowed suddenly, maliciously. 'Go on,' he said, 'call me a liar, cowhand.'

Raymond blinked a number of times as he tried to come up with a response to Ragnall's outline of future events, but the glut of information, delivered with such accuracy and self-assurance, had caught him completely unawares.

'I still hold the crossing,' he said belatedly and weakly.

Ragnall was nonplussed as he turned to look at the west where a flock of seagulls had suddenly taken to flight from a large tree a mile distant. 'And you can keep it,' he said, 'for that is all you will have if you remain here. Those birds,' he flapped a hand towards the gulls, 'were scared by the three thousand warriors I sent to outflank you two hours ago. They will have already crossed the river and, within an hour or two, they will attack you from the west, and then no amount of archers will prevent you from defeat and death.'

Raymond's eyes followed the Konungr of Veðrarfjord's outstretched arm and settled on the great tree in the distance. Birds squawked and flapped in fear and made for the safety of the sea. Raymond considered that he should copy the seagulls' example. However, before he could gather his thoughts Fionntán's hand landed upon his shoulder and began to pull him back along the causeway to where the shield wall still stood.

'Come on. We need to retreat...now,' the Gael urged.

'Yes, you must,' Ragnall laughed as he followed the two men towards the southern shore. 'Run back to your Lord Strongbow, and tell him that Veðrarfjord will never fall! I will tear down every stone and piece of timber at Dun Domhnall, and claim every cow that you have gathered there. Then I will march on your friends in Cluainmín,' he exclaimed. 'I have five thousand warriors at my back and I intend to use them to sweep clean this land of every foreign soul.' His face turned sour again. 'I will take Waesfjord and then bring fire to FitzStephen's little castle while he is in the west.' He stopped to watch Raymond and Fionntán clamber from the causeway up the bank of the river to join their companions. 'There will be nowhere safe for Strongbow,' he shouted in French so that all the warriors could understand. 'You are finished, you and your cowhand captain!' He spat disdainfully on the mud of the creek before turning on his heel and walking back towards his vast army.

332

As he watched Ragnall casually stroll away, Raymond tried to think what he should do. He had expected to be assailed by his warriors' questions about what had gone between him and the enemy, but they did not come. Instead silence had overtaken his conrois. That, if anything, was more disconcerting. They were stricken dumb with fear; mute in the face of their enemy's bravado, and the irresistible force arrayed against them. To remain, they all knew, was to die. To return to Wales was to return to ignominy and pitiable poverty in the service of their pauper lord.

The whistling arrow which struck the ground behind their lines came so suddenly and so loudly that it made each warrior jump in fear.

It was Bertram d'Alton who translated the arrow's significance: 'A rider approaches from the south!'

'Holy St Maurice, what next?' Raymond asked and swapped a wary glance with Fionntán before turning to look at the top of the distant ridge where he had sent a single archer to act as a lookout. 'Get your gear together,' he ordered, 'and get ready to move out. But for now, if anyone puts a foot on that causeway I want you to put an arrow in them.' With that he began running uphill towards the picquet line.

He could not believe that the flanking force despatched by Ragnall could be so close so soon, but then again, he considered, he had never actually believed that he would face a force even a fifth of the size of the one that currently threatened his small army. His armour thumped on his shoulders as he ran, his shield rolled around on his back, and his sword clattered against his thigh. The face guard of his chainmail coif twice struck painfully against his lip and, irritated, he whipped the headgear onto his shoulders feeling the breeze on his sweaty temples immediately.

'What's happening?' Raymond breathlessly demanded as he reached the small clearing on the hill crest where the lookout waited with the company's horses.

The archer already had an arrow on his bowstring, but had not yet drawn the weapon. 'A half a mile to the south-west, coming hard at us,' he replied.

'From Dun Domhnall?'

The archer shrugged and said something in his Welsh mother tongue that Raymond did not understand. 'Could be, could be,' he added in French as he squinted at the distant figure, 'though I am almost certain that the rider has long hair.'

The captain held up a hand to shield his eyes against the power of the sun in the south. 'So he is no Norman?' Raymond's mind was a forest of questions: who was the rider thundering towards the crossing? And what could his approach herald? If he pulled back to Dun Domhnall immediately, how long would it take? And how much time would be needed to load their gear onto *Waverider*? Would the tide be full enough to do that? How many hours would it take Ragnall to get his army across the causeway once the archers retreated? And where would he even take his army once they were at sea? The problems kept coming, threatening to overcome him, and no answers readily arrived to relieve his troubled mind.

'He could be of Cymru, like me,' the Welsh archer said encouragingly of the rider when he saw the worry on Raymond's face. He grabbed the long hair at the nape of his neck and gave it a tug to emphasise his point. 'You think it is time that we head home to Gwent?'

As the clip of galloping hooves came closer, Raymond turned to the archer and nodded. 'We can't do any more good here.'

The Welshman scowled at that. 'Begging your pardon,

for I haven't been in your employ for long,' he said, 'but Seisyll ap Dyfnwal always said that there was never a trap which Raymond the Fat...' He paused wide-eyed when he realised what he had said.

His captain shook his head to make clear that he was not offended. 'Go on.'

'Well,' the archer cleared his throat, 'he said that there was never a trap that *Strongbow's captain* could bumble into that he couldn't fight his way out of too.'

'Not until now,' Raymond said sadly. A roar sounded suddenly from behind them, louder than anything he had heard that day. Both he and the Welsh archer turned sharply towards the river and stared across at hundreds of Ostmen as they battered their axes on the wooden boards of their shields, shouting curses and singing battle hymns of their fathers.

'They make a powerful lot of noise,' the archer told him.

'And that's only half of them,' Raymond admitted.

'Well, they are terrible singers,' the Welshman said dismissively as if that was the most important weapon in the hands of a warrior. He turned away from the din of battle and nodded southwards. 'That rider is coming into my range. Shall I kill him?'

Raymond again squinted into the sunshine. 'I don't recognise the rider,' he paused and concentrated his eyes upon the figure, 'but I do know the horse!' he exclaimed. 'That's Rufus, the horse I bought in Cluainmín!' he stared at the shadowy figure as he slowed to a canter. At his side, the archer drew the bow back to his ear, awaiting Raymond's command to kill.

'So they've captured the fort?' the Welshman said as his arm quivered under strain from the taught bow. The rider was a hundred paces away, an easy shot for the archer. 'And they've sent this emissary on your horse – your own horse – to tell us of their victory, while we stood here and bartered with the Ostmen like fishwives.'

Rather than answer, Raymond put his hand on the archer's arm and gently forced him to lower the weapon. The Welshman's grip on the bowstring naturally lessened as it sank towards the ground but Raymond stepped in front of him anyway so that he could see better.

'Go down to the river,' he ordered, 'and tell Fionntán to send the men up here in groups of two; milites first and then the archers.' His companion looked doubtfully at him until Raymond again ordered him to go. His eyes had not left the dark figure on the horse, and there was some murmur of recognition on his face.

As the archer ran downhill to fulfil his instructions, Raymond jogged over to where his men had hobbled their horses. He quickly removed Dreigiau's bindings and sprang onto his back, kicking him into a trot. With his thighs striking the inside of his bucket saddle, he urged the reluctant courser upwards towards the summit where the rider had again slowed, this time to a trot.

'Alice!' he called and stood in his stirrups to wave his hand above his head. 'Alice?' he exclaimed again with disbelief and confusion apparent upon his face. He was finally close enough to see the features of her face, and despite his worry his heart jumped as a smile broke across her sweaty face for him.

'I found you!' she gasped and grasped for his hand. Her smile, however, fell away quickly as she looked past Raymond to see the enemy on the far bank of the inlet, still hollering their war cries. 'O Lord, protect us,' she said.

'What are you doing here?'

It took Alice a heartbeat to compose herself, and rip her eyes from the terrifying throng to look at Raymond. 'It's Sir Hervey,' she began, 'he plans to flee Dun Domhnall in

Waverider. You must come back to the fort. Now,' she stressed, 'or he will leave you here to be killed.'

'He wouldn't…'

'There is more,' Alice interrupted and leaned across so that she could lay her left hand atop Raymond's arm. 'Geoffrey spotted an Ostman vessel coming around the headland to the south.'

'A warship?' Everywhere he looked there were enemies, even within his own camp, Raymond realised and cursed loudly. This time he did not deride himself for breaking his oath to Basilia de Quincy, for there was little hope that he would ever have the chance to apologise to her.

'I'm sorry, Alice,' he turned his head away. 'I should never have brought you here. This venture was always going to be too dangerous…'

Her hand was soft as she reached out and gently turned Raymond's face back towards her. 'We can still escape if we race back to the fort. We must go now,' she emphasised.

The captain took a breath of sea air deep into his lungs and tried to convince himself that he had no choice other than to abandon his bridgehead and make a break for home. He had to admit failure. The thump of many feet coming up the hill forced him to abandon his considerations, and he wheeled Dreigiau around to look back towards the inlet. There he saw his warriors charging towards him as if the hounds of Satan were on their heels. And well they might, for behind them was the enemy. The Ostmen had crossed the creek, forging ahead despite the deep mud underfoot, and the fastest of them were already on the southern bank, screaming profanities and awaiting their comrades to join them.

'O Lord God save us,' Alice said, her eyes to the heavens.

Breathing out slowly, Raymond reached up to his

neck and forced his much-mended coif back onto his head. 'Alice,' he said calmly while he tied the leather cords at the rear of his skull. 'I need you to ride back to the fort with all haste.' She began to make a murmur of resistance, but he quickly cut her off when he shoved his spangenhelm onto his head. 'Please, Alice! We will catch you up, but I must make sure the conrois get to their horses.' Tight-lipped, Alice cringed as she was assailed by equal part worry for Raymond, and anger at being dismissed. However, rather than argue, she glanced only once at the enemy army before nodding curtly and turning Rufus towards the sun.

'Follow soon,' she told him. And then she was gone, trotting southwards.

Raymond forced his eyes from her back and made his way over towards the twenty horses, each secured by a single hobble above the hocks. They had spread out to find better patches of grass to eat, but each quickly raised their heads when Raymond and Dreigiau approached. He rode amongst the grazing horses and encouraged them to flock behind him. It took a minute for one of the younger coursers to fall in behind him at a walk, but thereafter their natural instincts stimulated more of the animals to join the snaking column. Raymond turned in Dreigiau's saddle to check that he had enough of the horses and then led them into a tight circle at a walk. Minutes later, the first of the archers met the captain and his wandering fleet of coursers.

'Thank Christ!' the tired archer exclaimed. He was visibly shaking with the effort of climbing the hill and sweat was discernible at his brow and through his clothes.

Raymond ignored his greeting. 'Find your horse, get his hobble off and get back up to the top of the ridge,' he told the warrior. 'Keep your eyes open for the flanking force to the west.' The Welshman nodded and quickly moved down the circulating line of horses. Raymond did not wait to see if his orders were carried out for Fionntán was part of the next group to reach him.

'Ragnall is not messing about. He sent at least a hundred across the causeway at once,' he described as he gasped for breath. Sweat spat from his top lip as he spoke. 'We shot all the arrows we could and then had to fall back. We didn't lose anyone, but we couldn't slow them down.' He grabbed the bridle of his horse and began loosening the rope hobble. 'What the hell is the plan, Raymond?'

The captain grimaced as he watched the last of his men struggle uphill towards him. 'An army is to our front, a flanking force to the west, and now a shipload of Ostmen is at our backs.' Raymond ignored the horrified look on Fionntán's face as the new information hit home. 'I don't know what an Irishman would do, but there's only one place for a Norman to be when he finds himself surrounded.'

'Behind the walls of a castle?'

Raymond nodded in answer.

'And then to the sea?' Fionntán asked as he snatched the hobble from his cob's legs.

'And then to the sea,' Raymond answered resignedly. He circled his horse away from Fionntán to see that all his warriors were either already in the saddle or climbing in that direction. All had the look of hunted men on their faces.

'Let's get moving,' he raised his voice so that the whole conrois could hear his words. 'A quick canter to the top of ridge and then a trot back to Dun Domhnall,' he told them for, yet again, the race was on and to come in second on this occasion would mean certain death. He whispered a single word to Dreigiau and they were off.

＊＊＊

The wind was against the tide and so sea spray spiralled over the bows of *River-Wolf* and collided in great torrents upon the wooden deck. The watery hammer-blows were nothing to the tumult which came with every impact of the white waves upon the ship. They curled and crumbled like rolling white vellum sheets and smashed into her hull as would a sword upon a shield. *River-Wolf* punched through each one, her dragon prow riding above the bowstave-high waves, dragged onwards by the wind, before again tumbling downwards towards the belly of the ocean and then soaring towards the sky.

'It's an unruly sea,' the ship-master, Amlaith, called as he clung to the steering oar. 'She's being a right bitch.' From his vantage point in the stern, Amlaith saw a rainbow appear above Jarl Sigtrygg as the sun struck the shower of saltwater and he took that to be a good omen.

Flexing his bare arms, the jarl hung from the forestay and howled in delight, seawater dripping from his two beard braids as his cloak billowed around his shoulders. He laughed each time the battle between wave and ship was fought below him, tensing his body before each impact before gasping in delight as his beautiful ship navigated the danger.

'Maintain this heading,' Jarl Sigtrygg bellowed at Amlaith. The foreigners' fort was dead ahead, less than a league, and he could see the closer, western beach which shone invitingly in the midday sun. He could even make out the Norman warriors milling around like ants on the green grass and on the tiny walls. At this distance their fort looked so flimsy that a decent gust of wind would knock it over! The rising waves momentarily hid Dun Domhnall from his sight and as *River-Wolf* broke through the next swollen wave, the jarl looked to the blue sky and began a prayer to St Olav for the protection of his crew. Impulsively, he added a short appeal for the support of Njord - the old god of the sea. Jarl Sigtrygg awaited some divine punishment, but nothing happened and he laughed, emboldened by the success of the treasonous act. He was Christian, but the ship-folk of Veðrarfjord had always gathered by campfires while on trading missions and told tales of their ancestors and their ancient deities. Huddled on strange shores, they had told of heroic deeds of the gods, and of seafarers who had journeyed the oceans for generation upon generation. They had sung of adventurers and of brave warriors who had come to Ireland and taken land for their own. Sorrowful, funny and full of daring, the stories flooded back to him now as his ship soared towards Dun Domhnall under full sail. Jarl Sigtrygg had often thought about the old gods, especially when he was surrounded by the awesome power of the ocean. Why had they vanished, he wondered? Why had his people chosen the meek Lord Christ over the many aspects of the Northman's pantheon? Jarl Sigtrygg could not see one feature of Christianity which spoke to him: timidity; forgiveness; abstinence; chastity; denial. He was filled with desires which the priests said were sins.

At his feet the woman captured at Dun Conán whimpered and huddled in the deep, dark belly of *River-Wolf*. Water clung to her woollen clothes as she gripped her children's hands to her face and whispered that Lord Jesus would protect them from harm. She told her tearful children to admit their sins and to remember that they had said prayers at a Holy Well. She lied to them and told her children that they would be saved through the loving grace of the Holy Trinity.

Jarl Sigtrygg scoffed at that. It was the sort of mewing, sycophantic whine that he believed Christ would want of

341

his followers. They offered Him their backs to thrash and in return He would give them everlasting life. He was the God of slaves, he reasoned. If there was an afterlife, their only way to get into the next world was to bow and snivel and obey, for they would never be accepted into Valhalla. The Valkyries would never allow a thrall access to the great feasting hall in the sky. Only the brave, who had proven themselves in battle, could share a table with the gods. Not that Jarl Sigtrygg sought that honour at Dun Domhnall. He pursued revenge and glory.

'Their ship will be on the eastern side of the headland,' he called to Amlaith and refocused his eyes to study the beach ahead. He had sailed these waters many times and, though he had never landed at Dun Domhnall, knew the lay of the land intimately. 'Keep her headed towards those islands,' he shouted down the length of the ship to the ship-master. Amlaith adjusted their course a little more eastwards on a course which would take *River-Wolf* past the rocky outcropping where the foreigners had their fort. 'If they are prepared for us to land on the western beach, we'll give them a surprise!' Jarl Sigtrygg laughed and began marching down the length of his ship. 'Get up, you sons of whores,' he called as he cajoled his eighty warriors to readiness, 'and prepare to get back on the oars. We've a lot of killing to do today, but we must make land before we can do that! Amlaith,' he shouted to the distant steersman, 'wait until the fort is off the beam, and then turn her at the point of the headland.' The jarl pointed one large finger at the eastern extreme of the promontory off the port side. 'The closer you get us,' he warned, 'the less we'll have to pull to get her onto the beach. The rest of you,' Jarl Sigtrygg shouted as he tightened up the steerboard side sheet, 'get your armour on and your weapons ready, for we will not have time once we hit the sand to be pissing around looking for our spears.' With that he strode across the deck to the port side and stared out at the headland.

If the Normans were ready to repel seaborne warriors, they made no sign of it, for only one warrior had left the walls to watch their ship. He simply stood above the precipice and examined his enemy in the distance. The foreigner's head and torso were wrapped in dark steel and his hand was upon his sword pommel. It was only when he realised that *River-Wolf* was not going to land on the beach to the west of Dun Domhnall that he disappeared into the depths of the headland to raise the warning.

'You're too late,' Jarl Sigtrygg shouted after him though the distance was too great for the foreigner to hear. *River-Wolf* was already over halfway past the sea cliffs and he was able to study their little stone and bracken houses up on the eastern end of the headland. There were certainly not enough shelters for the three hundred warriors that Ragnall had said they would face. At most, Jarl Sigtrygg guessed, there were a hundred and fifty perched out on the rocks and that realisation was followed by a surge of ambition in his chest. Every one of his eighty crewmen was a veteran of many fights and all had stood in at least one shieldwall. Could the foreigners possibly say the same? He thought back to the slave market in Cluainmín when he had first laid eyes on the Normans. Their leader, Raymond, had been a pudgy youth who landed a lucky punch before hiding behind Trygve's chair and whispering lies about him. If he was their best, then the rest of the warriors would be bloody useless. Of that he was sure.

'We're almost ready to come about,' Amlaith called, and Jarl Sigtrygg raised his head to signal that he understood. With a last look at the headland, now four boat lengths off the stern, he crossed to the mast and called six men to assist him.

343

'Now!' he shouted and released the halyard from the cleat to begin lowering the sail towards the deck. The strain on his upper arms was immense. 'Turn her into the wind,' he managed to grunt at Amlaith through gritted teeth and, as the ship-master pushed the steering oar away, *River-Wolf* swung back towards Dun Domhnall and the estuary. His foot planted on the kerling, Jarl Sigtrygg clung to the mast one-handed and ordered his crewmen to furl the sail to the boom. The job was made all the more difficult due to the crewmen's cold fingers and the high waves which struck from the leeward side. Hands grasped for the rail of the ship, such was the power of the tide smashing into the steering board side.

'Keep her turning,' Jarl Sigtrygg shouted at Amlaith when the soaked warriors finally completed their task. The power of the tide sweeping along the coast had already forced the ship dangerously back towards the sharp black rocks of the headland. Jarl Sigtrygg snarled at the menacing landmass and began hauling the furled sailed back up the mast. 'Get up there, damn you!' he roared at the dripping wet bundle of rope, linen and wooden spars as it ascended.

Amlaith did not even wait for his jarl to get the sail out of his way. 'Get your oars out!' he called, his voice full of urgency. 'Pull, you bastards,' he exclaimed.

With a growl of determination, Jarl Sigtrygg heaved the rope up the last few inches before lashing the excess to the carved stone cleat fastened to the mast. Panting and covered with sweat, he stared balefully at the foreigners' fort. 'I'm coming for you,' he whispered before turning his eyes on the beach below Dun Domhnall. 'Pull harder!' he called to his crew. 'Come on, you bastards, pull!' he exclaimed and sat down on a chest, extending an oar into the sea to help his warriors. '*To the oars, my boys, to the oars!*' he sang the old rowing song. '*We'll get this boat to shore. She needs a berth and I need a drink so we'll get this boat to shore.'* Soon the whole crew were howling the fast-paced tune though they were soon lost in the combined effort of both tasks. Their arms, legs and stomach muscles burned and most did not even notice when the headland stole the wind and the waves below them lessened.

Jarl Sigtrygg glanced over his shoulder at the beach and there he saw a tantalising target: the beached Norman ship. He recognised the vessel immediately as the one in which Raymond de Carew had sailed to Cluainmín, the one in which he had hidden for fear that Jarl Sigtrygg would try to murder him. She would provide no refuge for his enemy on this occasion, he thought as he pulled the pine oar through the water.

'How far is it?' he demanded of Amlaith. He had to shout so that his voice could be heard over the crew's continuing song.

'Eight ship-lengths,' the ship-master replied and the jarl looked to his right and was surprised to see that *River-Wolf* was almost alongside the point of the headland. He could see the old Celtic fort walls had been rebuilt. Seconds later, his ship passed the new stables and cow pens. The sight of the double embattlements above the black cliffs gave him pause for thought, but a call from Amlaith that they were nearing shore grabbed his attention before he could give them serious consideration.

'Stow oars,' Jarl Sigtrygg boomed as the ship continued to drift towards land, 'and ready yourselves for battle,' he shouted as he tossed his oar aside and quickly threw his great helmet upon his head. His heavy belt held all manner of sidearms and they rattled against his chainmailed thighs. He stared at the shoreline. A number of people milling around the beached ship had spotted the danger approaching from the sea.

'They are running away!' one of his crewmen laughed when he joined his jarl in the bows. Indeed, at least fifteen boys were dashing away from the Norman vessel, scrambling and pushing up the earth cliff-face like frightened ants.

The jarl also laughed and turned towards his men. Old and young, they shared a fury in their eyes, an excitement for battle and plunder. 'Kill anyone left on that ship,' he shouted, 'and steal anything of any worth.' A number of the men nodded in agreement. 'Then we burn it and attack the fort. Are you ready to kill the bastards who humiliated us in Cluainmín? Are you ready to get revenge for the crewmen who died in the English lands?'

As *River-Wolf* began to skid along the sandy bottom of the estuary, the Ostmen of Veðrarfjord roared their battle cry and waved their weapons above their heads. The ship had barely shuddered to a halt when Jarl Sigtrygg vaulted over the side to land in the shallows with a splash and a bark of pure hatred.

'Kill them all,' he screamed and charged out of the waves like a sea-raider of old. 'Kill them all!'

Raymond spotted the smoke before he saw those fleeing from the beach. A tall, swirling plume swept inland on the early afternoon breeze. It tormented the nostrils of man and courser alike as they trotted southwards along the grassy path under high sun. Generations of Gaels herding cattle between the highland pastures and their winter grazing territory by the brimming sea had caused the well-trodden track to be cut into the landscape, but it suited the mounted Normans well despite the grasping ferns and briars at either side. Dreigiau whinnied and shook his mane as the acrid smoke irritated his eyes, and Raymond soothed him by rubbing his rough hand along the horse's neck. His eyes did

346

not leave the pumping cloud of smoke, for he guessed its origin and what that entailed; there would be no maritime evacuation from Dun Domhnall for his army. The Normans and the Welshmen were surrounded and they were alone. There was no line of retreat.

Raymond turned in the saddle to reassure his men. They had also spotted the smoke and had guessed that it came from the beached *Waverider*. Panic was already evident. His warriors flapped hands in the direction of the inferno and babbled to each other in frightened tones like those of the gulls that plagued the pages for scraps at mealtimes in their camp.

'Asclettin,' Raymond called to his most senior man, 'take all the men except Bertram back to Dun Domhnall. Archers, find Borard and replenish your arrow supply. Stable your horses and then get up onto the walls and get ready to repel attackers.' His orders were delivered so sharply and loudly that his detachment immediately stopped talking and began listening to what their captain told them. 'Is everyone clear on what to do?' he asked and received affirmative responses.

'What about the gates?' Fionntán called from the midst of the column. 'They are still closed.'

The captain turned and shielded his eyes from the high sun as he looked southwards over the sparkling grassland. It spilled away from the walls of Dun Domhnall. Flies buzzed around his face, but he could not see if the outer gate was open or closed. However, he trusted the strength of Fionntán's eyes to discern the truth.

'Just get to the gates,' he told the slouching Gael. 'They will admit you.' Fionntán looked unconvinced, but Raymond ignored him and lifted his left hand to point at the smoke cloud belching skywards. '*Waverider* is on fire and that means only one thing – we will have to remain in

Ireland. Before you let yourself be worried, I will remind you that each of you helped me build the walls of Dun Domhnall. Each of you poured your sweat and effort into them, and you know how bloody hard they were to put up. Imagine how hard they will be to tear down! They will hold. They will be tested, no doubt about it, but they will hold as long as we stand together.' He let his last word ring in their ears and pulled to the side of the path, allowing each of his men to pass him. Raymond made sure that they saw the defiance in his eyes and, for their part, most returned his stare before kicking their mounts into a canter towards the distant battlements. Only two paused to speak.

'Why aren't you coming with us?' Alice asked as she reached from Rufus' back for Raymond's arm. He took her fingers in his own and gave them a supportive squeeze.

'Bertram and I will make sure those youngsters get safely back to the fort,' he told her and pointed to the small number of people, pages and esquires, fleeing back towards the wooden rampart from the beach. 'I hope that the Ostmen have paused to plunder all that they can from *Waverider*, but that will only stop them for so long.' He looked past his former lover to address Fionntán. 'Keep her safe?' he requested of his new friend.

'We'll see you both back at the fort,' Fionntán sniffed and turned to bid good fortune to Bertram. His face dropped almost immediately for, past Bertram's shoulder and less than a half mile away, he had spotted a warrior on foot as he emerged from behind the wooded ridge. Within seconds fifty more had followed him into the sun-soaked landscape to the north. 'The Gael are here,' he warned, and reached out to take Alice's bridle. 'It's time to go,' he ordered and tapped his heels into his horse's sides.

'Raymond!' Alice called desperately as she clung to her saddle, but whatever her words they were lost below the thump of their hooves.

Bertram shifted in the saddle to look at the enemy army as they poured towards Dun Domhnall, a hundred, then two hundred, and soon more than he could hope to count. 'Do you think it might be time to go, captain?' he asked nervously and rolled his leather reins around in his hands.

Raymond nodded and shrugged his shield from his back and onto his left arm. 'Forget about them,' he told his companion. 'It will take them some time to reach our walls. We will worry about the Ostmen on the beach and getting those lads – and ourselves – safely back behind the palisade.' Though what safety the walls of Dun Domhnall could provide against the horde of Veðrarfjord, Raymond did not know. He swept the gloomy thought from his mind and focused on the task at hand. Bertram copied his actions and hefted his lance from his shoulder and upright to vertical, balancing the end upon his right foot in the stirrup. He was a cousin of the powerful Staffordshire Verdon family and, like his captain, had little prospect of making his fortune at his home hearth, and so had taken a place in Strongbow's household with the promise of trappings and armour, and two square meals a day for both his horse and himself. He was a steady warrior who never let his temper get the better of him and this, to Raymond's mind, made him the best from amongst the conrois.

Both men squeezed with their legs to make their coursers start forward, and a click of the tongue saw them into a trot and then a canter. They had only been riding for a matter of a few minutes when Raymond saw the first Ostman, bearded and helmeted, as he rose from the beach like a demon clambering from the pits of hell. More enemy warriors quickly ascended onto the grasslands before the walls and began running, their colourful, circular shields bouncing on their backs as they galloped forward with steel

349

sparkling in their hands. The Norman boys had already reached the base of the palisade and were running along its length towards the outer gate, but the first Ostmen were only fifty or sixty paces behind them and, despite their armour, were quicker over the ground. At the other side of the small peninsular, the conrois, with Asclettin at their head, were almost to the outer gates.

'Why aren't our archers shooting?' an exasperated Bertram shouted towards his captain and waved his lance in the direction of the rampart. 'They could drive the Danes off in seconds!' He had to yell so that his words could be heard over the noise of their cantering hooves and the wind as it swept by.

Raymond did not answer immediately but guessed the reason for the oversight: Sir Hervey had been too engrossed in organising an evacuation from Dun Domhnall and had not readied his archers for a battle. He stole a glance at the wall and could see only the outline of spearmen atop the defences.

'We'll have to drive them away from the barbican,' he replied as both man and horse leapt over a small, watery ditch which interweaved the terrain. 'That'll give the esquires and the conrois enough time to get through.' He did not wait for his companion to realise what that would mean for them if they remained outside the walls when an army of several thousand arrived. Instead he aimed Dreigiau at a point behind the fleeing Norman youths and clipped his heels to the courser's flanks. A prayer to St Maurice tumbled from his mouth as he rode forward, asking forgiveness of his sins and pardon for leading Bertram and their two coursers towards danger.

Glancing over his right shoulder, Raymond saw that Asclettin's group had reached the outer gate, but they had still not been permitted to enter. In the circling mass of men and horses he caught sight of Thurstin standing in his stirrups, shouting up at the men on the barbican, threatening violence and then pleading with them to open the gates to allow the conrois through. Raymond did not wait to see if his warrior's plea was accepted. He fixed his gaze on his enemy. The long line of Ostmen, at least sixty in number, were still in pursuit of the Norman boys on a trajectory that would inevitably take them to the outer gates where the small conrois and archers waited.

'Keep going!' Raymond called to the boys as he and Bertram cantered past. He smiled briefly when he saw the sweat-drenched Fulk of Westminster with two tearful and grubby-faced pages thrown across his young shoulders. The boy, no more than sixteen, nodded and redoubled his efforts, bellowing encouragement at his fellows as Raymond and Bertram hurtled in the opposite direction. The captain's stare settled on the Ostmen who had reacted to the threat of the two horsemen and stopped to organise into a defensive formation, locking their shields together in a line and issuing a roar of defiance.

'St Maurice!' the Norman captain bellowed as he kicked Dreigiau into a gallop and stood in the stirrups, ready to strike down with all the weight that their thundering charge could provide. The Ostmen bared their teeth and gripped the leather straps of their shields, prepared for the clash of Norman lance, but the blow did not fall for, rather than waste his energy battering the pine boards and metal bosses of the sturdily made shieldwall, Raymond pulled Dreigiau out of the charge a few paces from the enemy line and, with a whoop, knifed along its length to attack the men who had not yet been able to immerse themselves in the safety of hastily constructed barricade of shields. Raymond lanced one man in the shoulder as he tried to lift his shield to defend himself while Bertram hunted down a beardless

351

youth as he tried to run for cover under a nearby bush. Both men were panting hard when they wheeled away from the Ostmen's shieldwall and planted themselves between their enemy and the outer gates.

A roar of bellicose anger erupted from the shieldwall as, still in formation, the Ostmen began inching towards the gates of the Norman fort.

'It is you, you bastard!' the voice called in French and Raymond turned to see his enemy, Jarl Sigtrygg, leap out of the shieldwall and remove his helmet so that Raymond could see his bearded face. 'I told you that we would meet again, you whoreson of a Norman,' he thundered. 'I warned you that there would be no place that you could hide.' He waved his men onwards. 'We're going to kill everyone in your pathetic little fort, but you'll be the last to die,' he screamed as he shoved his helm back on his head. 'You'll watch as I send them to hell!'

Raymond ignored the jarl, but noted his position in the shieldwall. 'Where are the archers?' he mumbled as he searched the walls of Dun Domhnall again. The Ostmen were an easy target for even a handful of archers, but not one appeared to force them into retreat. Instead one of the Normans threw a lance from the outer wall, but it fell well short, earning a cry of utter disdain from the Ostmen's ranks.

'Get some archers onto the wall,' Raymond cried towards the sentries on the wall. 'And for God's sake open the gates!' he shouted, indicating towards the barbican with his bloodied lance. He could not tell if the men even heard his words, and prayed that they would have the good sense to realise the predicament of those left outside the battlements.

'They're moving again, Raymond,' Bertram warned. A broken spear tip had been buried between the boards of his teardrop shield and the Norman grunted as he pulled it out

352

and tossed it into a patch of nettles.

'They can't move forward quickly and keep the shield wall intact,' the captain replied. 'So we need to worry them like a wild dog would a flock of sheep,' he said and hoisted his lance again. 'If they lose cohesion, give them a bite, but otherwise try to make them bunch up and slow down.' *And pray that we get some archers onto the wall,* he thought with a final look towards Dun Domhnall.

With that both men tapped their spurs to their coursers' sides and cantered towards the line of Ostmen. A cry from Jarl Sigtrygg brought the enemy advance on the gates to a halt and the Ostmen again steeled their resolve to meet the charge of the Norman horsemen. But neither Raymond nor Bertram went close to attacking the line of overlapping shields. Instead they divided and began circling the enemy in opposite directions at a trot, waiting for the opportunity to strike at anyone stupid enough to break the stability of the shieldwall.

'Move,' Jarl Sigtrygg bellowed in the language of his fathers. 'Move,' he exclaimed and his warriors edged forward again, slower than before as they worked to keep their shield edges locked together. Ostman insults bombarded the two Normans as they orbited their enemy like cats working to kill a vicious rat. The men of Veðrarfjord screamed abuse, claiming that the Normans were cowards, that they would not dare get down from their horses and fight like real men. They cursed their mothers and fathers, and called them curs and runts and worse. Neither Raymond nor Bertram reacted to the slurs, busying themselves by periodically kicking their coursers into action and charging menacingly close to the Ostman lines before wheeling away once the shieldwall had been forced to come to a shuddering halt.

'Keep going,' Raymond called to his companion as he

retreated back to a safe distance after one such ploy. 'Don't give them the chance to get marching forward!' If Sigtrygg's crew did build up a rhythm, he knew that he and Bertram would never be able to stop their advance. At its best, a stationary shieldwall was almost as strong as a castle rampart, though it could also be used in attack to devastating effect if its structure could be maintained. Raymond did not doubt that Sigtrygg's men would be experienced practitioners of the art.

He was already panting hard, and could feel that Dreigiau was similarly fatigued. Nevertheless he pressed the courser into another circuit of the enemy position which, he now realised in alarm, had travelled over halfway along the front of the rampart despite their efforts to stop them. He quietly cursed for he knew that his enemy's advance was inexorably moving towards his tired conrois.

'Come on, open up,' he moaned as his circuit forced him to turn his back on the outer gate. Insults which had blasted Raymond and Bertram now blended and developed into a raucous war song from which the men of Veðrarfjord took their pace. The stomp of their boots and angry crash of steel weapons on wooden shields echoed upon the earthen palisade as Raymond watched Bertram take his turn at attacking the shieldwall. Instantly the war song was quelled and the drumming feet brought to a standstill as the Ostmen turned to face the young miles' charge. Raymond looked on with pride as Bertram skilfully leant into the turn which took his courser towards the shieldwall before the slightest shift of his weight and a tug on the reins with his one free hand took him out of reach of enemy battle-axes. Bertram whooped in joy at the perfectly performed manoeuvre which had again brought about the desired outcome of stopping the shieldwall in its tracks.

Raymond smiled at Bertram's victory, but knew that the

standoff could not continue for ever and that if Sir Hervey did not allow them to enter, he would face a last stand before the gates of Dun Domhnall alongside eight tired horsemen, the Welsh archers now devoid of arrows, a handful of pages and esquires, and the woman he had sworn to protect from all harm. Their only path of retreat was through the closed gates. All other options had been taken from them.

It was at that moment that Jarl Sigtrygg acted.

'Now!' came his cry from amongst the enemy ranks and at either end of the shieldwall the Ostmen circled outwards to wrap around Bertram as he turned his horse towards them and make another charge upon their lines.

'Look out!' Raymond roared, but it was already too late. A heavy axe took Bertram's horse in the neck and the animal screamed in pain as it went down. 'No!' the captain yelled and cut back towards the enemy shieldwall. He stabbed down twice, kicking Dreigiau to keep him moving, but Jarl Sigtrygg was ready for the move and had ordered half his men to turn and form a second line between the two Normans. Raymond screamed as he battered the shieldwall with his lance, but he struck nothing other than wooden shields. As he fought, Raymond saw Bertram climb to his feet and draw his sword to defend himself, but it was thirty against one and he could see that his cohort was winded and hurt from the fall. The Ostmen had again stopped in their tracks and had formed into a circle around Bertram, whose injured leg gave way under him as he swept his sword back and forth in wild strokes at those who came forward to meet him. Screaming in agony, Bertram climbed back to his feet and deflected a spear thrust aimed at his chest, but he could not turn quickly enough to meet all those who desired to take his life and, as Raymond abjectly bellowed his companion's name, a bearded Ostman cut him down from behind before two more began hacking at him with axes as he fell to the floor. Raymond was powerless to prevent the death of his cohort, and he impotently stabbed his lance down once more before pulling on Dreigiau's reins and scampering away to a safe distance. He would've wept for Bertram d'Alton, but he was not afforded the time.

'Forward!' Jarl Sigtrygg called, more desperately than his orders had sounded before. He had stepped out of the shieldwall and had his axe pointed directly at Raymond de Carew. His men responded by abandoning their formation and, with a peal of joy mixed with fury, began charging at the Norman captain.

Raymond was momentarily taken aback by the change in Jarl Sigtrygg's tactics, and for several seconds simply sat astride Dreigiau watching the frenzied stampede. His eyes were drawn to their circular shields bearing hypnotic, swirling devices of all colours as they rushed towards him. Their glittering spear, sword and axe blades were pointed skywards and caught the light from the high, midday sun. They cast a churning dapple of reflections upon the grass before them.

At their head was Jarl Sigtrygg, his red hair wild as it flowed from beneath his iron helmet and across his armoured shoulders to swing furiously in the racing wind. He looked every inch the seaborne warrior of old as he bellowed his war cry and led his men forward. Raymond was reminded of his youth and of the stories that his father had told him and his brothers about the men from the north. *Vikingrs*, he had called them. They had been the scourge of Christendom and the underlings of the Devil. Watching Jarl Sigtrygg's attack, Raymond felt sure that he understood the same terror that had been inflicted upon any victim of those attacks.

He sucked air down into his lungs to calm his mind, and made ready to attack the unruly band. He knew that he could not stop them all, but Raymond was sure that from horseback he could avenge the death of Bertram many times over before his own life was claimed. He promised that Jarl Sigtrygg would be first and searched for his foe in the midst of the charging war band. His red, braided beard was easy to find and Raymond had half-turned Dreigiau towards the enemy leader when he noticed that Jarl Sigtrygg's eyes were not locked on him, but on a target behind him and to his right. He quickly swung around in his bucket saddle to see what had prompted the Ostman's wild charge.

'Oh no,' he wailed and, turning Dreigiau away from his enemy, he kicked his heels into his courser's sides, for disaster was about to befall the Norman bridgehead and it would require a miracle to save it.

Sir Hervey de Montmorency thought that he had seen war of every kind. As an esquire to Gilbert de Gant, he had seen Scots cast down by arrows on the fog-bound fields of Cowton Moor, while at Lincoln when King Stephen had been captured, he had experienced boring siegecraft as well as knightly combat on the field of battle. He had fought the war of the raider, prowling the countryside to pillage and harry minor lords, their villeins, churchmen and freemen alike, when the wars of the vying royal houses had raged and the barons of England had sought to proclaim their independence. Hervey thought he had seen everything that this world of constant war could throw at him, but he had never faced odds like those which stared at him across the peninsula in the land of Siol Bhroin.

He stood on the barbican of Dun Domhnall gaping out over the little copses of shrubs and smattering of tiny trees, piebald patches of foliage upon an otherwise unending carpet of bountiful green grasses, to where the enemy gathered and made ready to attack. The baying of their vast herds of cattle sounded like the trumpeting of those Gallic savages who had stormed Rome, and the barbarians' clanged their weapons on their shields and sang animalistic songs of defiance that were so different to the soft songs of his homeland. The clamour was supplemented by the all-encompassing sound of the ocean and the screech of the gulls that circled the headland searching for food. Noise and heat and stress assailed him from all sides. To his right he could hear the roar of flames as they licked clean the shell of his ship. The plume of smoke was carried away from the fort, but he could still taste the devastation of *Waverider* on the wind. She had been his last hope for escape, and now she was gone.

'For God's sake, open the gates,' the desperate voice came from below him again, but Sir Hervey had no eyes for the frantic conrois left outside the battlements. He was surrounded and he did not know how to save himself.

'Open the damned gates!' the voice pleaded and twenty more shouted similar demands of him. The stink of human sweat and horse faeces emanating from below the barbican pulverised his senses, adding to the others which beset him.

'Sir Hervey!' another anxious voice, belonging to Borard, called from the inner wall. He turned around and stared across at the other palisade.

'You need to get some archers onto the walls and kill those Ostmen. You need to do it now!'

'Shut up, shut up, shut up and let me think!' Sir Hervey groaned and put his hands to his face. Following Geoffrey of Abergavenny's warning about the Ostman vessel, he had waited apprehensively for the expected appearance of an enemy fleet from beyond the western landmass, and had despatched all of the archers in the fortress to the cliffs above the beach with orders to bombard them when they made land. Much to his relief no further ships had followed the first and when the vessel had swept past the western beach, he had convinced himself that the crew would trouble him no more. He had been wrong and while he had taken charge of the work to ready *Waverider* for withdrawal to Waesfjord, the Ostmen had struck. Having burned his ship they had climbed the cliffs from the beach and were now attempting to attack his gates.

'Let me think, please, let me think!' Sir Hervey whispered again and, from between his fingers, he watched the white smoke as it pumped from his stricken ship on the beach. He could see the top of her rigging as the flames tore through it. The mast was already ablaze and as he watched it cracked and crumbled from sight. He appealed to God for an escape route, for an army from Waesfjord, or a friendly fleet to appear on the horizon; anything that would save him from inevitable death. He had seen with own eyes what a victorious army did to a fallen enemy, and had taken part in those excesses too, but in a savage land like the one in which he found himself he believed that it would be worse again. The Gael were animals who would murder prisoners with their bare hands, or mutilate them by carving out their eyes or cutting off their genitals. At best a defeated foe could expect to be sold into slavery at one of the great markets at Dubhlinn or Veðrarfjord. Sir Hervey promised that he would throw himself from the cliffs rather than face such an end as that.

It was all Raymond de Carew's fault, he decided. It had been Strongbow's captain who had prevented him from launching his offensive against Veðrarfjord when the Ostmen were not expecting an attack. It would have been an unequivocal victory, of that he was sure. Instead of attacking the enemy, Raymond, the fat dolt, had ventured upriver to talk to Cluainmín where he had no doubt eaten and drank his fill before coming back to Dun Domhnall with little more than a verbal agreement of friendship – and how had that benefitted the Normans? Raymond had bypassed Sir Hervey's authority and had led the army to the brink of utter destruction.

He turned to look at his rival. He felt the hatred course through his veins at the sight of the younger man. The dullard was attacking the eighty-strong crew of the longship with only one other warrior by his side. As Hervey watched, the Ostmen quickly formed into a shieldwall but not before Raymond speared one of their number who lagged behind the rest. Sir Hervey loathed Robert FitzStephen, Raymond's uncle, and was jealous of his success in capturing Waesfjord the summer before. But Raymond he truly hated. Sir Hervey hated his good nature. He hated his plump, jolly face. He hated that like him, Raymond was a younger son without a penny to his name. He hated that he was enduringly carefree, as if he was too stupid to understand the injustices of the world which saw men like them spend their lives in penury whilst elder brothers lived in opulence. That Raymond had embarrassed him on the first day he had arrived in Dun Domhnall would not be forgotten, but it was that Raymond believed himself to be better than he that truly crawled beneath Sir Hervey's skin. He promised that if he was ever in a position to kill Raymond de Carew, he would take the opportunity.

Anger seemed to clear Sir Hervey's mind and he removed his hands from his face and turned towards the warrior who stood next to him. 'We'll send an emissary out to negotiate,' he ordered.

The man, Rechin, was one of the warriors that he had brought back following his last trip to England. He claimed

360

to have served in the north against the Scots, but Sir Hervey had not recognised any of the names of the lords he said that he had served. Sir Hervey was convinced that he was a deserter, perhaps from the Normans who had fought with King Malcolm. Not that it mattered, for Rechin had proved himself to be capable and loyal to the money which Hervey gave him from that earned by his four prostitutes.

'Why would they want to talk?' Rechin replied and looked at the army which gathered less than a mile from their walls. 'They outnumber us by at least twenty to one, and they've burned our only means of escape. It's time to fight,' he said gruffly and half-drew his sword from the scabbard at his side, testing the edge with his thumb.

Sir Hervey was about to argue, to tell him that it was pointless to battle such a force, but he stopped when he felt a strange sensation course through his lower limbs, the feeling that the whole barbican was moving beneath him.

'What is that?' he asked only for Rechin's answer to be lost beneath a cry of exultation arising from Raymond's horsemen. 'The gates,' Hervey exclaimed and leaned out over the outer wall to see the painted, wooden gateway swing open and Geoffrey of Abergavenny step out from the shadow and begin waving the conrois inside. 'You damn fool boy, close the gates!' he shouted towards Raymond's esquire as Geoffrey grabbed his pretty sister's bridle and physically dragged both woman and steed through. Yells of anger and the sounds of horses beginning to panic seeped through the hewn wooden walkway beneath Sir Hervey. The horsemen, still mounted, had knocked aside the archers and forced their way to the front where, in their hurry to escape the threat of the enemy, a bottle-neck had formed as each fought to find the safety inside the walls. Sir Hervey had to grab hold of the pointed post as the milites pressed into the small, noise-drenched entrance way. The barbican shook beneath him. Such was the crush that only a trickle of Norman warriors had been able to enter through the gate and even then the congestion seemed to have seeped between the battlements. A more distant cry of acclamation sounded and Sir Hervey turned sharply towards the pumping column of smoke.

'St Denis, protect me,' he whispered, his voice chastened by dismay, for the band of warrior Ostmen were no longer advancing in the slow, lumbering shieldwall. They were charging at the open entrance to Dun Domhnall like the berserkers of old. Long hair and beards flapped beneath armoured helms as the wild-eyed mob sprinted along the line of the fortifications, their shields a haze of many colours and their weapons a forest of steel upon them. A few of the twenty Norman warriors on the wall launched spears at the passing enemy ranks, but most fell short or missed the screaming, sprinting pack of Ostmen. Sir Hervey was momentarily frozen by fear, and merely stared open-mouthed at the stampede of leather-bound raiders from the sea.

'Hurry up, damn you,' the Frenchman finally stuttered in the direction of the horsemen, but their increased efforts to enter the fortress was nothing to do with his words, and did not speed up their progress.

'We need archers, where are my archers?' Sir Hervey demanded of Rechin.

'You sent them to watch over the beach,' the mercenary replied and pointed a stubby finger towards the west.

'Then get those gates closed yourself!' Sir Hervey demanded. 'I don't care if you have to kill all of Raymond's men, get them closed!'

Rechin hesitated. 'I'll need help,' he called over the commotion of horses and men all fighting to get through the small gap between the double entrenchments.

'Just do it!' Sir Hervey ordered as Rechin disappeared onto the battlements. He looked back to the terrifying charge of the Ostmen, now only fifty paces away, and knew instinctively that there was no hope for anyone in Dun Domhnall. Those trying to get through the outer gate would be quickly slaughtered by the Ostman crew and then, with the defences breached, they would turn their axes on those twenty Normans left on the outer wall - and that included Sir Hervey. It would be a massacre. He pictured the brutish enemy screaming heathen curses and clambering between the gaps in the crenulated wall to hack down anyone remaining alive in Dun Domhnall.

Sir Hervey was already scrambling down the ladder from the barbican to the rampart when the first Ostman blades fell upon the archers below, and he was running along the allure towards the inner gate, screaming for them to let him pass, when he heard the Gaelic war horns sound in the distance.

Death approached the Norman fort.

Noise, everywhere noise. Even blinkered by his coif and enclosed by his heavy steel spangenhelm, Raymond was assailed by sound. Monosyllabic peals of panic and rumbling, ascending anger, the thump of running feet, the screams of frightened horses, impact upon impact of weaponry, it surrounded him. His hot breath rasped around his sticky brow, unable to escape through the tiny circlets of steel which protected his jaw and neck. It was not enough to dull his ears to the clamour. At his back, the sea rolled and tumbled and slowly chewed at the black rocks upon which he had built his little fort. On the beach the inferno still crackled and hissed and roared in glory as it triumphantly consumed the hull of *Waverider*. And to the north Ragnall of Veðrarfjord's army gathered, their thick cattle-skin drums booming like thunder, intermingling with the flat, metallic din of horns and trumpets. But it was directly ahead, where the sharp, staccato clash of steel pierced most keenly, that Raymond focussed his attention.

Sir Reginald de Bloet, Walter's father, had once told Raymond that a clever warrior should be able to read the emotions of a battlefield like a good shepherd could the weather, or an experienced sailor might the tide. Any warlord worth his salt could pick a good battlefield, Sir Reginald had told him, and even the most cloddish could use the lay of the land to his advantage, but the best captains also knew how to clear their minds and listen to the sounds going on around him, to discern their meaning.

Read the emotions on a battlefield, he had told his esquire.

It had taken a long time for Raymond to realise the truth in the old man's advice. He had been midway through his knight-apprenticeship at the time, angry and newly impoverished by his father's loss of the Barony of Emlyn, and all he had wanted to do was to fight the Welsh rebels who had wronged his family. Sir Reginald had prevented him from running away and joining a battle that he was, at that time, ill-equipped to win, and so he had continued his education in the ways of the frontier warrior. It was only after experiencing hundreds of small skirmishes in the hills of Gwent by Sir Reginald's side that he had come to understand his master's words and what they meant, for battle was not glorious and ordered, it was a confusing tumble of action where dust blinds and rain deafens, where well-formulated strategies were defeated by unforeseen circumstances, and commanders lose all sense of control over their armies. Raymond had seen how, in the heat of combat, men quickly became disorientated and had even watched as members of the same conrois had hacked at

364

each other before realising they were on the same side. He had experienced the crush and the collapse of a shieldwall, and had seen the lost look on men's faces as they were squashed and jostled so that they no longer knew from which direction an enemy blade would fall. Yet Sir Reginald de Bloet's advice was true: only by deciphering the raw emotions of a battle could a commander form a clear picture and could anticipate how to emerge victorious.

When Jarl Sigtrygg's crew had made their unexpected charge, Raymond had been forced to flee out of their path rather than be swamped by their sudden move, and by the time he had Dreigiau settled and turned, the first Ostman blows were already beginning to rain down upon his outnumbered conrois in the shadow of the barbican. Swirling dust and shadow had partially obscured his view, but he had quickly spotted the yawning gates of Dun Domhnall over the heads of the charging crewmen of Veðrarfjord. The sounds coming from that fight – as well as the effect that he could see on the agitated men stationed upon the outer wall – told him that his conrois were dying and his fortress about to fall.

Raymond had rarely been afflicted by rage, but in that moment he felt it all: every insult and injustice, each blunder and regret, the bounds of his ambition, the fury of his passions, and the depths of his hates. Basilia, Alice, Sir Hervey, his father, Strongbow, poor Bertram d'Alton, Jarl Sigtrygg, and Roger de Quincy, all their faces came to him. *Cowhand*, Ragnall had called him. Fury rose in Raymond's chest and forced the stale breath from his lungs in short, ever quickening bursts. In his hand the lance was sticky with blood and shining sweat, but he barely noticed as he sought glimpses of the fight by the outer gate. Caradog's archers had wasted their stock of arrows at the causeway, yet they refused to submit and desperately defended themselves with short swords and hand-axes against the armoured Ostmen who attacked them. Beside the Welsh, his conrois had dismounted and fought alongside their old enemy in defence of the gates, and he could even see two of the older esquires, mere boys, with abandoned lances in their blood-covered hands. But it was to no avail, for the Ostmen outnumbered those defending the gate by four to one, and as Jarl Sigtrygg's men advanced Raymond could see twitching figures of Welsh and Normans left prone upon the ground, the trampled soil soaking deep red around them. One man cried out loud, his hands full of his blue innards as they spilled from below his leather hauberk to rest upon his lap. He cried for his mother in his native Welsh before he was silenced by a single downward cut of a battle-axe.

Raymond could feel the frenzy rising in his heaving chest, and from nowhere the words from the Song of Roland came to him: '*My sword is in its place at Roncevaux, scarlet I will it stain,*' he softly sang the boast of the Saracen general before he left to ambush Charlemagne's rearguard. '*Find I Roland the Proud upon my way I'll fall on him or trust me not again. And Durendal I'll conquer with this blade, Franks shall be slain, and France a desert made.*'

The great song was Raymond's favourite and he had delighted in its telling when it had heard it played by visiting minstrels to Strongbow's hall at Striguil. He had always thought it a fanciful story of Christian bravery victorious over Saracen deceit, of Roland's brave stand against an overwhelming horde of pagan warriors. Now the flowing, pugnacious verse came to the young captain and every memorised word spoke of primitive horror, not glorious combat. The acts of Aelroth and Olivier, of

Falsaron and Turpin, of Oger and Corsablis were played out before him as his outnumbered conrois engaged Jarl Sigtrygg's warband. And in the distance, Ragnall played the part of King Marsilla perfectly, bringing the main body of his army to bear as if he was singing from the same sheet music that Raymond imagined. In this fight there was no elephant horn for the Normans to summon help from afar. He had no magical sword to give him an advantage, and nor was Dreigiau a charger like swift Veillantif. He was not fighting on God's behalf against the infidels, and no saint would hear his cry for divine help.

I am no Roland, Raymond thought, and neither could any man in his conrois claim to be as skilled as Charlemagne's famed paladins. His warriors were outlaws and miscreants, reviled as invaders in their own country, and treated as criminals in that of their king. They were the sworn swords of a beggared lord sent west on a fool's quest for a crown. Yet it was not Strongbow's ambition, but Raymond's, that had brought the band of a hundred to this end; for he could see no conclusion other than the utter destruction of his army, his fort, and of Strongbow's dreams.

In this theatre, he played treasonous Ganelon, the bringer of destruction on his own kin.

Had the outer gates held, he might have been able to inflict enough damage on Ragnall's army to allow some of his people to live, to force his enemy to negotiate, but that was no longer likely and all that was left for Raymond de Carew to do was to die beside his comrades.

'*Shame take him that goes off: if we must die, then perish one and all!*' he sang, again from the Song of Roland, and thought once more of sweet Basilia de Quincy, of how she looked at the feast in Striguil. She would never understand that it was for her that he had set himself upon this path, to prove that he was a man deserving of her love, that he was a man worthy of her, a captain who warranted the hand of an earl's daughter. That dream lay in tatters. All his hopes relied on him winning great renown on the field of battle. But there could be no victory against this enemy. A hundred could not defeat five thousand.

It was for glory that Raymond charged; for ambition and greed, for revenge, and for love. It was for honour and hate and friendship. He felt the emotions collect in his throat and issue forth in an incoherent scream as his heels clipped Dreigiau's flanks and they jumped forward together, gaining speed as they cantered towards the huddle of Ostmen. He had no plan and no expectation of survival. He simply wanted to lose himself in the fight.

'Montjoie!' he screamed Roland's war cry as he stabbed his lance downwards towards the first Ostman who turned to meet him. As the bearded warrior tumbled to the ground, Dreigiau stamped on him while Raymond deftly reversed his weapon and struck three times at another assailant who came from his right side.

'On, Dreigiau,' he exclaimed and squeezed the courser with his knees. Together, man and horse forced their way further into the crowd of Ostmen and Raymond tossed the lance into the air and caught it so that he could use it overarm against the swarming mass of men. As he took an axe blow plum on his shield-boss, Raymond was dimly aware of his conrois fighting valiantly in a tight knot between the open gates. It was in that direction that he urged Dreigiau, rocking his midriff and squeezing his thighs to keep the tough little animal moving forward.

'Dreigiau, onwards!'

They were still twenty paces from where the packed ranks met when a rancorous bellow made Raymond turn in time to see the Ostmen ranks peel aside like the Red

368

Sea did before Moses, and allow a tall warrior to run at him. His hair was wild and long like his beard and he wielded his huge sword double-handed, ready to chop at the Norman. Raymond ignored his first impulse, to drop his reins and raise his shield, and instead threw his weight down upon his left stirrup, leaning as far as he could out of his saddle to stab at the maddened warrior before he could strike. The captain gasped in relief as the effort hit home, piercing the Ostman's leather jerkin above his heart and stopping him in his tracks. His respite was all too short as, due to the sudden shift of his rider's weight, Dreigiau lurched to his left, scattering enemy warriors from his path. Raymond's stomach muscles screamed in agony as he attempted to right himself without hauling on his reins, but he was only halfway back into the saddle when he felt hands grab him by the left shoulder and began hauling him towards the ground again.

There was little enough hope of reaching his conrois as it was, Raymond knew, but to leave the saddle would mean certain death and so he stabbed his lance into the soil and used it like a crutch to steady himself in his seat. Then, using the spearpoint planted in the soil as a pivot, he punched his assailant in the face with his fist still wrapped around the pine spear shaft. His enemy gasped and slumped against his shoulder, so close that he could feel the hot breath upon his cheek, the reek of salted fish and beer, and Raymond partially recoiled from the stench as he fought against the man's lessening grip and righted himself in the saddle.

'On, Dreigiau,' he shouted again at his tired and frightened courser who stamped his hooves and butted his head forward in answer to his command. Sweat poured from Raymond's brow and stung his eyes as he gasped down lungfuls of bitter air. Men scattered and fell before him as he forced his way through, stabbing right and left, but he could already see that he was too late for, even though he was almost upon them, he could only watch as the small Norman shieldwall began retreating beneath the barbican and then, moments later, broke under pressure and fled. The Ostmen's cry of victory boomed and echoed around the wooden enclosure as they swarmed forward to take their prize.

Raymond responded with his own roar of venomous ire, his voice puncturing their triumphant tumult as his charge had their lines. He knew that unless his men were given an opportunity to reform they would be slaughtered and he lunged left and right with his spear with greater resolve than before. Men tumbled aside rather than face him, but he barely noticed as he settled into the killer's rhythm – stab, withdraw, kick on, stab, withdraw, kick on.

'Montjoie!' he called again as he urged Dreigiau to turn sharply, using the courser's weight to knock two men from their feet as man and horse whirled in the press of men. And suddenly he was aware that there was breathing space between the gates, but Raymond could not take advantage of it as his horse, now thoroughly confused, exhausted and terrified, started to skip and bolt. White froth collected at the edges of Dreigiau's mouth and his eyes shone with fear.

'Easy,' Raymond appealed, but nothing he could say would calm the courser and, as he began to rear, the Norman captain was thrown clear of the saddle. His last sight, as he tumbled backwards towards the broken gates of Dun Domhnall, was of Dreigiau standing on his back legs as if he was battling the horde of Veðrarfjord like one of the boxers that had so impressed him at the spring fair in Germany two years before.

370

Then, all of a sudden, everything went deathly dark as Raymond impacted with the torn earth.

Ragnall Mac Giolla Mhuire, Konungr of Veðrarfjord, was a patient man, but that forbearance was being sorely tested. He had once negotiated for two weeks with Toirdelbhach Ua Briain, and his bevy of monks, to increase by a hundred the number of cattle that the King of Tuadhmumhain offered to secure Ragnall's vassalage. Offers, threats and bargaining by the Uí Briain had been met by his stubborn silence and in the end Ragnall had received what he considered a fair proposal for an alliance between their two kingdoms. A summer later he had bartered for almost a month to exact ten more slaves, as well as much-sought bird skins and cow hides, as tuarastal from the Meic Cartaigh of Deasmumhain. In return Ragnall had cast off the rule of the Uí Briain, and his fleet had gone to war against their erstwhile allies. The memory of that campaign, only twenty years before, went some way to soothing his frustrations. He remembered the hundred and ten sleek longships cruising west in the bright summer sunshine, their sails fat-bellied as a pregnant sow, and the sons of his city ready for war. His pride at the memory dragged a long snort of air into his lungs, and it was only the sullen lowing of a cow which interrupted his recollections and set his teeth to clenching in anger once again. Rapidly that whine was taken up by more and more of the dour animals, and the din increased as the slave-drivers and their masters added the crack of whips and coarse commands. Then the stink of the cattle assaulted Ragnall's senses and the Konungr of Veðrarfjord cursed irately as his frustrations with his allies finally got the better of him.

It had been a week of slow progress since departing

Veðrarfjord, first eastwards along the banks of the River Siúire in the company of Máel Sechlainn Ua Fhaolain's people, and then north, following the Bearú to the crossing at the monastery of St Abbán where they had met with the Uí Drona. Many years had passed since Ragnall had last marched to war alongside the Gael, and he had forgotten how astonishingly slow they could be for, though it was only an army that the konungr had demanded from his Uí Drona and Déisi vassals, what had come to his aid was a civilisation on the move. It seemed to Ragnall that the lands of the two tribes must have been emptied for with the two thousand spearmen came women, children, clerics, slaves, hostages and foster children, poets, brehons, craftsmen, and others of every rank and custom possible. Each had a cart bearing his family's property and each had his herd of cattle. The Gael did not deal and trade in coin like the men of Veðrarfjord, they transacted in livestock. Of a more difficult form of movable wealth, the konungr could not think! Thousands of heifers followed the army, forced onwards by a mass of slaves and stockmen armed with whips. And it was not only the chiefs and their sons who brought their herds, it was their wives – multiple wives in many cases – and his warriors too, and of course each herd had to be kept separate even from those owned by members of the same extended family. The animals were everywhere and with each step the stink and noise seemed to intensify, hour after hour, day and night. The Gaels fought over fodder and pastures, they fought over access to water. They argued about trade, methods of making butter and oatcakes, and who had the best bull. They disputed in what order they should cross streams and to which saints and spirits to make offerings to keep them safe when doing so. In fact the only thing that united the tribesmen was that all wished for a quick resolution to the campaign so that they could make ready for the harvest, quickly approaching. Nevertheless, cousins, nephews, brothers and uncles, stared balefully at each other, fingering spear shafts and speaking in suspicious tones. Old quarrels started in their great-grandfathers' time soon spilled over into violence as they marched and two days before Ragnall had watched as two rival sects of the Uí Fhaolain had fought a vicious, impromptu battle as they had stopped for the night. It was only the intercession of a gaggle of churchmen under the Bishop of Laighin that had stopped the fight before a death occurred. It transpired that thirty years before the two combatants' chiefs had fought each other for rights over a summer pasture in the high hills to the west. It was a common enough tale for amongst the Gael any man, though he had only a single warrior to stand alongside him and a herd of ten cattle, though he was a king and every other a rival. That the two kings, Donnchadh Ua Riagháin and Máel Sechlainn Ua Fhaolain, had managed to get their respective *armies* this far, intact and ready to fight despite the enmity within their ranks thoroughly impressed Ragnall of Veðrarfjord.

His own army, by comparison, had been easily raised, for the threat to their city was real and nearby. Ragnall's father had been only a boy when the men of Laighin had last attacked and burnt Veðrarfjord to the ground. It had been before his forefathers had accepted the light of Christ into their hearts, yet the townsfolk still talked of the death and destruction of the outlying farms, the disease and famine which had followed. It was as if the attack had happened in their own lifetimes and as a consequence his jarls had been quick to raise warrior bands of freemen and to offer ships to transport them across the bay. The Ostmen did not have their families amongst their ranks, and nor were they beleaguered by the petty differences which dogged the Gael. They were not slowed by cattle.

Now that Dun Domhnall was in sight, Ragnall at least knew that his frustrations with his allies would soon be over. He would destroy the foreigners' little fort and then move against Cluainmín and impose his rule over Trygve's people and his precious silver mine. Then, it would be on to Waesfjord and the skeleton garrison holding FitzStephen's castle. Two more weeks, he mused, and the threat of the invaders would be gone for ever. However, it was not in Ragnall's nature to look too far ahead and he refused to allow his focus to wander from the business at hand. Before him the breeze repeatedly forced the long grass downwards as if the land was bowing in submission to the Konungr of Veðrarfjord and he took that to be a favourable portent. Ragnall added a prayer to St Olav to guide his hand before turning his eyes back on Dun Domhnall. From half a mile away the foreigners' fort looked insignificant and fragile, as if a stiff breeze off the ocean could knock down the timber walls and so allow his army to swarm all over the headland.

'Are the Uí Drona in position yet?' he asked one of the jarls who stood alongside awaiting the order to attack. Like Ragnall's son, he was named Sigtrygg though he was of Norse stock and old in years. He had been nicknamed Sigtrygg Fionn in his youth due to his shock of blond hair which had hung long and loose across his mailed back. Now it was grey and lank, but the nickname remained.

'Not yet,' the old jarl replied. Sigtrygg Fionn stared southwards, his right hand across his brow to shield his eyes from the afternoon sun. 'My warriors are ready, as are Jarl Amlaith and Jarl Gufraid's men.'

Ragnall scowled and ignored his words. Instead he watched the plume of smoke as it pumped skywards from the beach hidden below the headland. 'My son's work, I suppose?'

Sigtrygg Fionn nodded and shifted uneasily. 'He sailed right up to the beach and burned their ship.' Although the jarl had not intended it, his konungr heard a reproof in Sigtrygg Fionn's statement.

'He is a stupid boy, and anyone who thought to attack them from the sea is as stupid as he,' Ragnall replied. 'But our enemy has proven himself to be even stupider again, for they allowed him to get off that beach.' His eyes narrowed as he imagined what had occurred while his army had made their way across the causeway to the north; his son beaching his vessel and setting fire to that of the Normans; warriors leaping from the shallows to chase those stupid enough to have found themselves outside the fortifications. That the Norman commander had not sent his warriors to stop Jarl Sigtrygg climbing up from the beach was bad enough, but to have opened the gates to allow those attacking to gain a foothold, stunned Ragnall. Yet it was the only explanation that he could envisage for his son's success.

He remembered the plump youngster who had met him on the causeway and had claimed to be the leader of the foreigners; a mere boy named Raymond who had been easily outmanocuvred and overawed. Ragnall decided that his opponent had probably grown up in a noble household, the type which his spies described as being common in the English lands – a pampered, soft boy, who had been promoted too early to command and thought of war as a game to be enjoyed as entertainment. Somehow, the konungr felt insulted that this was the captain that the Earl Strongbow had sent to prepare the way for his conquest of Veðrarfjord.

I shall make the boy pay for that slur, he thought.

His eyes settled on the gates of the fort where the battle was taking place. Axe blades flashed through the swirling dust and smoke from the burning ship, while cries of pain, anger and triumph reached even to the eight hundred warriors perched on the crest behind Ragnall and Sigtrygg Fionn. As he watched he saw a single Norman horseman barrel into the midst of the packed ranks of Ostmen, his crimson and gold surcoat and strangely shaped shield bright amongst the dull coloured leather, chainmail and wool coverings of his enemy.

'Brave lad,' Ragnall murmured as he recognised Raymond de Carew. Perhaps he had misjudged the Norman, he considered.

Beside him, Sigtrygg Fionn rocked his weight from one foot to the next impatiently. 'We shouldn't wait for the Gael,' he told his konungr. 'We should help your boy now. If we commit our eight hundred, it would be over in minutes.'

'Why did no-one tell me that there were two sets of fortifications?' Ragnall asked rather than acknowledge Sigtrygg Fionn's words.

'You have eight hundred of Veðrarfjord's bravest sons at your side,' Sigtrygg Fionn hissed irritably. 'What would it matter if they have three walls, twice as high? The foreigners have shown that they are incapable of holding them against proper fighting men.'

Glowering at his jarl's impertinence, Ragnall spat on the grass at his feet. It was clear – despite his attempts to change the subject – the fort was indeed ready to fall, as Sigtrygg Fionn said, for no fort could hold once the outer gates had been breached. Still Ragnall hesitated. It wasn't that he was afraid of defeat or even death. He feared his son.

Many in his army would, like Fionn, think that his son's

actions were heroic rather than foolhardy. For if the foreigners did capitulate, it would only be Jarl Sigtrygg's daring attack from the sea that would be remembered by his warriors. The recollections of poets and minstrels rarely hung on the folly of an enemy who had allowed the hero to capture their gates. They never noted a commander's good fortune. They would speak only of the audacious acts of the young prince who had ignored his father's hesitancy and captured the enemy fortress.

Old, they would say of Ragnall, *old, dithering and fallible*.

Whether or not his son had the brains or ambition to take advantage of such a state of affairs and depose his father hardly mattered; the Konungr of Veðrarfjord knew from experience what happened to a ruler who was shown to be weak. His own family, the Meic Giolla Mhuire, had seized control of Veðrarfjord in such circumstances. Ragnall, for one, had learned the lesson that he could never allow a rival to rise to challenge his rule, no matter how seemingly insignificant and closely related.

His eyes settled on the walls of the Norman fort, shrouded partially in smoke and dust, where his son battled, not only for victory over the foreigners but potentially for his father's throne as well. Ragnall knew that if he sent his army forward to help his son, that victory would be assured. However, if he did nothing then Jarl Sigtrygg might yet be forced to retreat and Ragnall could send his eight hundred men forward and claim the triumph for his own. If, on the other hand, Jarl Sigtrygg emerged victorious with only his crew at his side, it would cost many crewmen's lives. Son or no, a weakened rival to his crown could then be easily toppled before he could regain his strength. After all, the memory of a dead man's glory would be no threat to the konungr.

'Ragnall?' Sigtrygg Fionn appealed again. 'We should

commit to the attack now.' His voice was slurred and the smell of ale was strong from his breath.

The Konungr of Veðrarfjord stole another look at the battle before the gates of Dun Domhnall and shook his head. 'We wait for the Uí Drona.' Though the jarl said nothing, he could sense Fionn's impatience and suspicion. 'The boy has to prove himself sometime,' Ragnall said offhandedly. 'It was his choice to sail ahead of us, against my orders. If he succeeds in taking the walls then the fort will fall and we will have accomplished what we came to do. If not then, as you say, we have eight hundred other warriors and two thousand Gael to throw against them. The fort will fall one way or another.'

'Jarl Sigtrygg could die!'

'I have other sons to replace him.' *And neither is as troublesome as Sigtrygg*, he thought, picturing his two teenage sons, safe behind the walls of Veðrarfjord with his most recent wife. There was too much of Sigtrygg's mother in his eldest son, of that Ragnall had decided many years before. She had come to his bed as part of a long-abandoned pact with her father, the King of the Uí Chinnéide, and she had proven to be as pig-ignorant and uncontrollable as her father's people. She had eventually succumbed to sickness when Jarl Sigtrygg was on the verge of manhood, though Ragnall had not mourned her loss for long. Although big and strong for his age, the konungr had found her son, Sigtrygg, to be as dumb as an ox with a temper to match, and so he had given him to one of his lesser jarls to foster, and told him to make a sailor of him. He had hoped that the sea would douse his son's fiery temper, but when he had returned to his father's hall that spring, ten years after he had been sent away, Jarl Sigtrygg had proven to be the same hot-headed bully the had been in his youth.

378

The boy had, however, grown into a giant of a man and even on a ship with a crew of hardy men he had been accepted as their captain. Initially his father had been impressed by the man that Jarl Sigtrygg had become, and thought that the boy could yet be turned into something of use. Then the pig-eyed youth had begun making demands of the konungr. First, he had demanded food, wine, and lodgings. Then, when he had grown tired of those, he had demanded recognition as Ragnall's eldest son. He had demanded responsibility and land. He had not demanded a wife, but that was what his father had given him; an old widow with a voice that could've cut a silver coin in two as well as any axe. She also brought slaves and a farm, half a day's walk from Veðrarfjord, and the title of jarl to their marriage bed, and for a while Sigtrygg had seemed happy with the wealth derived from his new manor. But all too soon rumours of raiding and pillaging of trading vessels began to abound. Ragnall had tried to quash those tales, to blame it on their enemy in Cluainmín. However, when traders had started to avoid Veðrarfjord and take their wares to safer ports such as Corcach, Waesfjord and Dubhlinn, Ragnall had known that he had to act lest the merchants of the city turn against him. Jarl Sigtrygg had been hauled before an assembly of the people in Ragnall's feasting hall to face charges. Exile and confiscation of his lands was the consensus from the freemen who spoke against Jarl Sigtrygg, and it would've been the death of him, Ragnall had known, even as he had pronounced the verdict, for none of his crew should've followed his son into penury and the wandering life of an outcast. What misguided impulse had caused Ragnall to offer twenty pounds of silver to save his son from that sentence? He still did not know! Yet the merchants of Veðrarfjord had accepted the offer as fair compensation for their losses that

379

summer, and Jarl Sigtrygg had been released. His son had not even thanked him for saving his life. Rather he had stomped off, gathered his crew, and disappeared into the west for three months.

'Blasted boy,' Ragnall murmured.

Rumours of Jarl Sigtrygg's raiding had soon returned to the city; of a monastery in Tuadhmumhain burned to the ground, of a village in the Uí Maille lands far to the north put to the sword, and of a massacre at an Ostman village on Kerlingfjord. When he had finally returned, Jarl Sigtrygg had denied any involvement in those attacks before dumping a small fortune in good English silver coin onto the floor of his feasting hall to settle-up his debt to his father. Not one word of thanks had passed his lips, and for good measure the ungrateful swine had demanded payment for news from England; news which, he claimed, his father would consider of the highest importance. The konungr had agreed, though his son's information only confirmed the whispers that Ragnall had already heard from his slave traders in Bristol and Chester: that the Earl Strongbow would bring an army to Ireland, and that he planned to take Veðrarfjord for his own.

A roar of triumph sounded from Jarl Sigtrygg's war band, startling Ragnall from his reminiscences and his warriors into sudden conversation as they awaited their konungr's order to engage with the enemy. Sigtrygg Fionn noted his army's demeanour and pumped his axe into the air, shouting the name of his city each time it reached its highpoint.

'Veðrarfjord!' the jarl shouted again and again, and the warriors joined his call to arms, beating their weapons on the back of their shields and shouting curses in the direction of the fort walls. Sigtrygg Fionn was not so stupid as to countermand Ragnall's orders, but he worked the eight hundred warriors to frenzy and soon men began streaming past their konungr to join the fight by the gates.

Ragnall was a patient man, but he ground his teeth in frustration. His allies amongst the Gael could not be roused to speed while his jarls could not be prevented from plunging into the fray at every opportunity.

'Lead them on, then,' he shouted at Sigtrygg Fionn, for what else could he do? His army was on the move and could not be stopped from joining his son's attack on Dun Domhnall. All Ragnall could do was to make it seem like it had been his order to send them forth. Sigtrygg Fionn grinned as he accepted his konungr's order and began bellowing the name of their city and invoking the name of the saints who would grant his people victory.

'Onwards!' shouted Ragnall of Veðrarfjord as he watched them charge the short distance towards the Norman fortifications. Despite his reservations about helping his son win glory, he watched with great pride as his folk marched towards battle. They sang as they pushed forward. It was the song of their people, of the founding of their city three hundred years before.

One youngster stepped out of the cluster of men and vomited. An older man, an uncle or his father, slapped him twice on the back and pulled the boy back into line.

'Onwards,' Ragnall murmured as he watched them go. It was only the sound of savage drums, deep and disjointed, that made him turn his back on his army and Dun Domhnall. On the bluff at his back the Gael had finally arrayed for battle. Two and a half thousand warriors walked towards him, ready to attack, and for the first time in many days a smile broke across the Konungr of Veðrarfjord's face for he knew now that victory over the foreigners was inevitable.

Light began to seep in, like sunshine behind thick cloud,

dazzling yet dull, uncomfortable. Then noise started to force its way past the blur to assail his ears. The sensation lasted only seconds. His head began to spin and his stomach churn. Then, a gust of alarm as he realised that he could not breathe. Raymond choked and panicked and attempted to grapple at his midriff, but only the fingers of his right hand found his chainmailed chest and searched for relief from the pain. His left arm was pinned down and, as he tried to sit up and force air into his lungs, he wondered if he had lost the limb. He did not wish to open his eyes. He did not want to confirm his fears.

'Wake up,' a voice shouted desperately, if distantly, from above. 'Please, wake up!'

He felt his shoulders shake before he was slapped twice across his cheek. Raymond was sure he was dying for no air was flowing down his windpipe, and his left arm was in agony. He felt his eyes bulge and reel below his eyelids while his tongue floundered like a landed trout, but finally, as he rolled over onto his left shoulder, a blast of cold, stinging air fought its way down into his chest, and for several seconds he heaved in and out ferociously. He swallowed back the desire to vomit and clung to the tough leather clothes of the figure kneeling at his side. The person was atop his shield which, still strapped to his forearm, pinned the captain to the ground. Despite his efforts to breathe he realised that he had not lost his arm and thanked the saints for that blessing.

'Raymond!' the youth appealed and shook him again by the armour at the nap of his neck.

He quickly recognised that that voice belonged to Geoffrey of Abergavenny and he opened his eyes to look at his esquire. He immediately wished that he had remained unconscious.

His last memory had been of a much different scene to that which he now observed. His brave courser was nowhere in sight, and in Dreigiau's place was a lone warrior. He stood between Raymond and the packed ranks of Ostmen enemy. The figure was flanked on either side by the torn-down outer gates to Dun Domhnall, a shield on his arm and sword in his hand. But as Raymond and the Ostmen watched, the warrior stabbed his sword into the soil and removed his spangenhelm, casting it at the feet of his enemy while loudly extolling the heavens for strength and support. No-one, other than a man shorn of his wits, would begin a fight without a helmet, especially when faced with such odds as those against the lone warrior. It was suicide, Raymond thought. It was eighty against one.

He only understood when the figure dragged his chainmail coif from his head so that the enemy could clearly see his face.

'God grant this poor sinner redemption,' William Ferrand wheezed towards the sky, oblivious it seemed to the threat of the men to his front. 'Holy David, hear my prayer and give me the strength to stand when all others flee.' As always, Ferrand's voice was little more than a gravelly rasp, yet it carried even to where Raymond slumped under the shadow of the barbican. 'Give me a good death,' the leper continued 'Give me back my honour.'

Though only one man now stood between them and their victory, Raymond could see that Jarl Sigtrygg's crew was hesitant. They encircled the yawning gates of Dun Domhnall, but none was willing to come forward and fight the spectral figure drawn straight from their foulest nightmares.

'Look,' Geoffrey whispered, staring over his captain's head and down the length of the double fortifications.

There, two hundred paces away, the second set of gates was opening to allow the survivors of the Ostman attack to pour through. Gasps of elation carried to Raymond and Geoffrey's ears as the surviving Welsh archers and Norman horsemen attempted to force their way inside before the enemy forced their way past Ferrand.

'We must hurry,' Geoffrey insisted and began to help his captain to his feet. 'We need to get inside before the enemy attack again.'

Raymond leaned hard on Geoffrey's shoulder as he climbed to his feet. Bodies were everywhere, both Ostmen and his own people, and the ground shone with blood. Injured men's groans of agony echoed around the small space between the wooden walls while the smell of excrement almost made Raymond gag. He shook his head sharply to clear the daze caused by his fall from Dreigiau's back. His helmet had come away, but he had no time to assess his injuries for he could see that one of the Ostmen had finally steeled himself to fight against the ghoulish Ferrand.

It was Jarl Sigtrygg.

The giant warrior did not speak as he strode forward. On his arm was a circular shield and in his right a long axe and, as he looked Ferrand up and down contemptuously, he said something in Danish which earned a small laugh from his men.

'Go, sick man,' he then told the Norman. 'Run away or I will kill you.'

Ferrand did not move, but mumbled a prayer to St Maurice as he prepared to meet the Ostman in battle.

Geoffrey whimpered at the sight of the jarl and hauled furiously at Raymond's arm. 'We need to run if we are to get into the fortress before the enemy reach the gates.'

'No,' Raymond croaked. He could see that the inner gates remained open and that there were still men attempting to gain entry. He turned his eyes towards the eighty-strong crew of Ostmen and then back down the length of the alley between the two walls. He gauged that if Jarl Sigtrygg was to send his men down between the fortifications and attack the gates the fortress would surely fall. 'You go and I'll be right behind you,' he told the esquire, pushing the boy in the direction of the gates.

'Come on then,' Geoffrey exclaimed, skidding to a halt a few steps away, and urging Raymond to follow as he had said that he would.

The captain merely shook his head. 'Go on, Ferrand and I will catch up. Make sure those gates are closed.' With that Raymond sucked another chest full of air in through his nose and drew his sword from his side. 'Go,' he ordered with more force than was necessary, and watched as the shocked esquire took a few steps towards the gates. Raymond did not have time to feel guilty, and turned his back on Geoffrey, locking the edge of his shield to that of Ferrand.

'We will stand together here,' Raymond told the leper, 'the sick man on the left and the fat one to his right. We'll hold them here and let our people get safely inside the bailey.' As he turned to make sure Ferrand understood, he spotted the last emotion that he thought possible in the leper's rheumy eyes: happiness.

'God has given me a chance to keep my oath,' Ferrand wheezed, tears of joy pouring down his gnarled and discoloured cheeks. 'I told you that I would fight alongside you, whatever the odds. Eighty men against two – God will grant us good deaths,' he said and turned back to meet Jarl Sigtrygg's angry porcine eyes.

'God grant us good deaths,' Raymond repeated and pictured Basilia de Quincy.

'Montjoie!' he shouted and lifted his shield to meet his enemy's blade.

Strongbow watched as his army sloshed through the ford of the sparkling River Cleddau and into the small town of Haverford on the far bank. Pride bubbled in his chest at the sight of the men who followed his family's crimson and gold colours. Eight hundred warriors! Such an army had not been seen in Wales since King Henry had forced the native princes to submit to his will six summers before. Strongbow had, of course, not been part of that campaign, the king neglecting to request his presence or that of his diminished household. The earl felt his shoulders stiffen as he recalled that particular insult. It had saved him a great deal of money and trouble, of course, but the affront still found its target. Assailed by atrocious weather and complications with supplies, Henry had been forced into an embarrassing retreat by little more than a handful of Welsh bowmen. A smile broke across Strongbow's thin lips before he could think better of it; many good men had perished under the Welsh arrow-storm as Henry's army had crept back towards Shrewsbury. Worse, the Welsh, emboldened by their victory, had soon overrun more fortresses, killing, raping and pillaging as they had passed through Powys.

No, he chastised, *that is not a memory to be enjoyed*.

The lesson taken from that campaign, however, had to be acknowledged: that a force of only a few archers could meet a host and emerge victorious. Raymond de Carew had believed that to be true and had used his friendship with Seisyll ap Dyfnwal to hire a small troop of bowmen for his vanguard now across the sea in Ireland. Strongbow had no friends among the Welsh, and he refused to go on bended knee to beg assistance from any man, let alone the bandit Seisyll. Instead his requirement to find archers had led him into Little England-beyond-Wales.

They told strange stories about those lands to the west of Pembroke, where the tongues of English serf and Cymric prince were predominant, and only a few barons of breeding spoke French. Traders described strange men, hermits, druids, and ancient evils that could no longer be found in Christian England or Gwent but still lived in the extreme west. They said that Little England-beyond-Wales was a place where faery folk and fantastical beasts still resided, and where forests emerged from the sea at the turning of the tide. They spoke of trolls who lived in the mountains and of spirits that inhabited rivers. It was only the light of Christ in St David's and the Norman manors and castles which kept the evil at bay. Here, Strongbow was sure he would find a company of bowmen to rival any in Christendom.

From the hall, high up on the plateau to the north of the crossing, Strongbow watched as his army's vanguard emerged from the river and passed into the darkening streets of the market town on the far bank. He hoped that his captain, Robert FitzBernard, had taken the necessary steps to prevent any of his warriors from disappearing from the column and into one of the many dank taverns of thatched Haverford. His army would only be in the town until dawn when they would make the final leg of their journey to the port of Melrfjord where they would prepare to take ship to Ireland. He could not afford to be without even one of those who had agreed to join him on his expedition and he knew from his youth how an army's ranks could thin as men deserted their duty for a night's drinking, never rousing from their drunkenness until it was too late and their comrades departed.

'Lord?' a tall man in green vestments hailed Strongbow as he marched into the great hall. Like many Flemings, his French was spoken with the distinctive clipped Germanic tone of his ancestors. He set aside a heavy bow and arrow bag as he came in, trailed by the short, stout steward who had first greeted Strongbow at the manor house door.

'Greetings sir,' the earl replied, inclining his head slightly in the man's direction. Strongbow had never trusted the Flemish as a race, not since he had seen first-hand the depravity of their kind during the reign of King Stephen, but he forced a friendly smile onto his face as he confronted Maurice, the lord of the manor of Prendergast. 'Your steward was kind enough to show me into your hall to await your return.'

The Fleming slowly nodded his head as he backtracked towards a table and began sorting through a number of rolls of paper, storing them in a box. 'I'm afraid that my household is quite unprepared for a visit from a person of your eminence, but I can ready a room for you? I suspect that I will not be able to house all your companions.' Maurice waved a hand in the direction of the army in the belly of the valley and smiled. Strongbow did not share in his attempt at mirth and Prendergast quickly changed tack: 'Might I offer you some small beer instead?' Without waiting for a reply he waved his steward forward and, as his mug was filled, he began whispering furiously in his own language into the man's ear.

Strongbow would've gladly accepted wine but, rather than be impolite, he accepted a cup filled to the brim and slowly sipped at the cloudy brown liquid. 'I am honoured by your offer of hospitality, sir,' the earl began, 'but I have already agreed to stay...' He indicated through the open window at his side towards the church half-hidden behind Haverford Castle on the hill opposite. A morose look passed over Prendergast's face as both men stared at the town on a high spur of land across the river. Strongbow suddenly remembered hearing news of some trouble between the two neighbouring lords, a squabble over the theft of animals and an abandoned marriage proposal from a few years before. 'I will not be the guest of Richard FitzTancred,' Strongbow described quickly to ease any awkwardness. 'I am to stay with the archdeacon at St Martin's Church. My army will camp to the south of the town tonight.'

Prendergast smiled politely and for many minutes neither man said anything. Instead each supped silently at their beer and stared out of the keep's south facing window as the army marched through the town opposite. The murmur of conversation between the warriors reached even to Prendergast's manor house, two long bow shots away.

It was the Fleming who broke the silence: 'Lord, I know what brings you to my hall, and I do not wish to waste your time, but I will not return to Ireland with you.'

'I was led to believe that you had acquired a large estate there.'

Prendergast nodded. 'I also acquired enemies – Robert FitzStephen and King Diarmait – and I don't think either would permit me to visit his domain again.'

The Fleming had been Robert FitzStephen's second-in-command, Strongbow knew, and had fought alongside the Norman when they had stormed the walls of the Norse city of Waesfjord the year before. But something had triggered a breakdown between the two men, leading Prendergast to flee FitzStephen's side, along with almost a third of their army, and join the service of their enemies on the eve of battle with the High King of Ireland. FitzStephen had somehow managed to win that fight despite facing overwhelming odds and Prendergast had returned home to Wales in defeat with barely the clothes upon his back to show for his efforts across the sea.

The Fleming stepped forward suddenly and put his hand

on Strongbow's sleeve. The earl was taken aback. A man of Prendergast's lowly standing should not have thought it appropriate to act like they were equals.

'I have to warn you,' Prendergast told him, 'that I have seen things in that savage land of which even the Devil himself could not conceive. No matter what glory or realm which you think you will win, I promise you it will be fleeting. These Gael do not forget and are vicious in their search for retribution. I have seen it,' he told him earnestly. 'With God's grace I lived to tell the tale, but I will not go back.'

Strongbow frowned deeply, not because of Prendergast's warning, but because he was angry and frustrated. He did not wish the Fleming to see the effect of his words, but his ire bubbled. He wanted to call Prendergast a coward, to challenge him to prove his accusation of spinelessness wrong, but he could see that it would do no good and so he held his tongue. He refused to beg and barter like a cloth merchant on Gloucester's wharf to secure the services of Prendergast's two hundred-strong archer warband.

Prendergast had turned away and was waving his mug in the air to attract the attention of his steward bearing the jug of beer. He did not even think to excuse himself before leaving the earl's side. He roared in the English tongue at the servant on the far side of the room. Strongbow sighed at the small insult and began staring out the window at the town of Haverford. A shadow, cast by the high cliffs above the crossing, seemed to cover the whole of the thatched settlement. Atop that natural motte sat the castle like a squat owl eying a fat mouse at its feet. As with Striguil, Haverford's castle was perfectly placed to command the river crossing and anyone who chose to use its course to travel further inland. The similarity with his home led

Strongbow's mood to darken further. Haverford was one of the castles which belonged to the Honour of Pembroke, the estate and earldom which his father had won, and of which Strongbow had been unfairly deprived by King Henry. The anger at the injustice burned brightly in his chest. Cilgerran, Emlyn, Pembroke, Manorbier, and Tenby were some of the great Marcher castles that should have been part of his Welsh fief. Instead they were held by low-born royal constables like Richard FitzTancred who sent the profits from his estates to the crown treasury or, more likely, stole it to enrich themselves while he, the lawful owner, was almost ruined. His lips squeezed to white as he fought the all-too-familiar anger.

Had he been earl in deed as well as name, Pembroke would've provided him with two hundred knights' fees, a thousand spearmen and as many archers as he required, while those from his share of the Giffard lands scattered across England and Normandy would've given half that number again. Strongbow closed his eyes and remembered a time when that power had been his, almost unmatched by any man in the kingdom, before the ascension of Henry FitzEmpress to the throne. He recalled riding at the head of a column of chainmail-clad warriors all sworn to the House of Pembroke, two thousand knightly pennants flying above their spears. He had been a boy, eighteen years old and raw, when his father had died, but King Stephen had treated him with great respect and in turn Strongbow had raised an army of thousands to serve the goodly monarch against his rebellious subjects in the north. It had been the earl's proudest moment, exciting and terrifying in equal measure, as he had led his army in defence of his king's throne. He had not had to scrape and bow to the likes of Maurice de Prendergast, men not worthy of his lineage, but had ordered them to do his bidding. That time had passed, but it would come again, he promised.

He reordered his thoughts to the present as Prendergast returned to his side, his mug refilled without bothering to offer his guest the same. Behind the Fleming, more men had made their way into the hall, talking loudly and bawdily as they entered. Not a few threw interested glances in Strongbow's direction, but most simply sat down at the tables scattered around the room and called loudly for ale. It was obvious to the earl that Prendergast considered their business over and rather than spend any more time bartering and rebuffing his guest he had simply decided to make Strongbow feel awkward by inviting his captains into the hall.

The manor house was, to Strongbow's eye, closer in design to a barn than the great hall at Striguil. The building was dry and stoutly built, and in a defensible position, but its lord had either not the sense or the finances to build a proper keep. Even the wooden walls which surrounded its bailey were in need of repair. A man with two hundred archers at his disposal was a powerful man on the March, but that, Strongbow decided, did not make him a rich one and a lord who could not pay his troops would not command them for long. That he knew from experience.

'I am sorry that I cannot help you,' Prendergast continued and slumped into a wicker chair, causing it to squeak and stretch beneath his weight. His beer sloshed from his mug, onto his hand and he grimaced as he wiped his fingers clean of the liquid on the thin table top before him. 'But I will pray that your endeavours will bring you success, Sir Richard.' A self-satisfied hint of smile twisted the edges of Prendergast's mouth.

Strongbow summoned his courage. 'I regret that you feel the opportunity in Ireland too dangerous for your men,' the earl said. He had never had a strong voice but he now forced it to pierce the hubbub of the hall. 'I had thought the men of Flanders hardier than that, but nevertheless I will visit with Richard FitzTancred at Haverford Castle this very hour and hope that his stomach is sterner and his ambition greater than that which I have found here at Prendergast.' With that he turned on his heel and made for the door. His stomach churned as he realised that the clamour in the room had abated following his words and that all eyes were on him as he strode through the main hall. He kept his head high as he made his departure, picking a path directly towards the main door while being careful not to walk too fast or to appear apprehensive.

However, when a tall warrior rose from the bench and placed himself in his path, the earl began to worry that he had indeed miscalculated with his stern words.

'Out of my way,' he squeaked at the man before clearing his throat and trying again, more forcefully. 'Out of my way, I say.'

The Fleming's only response was to step closer and place a big hand on Strongbow's chest, preventing him from leaving. The earl felt uneasiness pucker in his stomach. He was alone in this fortress amongst foreigners, foreigners who he had insulted. He gathered his courage to make another effort to move the warrior:

'You will get out of my path,' he stated, but the bearded man merely shook his shaggy head.

'Wait, sir,' he said and raised his chin to address Prendergast. 'I don't understand why you would turn down this opportunity, Maurice. Did you not see the size of that army?' the Flemish warrior continued, earning a number of supportive grunts from his fellow captains scattered around the feasting hall. 'We were able to claim Waesfjord last summer with an army half the size of the one that Lord Strongbow has mustered.' The man kept his palm firmly on

393

the earl's surcoat as he turned towards the hall to encourage the like-minded amongst the warriors to support him. 'Why would we not want to go back to Ireland?'

Maurice de Prendergast could not have missed the number of his followers who grunted encouragingly at the man's words. 'I did not think that you would speak against me, Osbert de Cusac,' he said reprovingly, but his words were lost immediately as another man, younger than the first, weighed in:

'I still don't know why we left FitzStephen's side in the first place!' the second man snarled. 'I barely made it back home with more money than I had when I landed in Ireland.'

'That was only because we sold our horses to those crooks in Veðrarfjord,' Osbert butted in again.

Strongbow, momentarily forgotten, watched quietly as the Flemings argued his cause for him. He stole a glance towards the dais where Maurice de Prendergast had climbed to his feet in an attempt to calm his warriors down. He held up his hands to achieve quiet and allow him to speak, but the discussion had already started between the warriors below.

'The summer is already upon us,' Osbert barked, 'and no offers have come from Philip FitzWizo for our service. We all heard how Rhys ap Gruffydd raided Llandissilio two weeks ago. Yet our lord in Wiston did not summon the men of Prendergast to help him fight our enemies.' Osbert pointed an accusatory finger at Maurice. 'There is something amiss when he does not bid his best warriors to join him in a fight! And now another offer falls right in our lap,' he said, finally removing his hand from Strongbow's chest and stepping back to allow everyone to see the Norman baron, 'but Maurice wishes to let it pass him by so that we can sit on our backsides all summer and grow poorer.'

Amid the growls of agreement and ire, Prendergast was finally able to speak. 'There will be other offers, of that I am sure. I have never let you down. Did I not get a good price from the Bishop of St David's for our services? Did I not earn us land south of Waesfjord from Robert FitzStephen? Remind me, Osbert, who it was who found work with Donnchadh Mac Giolla Phádraig when our allies betrayed us?' He nodded his head. 'That is correct – me. And I will find us riches again. We need not go back to Ireland.'

As Strongbow looked around the faces in the manor, he could see that Osbert was losing the argument. Maurice de Prendergast was obviously a good lord and his men trusted him. In many ways the Fleming reminded Strongbow of Raymond de Carew and he felt a pang of jealousy rise in his chest. His father had possessed that power too, he remembered.

'If your lord, Maurice, says that he can get you service in Wales, I believe him,' Strongbow told the room of warriors. All eyes turned to look at him. 'From what I have heard he has won you much, if not in terms of great wealth, certainly in renown.' He allowed his words to traverse their minds. 'I do not offer any man fame,' he said with a shake of his head. 'I offer only riches and unless Maurice de Prendergast can promise, here and now, to lead you to capture both Bristol and Chester this summer then he cannot match what I offer to those who follow my banner. I mean to take both the Danish cities of Veðrarfjord and Dubhlinn.' He stressed the names of both the famous Scandinavian settlements in Ireland. 'You have seen Veðrarfjord for yourselves and Dubhlinn is said to be four times as big. That is what I offer in return for your bows. So you can stay here in hope of employment or you can join me and become rich. You have until I reach the ford to

395

Haverford to make your choice.'

Again the room descended into the murmur of debate and argument and, with a final nod in Maurice de Prendergast's direction, Strongbow strode from the hall without a backwards glance. He managed to hold off the panic as he climbed down the stairs to the ground floor. He was even able to swap some small talk with an esquire as he retrieved his palfrey from Prendergast's small stable, but, as he passed through the gate in the defensive walls, worry reached into his stomach and twisted his guts. He had half expected to be called back before he had reached the main door of the manor house, to be told that the Flemish captains had convinced Maurice de Prendergast to take up his offer and follow him to Ireland. That he had made it to the outbuildings without one of the warriors dashing to stop him and beg him to reconsider made him worry that he had misjudged the temper of the room and Maurice's hold over the Flemish bowmen.

'Slow there,' he whispered to the mare and pulled on his reins as he passed through the gates. He wanted to turn in the saddle to see if anyone followed him but he knew that he had to keep up the facade of confidence, his eyes straight ahead and fixed upon Haverford Castle. He emerged from between the heavy timber gateposts into bright sunshine, but his mood was anything but good. Strongbow had set the gates as his Rubicon and beyond them his hopes of securing a company of archers would be over. Before he had departed for Ireland, Raymond had made the earl promise that he would use all his efforts to engage a warband of bowmen, saying that with even a hundred more he would conquer a realm as large as Strongbow could imagine. Without them, his captain had told him, their campaign would be short and unsuccessful.

Strongbow felt a bead of cold sweat separate from his

hairline and run down his face. He had not admitted as much to Prendergast, but he had already asked every Norman baron in Glamorgan to permit him to employ their archers, and had been turned down at every hall because he could not pay silver up front. It was the work of William de Braose, he was sure. Strongbow had hoped that in Little England beyond Wales, rather than the infuriating obstinance of landed lords, he would find desperate men willing to take any chance to plunder loot at his side. Strongbow had thought to inspire them as Raymond had Seisyll ap Dyfnwal with stories of great lands won by warriors with no less right than they. He had failed and now all he had accomplished and built in the last weeks and months seemed constructed on unstable foundations. He worried about the men he had appointed to high command and those he had chosen to stay behind. He worried about the condition of the ships that he had procured at Melrfjord and he worried about being cheated by all who surrounded him.

He wiped the perspiration from his brow as his mount began walking down the hillside. He felt his weight shift onto his hips as he leaned back in the saddle. On each side he watched as English serfs toiled in bountiful fields, spreading manure and buckets of water amongst Prendergast's wheat crop.

It had all been for naught, Strongbow decided. He had reduced himself to penury for a folly that could never have resulted in success. He had gained an army to conquer a kingdom, but without archers he knew the odds were stacked against him. Doubt assailed Strongbow.

Only that morning a brute sent by the moneylender in Gloucester had caught up with his army, thundering along the length of his column on a palfrey worth more than that beneath the earl. The newcomer had demanded that

Strongbow hand over silver before he set sail for Ireland in part payment of his debt – even the Godless Jew had realised the recklessness of the campaign and wished to extract what he could before the opportunity was lost for ever. What the debt collector did not know was that the earl had exhausted every single line of finance, and had called in every favour owed to his house. He had nothing left to give. Yossi's man had argued, of course, had called Strongbow a liar and so the earl had ordered Milo de Cogan to hurry the man, as well as his six gruff and heavily armed companions, down the road without a penny.

Strongbow's poverty remained. It seemed so long ago that Diarmait had made the offer to name him his heir to the kingdom of Laighin. Now he could not even afford a single sheep to load onto his ships for his army to slaughter when they made land in Ireland. If Raymond had not been successful in maintaining his bridgehead or, worse, had not obtained enough animals for them to eat, then Strongbow and his army would face starvation. They would have to range far and wide foraging for food. Spread thinly, his men would be easy pickings for any army arrayed against them.

Strongbow was so lost in his thoughts that when the shout came it almost made him tumble from his saddle in surprise.

'Lord Strongbow!' the Flemish esquire shouted from the manor house gate. 'Please wait!'

He did not turn immediately, but he did bring his horse to a complete stop. Instead of addressing the boy Strongbow closed his eyes and murmured a prayer to St Benedict in thanks for sending his munificent aid. For he knew the message that the boy would carry: Maurice de Prendergast had reconsidered his decision. He would follow Strongbow to Ireland. And the crown that had seemed so uncertain could still be his – as long as Raymond de Carew remained true and his bridgehead secure.

It was the sudden coldness as it caught in his throat that Raymond noticed first, not the darkness. Only moments before he and Ferrand had been bathed in blazing sunshine as it poured over the inner wall, but now his breath misted before his eyes as their fighting retreat took them backwards between the two battlements towards the inner gates.

Not that Raymond felt cold. His shoulders and legs burned with effort as he fought against Jarl Sigtrygg's crew. His mind was a blur as he attempted to keep his shield locked with that of Ferrand as well as to strike out and to block the Ostmen's attempts to kill him. Together, he and Ferrand filled the whole width between the two fortifications, but the weight of men who opposed them was immense and they were pushed inexorably backwards by the wave of colourfully painted circular shields. The only thing in the Norman duo's favour was that so many of Jarl Sigtrygg's crew attempted to kill them that they got in each others' way.

Nevertheless two men could not hold out for long against almost eighty and step by step they fell back down the alleyway. Neither Norman had the chance to steal a glance behind them, to discover if the gates were open or closed, rather they could only block and stab before retreating again. Raymond had not even the breath to call Roland's war cry, but breathed hot sweat through his chainmail coif as he felled his closest opponent. Another Ostman quickly took the place of the fallen man, leaping over his comrade to engage his retreating enemy. Raymond jabbed twice, low and hard, at his midriff and when the leather-clad Ostman dropped his shield, anticipating a third attempt, Raymond brought his sword pommel down hard on the man's left shoulder, breaking the bone and sending the man to the ground. He wasted no time and withdrew another step to again lock his shield with that of Ferrand, battling equally hard to his left.

'Stay beside me,' Raymond wheezed in the leper's direction as another warrior armed with a spear disentangled himself from the crush and threw himself upon their shields. The impact rocked both men onto their heels. The Ostman was soon joined by another bearded raider wielding a two-handed axe. He yelled something unintelligible as he swung the weapon in circles around his head to build up momentum, but he only succeeded in forcing the warriors behind and beside him to duck lest he cleave their heads in two. When his axe did fall Ferrand stepped back suddenly, allowing the blade to slam into the pathway at his feet. Woodchips and loose stones scattered everywhere but neither Norman was hurt. The Ostman was unbalanced and abandoned his weapon to slam his shoulder into Ferrand's shield, tackling the leper backwards beyond Raymond's vision.

'Ferrand! Are you alright?' Raymond called desperately as his small shieldwall disintegrated. He heard no response and Raymond dared not turn to see if Ferrand still lived for another warrior had pulled the axe from where it was buried in the ground and now threatened him alongside the younger man armed with the spear.

The axeman struck first, shouting a challenge as he hooked the blade over the top rim of Raymond's shield and attempted to rip it from his grasp. By his side, the spearman waited for an opening to stab the Norman's defenceless midriff.

'Ferrand!' Raymond appealed again as he fought the weight coming onto his left arm. He knew that he could not lose his shield, nor could he stab at his assailant lest the other man spear him in his undefended flank. Both his arms quivered with effort, his left from exertion, the other from yearning to attack.

Suddenly a high-pitched scream sounded from his side and a slight figure bounded past Raymond to plant a bloody dagger in the axeman's upper arm. The pressure immediately relented as the Ostman fell to the floor in agony, but Raymond didn't give the second warrior a chance to gain an advantage and gave him two huge sword cuts which forced him backwards into the crush of his crewmen. He then turned and stabbed downwards to take the axeman's life.

'I told you to run!' he shouted as he pulled Geoffrey of Abergavenny to his feet, forcing him behind him again. The boy was pale but he stooped to pick up a fallen spear.

'I'm your esquire,' Geoffrey exclaimed. He had to yell in order to make himself heard over the noise coming from the Ostmen. 'I should be at your side when you go into battle.'

'This isn't a battle,' Ferrand hissed as he righted himself beside Raymond. 'It is a damned street brawl.' He noticed his captain's apprehensive glance at his shoulder where blood was seeping through the links in his coat of steel. 'I'll be fine. I could fight on all day,' he insisted, but his hand went briefly to the wound.

Raymond knew that they could not hold off the Ostmen for much longer. Though it felt like hours, they had only been fighting for a matter of minutes and Raymond could see that Ferrand was tiring. There were simply too many for two men, one a leper, and an esquire to fight. He glanced past Geoffrey to where, thirty paces away, the last of his conrois and archers were finally disappearing through the inner gates to the relative safety beyond.

'Geoffrey, go now before the gates close,' he ordered, but the boy refused to budge. Raymond looked over his shoulder at him. 'I need you to make sure that the gates will be closed and that no one keeps them open to wait for Ferrand and me. Go!'

But instead of running to the salvation of the bailey Geoffrey's eyes widened in alarm forcing Raymond to recognise another threat approached him down the path between the fortifications.

'Go!' he told his esquire again before hefting his weapons and turning to meet the next charge of the Ostmen. Instead only one man approached. Jarl Sigtrygg did not run but stared menacingly at the two Normans who blocked his path. Raymond felt Ferrand tense at his side. Even the Ostmen of Veðrarfjord had quieted as they watched their giant leader walk forward. They expected to see him sweep aside the stubborn resistance of the Normans and lead them in an attack on the inner walls of Dun Domhnall. However, rather than attack he put his hand to his ear and arched his neck as if listening to the wooden fortification to his left.

'Do you hear that sound?' Jarl Sigtrygg asked and, for the first time since the fight between the walls of Dun Domhnall had begun, Raymond noticed shouting and the thump of feet coming from beyond the outer defences. 'That is the sound of eight hundred of Veðrarfjord's best warriors marching towards your little fort,' Jarl Sigtrygg told the three Normans, his braided beard curling into a smile. 'They are coming to kill you and the sick man. Then we will storm the gates and kill all inside.' He dropped his hand and took his axe from his belt, tossing it into the air before catching it and pointing it at Raymond. 'The good news is that you will not have to see any of that,' he sneered as he brought his shield up to eye level and stared malevolently over its rim at his enemy. 'Time to die, Raymond the Fat,' Sigtrygg shouted at his opponent and that was the signal for six spears to be launched from the crowd behind the jarl. Two soared overhead but the rest struck their target, forcing Ferrand and Raymond to raise their shields to defend themselves from the projectiles.

Jarl Sigtrygg reacted immediately, using the brief distraction to jump forward and smash his shield boss into Raymond's. Jarl Sigtrygg's frenzied axe attack did not allow the Norman captain a chance to hit back. Instead Raymond crouched, protecting his head, with both hands pressed against the back of his teardrop shield and his cheeks puffing with effort. The weight of the giant jarl was like that of a stampeding bullock as he attempted to trample Raymond into the ground.

A second man, wearing a bright orange woollen shirt, joined his jarl, colliding with Ferrand as the leper raised his sword arm to slash at Jarl Sigtrygg's head. The blow missed its target as Ferrand was rocked back on his heels and into Geoffrey who, having speared Sigtrygg's crewman in the shoulder, was knocked aside in a tangle of bodies. Raymond was almost taken down by his fellows, but he kept his feet as Geoffrey, Ferrand and the injured Ostman tumbled into his legs. Jarl Sigtrygg's onslaught continued and he was keening now, cursing Raymond for his timidity. The Norman could hear the Ostmen of Veðrarfjord begin to roar their support for their jarl, urging him to lead them to victory.

'Come on,' Jarl Sigtrygg shouted. 'Come out from behind that shield!' A massive set of fingers appeared and gripped the top of Raymond's shield close to his head.

He knew what was about to happen; that Sigtrygg would force the top of his shield down and deliver a killing blow to his head with the axe. And he could tell that the jarl was

stronger than he. Raymond's head shook and his vision
swirled as he gripped his teeth and clung onto the straps
pinned to the back of his shield with both his hands, but
nothing he did could turn the fight in his favour. The
inevitability of Jarl Sigtrygg's victory over him forced a
roar of frustration and effort from his throat. But in that
second, an idea came to him. He acted upon it immediately.
He simply let go.

What happened next was a blur. Raymond was aware
that he had fallen backwards and that his temple had
cracked onto something hard as he had landed. Punch-
drunk, he knew that he had to rise and finish Jarl Sigtrygg
before his enemy had the chance to recover and do the same
to him. But his legs would not respond and he toppled to
his knees with dizziness. He fought the sensation, but he
found it impossible to focus his eyes and, as he blinked and
clung to the struts which held up the fighting platform, he
was aware of a strange sound which suddenly punctured
his daze. It was like the sound of a hundred serfs with heavy
flails threshing wheat. He had heard that noise often during
summers spent overseeing Strongbow's estates though he
could not imagine why the task would suddenly be
performed during a battle.

'It's too early to have brought in the harvest,' he slurred
and collapsed from his knees onto his backside. He
attempted to open his eyes again but they continued to roll
in his head. 'One more month at least,' he babbled as the
thwack of wood continued to echo around him though it
was now swamped by screaming. Raymond barely had
time to register the cause of the new sound for, at that
moment, a set of hands slipped under his armpits and he
felt himself being dragged away, his heels trailing on the
wood chip ground.

'But the serfs,' he garbled and flapped his left hand

towards the sound of the flails.

'Have you lost your senses, you dolt?' wheezed Ferrand. He grunted with the effort that it took to lug his captain away from the fight between the battlements towards the open gates to Dun Domhnall.

Fighting the urge to vomit, Raymond forced his eyes open and found that he had regained control over his sight and was staring straight up into Ferrand's crumbling features. His mind quickly reordered as he stared at the leper's upside down face, bounded on all sides by the brightest blue sky that he had ever seen. He remembered talking to Ragnall of Veðrarfjord at the estuary and fighting alongside Bertram d'Alton as *Waverider* burned. He recalled Dreigiau bucking and Geoffrey of Abergavenny stabbing at the axeman, and all of a sudden he did not feel sick or disorientated any longer. His head flopped forward so that he could look back down the length of the battlements. Raymond half expected that he would find Jarl Sigtrygg standing above him ready to deliver a killing blow to both he and Ferrand, but instead he instantaneously understood that the sound that had so confused him was not that of flails dividing grain from chaff. It had been the sound of bowstrings striking against elm bowstaves.

From the inner wall of Dun Domhnall Welsh archers were shooting downwards onto Jarl Sigtrygg's crew and Raymond knew instinctively that no warband could live long under that arrow storm. A strange sensation of sadness almost overtook him as he watched the death of an enemy that, a matter of moments before, had been trying to kill him. The sun had shifted position in the sky and the rays now poured directly down between the two battlements, almost blinding him. He was thankful that he had to turn away from the slaughter.

'Let me go,' Raymond complained towards Ferrand. 'I

can stand up now.'

'Be quiet. We are almost there.' Ferrand hissed as he dragged Raymond to his left. Suddenly Raymond's world went dark. The Norman captain's feet collided with wood before he was dumped unceremoniously onto the hard earth back in the dazzling sunshine.

'Close the gates,' Ferrand cried, now closer to Raymond's ear than before. The captain realised that the leper had crumpled to the floor due to his exertions and had dragged Raymond on top of him. Ferrand's gnarled hand slid across his chest as the creak of wooden gates sliding shut sounded to Raymond's front.

'You are safe now,' an exhausted Ferrand rasped. He held Raymond firm and patted his chest like a mother would do a scared child at night. 'They cannot get to you. You are safe now.'

Raymond tried to roll off Ferrand, but the leper's grip around his chest was immense and it was several seconds before he would allow his captain to break free. When he did Raymond immediately turned to comfort the man who had stood alongside side him when the likelihood of survival was lowest. Ferrand was now prone on the ground with what Raymond took to be a satisfied smile across his broken and gnarled face.

'Ferrand?' he called and shook the leper. 'William, are you alright?' There was no answer from the warrior and Raymond feared that Ferrand had got exactly what he had asked for on the morning that they had first landed in Ireland. He quickly looked around for assistance. Men were running this way and that in disorder and no one was paying any heed to Ferrand's plight.

'Geoffrey, bring me water quickly,' he called, but his esquire was nowhere to be seen. He made a mental note to reprimand his apprentice for being absent when he needed him and turned back to Ferrand. He stared at the man's face, wracked by disease, and wondered if it would be better that the warrior die now. He bowed his head to say a prayer to St Michael. 'He kept his oath and I pray that God was indeed watching when he recovered his honour. He saved the fort.'

A cheerful chuckle issued from the man lying beside him.

'We did that together,' Ferrand rasped. 'I only wished to save you,' he closed his eyes, a smile prominent on his ghastly face. 'And you are safe now.' His head flopped onto his shoulder and as much as Raymond tried to rouse him, Ferrand would not open his eyes again. Closer inspection allowed him to feel breath coming from his lungs. In the end Raymond's only option was to drag Ferrand away from the gates and lay him on the ground by the cattle pens above the beach. The animals, scared by the fighting, mooed and gathered together by the wattle fence as far from the battlements as they could get. The beasts were secure, but the twisted wooden rods squeaked and strained as the cattle pressed against the fence. Raymond momentarily wondered if Ferrand would be trampled if he remained beside the enclosure.

'Be safe, my friend,' he told the leper as he stood straight. The rigging and mast had gone, but *Waverider* still burned by the seashore and Raymond watched as the flames licked the fire-blackened sheer-strake on the steering board side. It was mesmeric as the slight wind off the sea made the fire roar. Even from a hundred paces away, he could feel the heat on his face and he closed his eyes, allowing the sour smoke to tease his nostrils. Raymond knew that he had responsibilities on the fortifications, but for a few seconds his army's plight and the pain in his arms and head disappeared as he concentrated on the thump of small waves against the cliffs and the grumble of flames as the fire consumed *Waverider*.

His trance was disturbed by the screams of injured men emanating from between the walls of Dun Domhnall. He tried to ignore them by closing his eyes, but they easily penetrated his thoughts and with a sigh Raymond opened his eyelids, returning to real life. He was amazed to see that *Waverider* had moved, only a matter of ten paces, but she was floating into the bay, revealing the undamaged Ostman vessel behind. The sight of *Waverider* escaping into the small waters somehow cheered him.

'Go on,' he urged the burning ship, 'Get out of here.'

Fully laden, *Waverider* only needed a draught of a few feet to float and, with her rigging and contents having burned away in the inferno, she needed even fewer now. Her prow swung northwards as he watched and she came to rest atop the dark rocks hidden just beneath the surface in the bay. He urged her to break free, his attention completely overtaken by the burning ship's efforts to escape, and he cursed the tide for not rising faster. Despite the roar of flames he could hear *Waverider*'s hull scratch along the rocks and then suddenly she was free again, squeezed between the oncoming tide and the underwater features in the bay so that she again travelled northwards.

Raymond would've cheered then, captivated as he was with the ship's progress, but at that second a new noise broke through the din of battle and forced him to turn away from the sea.

Alice screamed his name.

'Loose!' Borard shouted again. Welsh bowstrings slapped sharply against ash heartwood staves and arrows lanced into Jarl Sigtrygg's crew. The archers barely had the need to aim for they couldn't miss the enemy crammed into such

408

a small area as that between the fortifications. Instead the fifty men on the wall concentrated on shooting as fast as they could, letting loose a hail of arrows onto their enemy. In a matter of seconds hundreds sliced into the Ostmen.

'Lay it on,' Borard snarled as the Welsh archers grabbed for more arrows from the bags at their hips. Another flight whistled through the air to thump into the enemy below, striking face, torso and limb. Those had barely struck before another soared and struck home to rattle wooden wall and shield. The screeches coming from the wounded appalled Borard but he again ordered the men to unleash their fury on the enemy. 'They would do the same to you given half a chance,' he shouted. 'So lay it on them, you Welsh bastards!'

'They're running away!' one of the archers said before nocking another arrow and leaning over the pointed stakes of the wall to shoot one of the retreating Ostmen between his shoulder blades. He whooped as it hit home. So close were the targets that the Welsh arrows powered through the weak points in the shields. They ricocheted and scored through limbs held aloft. They clanged as they struck helmets and cleaved flesh as they passed through hardened leather armour like it was no thicker than vellum parchment.

The Ostmen were brave, but they knew that only death awaited them between the walls of Dun Domhnall and soon those closest to the outer gates had turned and fled to find shelter from the arrow storm on the far side of the fortifications. Quickly, more survivors began to make off in that direction, their colourful circular shields held across their backs to defend them from more Welsh arrows.

'Cease,' Borard shouted when he judged the fight to be over. Even with his order it still took several seconds to get all the Welshmen to stop shooting. 'Save your arrows.

409

They are finished,' he called and cursed the archers' native cruelty as they continued to kill the retreating men. It was only when their senior men translated his order that the Welshmen ceased their salvo.

Below Borard there was little movement. It was difficult to tell where one body ended and the next began. Arrows sprouted indiscriminately from flesh and from earth. It was like a terrible harvest. In the few minutes since they had begun their aerial onslaught the seventy archers had all but exhausted their supply of arrows and over two thousand peppered the small area below. Even the archers were quieted by the carnage which they had wrought. Groans and wailing resonated from between the walls.

'Raymond?' Borard called into the carnage and desperately searched the crush for any sign of his captain. It seemed like only moments before that Raymond's esquire had opened the outer gates allowing the Ostmen to pierce Dun Domhnall's defences. Borard had been certain that the outer wall was about to be captured and so he had leapt from the inner allure where he had been stationed and sprinted to the western extremity of the headland. There he had gathered the archers, who had been sent to watch over the western beach by Sir Hervey, and had brought them back to the wall. He thanked God that he had arrived back in time to stop the Ostman crew, but it had been a close run thing. Borard raised his eyes from the slaughter to look over the wall at the horde which approached the fort; a wave of hard leather and iron about to crash into the broken walls of Dun Domhnall.

'Raymond!'

Borard did not want to consider what would happen if command of the warband fell to Sir Hervey de Montmorency. His last sight of Strongbow's uncle had been of him galloping away from the attack of the Ostman crew, up the outer wall towards the inner gate. Might he be dead too? And to who would the captaincy fall then, he wondered. Walter de Bloet, he supposed, given that he was Strongbow's kinsman.

'Raymond!' he called again, more desperate than before. He was becoming ever more anxious. Sunshine dazzled him while flies and sweat annoyed his face. In the distance, drums and horns irritated Borard's ears. His stomach called out for ale. 'For God's sake, Raymond, are you alive down there?'

As he was beginning to lose all hope he spied his captain's shield. It was lying face up near the inner gates which, praise be to God, had again been closed in the face of the enemy. Of his captain he could see nothing and he prayed that he had made it through the gates and into the bailey before the archers had begun shooting. Several arrows stood proud in the crimson and gold shield. The last time he had seen him, Raymond had been outside the defences and on horseback alongside Bertram d'Alton. How he had managed to fight his way through the Ostman crew so that his shield was a few paces from the inner gate, Borard could not imagine. He turned away from the allure and looked down into the bailey. The survivors of the ten-strong conrois were strewn around the grass, tending to wounds and their horses. Esquires and pages ran to and fro, nervously handing out assistance and awaiting instruction.

'We need to get someone out there, between the fortifications…' His voice faded away for not one of the soldiers gave an indication that they had understood his order. He snatched his padded linen cap from his head and wiped it across his sweaty face.

'*Uffern ddiawl,*' one of the Welsh archers exclaimed and poked Borard in the arm with the top of his bow.

'Oh, what now?' Borard asked, angrily turning his back on the bailey to follow the archer's outstretched arm as he gesticulated down into the valley between the walls. There he saw a man climb from his knees to his feet bearing Raymond's shield. For a moment Borard's heart leapt as he saw the crimson and gold armorial rise, believing Raymond to have survived by lying beneath the shield as the arrow storm had passed over him. Then Jarl Sigtrygg's angry, bearded face appeared over the top.

'Someone shoot that bastard dead,' Borard ordered and two men close to him obediently nocked arrows on their bowstrings.

Jarl Sigtrygg surveyed the movement atop the wall and, guessing what was about to happen, ducked down to his knees behind the shield so that Borard could only see the top of his helmet. He turned to the two Welshmen at his side on the allure.

'Ready?' he asked and received curt nods in response. 'Next time he looks up I want to see an arrow in each of his eyes.' He turned back towards his enemy. 'On my command then.'

If the Ostman had killed his friend Raymond, Borard would make sure Jarl Sigtrygg would pay with his life. He urged his enemy to raise his head but the Ostman positively refused to give the archers a clear shot. Borard could see him rummaging around at his feet, but Jarl Sigtrygg's shield blocked sight of what he was up to. One of the archer's at his side murmured something in his own tongue which the Norman did not understand. A flurry of movement amongst the bodies saw Jarl Sigtrygg suddenly climb to his feet again and cast aside Raymond's shield.

In his eagerness Borard almost dropped his hand to command the two men to loose their arrows, but he managed to stop himself when he saw that Jarl Sigtrygg had sheltered behind a shield of a different kind, one that could not be pierced. And to Borard's right Alice of Abergavenny screamed in horror.

Raymond skirted the cattle pens at a gallop, ignoring the terrified animals' calls as he dashed the short distance to the inner gates. Men slumped inside the walls called questions in his direction as he passed by, but he did not stop, save to stoop for his sword which he had abandoned below the barbican. He threw himself at the ladder leading to the battlements, hitting the fourth rung before clambering upwards. The whole structure seemed to judder as he hauled his weight onto the timber platform above.

Momentarily blinded by the late afternoon sun pouring down, Raymond turned away and searched for Alice on the inner barbican, but he could not see her and it was only when she screamed again that he caught sight of her. She was at the far end of the allure, clinging to the top of the timber posts and wailing over the wall in the direction of the outer gates.

'Raymond!' One archer hailed him and clapped a big hand on his shoulder, and within seconds the captain was surrounded by smiling Welshmen offering greetings and jabbering in their own tongue in his direction. He had to weave between the outstretched arms as all along the rampart the archers leapt to their feet to cheer his safety, clapping their hands, slapping his back, and cawing happily. The captain returned their welcome as he attempted to push past as fast as possible and go to Alice's aid.

'Raymond, thank God you are alive,' Borard exclaimed as he planted a bear hug across his friend's chainmailed shoulders. Raymond could only watch as Alice sank to her knees on the walkway, crying uncontrollably.

'You must save him,' she whimpered.

Raymond shrugged off Borard and grabbed Alice by the shoulders, lifting her into his arms.

'What has happened?'

It was his friend Borard who answered. 'See for yourself.'

Reluctantly, he let go of Alice and rose so that he could see over the battlements to where Borard had indicated with a lift of his chin. He had known that an army was approaching their walls, but Raymond's mind struggled to comprehend the sheer number that his eyes now beheld. It was a great flood of men, a tidal wave of steel and toughened leather against which even Noah's great works could not have stood. The whole headland seemed to quake beneath their feet and from a quarter of a mile away the roar of their war songs was deafening.

It was a horde.

Drums rattled and trumpets blared as the warriors thumped the back of their shields to increase the noise assault on the wooden walls of Dun Domhnall. Jarl Sigtrygg had not been lying when he had taunted him during their fight between the walls, Raymond realised. An army of thousands approached the small Norman contingent crouching behind the fort's creaking walls.

'St David, preserve our souls,' Raymond hissed as he stared at them. 'It looks far worse from up here than it did from horseback.'

'Aye. There is a terrible lot of them,' Fionntán told him as he joined the captain on the wall, 'but that's not why Lady Alice is upset.' He spat a long stream of spittle into the gap between the ramparts, nodding his head in the same direction.

Raymond felt his stomach squeeze in anger and fear for

there, not ten paces from the outer gates, was his enemy, Sigtrygg. At the jarl's front was Geoffrey, with a knife pressed to his windpipe, the boy's body held firm between Jarl Sigtrygg and any Welsh arrow which might otherwise have struck him down. Tears streamed down Geoffrey's face as he gripped Jarl Sigtrygg's muscled forearm.

'Shoot and I'll kill the boy,' the jarl shouted up at the inner wall in the French tongue as he continued to carefully pick his way between the bodies of his crewmen towards the outer gates. Hands clawed at his leather-covered thighs. The jarl kicked his wounded crewmen away and struggled towards the gates.

'You'll not get an arrow away without hitting Geoffrey,' Fionntán confirmed.

'You must save him,' moaned Alice. 'You promised that you would keep him safe! At least William de Braose kept him locked up in a monastery – Geoffrey did not end up with a knife to his throat.'

Raymond stared deep into Alice's eyes. She held his gaze for several seconds, daring him to act, before her rancour turned to desperation and then to sadness as she broke down again. Her tears appalled Raymond and guilt scored through his body as he looked down on Geoffrey's predicament. Jarl Sigtrygg was a few paces from safety under the barbican and if he was going to rescue his esquire Raymond knew that it would have to be immediate.

He turned to a Welsh archer close by. 'Quickly, bring me rope.'

Borard was not quick enough to stop the young man from disappearing in response to Raymond's order, but he did understand its implication.

'You are not going down there,' he told his captain.

Raymond ignored Borard, putting a hand to the side of his mouth. 'Hurry up!'

415

'You are not going down there, Raymond,' Borard repeated.

'I have to save Geoffrey. I promised I would keep him safe.'

Fionntán shook his head. 'You will be killed.'

'I have the beating of Sigtrygg.'

'He will lure you outside the walls where he still has some of his crew. They will kill you and then he will finish the boy off too,' the Gael said matter-of-factly. 'You will be killed.' His eyes flicked towards Alice. 'You cannot save Geoffrey.'

Raymond shot Fionntán an angry look. 'Rope!'

The Irishman threw his hands in the air as the archer returned and handed Raymond a long length of sturdy rope taken from *Waverider*. With another venomous look at Fionntán, Raymond looped the rope around one timber column and knotted it tightly. He then cast the remainder over the side of the battlements.

'You are our captain,' Borard attempted. 'If you go down there you condemn us all to death.'

Raymond ignored his friend and placed his hands on the top of the wall, preparing to hoist himself up and over with three shallow breaths through his mouth. As he steeled himself to jump Borard's palm landed on his own right hand. The delicacy of the warrior's gesture surprised Raymond and stopped him in his tracks. He turned to look into Borard's dejected eyes.

'You would rob us of our captain when our need is greatest,' he said.

'There are better men than I who can lead you,' Raymond said weakly as he turned away from Borard's accusatory gaze to look at Jarl Sigtrygg. The Ostman was almost at the gates and Raymond bared his teeth in desperation. In a few seconds his enemy would have made it to safety. In moments Geoffrey would be dead. 'Sir Hervey wants command? Then I give it to him.'

'Do you actually believe that Sir Hervey can lead us to victory over the host of Veðrarfjord? For not one other man here trusts that he can. Yet if you tell these hundred souls that you will lead them to success, they will trust you, Raymond, and they will fight beside you without a moment's hesitation.'

'I am not their lord,' he protested as he hoisted himself up onto the top of the wall, throwing his right leg over so that it dangled over the wall. 'They have given me no oath.'

Borard smiled. 'A good lord needs no oath and nor would a good soldier offer one. It is enough that we can trust each other to stand at his side no matter the odds. I have done that for you, Raymond de Carew. Now I need you to lock your shield to mine and to stand beside me. Here and now at Dun Domhnall.'

Raymond paused as he sat astride the walls of his fort, his chin hitting his chest as he tried to decide what he should do. Below him, Alice still sobbed for her brother, inconsolable with Fionntán at her side. He raised his head and looked past her, down the length of the inner wall lined with archers. They were hard men, the Welsh, but each looked terrified as they watched Ragnall's army approach. Those closest grabbed glances of their captain and Raymond felt the impulse to explain himself to them, to make sure that they understood that he was not running away, that he only intended to save his esquire. They would understand that he had a responsibility to the boy, he told himself. *These men*, he thought, *who spoke a foreign tongue and had crossed the sea to a strange land on the promise from him, an invader of their country, that together they would win great riches*. Those men would understand him leaving their side when faced with

417

annihilation by an army twenty times larger than their own.

'Damn you, Borard,' Raymond whispered through gritted teeth and shifted his gaze towards the outer gates. Jarl Sigtrygg had reached the barbican and there he paused, turning towards Raymond, perched high above him. The Ostman's small, angry eyes met those of the Norman.

Jarl Sigtrygg did not smile as he did it, but neither did he take his implacable eyes off the Norman captain. The slice of the knife across Geoffrey's throat was deliberate and slow and blood gushed from the wound and down Geoffrey's surcoat. When it was done Jarl Sigtrygg cast the dying boy onto the ground. The jarl tarried a second longer, his eyes still locked on Raymond, before stepping backwards into the safety of the shadow cast by the barbican where no Welshman's arrow could find him.

By Raymond's side, Alice again began to scream.

Chapter Twelve

Fionntán grabbed Alice and pressed her face to his shoulder. Her agonised moan was muffled, but the lithe Irishman did not wait for her to struggle, lifting her legs and marching away from the scene of Geoffrey's death with Alice bundled up in his arms. As they passed Raymond, still astride the inner wall, Fionntán gave him a livid look.

'I have her. You deal with the Dubhgall.'

Raymond ignored him and reached for Alice. 'I'll kill Jarl Sigtrygg. I swear it! I will get revenge for Geoffrey.' He twisted his seat on the wall in the hope of catching Alice's notice, but she and Fionntán were already ten steps away, the archers moving out of their path as the Gael carried Alice towards the ladder and off the fighting platform.

Shame, sorrow and jealousy scored through Raymond. He wanted to chase after Fionntán, to rip Alice from his grasp and explain himself to her, to apologise and to tell her that he should have acted faster to save Geoffrey, that he should have bartered or negotiated, or even challenged Jarl Sigtrygg to single combat rather than simply watching from the safety of the wall while her brother was murdered. Raymond's chin dropped to his chest. He closed his eyes. Alice had trusted him and he had failed her. He knew that she would never forgive him.

The noise from Ragnall's army suddenly reached a crescendo and Raymond turned his head to look at the enemy multitude as they marched on his walls. They seemed to fill the entire headland as the warriors streamed down from the north. Steel links of Ostman armour and metal blades sparked under the late afternoon sun while their colourful circular shields revealed where the men of Veðrarfjord were deployed amongst the mass of Gaelic warriors. Raymond was awed by their number, by the noise issuing from their drums and horns, from the stomp of their feet and the bellow of their voices. For almost the first time in his life Raymond was wracked by indecision and doubt. He simply stared across the outer walls at Ragnall's army without any thought of what he should do to stop the coming onslaught.

From his vantage point, he could already make out the features of those closest. They were Ragnall's Gaelic allies, judging by their dress, and they had quickly outpaced those more heavily armed behind them. They wore long shirts bound at the middle which, like their strangely trimmed hair, billowed in the wind as they dashed towards the Norman fort. Some had removed the top half of their clothing so that it hung from their belts around their bare legs. Raymond could hear pipes playing and spotted one of the bearded performers at the front of the charge, his instrument under his right arm and a heavy javelin in his left. As he watched, the piper pointed his weapon in the direction of Dun Domhnall's outer barbican and, like a murmuration of roosting starlings, the Gaels followed his order and flocked towards the yawning gates.

There would be no siege of his sea castle, Raymond realised, no pause for respite. Ragnall's army would not call a halt to their advance outside bow range and there make camp as would any besieging force in Henry's kingdom. There would be no envoys and no parley, no exchange of threats or bombastic claims of martial strength. There would be no enticements to surrender.

Ragnall would not spend a moment constructing defensive ditches, inching forward day-by-day to increase the pressure on the defenders and the likelihood of assault on their walls. The Gael would not dig tunnels to undermine his walls. They would not build counter-castles or siege-towers. They would seek to destroy his fortress with an overwhelming deluge of men that would fall upon his walls like the Red Sea closing over the army of Egypt.

The piper was still playing, his song a manic crow-caw of sounds only just audible above the tumult of men who dovetailed towards the gates. It was not only their leader who was ardent in his desire to attack. Raymond could see that each of the Gaelic warriors competed to be the first to reach the walls. They saw no outcome other than the annihilation of Strongbow's bridgehead. Raymond felt the anger rise again. His enemy felt that they only had to raise their hand and Dun Domhnall's fortifications would fall. Using the taut rope in his left hand to steady him, Raymond clambered to his feet on top of the inner rampart. He felt the wind off the ocean catch his hair and his bright surcoat as he stood taller even than those men stationed on the barbican above the inner gate. He wished for the enemy to see that there were still fighting men behind the walls of Dun Domhnall. The tails of his crimson and gold surcoat flicked wildly. He could feel his own army's eyes settle upon him and he drew his sword from his side and pointed it at the horde of Veðrarfjord.

It was Borard – dependable, honest Borard – who first began to cheer, but his call was quickly taken up by the Welshman next to him and then the warrior beyond that began to hurl abuse in the enemies' direction. Soon ten, and then twelve men, were shouting defiance over the timber embattlements, and Borard was walking down towards the inner barbican slapping men on the back and urging them to show the enemy that there was fight in Raymond's army, that they would battle to the last man.

Their captain stood tall, like a great battle standard which cast its shadow over half the bailey of Dun Domhnall. The bright colours on his chest reflected the sun's orange rays so that it seemed like Raymond glowed with power. As he turned to cheer defiantly with his men, he caught sight of the herd of frightened cattle still bounded by the twisted wattle fence close to the cliffs. Their sight caused a ploy to form in his mind. Strands of other ideas gathered together into a coherent plan and he put his hand to the side of his mouth and screamed for Borard to attend him. Providence had sent him a strategy that would turn the tide in the Norman's favour, and he prayed to St Maurice and St David that it had indeed been heaven that had sent him inspiration in his hour of need. For it was a most desperate gambit that he had concocted, and it was only with divine help that he believed it could work.

'This is my castle and you will break like a wave upon its walls,' Raymond whispered in the direction of his enemy before leaping down onto the fighting platform. He had many preparations to make and only minutes to save his army from utter annihilation.

The yells of the charging Gaels seemed to bounce off the flat timber palisade at Jarl Sigtrygg's back to ring in his ears. He could no longer hear the booming ocean over the din, and he grimaced. His clenched teeth seemed to rattle in his head and he snarled as he wrapped his forearms around his ears.

At his side, his remaining crewmen looked nervously at the mass of savage Uí Drona and Déisi as they ran headlong in their direction, swarming across the headland like a stampeding herd of cattle.

'We need to get out of their way,' Amlaith shouted in his direction. Though only arm's length away Jarl Sigtrygg's ship-master had to lean close to his jarl's ear and repeat his comment to make himself heard. 'If they don't trample us they will cut us down as soon as look at us, the bastards.'

Jarl Sigtrygg agreed and, with a look towards the top of the rampart to make sure none of the foreigners' archers had appeared, he led his men along the bottom of the fortifications. Every few steps Jarl Sigtrygg stole a glance at his allies as well as of the empty battlements above him.

'Where are the Normans?' Amlaith shouted. They had neared the middle of the rampart.

'Probably jumped off the cliffs to escape,' Jarl Sigtrygg barked as he chanced another look up at the outer wall of Dun Domhnall. 'Come on,' he told his men and, without waiting for them, began running away from the Norman defences His chainmail thumped onto his toughened leather armour as he galloped northwards. Jarl Sigtrygg cursed as he realised that he had lost his shield in the melee between the walls and had no cover should an archer shoot at him. He fought the urge to turn and look at the stockade, and doubled his efforts to get out of range of the cursed bowmen. Sweat poured from underneath his helmet, picking up the dried perspiration from his earlier efforts to sting his eyes.

It was only a few seconds later that Jarl Sigtrygg passed the first Gaels as they ran in the opposite direction. They had already changed their course towards the open gates of the foreigners' fort and were getting ever further away from the jarl and his crew. A few on the periphery of the army noticed the small group of Ostmen as they passed, but only one Gael slowed, and then only briefly, raising his short axe and tiny buckler shield in their direction. Whether it

423

was in salute or as a threat Jarl Sigtrygg could not tell, and he did not stop to find out, but led his men away towards the estuary to the west.

Somewhere in the midst of the Gaels, a piper's jaunty tune encouraged them onwards towards glory. Jarl Sigtrygg scowled as he considered how close he had come to taking the foreigners' fort with only his eighty-strong crew. Now it would fall to the Gael, of that he was sure, and the victory that should've been his would go to another. The jarl turned his head and spat. All the slaves taken by the Uí Drona and Déisi would be given over to Ragnall, he thought sullenly, while he, who had taken the outer rampart, would leave with nothing; no riches, no glory, and only a third of the crewmen who had followed him into battle.

'Get back to *River-Wolf* and make sure she is ready to depart these waters,' he ordered Amlaith as he slowed and finally came to a stop close to where his crew had come up from the beach. It seemed like hours had passed since he had landed his vessel below the headland and set the Norman ship on fire. 'The tide is at its height,' he remarked.

Amlaith had his hands on his knees and sweat spat off the ends of his moustache. 'You want to leave? What about the slaves you promised us?'

'There will be no slaves. Ragnall will keep them all. But we can still make it to Dubhlinn to sell the three we took from Dun Conán and lessen our losses.'

'"Lessen our losses?"' Amlaith repeated. 'We lost over fifty oarsmen today! How do you suppose that we will even get to Dubhlinn? Do you think twenty-five can do the work of eighty at the oars when we enter the river?'

'You are the sailing master. I am the jarl. I tell you where I wish to go and you get me there. No excuses.'

The ferocity of his retort shocked Amlaith, who did not argue. Instead he turned and made for the beach, calling the remaining crewmen to follow him from the headland so that he could attempt to get *River-Wolf* afloat.

Jarl Sigtrygg watched them go, his temper flaring at Amlaith's brief show of defiance, but he calmed down by swearing to put the ship-master in his place as soon as he was able to do without his skills. His father was another against whom he promised to have a reckoning and he turned on his heel to see if he could identify the Konungr of Veðrarfjord amongst those attacking Dun Domhnall. He had to shield his eyes from the sun, now burning in the sky to the far south-west, but he was able to spot the white raven standard in the distance above the heads of the attacking army. Ragnall and his jarls were at the back of the advance and Sigtrygg felt his lip curl into a sneer as he watched the old cowards walk calmly forward to claim victory – his victory – and rob him of his vengeance against Raymond de Carew.

He guessed that Jarl Gufraid, his father's cousin, would be at Ragnall's side and Jarl Sigtrygg, who men called *Fionn*, too. Suspicion had been growing in his chest since his escape from the archers' threat; a suspicion that he and his men had been betrayed, and he guessed that if there was a conspiracy against him Gufraid and Sigtrygg Fionn would be behind it. They were the men who had spoken against him when he had been exiled from Veðrarfjord months before. At that time Jarl Sigtrygg had guessed that it had been their plan all along to supplant him and deprive him of rightful position and responsibility in his father's city, but now he wondered if they had also convinced Ragnall to abandon his son during his attack on the foreigners' fort. The more he considered the notion the more it worked its way into his feelings of injustice. Jarl Sigtrygg did not doubt that Gufraid and Sigtrygg Fionn would already be working their poison into Ragnall's ear, spreading more lies about him. He knew the circumstances of his defeat at the gates of Dun Domhnall would act against him, as would his flight from Dun Conán, but if his father could not see that it had been for Veðrarfjord's benefit that he had acted then he was a poor king indeed.

Even from half a mile away, he could see Sigtrygg Fionn at his father's side. He wanted to race over to Ragnall and accuse the other jarls of holding unnatural influence over the konungr, to force them to unveil their enmity towards him in front of his father; to dare Sigtrygg Fionn to defend his name with the strength of his battle-axe. But he knew that he could do nothing. Without a crew of fighting men he did not have the power to back up his claims and he cursed the luck that had led to his men being cut down by arrows when on the cusp of victory. Somehow, he swore, he would build a new crew and then return to Veðrarfjord to oust his father's faithless jarls. He would make Ragnall Mac Giolla Mhuire understand in whom he should place his trust.

A roar of rage dispensing from the walls of the fort made Jarl Sigtrygg turn away. From his position he watched as the Uí Drona and the Déisi poured through the outer gates and into the passageway between the ramparts. The first men barely broke stride as they waded over the bodies of his crewmen to attack their foreign enemy. Despite his innate hatred of the Gael, he felt his head nod in admiration at their bravery to charge headlong into a place where so many had already fallen. He suddenly realised that he was holding his breath and forced himself to exhale, angry that his experience under the Norman arrow-storm had any lasting effect on him. Nevertheless he could still feel the cloying expectancy that at any second he would hear the slap of bowstrings and the howl of death emanating from between the wooden walls. When this did

426

not occur, Jarl Sigtrygg began to wonder if the Normans had exhausted their supply of arrows to decimate his crew. He shook with fury at that realisation, his ire quickly moving from the foreigners to the Gael and then to his own crew's inability to defeat the two men who had stopped their charge on the inner gate. Raymond de Carew's unctuous face and his nauseating yellow and red robes returned to his mind's eye. The Norman had challenged him and now Jarl Sigtrygg would never have the chance to show him that he was the superior man. As the thought rolled around the jarl's mind it picked up speed and impetus. For several seconds Jarl Sigtrygg considered joining the attack on the fort, to fight his way to the frontline and to hunt out his enemy. He would kill the bastard who had murdered his crewmen and broken his nose. He would slaughter the cur who had defied him.

It took Jarl Sigtrygg several moments to calm down, but when he did he realised that there was no way that he would be able to force his way to the fore. Ragnall's allies continued to cram into the fort, but Jarl Sigtrygg could see that the flow had slowed to barely a trickle. Behind those men inside the walls a logjam had formed and hundreds stood immobile awaiting the opportunity to test their blade against the few foreigners who had dared raise their banners in warfare.

As Jarl Sigtrygg watched some of those outside the rampart broke away from the press and began to scale the outer wall, using the shoulders and heads of their kin to aid their climb to the top. Several were slingers for – their ascent completed – he could see their rhythmic dance as they built up the force to unleash their bombardment upon the inner fortifications. The few Normans opposing the Gael must've known the futility of their position. Jarl Sigtrygg counted only sixty on the battlements, their feeble efforts largely confined to throwing items down onto the heads of those below. He spat on the ground. Vengeance and glory should've been his, but they had been taken away by the cruel hand of fate.

At least Raymond will die, he thought. *Not by my hand, but he will be no more.*

For Norman defeat was inevitable. A hundred could not overcome three thousand.

'Here they come!' Borard's bellow could not hide the fear he felt as the enemy poured through the outer gates and between the fortifications. 'Get ready to repel them from our walls!' Few of his men could hear his cry, such was the tumult echoing from the army beneath, but Borard could see the sixty Welshmen ready themselves for the oncoming violence. With no arrows remaining, the archers had taken up spears, axes, and maces. Two senior men had vicious short swords in hand.

'Easy, boy,' Borard told the lad closest. He was taking deep breaths and was shaking like a leaf in the wind. *And well he might*, Borard thought. The boy, like his kin, was a killer with a bow in hand, but it took a different type of training to slay an enemy up close. Few, if any, of the Welshmen were practised in hand-to-hand combat, but Borard did not have the time to tell the youth what to expect when one took a life in this sort of fighting. In Raymond's service he had killed twelve men and Borard remembered the details of each one; the sound and impact of steel and wood as he had speared a Welshman's flesh the summer before, the strain and horror in the German bandit's eyes as pain flooded his dying body in the spring of 1168. He recalled the smell of shit and blood and days-old sweat as an Englishman had slumped against his shield during a brawl over some sheep near St Briavels, Borard's weapon buried in his breast. And from those below he recognised the furore of terror, excitement and anger as they ran towards the frontline. He knew that from some of those he would soon hear the blubber of sorrow as they left this world for the one beyond.

'Do not hesitate,' he told the boy instead. 'If some ugly savage with strange hair comes over that wall, strike and strike true. If you give them a second chance they will skewer you.' The youth gave no indication that he had understood the words, instead closing his eyes and mumbling a prayer in his own tongue.

Borard had taken a place directly opposite the outer barbican on Raymond's orders and it was from there that he would command the defence of Dun Domhnall while his captain put his plan into action. Borard's task was simple: he had to hold the two hundred-yard-long inner wall with sixty of the seventy archers left in the fort. Without one arrow between them, that was, and against a force of thousands.

'But', Raymond had told him, 'the enemy will be lucky to be able to get more than two hundred to the wall at any time. So you'll only be outnumbered by three to one.'

With that terrifying assessment still ringing in his ears, Borard had watched his captain gallop off down the palisade, to what end he did not know for Raymond had not fully disclosed the plan he said would save the garrison. Borard had fought beside him for long enough to know that he would soon discover it. That Raymond had trusted him to command the defence of Dun Domhnall both encouraged and daunted him, and Borard prayed that he would play his part as best as he was able. He owed Raymond, and refused to countenance even the thought of surrender or defeat.

'Get ready,' he shouted and waited while the order was

echoed to all the men under his command. The torrent of warriors still poured down between the walls like the Afon Gwy the day after heavy rain had fallen upon the Cambrian Hills. Those at the front of the assault were pushed onwards by those behind while outside the walls he could see a great multitude of men awaiting their chance to force their way into the fortress. Not one could lay a hand on the men above, but all found the breath to scream insults before being swept onwards towards the inner gates. Borard could see that many had a handful of short darts for throwing as well as a larger spear or short axe for the close quarter fight.

It was when he heard the first strike of axe upon the wooden gates to Dun Domhnall that Borard gave the order.

'Now!' he shouted and stooped down to pick up a large block taken from their store of firewood. All along the rampart the Welshmen copied his actions, launching wooden blocks the size of helmeted heads down onto the foreigners beneath.

Borard roared with effort as he lobbed his projectile over the edge of the battlements. He did not see it strike but he knew it could not have missed, such was the jam of men in the passageway between the walls. Each of Borard's warriors had gathered large blocks, stones and broken timbers, onto the allure yet within seconds each had exhausted his store. He had cursed Raymond's name when the captain had given him the task of cutting and collecting the wood pile from the forests further inland, but now he thanked whatever saint had given the captain foresight; the cries from the attackers let him know that the bombardment had caused real damage.

'Come and help me,' Borard shouted as he tried to lift his last piece, a long length of driftwood, from the allure. It took two of the archers' assistance but they soon were able to get the heavy missile over the edge of the rampart and

Borard saw it strike home, taking down three men. He watched the trio of Gaels as they disappeared below the slow-moving river of men, tripping two more, their screams engulfed by the stomp of feet. For a second Borard felt unsteady on his feet, and he cursed his timidity before realising that it had been the press of bodies beneath that had caused the fortification to shudder rather than any swoon that had come over him. All the archers had felt the movement for Borard could see that many had grabbed onto the rampart to steady their stance. He could see uncertainty on their faces at the sudden reverberation beneath their feet and he, like them, wondered how long the timber walls could hold before they were torn down by Ragnall's vast army.

He had only turned to order the archers to prepare for men scaling the walls when the first bare-chested man appeared in front of him. Despite his words to the boy, his arrival shocked Borard so much that by the time he had hefted his spear the warrior had already clambered on the palisade beside him. He was, to Borard's mind, the strangest-looking human whom he had ever set eyes on. His red hair was shaved from both sides to leave a knotted ridge down the middle of his head, giving him a reptilian appearance. His beard had been trimmed so that it only surrounded his mouth. Strange shapes were painted in dark ash upon his bare chest.

Borard's shock was momentary and he stabbed at the Gael, but the nimble-footed warrior danced out of the way and cut at the Norman with a short axe in his left hand. Borard barely had his spear in the way of the second attempt before the weapon was knocked from his grip, clattering onto the palisade. The red-headed Gael had a large hand planted on the middle of Borard's chest before he knew what was happening. The axe was raised, ready to

431

strike, and Borard could only grip onto the man's forearm and yell incomprehensibly as his enemy tensed his arm to deliver the blow that would claim his life.

A loud thud sounded. Blood splashed his face. He did not know what had happened, though he felt the grip on his chest relent. Borard furiously swiped at the blood from his eyes, ready to grapple with his adversary with his fists if necessary. He was able to open his right eye first and found the Gael prostrate on the allure at his feet, seemingly dead.

'Get down!' came a shout. 'Slingers!'

Borard immediately ducked his head below the level of the rampart and dropped onto his backside where he listened to the staccato whack of stone striking timber palisade. He could feel the fortifications tremor behind him with each impact while more landed with soft thuds in the bailey to his front. The rocks were accompanied by short darts cast from assailants on the outer defences. Borard kept his head down and, as he dabbed the blood from his face, he poked the red-haired Gael who had attacked him with his foot. The man was either dead or out cold. Next to the man's head he found a rock the size of a fist which had struck his opponent full in his face. The Gael's mouth was a mess, his front teeth shattered in his head. A moan of agony escaped from his smashed face and Borard could see his hand begin to twitch. He snatched the axe from his hand and buried the blade in the back of the man's neck. Breathing deeply, he clambered to his feet and shoved the Gaelic warrior's body over the edge of the allure so that it fell into the bailey.

Up and down the wall Welshmen were fighting their own duels with those Gaels who had managed to scale the inner defences. The enemy whooped like fiends as they leapt over the fortifications to attack. It was as if they were possessed by madness. Several of the Welsh archers were

432

already down, their prone bodies lying across the allure with horrific wounds. He could see at least two more wounded lying twisted in the bailey where they had been cast by the enemy.

He tucked the axe in his belt and scooped up his spear, nodding to the boy next to him as he walked past. An archer ten paces down the allure had a body at his feet and was hacking at another man as he attempted to climb over the wall. Close by, two men wrestled on the allure, rolling dangerously close to the edge of the platform. Borard stopped to help the Welshman only to find that he could no longer tell friend from foe. It was only when one appealed to him in stuttering French that he acted, stabbing the other man in the nape of his back as he tried to throttle the life from his foe. Borard pulled the bowman to his feet as another helmeted head appeared from beyond the wall to attack.

'Keep fighting!' he shouted and pointed at the bearded face. Close quarter fighting had broken out along the entire length of the palisade and where Borard saw an opportunity to help one of the Welshmen he took it, but he could already see that his men were tiring from their exploits. The enemy kept coming over the wall and it was all the Welsh archers could do to keep them at bay. Another dart zipped past his head as he shoulder-charged another Gael, sending the man tumbling head-first into the side of one of the turf-roofed houses below.

'Keep fighting!' he shouted again. His head spun from his efforts. 'We only have to keep it up until darkness falls!' Borard wasn't entirely sure how long it was until sunset, but he recognised that the sun was already to the west. 'Lay it on them!'

It was as he lifted his hand to shout encouragement to the Welshmen that a javelin cast from the outer defences struck him in his left shoulder blade. Borard screamed in pain and dropped to his knees. Anger and pain coursed through him as he pulled the weapon from his flesh. He barely had time to notice how deep the rent to his armour as another set of bare feet landed next to him and he had to rise and grab the Gael's arms before he could bring his falchion down upon his head. Sweat poured down Borard's brow and streamed between his clenched teeth as he fought with his enemy. Pain scored across his back. He could feel his grip faltering and before he lost hold he brought his knee up into the Gael's thigh. The man cried out in pain and the split second distraction allowed Borard to elbow the man above the eye with his mail-clad arm. The Irishman stumbled away from him and became embroiled in another fight.

The pause allowed Borard some respite and he clung to the battlements with both hands, breathing heavily because of the pain dispensing from his wounded back. He had to fight the desire to close his eyes as he rested his head on the gap between two sharpened timber trunks. He found that he could see the whole way to the inner barbican between the walls through the shaped timber posts. The whole avenue between the fortifications was filled with men. They shouted and surged, cursed and climbed, killed and were killed. There were always more attackers to take the place of the fallen. He saw how great sections of the allure on the outer wall had collapsed but it had not stopped the enemy. Gaels who had hurled all their darts and throwing axes had taken to flinging pieces of the wreckage across at the Welshmen opposite. One had even built a fire and Borard watched as the man tried to encourage a flame from the small pyre. He was close enough to the inner gates now to see the effect of so many men pressing against them. The heavy timber boards were reinforced with spars on the inside, but the weight of so many was causing them to bend and warp inwards as the pulsating mass gushed forwards again and again. He knew that in a matter of moments the gates would be forced and the Norman fort overrun. A dam can only hold back flood water for so long. Their only hope was that Raymond's plan would save them.

Borard had barely the energy to lift his arms in defence as another Gael scaled the rampart and collapsed on top of him. Rolling to the floor, Borard hugged the man to his chest rather than fight, refusing to let him go or allow him to take hold of a cudgel in his belt. Instead the Norman officer gathered his breath and summoned all of his remaining energy.

'Raymond!' Borard screamed. 'Raymond!'

It was only a matter of minutes after he left Borard's side that Raymond heard the signal that the enemy had penetrated the outer walls of Dun Domhnall. Not that he needed warning; their feral screams rang over the headland. It was a sound that heralded Norman doom.

'God's teeth, there is a lot of the bastards,' Caradog commented as the river of men flooded down the passageway towards the inner barbican where he and his nine best archers stood with Raymond. The rabble of men screamed and shouted up at the defenders. Their voices rattled the walls. The enemy had begun casting their darts and javelins up at the battlements, and Caradog did not want his warriors wasting those few arrows that they had left.

'Hold fast,' deep-voiced Caradog told them. 'They'll get what's coming to them soon enough.'

As with Borard, Raymond had quickly outlined the ten archers' place in his scheme to Caradog and then together they had spent several frantic minutes collecting every available arrow onto the barbican for the Welshmen to use. Many of those sixty left with Borard had been furious at having to hand over the arrows and more than once Caradog had been forced to step in to assure his folk that Raymond was not trying to get them killed by robbing them of their primary weapon.

'Hold until I give the signal,' Raymond insisted in Caradog's direction as he made for the ladder that would take him to the bailey. 'Then give them every arrow you have left.' He paused as he swung his feet onto the rungs and locked his gaze with that of Caradog. 'Borard will hold them, you make a gap, and I'll deliver the killer punch. Hold until you see the signal.' He waited for the Welshman to nod his head and confirm that he understood before he began climbing downwards.

That the fate of the fort now lay in the hands of those Welshmen who had, a month earlier, been his most ardent of enemies, was not lost on the captain. He hoped that Caradog's kinsmen realised that Ragnall would not distinguish between any of those inside the fort, be he Norman or Cymric. They would live or die together. As he turned to take the second ladder from the allure to the floor of the bailey, he glanced at the frighteningly few men who would face the initial charge of Ragnall's army and prayed that the sixty archers under Borard's command were up to the task. It would all be for naught if they could not hold back the horde until he had made his final preparations. The din from the enemy was thunderous in volume and Raymond could feel the weight of the men between the walls rumble through the wooden fortifications to make the ladder shiver in his fingers. He fought back the urge to glance at Ragnall's army over the battlements for he knew that it would do no good whatsoever. He had set his plan in motion and all that was to be done was to follow it through.

Now the wine is drawn, it must be drunk. The old Norman saying went some way to allaying his fears though he would happily have had a mug of wine at that moment rather than merely repeated the words.

His resolve lasted until his feet touched the bailey and saw the enemy's effect on the gates. It was dark beneath the barbican, the sun having traversed the sky to lie low to the west, but every few seconds Raymond could see a long, vertical shard of light squeeze between the gates as each impact thumped against the outside. Had he more men he would've sent them to brace the inside, but he could spare no-one to secure the gates.

Misgivings assailed him.

'St David, allow me five more minutes,' he begged at the sky. With effort he backed away and forced his stare from the gates. It was then that he spotted a group of pages huddling together under the fighting platform close to the hay barn. Rocks and darts thrown over the wall, as well as broken bodies of fallen warriors, lay all around them.

'Boys!' he shouted and waved a hand in their direction indicating that they were to follow him towards the cattle pens. The pages, all under thirteen years old, looked terrified as they reluctantly broke from cover, but Raymond did not have the time to ease their fears. They squealed as a sudden barrage of rocks plummeted over the rampart and thudded into the bailey nearby.

'Get a brazier going and collect some torches. Then come back and hide in there,' he ordered, pointing towards the space between the twisted fence of the cattle pens and the white daub wall of the marshalsea. 'I have a task for you all and it may be the difference between the fort falling and our victory. Make sure and return.' The pages nodded before running off to complete their task.

Raymond was met at the door to the marshalsea by his

remaining milites and their esquires. Questions and demands accosted him as he entered and it was all that Raymond could do to not scream at his warriors to be silent.

'Why are we hiding here while the enemy attack?' Asclettin demanded of his captain. He, like all the seven remaining members of Raymond's conrois, was ready to fight. He had his chainmail coif up and his spangenhelm propped under his arm. His sword was belted to his hip.

'Those Welsh bastards aren't to be trusted with the defence,' Dafydd FitzHywel, Cymric himself, added.

Thurstin nodded in agreement and picked up a lance from the weapons rack nearby. 'Borard needs us on the wall, Raymond. We are going. Now.'

It was the unrest of the coursers and remounts – rather than Raymond's appeal – that quieted the conrois. Each owed his livelihood to his horse and their care was paramount. Almost as one the milites turned to calm their mounts rather than race to the walls.

'It's time for their evening feed,' Christian de Moleyns said, and ordered the esquires behind him to give each horse some mixed oat and bean bread to satisfy their hunger.

'I have a plan,' Raymond told his men as the teens, led by William de Vale, the most senior, went about their work. 'I think it can stop the attack, but we need to act quickly if it is going to accomplish anything.'

It was Asclettin who hissed a reply. 'Well, spit it out then.'

'We ride out and attack the enemy.'

For many seconds no-one replied to Raymond's statement. The only sounds were those of the battle going on outside and those of the horses eating. It was almost inevitable that Walter de Bloet broke the silence:

'You want us to open the gate and to charge into that

host?' he asked, lifting his left hand to point towards the sound of Ragnall's mass of warriors. 'We would be surrounded and cut down in seconds. No! We will take every man and boy onto the palisade to help Borard. We do not have time for your nonsense, Raymond.' A frustrated groan escaped from between his teeth. 'I cannot believe Strongbow put you in charge of his conrois!'

'But he did give me the responsibility, Walter,' Raymond stated as forcefully. 'Not you, his nephew, not his son-in-law, Roger de Quincy, and not his uncle Sir Hervey. Me.'

The conrois and the esquires had stopped what they were doing to listen in to the discourse. It was an argument that had been building between Walter and Raymond for two years. Both men had been part of the conrois led by Walter's father, Sir Reginald, which had accompanied Strongbow and King Henry's daughter to Germany for her wedding to the Duke of Saxony. Barely a day after crossing the frozen Rhine, they had been set upon by bandits. The young princess had not been hurt and the brigands had been chased off. The only casualty had been old Sir Reginald who had taken a spear to his side. Everyone had expected Walter, Sir Reginald's fourth son, to succeed to his father's role as captain, but Strongbow had intervened and to the surprise of all had advanced the younger, less well-connected Raymond to the position. If anything, the death a month later of Walter's childless uncle, the Lord of Raglan, and his elder brother's elevation to that lofty station had made Walter's jealousy of Raymond even worse.

'I was made captain,' Raymond insisted again. 'Above all of you...'

'Proving nothing except Strongbow's foolishness,' Walter de Bloet answered sullenly.

Raymond watched the reactions of his conrois. Asclettin bared his teeth in embarrassment at Walter's words while Denis d'Auton started to intercede on Raymond and Strongbow's behalf. The captain held up a hand for silence.

'Perhaps Strongbow was foolish, Walter,' he said. 'Or it could be that he felt that having lost so much to King Henry that he had to be able to trust those in positions of power in his household if he was to hold onto what little he had left. You know as well as I do that Roger de Quincy and Sir Hervey would do anything to get their portion of Strongbow's estate. So neither of them could be trusted as captain...'

'And me? Now I cannot be trusted? What have I ever done other than serve him to the best of my ability all my life? What have I done to deserve such contempt?'

Raymond closed the gap between him and Walter, planting a large hand on his chainmailed shoulder. 'You have an elder brother who would claim Striguil if Strongbow died. You are his nephew and a threat.' He urged Walter to understand, but he could see that his resentment at being overlooked was never going to disappear. He didn't have time for Walter's interruption and nor could he do without his sword if his plan was to succeed. So he tried another course.

'In me the earl sees a man without connection to his house, a man totally reliant on his purse. He perceives me to be one of the few men in his employ who can be controlled. Raymond le Gros. Raymond the Fat. Raymond the cowhand.' He pursed his lips as he spoke. 'That is why I was made captain, Walter, rather than you.' He took a deep breath and raised his voice so that everyone in the marshalsea could hear. 'But I want to be much more. In this land we all have the chance to be more than mere milites or

440

esquires in Strongbow's household. Here, in Laighin, he who is brave enough can become a great lord and gain vast domains.' He looked deep into Walter de Bloet's eyes. 'Here we can be our own men. We need not be beholden to another, be he uncle, brother or lord.' That seemed to cause a change in Walter's manner and Raymond could feel his shoulders relax under his hand. 'But we must first prove ourselves to Strongbow and we can only do that by demonstrating our skill in battle.' He walked past Walter so that he was amongst his men. 'We must preserve this bridgehead. At all costs, we must do that. Perhaps you are right and the best thing to do is to climb up onto that wall and fight them hand-to-hand.' Several voices grunted approval to this plan, but Raymond stamped out the spark of opposition before it could grow. 'No!' he exclaimed. 'A hundred cannot defeat three thousand – not in a fair fight. There are too many in Ragnall's army to defend that wall, no matter how hard and how long we fight. But I know a way to take them on and I promise you it will be successful.'

'You want us to attack,' Amaury de Lyvet said, 'but I don't understand how we can force them back, Raymond. There are only seven of us,' he reminded his captain.

'Thirty,' said one amongst the esquires. Raymond recognised him as Fulk, the butcher's apprentice from Westminster, who had performed so bravely during Jarl Sigtrygg's initial attack. 'That is if you include us.' He puffed up his chest, daring the older man to deny him his chance to prove himself in battle. Behind him his fellow esquires, both older and younger, looked aghast at the boy's swagger.

'Even with thirty it is quite impossible,' Amaury stated with an irritated look towards Fulk. 'I want to avenge my brother, but that would be madness.'

Raymond nodded his head. 'How many more would it take for you to follow me into the fight?'

'A hundred,' Walter de Bloet interjected. His tone betrayed much of his old insolence.

The captain turned to look at his rival. 'And if I can promise you fifty of the strongest, most unstoppable cavalry to ride ahead of you into battle outside the walls, would you follow them?'

Walter looked suspiciously at his captain. 'If you can magic up fifty, I will lead the conrois myself.'

'Then get ready to charge for I shall hold you to that vow.'

'Raymond?' the page asked and reached out to tug at his sleeve. 'Master Raymond, sir?'

The captain was lost in his thoughts and did not answer immediately. Before him a brazier burned black and orange. He stared into its depths. The moment had arrived for him to set his plan in motion, to see if his small army's will to survive was greater than the enemy's desire to kill. It was time.

'Master Raymond?' the page tried again.

In his hand was an unlit torch. He knew that once he pushed it into the glowing heart of the fire there could be no turning back. For if his plan failed to drive the enemy from before their walls there was no contingency plan, no alternative stratagem.

There was victory or there was obliteration.

And yet Raymond hesitated. His scheme had many parts and it relied on each man playing his role to perfection: Borard and his Welsh warriors holding the wall; Caradog and his archers' expertise on the barbican; Walter de Bloet and the conrois, now mounted and ready for battle; and Raymond the Fat and his team of seven pages with the most

442

important task of all. If any should fail, it would mean their downfall.

'You made sure that the marshalsea was clear of horses?' he asked the boy a third time. 'You moved Ferrand to a safe distance?'

He nodded in reply. 'Into the old fort, master. Sir Hervey shouted at us, but we didn't listen and came back as you said.'

Raymond clapped the page on the shoulder. 'Remember as soon as it is done you will have to help me again rather than run up to hide with Sir Hervey.' It was a caustic statement, but the boy did not seem to notice. If his plan failed all his warriors and horses would have to join Strongbow's uncle behind the stone walls of the citadel. There they would await defeat for, without access to the well in the bailey, they could only hold out as long as the small store of wine lasted.

That would not be his doom, Raymond promised. Events had conspired to give him a chance to prove himself at the edge of the world and he would not allow the moment to pass him by. He would not fail his men or Strongbow.

Raymond took a deep breath and plunged the end of the torch into the heart of the brazier. The flames took a few seconds to catch hold in the greased wool wrapped around its tip, but the pungent smell soon hit him and he pulled the torch from the wood fire. He invited the seven pages to light their brands while he turned and looked towards the far side of the bailey. There, Walter de Bloet readied the thirty horsemen. He raised his arm to signal to Walter, waiting for his waved reply before he dropped his arm.

'Get in position, boys,' Raymond told the pages and watched as they scampered off around the cattle pen towards the barbican, armed with nothing other than burning brands.

Raymond de Carew turned his eyes towards the sky. 'St Maurice, if you are up there and are listening, now would be a good time to send us your aid.' With that he turned and launched his flaming torch onto the reed-thatched roof of his own marshalsea.

Ragnall Mac Giolla Mhuire watched from afar as his army pressed home their charge. How many had fallen or how close the enemy were to succumbing, he could not tell. He was not unduly worried, however. Hundreds of his warriors stood outside the walls of the fort. Each pushed for his opportunity to prove himself in battle. Each wanted to claim the life of one of the foreigners who dared threaten the sovereignty of Veðrarfjord and her allies. Each wanted victory. The noise was colossal, the heat from the early evening sun immense. Yet his army still attacked, cramming into the alley between the twin fortifications.

'My folk will camp inside the fort tonight. Your people can stay outside the walls,' Ragnall told old Donnchadh Ua Riagháin. There was no elevated spot on the isthmus from which he could watch the battle unfold so Ragnall, Donnchadh and their followers had taken up a spot behind their attacking armies. They could not see what was happening within the walls, but none doubted that victory was close at hand.

'My people will go back across the river to tend to our beasts after the battle is over,' the King of the Uí Drona replied. 'There'll be too many ghosts wandering on this bank looking to plague the living with their woes.'

Donnchadh's Brehon nodded at his king's good sense. 'But no spirit can cross water.'

'St Moling will protect us,' a priest amongst the Uí

444

Riagháin entourage confirmed.

The konungr considered it good sense and felt glad that he had brought his own bishop with him from Veðrarfjord to keep Normans' spectres at bay through the night. 'And the dead?' he asked.

'The fallen will keep until morning,' replied King Donnchadh.

'Your people must be ready to travel upriver early tomorrow afternoon. Trygve will try to negotiate and I'll give him one night to see what he offers. If it is not enough to change my mind we'll tear down Cluainmín's walls as we have these.' Ragnall flapped a hand dismissively at Dun Domhnall. 'Then it is on to Waesfjord.'

'And at that time my folk can return home?'

Ragnall paused. That was the deal that he had struck with Donnchadh and the Uí Drona, but he hesitated now. Having almost a thousand spears at his command made him a serious power in the region and, given that he had ten high ranking Uí Riagháin hostages held behind Veðrarfjord's walls, he saw no immediate reason to commit to releasing Donnchadh's people from his service.

'The Uí Braonáin are as restless as ever on our borders. Not to mention Diarmait Mac Murchada's folk and his foreign mercenaries – they could pass through our lands at any time. My warriors are needed to defend our homes,' warned Donnchadh.

'Most of your herds are here,' Ragnall countered, 'and if my sources are correct the Uí Braonáin king is with the Meic Giolla Phádraig far to the north, trying to enforce their authority over the Uí Mordha of Loígis.' He turned and raised an eyebrow. 'If your enemies attack, it will be when you have brought in the harvest, as well you know. If you want my ships to come to your aid then, you might want to think about how long you choose to remain in the south. Gufraid!' the konungr suddenly called, denying Donnchadh the opportunity to respond. The contemptuous act was not missed by the King of the Uí Drona and grumbles of discontent soon surfaced amongst his derbfine who collected at his back.

'Ragnall?' the konungr's cousin, Jarl Gufraid, asked as he stepped forward from the senior men of Veðrarfjord who gathered, like the Gaelic chieftains, at their leader's rear.

'I can see smoke coming from the fort.'

'You think the Déisi are trying to burn down the foreigners' gates?' asked Jarl Gufraid.

Ragnall screwed up his eyes. 'The smoke looks white.'

'Like burning straw?'

The konungr nodded. 'Follow me,' he commanded and began walking away from the outer gate so that he could see what was happening beyond the defences. Though the Uí Drona did not follow, fifty men – the great and the good of Veðrarfjord – trailed behind their king as he walked eastwards towards the beach.

'Our army must have broken through the inner gates and set the houses alight,' Gufraid stated. He had to shout so loud was the clamour that rang from the opposing armies between the walls. 'The fight is over.'

Ragnall scowled at Gufraid's optimism and kept walking, his eyes locked on the archers hanging from the Norman barbican above the inner gates. Smoke poured over them as they concentrated all their efforts on sending wave upon wave of arrows down upon his warriors, unseen behind the outer defences. Ragnall contemplated that the foreigners' actions could indeed be those of desperate men, battling hard to prevent catastrophe, and that the gates had indeed been forced as Gufraid believed.

'If we are victorious why has there been no shout of

446

acclaim?' he asked, though no one could hear him. The konungr had been in many battles and on each occasion the moment of an enemy's collapse was marked by a cry of adulation from their victorious foe. He had heard none issue from between the wooden walls. As Ragnall turned to dispute his cousin's assertion, a new sound added to the deafening uproar: the wail of cattle calls and the thunder of hooves. The konungr's face twisted into a sneer of pain as the overpowering noise beset his ears.

'What is happening?' he called as he bowed his head. No one answered for none could hear his words. One of Gufraid's men dropped his spear in order to cover his ears from the booming sound. The jarl shouted inaudibly at him, pointing over his konungr's shoulder in the direction of the Norman stronghold. Ragnall looked back at the barbican and could see through the smoke that the archers had stopped shooting their arrows and were clinging to the timber posts as if the earth shook beneath them. The same effect could be seen to traverse along the long wall of Dun Domhnall as, one after another, the foreign warriors' swordplay was forgotten and they dropped their weapons to grab hold of the wall to steady their stance. More than one, Ragnall could see, fell from his station while timbers on the outside wall strained and collapsed outwards onto the grassland. Fine dust pumped and tumbled from the trembling ramparts. Screams of terror sounded. Shrieks were abruptly silenced.

Ragnall had been expecting a cry of victorious acclaim; the signal that the fragile fort was about to fall, but now he could sense an unseen menace. He could feel its approach. He could see its effect. His gnarled fingers were sweaty as they gripped the hilt of the short sword at his belt. Most of those crowded outside the walls were unaware that anything had changed and continued to surge towards the bottleneck at the outer gates, Gael and Ostman urging each other on to deeds ever greater, the bravest warriors from their three peoples, united only by their enmity with the foreigners and the precarious alliances between their masters. They were the first to perish.

Ragnall Mac Giolla Mhuire, Konungr of Veðrarfjord, had seen power in his long life. He had seen mountains of fire on Iceland that suddenly exploded from the sea with such ferocity that the waves turned to steam before them. He had observed feeding whales slam onto the surface of the ocean to scatter waves as tall as a man. Yet nothing prepared him for the impact of the stampeding herd of cattle as it burst from the outer gates of Dun Domhnall and collided with his army.

The terrified cows wailed and moaned as they charged, led onwards by a brown bull as large as Donn Cúailnge himself. He was like a great ship blasting through icy waves, his shoulders lifting high as he struck men with his great shaggy head. And behind him came fifty more beasts who wished only to escape the flames which reached high above the barbican on the inner wall. The cattle barely broke stride as they pummelled men beneath their hooves. The air trembled with their strained wails. The atmosphere stank of panic and smoke.

Ragnall, Donnchadh and their followers looked on appalled as the cattle tore a ragged gap ten paces wide through the middle of their army to leave a bloody trail of broken bodies behind them. Nothing could stand in their way. None could survive as the crazed animals carved a gory swathe through the packed ranks of men. It was not only those caught in their path that suffered; the force of the stampede sent men tumbling onto their backs though they stood twenty feet away from the herd's course. Those men in turn knocked down their neighbours. The slap of flesh and bone upon skin, hoof and sinew, and the screams of pain from both man and beast rocked the headland. Ragnall watched helplessly as men were tossed headlong into the air only to fall amongst the brown mass of stampeding animals. One Gael attempted to spear a cow in the flank. His weapon snapped in two and another horned animal gored his bare chest. He too disappeared beneath the wave.

And on the cattle's heels came the Norman horsemen, hollering and shouting as they emerged from the darkness and smoke emanating from between the walls of Dun Domhnall. Some had fiery brands in their hands and they launched them at the backs of the petrified animals so that they could draw their weapons. Everyone had heard tales of the Wild Hunt, the phantasmal, savage pack of riders, who haunted the countryside at the Devil's beckoning. And, for a moment, as he watched the horsemen cut through his army, Ragnall could believe the stories. The foreigners seemed to float above the ground as they passed through the ranks of infantry, stabbing this way and that, taller by half than any other on the battlefield. It was as if man and beast were one, and they howled like animals too, devilish, dark and delighting in the death that they brought down upon the packed ranks.

They drove the cattle on, poking at them with spears and scaring them with fire before turning away in packs of five to attack their dazed enemy on different parts of the battlefield. The thirty horsemen were outnumbered by hundreds to one but already Ragnall could see scores of his warriors on the periphery were fleeing from the Norman counter. Like foxes in a chicken coop, the foreigners seemed to revel in the kill, and their demonic cries seemed to infect his army with terror. More and more men turned to flee and, as the herd of cattle finally forced their way free of the crowds and continue to run northwards, Ragnall watched as his whole army began a stampede of their own. They were running for their lives. The hunters were amongst them. The scent of blood was on the wind and they were running.

It was as if a spear thrust had been driven through the heart of his army. For the first time in a long time, Ragnall felt fear. A king who went to war and returned without victory did not remain king for long, he knew. He had taken hundreds of the finest men of Veðrarfjord into battle and who knew how many still lived? He took a step backwards and collided with Jarl Gufraid. The konungr had no words for his kinsman, no strategy to turn the defeat into triumph. He needed time to think.

Raymond de Carew gave him none.

'Loose,' the Norman captain shouted at Caradog's company of archers as they emerged from the outer gates behind the cattle and horsemen. At his side the Welshman spanned their yew bows and drove ten shafts into the group of Gaels closest to them. The men were twenty paces away and their arrows easily punched through shields and toughened leather armour.

'Nock,' Raymond called to the archers, watching as they prepared more arrows. However, the survivors of their first flight were already bolting and Walter de Bloet had spotted them. He called to his detachment of esquires and led the horsemen amongst the Gael as they sprinted away from the battlefield. The boys whooped and chivvied with spearpoints as they ran amok amid the enemy. Their aim was not to kill, but to disperse. They had to take advantage of the disorder. Satisfied that the group of Gaels would not return, Raymond instead scanned the landscape for other clusters of enemy.

'There!' he shouted and pointed at a group of Ostmen

loitering to the right of their position, below the outer barbican. He waited for the archers to adjust their aim and span their bowstrings again. Their arms trembled. 'Loose!' he ordered and watched as the black blur of ash shafts scythed across the green grass backdrop towards their target. The impact of the arrows was no less impressive than that of the cattle for, though only a few men had tumbled to the ground, their effect was to set the hundred-strong company of Ragnall's men running for their lives, Christian de Moleyns' detachment on their tails.

'We're down to our last few arrows,' Caradog shouted in the captain's direction as he set another to his bowstring.

Raymond signalled that he understood and indicated towards another group of Gaels – whether Déisi or Uí Drona he could not tell – who had sought shelter on the edge of the cliff face to the west. Leaving Caradog to take charge, Raymond turned and disappeared into the fetid darkness between the ramparts.

'Loose!' he heard the Welshman call.

The scene between the walls was one of utter devastation. Raymond had to force down rising bile as he carefully picked a path between the torn timbers and broken bodies. The crush of men between the walls had been such that none could have survived the charge of cattle. Splintered weapons lay everywhere. Broken bones jagged from beneath beaten flesh. Pummelling hooves left great welts and bruising on dead men's ribcages while limbs were contorted in ways that appalled Raymond. The stench was almighty, though masked somewhat by thick smoke from the burning marshalsea which drifted this way and that, speared by shafts of fading sunlight which had found gaps in the tumbledown rampart. Although the noise of the battle was still evident, it was the roar of the distant inferno that was loudest between the walls. He came across

451

the carcass of a cow which, having tripped during the stampede, had been crushed by those coming behind her. Flies already swarmed around her lifeless face and those of men trapped beneath her.

'Boys?' Raymond coughed as he called into the smoky recesses. He could discern no answer but as he moved further down the path he saw them. With their tiny frames and colourful clothing, the pages looked like angelic spirits come to claim the souls of the brave men who had died beneath the stampeding hooves. The pages moved quickly through the smoke, disappearing from view here and there as the billowing fog wrapped around them, only to reappear like spectres a few seconds later. Each had wrapped cloth around their faces to protect them from the smoke and the stink as they went about their duties.

Having set fire to the marshalsea, he and the pages had directed the stampeding herd of cattle out through the gates. It had been a close-run thing, but the boys had proven their mettle by standing firm with nothing more than lighted brands in hand to scare the animals towards the gates rather than allow them to disperse into the bailey. In the confusion he had lost two cows over the side of the cliffs, but that was a price Raymond was willing to pay in order to clear the way for Walter de Bloet and his mounted milites and esquires to launch their attack.

'Boys!' the captain called again before wrapping the inside of his elbow around his mouth. With his other arm he waved for them to attend to him. The pages, compliant as ever, jogged the short distance to join him. The three youngest were the last to arrive. They had armfuls of undamaged arrows which had been retrieved from the killing zone between the walls. The four other boys had small knives in their hands and were red to their elbows. It had been their task to cut the arrow shafts free from wherever they could find them, whether timber or men's flesh.

'Take the arrows to Caradog at the gate,' Raymond told the pages, 'then I need you to come back to search for more.' The three youngest boys nodded and ran off towards the outer gates before disappearing into the bank of smoke with their precious cargo. Raymond handed his flask of water to the remaining pages and told them to finish it all. Theirs had been a nasty duty, but it was nothing in comparison to the task given to Fulk, the butcher's apprentice from Westminster. He approached more sedately, a spear held in both hands. The captain noted blood on the spearpoint and Fulk's white face.

'It was a mercy,' he told his servant. 'It was no different to putting a dying animal out of its misery.' He knew it was not true, but he hoped that his words comforted Fulk. 'How many men did you…?'

'Four men.' Fulk's lip trembled as he spoke and Raymond squeezed the boy's shoulder to comfort him.

'Well done,' he told him. 'There will be an extra tot of wine for you this evening. Make sure the pages keep at their task – we will need all the arrows we can find – then run and tell Master Borard that his men must repair any damage to the inner gates as best they can.' He waved a hand towards the top of the rampart above him where, he supposed, Borard and his men had collapsed to tend to their wounds and to recover from exploits. He coughed again as the acrid smoke stung his throat. 'That is,' he wheezed and pointed to the orange haze at the far end of the battlements, 'if the fire has subsided enough.'

'You think that the enemy will return?'

'I want to be prepared,' he replied and slapped Fulk on his shoulder once before turning and making his way back down the passageway towards the outer gate. It took him some minutes to reach the barbican, coughing and spluttering the whole way.

'So much for arrows,' Caradog told him as he stepped beyond the outer battlements. Raymond gazed in the direction indicated by the Welshman's outstretched arm, but could see nothing through the blanket of white smoke which poured over the fortifications. It shrouded the entire headland from their view. So complete was the mantle of smoke that, for all Raymond knew, they could be the last men alive outside the walls of Dun Domhnall.

'Can't shoot at what you can't see,' Caradog told the Norman. 'You hear that?' the archer said suddenly, tilting his ear towards the grassland beyond the smoke.

'What is it?' Raymond asked and felt his tired body tense.

Screams sounded in the distance and blended with the occasional call of cattle and seagull's whine, but otherwise the loudest noise that he could hear was still the crackling staccato of burning timbers from the marshalsea. 'Is it the enemy?' he asked and strained his ears. His eyes flicked to down the line of archers and could see the fear surge through the nine men. Each knew that any further attack would surely see their fort fall.

'I thought I heard...' Caradog began before his voice drifted away and he looked at his captain, his eyes weighted with unease. 'Perhaps not...'

Tired and sore as he was, Raymond could feel dread nagging at his soul. He had to know if there was any further threat to Dun Domhnall and he growled once before darting out of the line and plunging into the bank of smoke. He could hear Caradog calling him back, but he ignored the Welshman's warning and stomped onwards. His eyes were watering terribly because of the irritation so he concentrated on the sounds that surrounded him as he picked a path through the carpet of bodies which appeared through the smoke. Unlike those caught between the walls, out on the open expanse of the headland there were more injured than slain by the cattle. Those men who had been in their path and still lived moaned in strange languages and sought Raymond's help. He ignored them all.

Though he did not fear attack from the wounded, he kept his right hand gripped upon his sword's hilt. The smoke mixed with the stink of stale sweat, blood and excrement, forcing him to again wrap his chainmailed forearm around his face. He gagged and coughed and almost fell over in surprise as, a few paces to his right, a bare-chested Gael covered in blood rose to his feet. Raymond only had the chance to half-draw his sword before the man stumbled away towards the beach as if drunk. The captain breathed relief and returned his sidearm to the scabbard as he watched the man disappear into the gloom. Nauseating smells assaulted him again.

This way and that he caught glimpses of the gruesome scene as the wind swirled smoke around the peninsula. He had never imagined that the stampeding cattle could've caused so much destruction. As he walked on the same path that they had taken he saw the effect of their charge upon the packed ranks of Ostmen and Gaels. More, he knew, would've been trampled by their own folk in their efforts to get out of the way of the charging animals and to flee the battlefield. But had it been enough?

His contemplations – as well as his progress – were suddenly halted as his ears prickled in warning. Ahead, somewhere in the smoke, he had heard an agitated voice cry out. Raymond licked his dry lips and his eyes flicked this way and that as he attempted to discern what the noise meant. He still feared an attack and knew that if even one leader amongst the enemy could muster together a force of some hundred men his counter would fail. His exhausted and battered warriors could not face another assault on their walls. Raymond's mind conjured a great silent army of Ostmen beyond the smoke with Jarl Sigtrygg and Konungr Ragnall at their head, their great battle-axes ready to cut down upon the few remaining enemy within the damaged fort.

As he had before the walls of the fort when Bertram d'Alton had fallen, his mind wandered to the words of the Song of Roland, and Olivier's famous lines: '*Pagans from there I saw. Never on earth did a man see more.*' He hummed the song as he took another step forward. His breath was shallow and the smoke acrid. '*Against us their shields a hundred thousand bore that laced helms and shining hauberks wore.*'

It had all been for naught, he decided, and he again cursed himself for leading his warriors to this sad end on the edge of the world. Internally he apologised to his men, the Norman conrois; to poor Geoffrey who had fallen to Jarl Sigtrygg's hand, and to Alice of Abergavenny who he had loved; to the pages and the esquires who would never see old age, and to Caradog and his archers who had remained at his side when they could so easily have taken flight.

'*And, bolt upright, their bright, brown spearheads shone. Battle we'll have as never was before.*'

The words to the song tumbled from his mouth as he staggered forward through the broken bodies of the fallen. Ahead he heard the voice cry out again, enraged and close-by. He turned his eyes to the sky and apologised to St Maurice and St David, his family's protectors, and asked them to protect his lord, Strongbow, who he had failed.

'*Lords of the Franks, God keep you in valour! So hold your ground, we be not overborne!*'

He sang the last few lines at the top of his voice as he drew his sword from his scabbard and raised it, ready to fight the smoke-cloaked figure emerging ahead.

'Basilia!' he called as he prepared to land the sword stroke.

'Raymond!' William de Vale cried as he collapsed to his knees in shock at the sudden appearance of his captain before him. William's hand left the reins of his courser so that he could appeal for Raymond to stop and his captain gasped in relief as he pulled out of the sweeping cut, dropping the point of his blade to the ground at his esquire's side.

'Thank God it is you,' William exclaimed and got to his feet. 'I thought that I was dead.'

Raymond ignored William's words and grabbed him by his shoulder. 'The enemy? Where is the enemy? Are you all that remains of the conrois?'

'Come and see,' William said, turning his horse around and indicating that Raymond should follow. A coughing fit prevented his captain from demanding an immediate answer from the esquire, and it was only when they cleared the bank of smoke that Raymond understood the full extent of their situation. He had to blink many times, not only because of the smoke, but because he did not believe the evidence that his eyes provided. The landscape was empty, save for an ever-thinning number of bodies which peppered the headland as far as the green horizon.

The enemy had been swept away as if by an ebbing tide.

He felt neither joy nor anguish as the evening sunbeams settled upon his face. He felt only fatigue. The pain, he knew, would come later. Raymond legs suddenly felt strange and he collapsed to his knees amongst the slaughtered and the smoke, words of thanks to heavenly saints tumbling from his mouth. It had worked. His plan

457

had worked, he realised. Against all the odds they had won.

'The creek is at high tide,' William interrupted his captain's mumbled prayers.

'High tide?' The captain could not believe that it had been six hours since he had talked to Ragnall of Veðrarfjord on the causeway. It seemed like mere minutes had passed, but, sure enough, he now recognised that the sun had moved far to the west. Night was falling.

'The causeway is completely under water,' William continued. 'Some of the enemy swam across as Walter de Bloet led us over the hillock, but most fled inland to the west.' He held out a long finger in the direction of the setting sun. 'A lot of Ostmen are trapped on this side, however, as they won't throw away their armour to make the swim. They look like they will make a fight of it so Walter de Bloet ordered me back here to bring the archers to finish them off.'

Raymond nodded although the thought of more bloodshed sickened him. 'Go back and tell Caradog what you have seen,' he ordered William. The esquire yawned widely as his captain spoke, but nodded to indicate that he understood his orders. 'Tell him I will lead them forward myself,' Raymond added.

William's hand went to his courser's muzzle. 'I can't believe that we won,' he told his captain, sweeping an arm over the dead men strewn across the grassland. 'Who would've thought that we could have beaten them?'

'We have survived,' Raymond corrected him, 'that is all. I thank God for it, but we are far from victorious.' An image of Jarl Sigtrygg's callous murder of Geoffrey of Abergavenny appeared to him followed by Alice's screams and her accusatory eyes. 'Just because we are still standing does not mean we have not suffered a defeat.'

'But victory will come later?'

Raymond nodded his head. Strongbow's dream of conquest indeed remained alive. His small vanguard had endured attack by a force many times their number and had held their ground. Their bridgehead had not been overborne. His mind drifted to an image of Basilia de Quincy, more distant than it had ever been before, and he prayed that news of his great deeds at Dun Domhnall would soon reach her ears. He hoped that she would hear the tale of his daring and remember his last words to her in Striguil. He was fighting a campaign on two fronts, he now realised. The first was to his front against an enemy who he could meet with sword and shield and spear. It was a battle that would only end when he placed her father upon a throne. The other struggle would be fought on far more troublesome terrain and relied on many factors beyond his control. It was a form of war in which he was but a novice, the rules less defined. It was a battle that was waged not with steel, but with status, wealth and reputation. Those that he would challenge in that arena were seemingly unassailable, rich beyond his dreams with families of the greatest repute. But if he was to earn what he really wanted from life he had to rise to meet those standards, he knew. To merit the love of Basilia, the daughter of the Earl Strongbow, he would have to become a lord of battles.

'I will send the Welshmen out to you,' William interrupted his thoughts and, with a click of his tongue, he got his courser moving back towards Dun Domhnall's gates.

'Wait.' Raymond reached out and stopped him. The thought of the fights to come had given him new vigour and he abandoned the downcast mood which had threatened to overcome him. To attain his goals he would need help. He would not be able to accomplish his aims on his own. He would need men as ambitious and as desperate as he at his side if he was to succeed.

'From this moment on,' he told William de Vale, 'you are no longer an esquire in the service of Earl Strongbow. You will receive no more pay from Striguil.'

William looked shocked and confused at Raymond's words, worried, it seemed, that he had somehow offended his captain, and he shook his head as if trying to understand what he had done to deserve such treatment. 'I don't follow, sir.'

Raymond smiled at William's reaction and quickly rummaged under his chainmail. 'You will no longer be an esquire to any man,' he said and produced a silver coin from beneath his gambeson. The money sparkled as it tumbled, thrown by the captain towards the boy. William caught it first time. 'You have proven today that you are much better than the lowly rank of esquire. You proved that you are a warrior.' William still looked confused as he stared down at the coin in his hand. Raymond sighed and shook his head. 'I'm giving you a promotion,' he told him.

'I'll be miles?' asked William excitedly before his eyebrows furrowed again. 'In whose retinue?'

Exasperated, Raymond threw his hands in the air. 'In my conrois, you dullard! If you accept, you will be the first miles sworn to my service. Not to Strongbow, but to me.'

'You have no money or land,' William replied.

Raymond nodded. 'But I have a victory and my reward will come later when Earl Strongbow follows us across the sea.'

William still looked ambivalent, but nodded his head as he regarded the coin. 'Alright, count me in, Raymond. I'm your man. I'll go and get Caradog and his archers – then what would you have me do, my Lord?'

Strongbow's captain smiled happily when his new miles addressed him by that title. 'I'm no lord yet, William. I am still merely Raymond the Fat,' he told his warrior.

'But soon?'

Raymond smiled and nodded. 'It will depend on when the earl joins us,' he told him and turned towards the sea. To the west he spotted a single sail, headed west towards Veðrarfjord, but otherwise the waves were empty of shipping.

Flames still roared in the marshalsea, pumping ash and obscuring heat waves high into the blue sky. A break in the blanket of smoke revealed the small fort perched on the edge of the cliff face. Even to Raymond's eyes the hastily constructed battlements looked fragile and insubstantial, much like the company of Marcher warriors who had manned them. They had taken damage – that he could not deny as he caught sight of the battered Welsh archers slumped between the tumbledown gates and broken battlements – but they had withstood a storm.

He would build the walls again, higher and stronger than before. He would send out his milites to recapture his herds, and his archers to cut wood staves for more arrows. He would tend to his men's wounds and revisit Trygve in Cluainmín to barter for supplies. Trusted men would make contact with his uncle, Maurice FitzGerald, in Waesfjord and then travel back to Striguil to tell the story of their stand against the horde of Veðrarfjord. He would remain vigilant and await the coming of Strongbow.

Ahead loomed a campaign of conquest, and Raymond promised that he would be the man to lead it.

suddenly by Caprad and the . . . be told my sacrifice
. . .

Ragnall smiled and recalled. He will do good, was when
the sun . . . ns out. He . . . and turned towards the sea.

To the castle wall . . . heeded with an arm
Vedrarfjord, but offered the . . . were empty of
subject

Epilogue

Tallow lamps burned behind shuttered windows as Ragnall and his followers marched up the timbered High Street in Veðrarfjord. Their clattering feet startled dozing pigs and geese hidden in the allotments along the thoroughfare. Their noise brought townsfolk to the doors of their thatched homes to investigate who was about the streets when the city was asleep. Despite the darkness, the stone palisade topped with timber posts was outlined black against the night sky. The summer sun had given way to mist which partially hid the stars from the konungr's sight, but the moon's haze was brighter still and it lit up the heavens over the River Siúire. Ragnall's hall, and the great tower which his namesake had built five generations before, stood proud and dark against the glowering mist, and it was in that direction that the konungr led his company.

'Where the hell is everyone?' Sigtrygg Fionn asked as he shivered into the neck his heavy cloak.

Ragnall growled rather than answer. It had been four days since his army had fled from the field at Dun Domhnall, four days of humiliating retreat. Few of the men who had stayed with Ragnall had slept or eaten in that time and tempers had long since become frayed. After the cattle stampede had torn apart his army, the konungr and his jarls had tried to rally their men, for they had known that even a few hundred warriors could still have turned the day in their favour. But every time they had marshalled a small body of warriors, the Norman horsemen had come speeding

462

through the smoke to break-up their formation and send them running.

In the end Ragnall had led a group of sixty westwards to escape the rout. The Normans had not tracked them, but screams in the distant east had told the konungr that some, whether Ostman or Gael, had been caught by the vicious foreigners. The greatest danger, as they had turned north towards Dun Conán, had come not from the enemy but from their erstwhile allies. Twice, as they forced their way through the forests of Siol Bhroin, Ragnall had been attacked by some of the more rebellious sects of the Uí Drona. On both occasions he had been lucky to escape. Like wolves, the Gael had come in snarling packs that first night, testing the edges of the Ostman lines and picking off any man who fell behind. They had not been able to pause, to rest, or build a fire that first night, but had pushed onwards. The first sign that they were in real danger had come at sunrise the day after the battle. It had been a red sky that dawn, and that had always been the herald of ill fortune. Ragnall had feared the worst, but they had covered the last mile or so in daylight and it was only upon arrival at Dun Conán that he discovered their true predicament. Few ships remained on the beach, and those that did were burning. Everywhere bodies, both Gael and Ostman, marked zones where impromptu battles had been fought between vying companies of men in the darkness of the night. Defeat had brought about disputes. Fear had led to looting. To the victors had gone a ship and the safety of the river. With no other means of escape, Ragnall had led his men northward, back along the route that he had followed just days before beside the Déisi and the Uí Drona and their vast, lumbering column of camp followers. The sight of the well-trodden paths through the forest had reminded him just how large his army had been and the magnitude of the disaster that had befallen them.

They had finally made it back to Veðrarfjord that evening, the fourth since their defeat. There were now just fifteen men at Ragnall's back, the rest having died by the banks of the Bearú or gone with Jarl Gufraid to his manor upriver.

Ragnall needed news. He desired it more than food or rest. He had to know what had become of his army, and how many had returned to Veðrarfjord. He had to know how many ships had survived the brawls at Dun Conán, and what the jarls were saying of his defeat. Ragnall needed information if he was to re-establish his authority over the city in the wake of the rout at Dun Domhnall.

The konungr stole a glance of one of the men who had come to the door of his longhouse to check on his animals. His face was shrouded by the light emanating from a fire within, but Ragnall could see recognition and anger emblazoned upon his brow. Perhaps he was a father who had lost a son to the foreigners' blades? He supposed that few of the townsfolk would've escaped loss, close or distant, because of their defeat and he promised that the invaders would pay.

'At least there is no sign of the Englishmen,' Sigtrygg Fionn spoke at his shoulder. 'I half expected them to follow up their victory by crossing the river to besiege the city.'

Ragnall ignored the comment. To have scolded the jarl for his stupidity was to remind all his followers that their konungr had lost to little more than a handful of enemies. It would've served no purpose other than to have embarrassed both ruler and subject, and Ragnall knew that he would require all the help he could if he was to keep his position. To his right the high roof of St Olav's Church soared against the dark sky and Ragnall crossed his chest and prayed to his city's saintly protector to grant him grace over the coming days and weeks.

His hall was the biggest in the city. Built upon a small hillock, it had once been defended only by the confluence of the Siúire and the vast impassable marsh which it fed. However, the great wealth of Veðrarfjord, as well as the enmity of the local Gaelic lords, had permitted the erection of a wall, three times as tall as a man, around the city. Ragnall's hall, the hall of the konungr, had been enclosed on two sides by the meeting of the east and north walls. At the building's back stood the mighty tower which shared his name.

The konungr was pleased to see smoke and firelight seeping from behind the closed window shutters and he swore that he could identify the hint of cooked meat on the evening air as he advanced on the twisted fence which defended the southern approach to his home. Weariness threatened to overcome him so close was he to his destination. He could not wait to look upon his wife's face, to see his young sons Ragnall Óg and Óttar.

He increased his pace as he climbed the path towards the stone entrance to his hall, some of his troubles departing as he thought of his warm bed, good food and drink. He could positively feel the heat stored in the thatched roof and wooden walls as he listened to the voices within. A smile spilled across Ragnall Mac Giolla Mhuire's crooked face as he reached out to push open the heavily decorated doors. He was momentarily dazzled by the brightness and smoke inside the large room, and had to shield his eyes from their effects.

He immediately knew that something was wrong in Veðrarfjord for the noise in the hall suddenly abated as he and his men entered. As Ragnall's eyes drew accustomed to the firelight he lowered his hand to find that every eye in the hall had turned to look at him. Few had welcoming

465

looks upon their faces.

'Ragnall,' Jarl Sigtrygg's voice boomed around the hall and the konungr's eyes were drawn to the dais where his giant of a son climbed to his feet. 'It is good of you to join us finally. There have been some changes in your absence.' His voice positively flowed with menace.

Ragnall felt hands closing around his left arm and he turned to find it locked in the grip of Máel Sechlainn Ua Fhaolain, King of the Déisi. There was no friendship in the Gael's eyes as he raised a savage sword to touch the konungr's chin. A scuffle had broken out behind him and Ragnall craned his neck to see that his few remaining followers had been surrounded by more of the Uí Fhaoláin, their spears pressed to his warriors' chests.

'What do you think that you are doing, boy?' Ragnall raged in his son's direction. 'What right have you to do this to me in my own hall?'

But Jarl Sigtrygg did not answer. Instead he looked to his left and nodded once. Ragnall twisted away from Máel Sechlainn's clasp in time to watch as his friend Sigtrygg Fionn was cut down by two Gaels and a man from Jarl Sigtrygg's own crew. The old man had not had time to even draw his sword before he was felled.

'Is Gufraid amongst their number?' Jarl Sigtrygg called from the dais. Receiving no answer, the jarl cast his eyes over his father's remaining men as he strode down the hall, to make sure that his rival was indeed absent. 'No matter, I have made hostage of his sons and he will support me or they will die.'

'You have no right to do this,' Ragnall hissed at Jarl Sigtrygg and struggled against Máel Sechlainn's hold. He saw a look pass over his son's face and for a moment Ragnall thought that he too would follow his friend to heaven. Instead Jarl Sigtrygg leaned towards his father and spoke softly in his ear.

'Silver buys friends as quickly as defeat loses them,' he told his father. 'I rule in Veðrarfjord now and when I save this city from the foreigners I will be konungr.' Jarl Sigtrygg was smiling slyly behind his red beard when he stepped away from Ragnall. 'Take him to the tower,' he told Máel Sechlainn. 'Put him with his wife and sons. Then come back to my hall, for we have plans to make if we are to save the city.' Around him men shouted and raised their spears and axes in defiance. 'We must prepare for war on the streets of Veðrarfjord,' Jarl Sigtrygg yelled. 'We must prepare for the coming of Strongbow.'

Historic note

Very little is known about the life of Raymond de Carew before his landing at Dun Domhnall in May 1170. He was a younger son of William FitzGerald, a Welsh nobleman whose lands included Cilgerran Castle in the Barony of Emlyn as well as Carew Castle just north of Pembroke. It was from the second fortress that his family derived their surname and amazingly, some 845 years later, the descendants of Raymond's elder brother still own the ruined fortress (though it is administered by the Pembrokeshire Coast National Park). Raymond's extended family included the Bishop of St David's, the Constable of Pembroke, and Robert FitzStephen who led the first Norman advances into Ireland in 1169.

At the age of seven Raymond, like all boys of his rank, would've been sent to serve in a noble household and begin the long road to becoming a knight. The Raymond portrayed in *Lord of the Sea Castle* is probably ten to fifteen years younger than his real-life counterpart but, given his father's feudal ties to the House of Pembroke, it is likely that he would have been sent to serve Richard Strongbow's father or mother as a page around 1140. At this time Gilbert Strongbow was one of the most powerful men in the whole of the kingdom and still possessed Pembroke Castle as well as the vassalage of many knightly families. As a page, Raymond would've received training in courtly manners as well as learning the basics of combat. This 'education' would've been repaid by serving food, cleaning armour, running messages as well as a hundred other small tasks. It was perhaps during this period that the chubby Raymond received the nickname of *Le Gros* which he would bear for the rest of his life.

At fourteen Raymond would've graduated to the role of esquire, at which time he was given better training in martial practices as well as greater responsibility over his lord's weaponry, armour and animals. Older esquires would often become pseudo-knights, serving in the same capacity, but at a lower scale of pay, in his lord's band of horsemen. At twenty-one he would've either advanced to the rank of a knight or become a miles – a Norman cavalryman who performed the same duty as a knight without the accompanying noble rank. I can find no reference that Raymond was ever afforded the rank of knight and have surmised in these pages that his father's loss of the barony of Emlyn in 1164 may have made it quite impossible for Raymond to pay for all the trappings and expenses essential for this elevation.

It is probable that Raymond was part of the retinue which followed Strongbow to Germany in early 1168 when he accompanied King Henry II's eldest daughter Matilda to her marriage in Saxony. The attack by bandits mentioned in these pages is entirely fictitious, as is his enmity with Walter de Bloet. The lord of Raglan Castle in this period was from the Bloet (later Bluett) family and, given Strongbow's lack of an heir, he would have, in all probability, inherited Striguil.

Raymond's good service to Strongbow's family meant that in 1170, when he needed a trusted man to lead his advance party to Ireland, he was the man selected. Baginbun Point is well worth a visit and is easily accessible through Fethard-on-Sea in County Wexford. The fort (called Dun Domhnall in 1170) is much as described in the novel, with beaches on both sides and bounded by high cliffs. The remains of the earthworks that Raymond and his men created are still there, as well as a small plaque to remember the occasion. Raymond actually landed in Ireland around May 1st, but I have postponed this in *Lord of the Sea Castle* to July 1st to allow Raymond to attend the coronation of Henry the Young King at Westminster Abbey on June 14th. As far as I know there was no tournament before this ceremony. Henry the Young King was only fifteen at the time and there is no way that he would have been permitted to take part in such a dangerous sporting event. He did go on to make something of a name for himself in later life on the tourney circuit under the tutelage of the famous William Marshal who did, as portrayed, become his teacher at the behest of King Henry II in 1170.

Hubert Walter is another character plucked from history to appear in this novel. The younger brother of my own paternal ancestor Theobald, Hubert was, it seems, already a man of significant influence at court in the 1170s thanks to the patronage of his uncle Ranulph de Glanville. He would later rise to become Archbishop of Canterbury under King Richard I and became so authoritative that, upon Hubert's death in 1205, the chronicler Matthew Paris has King John remarking that "for the first time I am king" to indicate his subject's power.

It was probably in June or early July that Raymond's fort was attacked by a force of between two and three thousand men. The bulk of the army seems to have been drawn from the Uí Drona tribe who were led by the Uí Riagháin (O'Ryan) from modern County Carlow and the Uí Fhaolain (O'Phelan) who ruled the Déisi and hailed from what is now County Waterford. However, command seems to have fallen upon three Ostmen from Waterford called Ragnall Mac Giolla Mhuire and two named Sigtrygg. Little is known about any of the Ostmen leaders and though the names are taken from history, the deeds of Ragnall, Jarl Sigtrygg and Sigtrygg Fionn in *Lord of the Sea Castle* are all fictionalised. There was an Ostman town at Cluainmín (Clonmines) though the character of Trygve and Raymond's time at the longfort is totally invented. The town has since disappeared but it continued to thrive well into the seventeenth century.

The fighting at Dun Domhnall is as close to the historical record as I could possibly make it. Raymond did sally out of the fort to attack the enemy as they journeyed southwards from Waterford (possibly in the townland of Battlestown). The attack of so few horsemen did not prove enough to stop the Gael and Ostmen, and, according to the chronicler Gerald of Wales, the Normans arrived back at Dun Domhnall so hotly pursued by their enemy that the gates could not be closed. Raymond and the leper William Ferrand took on the entire army in Gerald's retelling, but he leaves out Raymond's ruse using the cattle. This trick is, however, not lifted from the film *Zulu*, but from *The Song of Dermot and the Earl* written in the early 1200s. The source gives no indication if the Normans deliberately caused the stampede or simply took advantage of the animals' terrified reaction to the noise of the battle going on around them.

The Song of Dermot and the Earl also introduces Alice of Abergavenny to the story. In this version Alice is a 'wench' driven mad by the death of her lover in battle and snatches up an axe to behead all the Ostman prisoners. In Gerald of Wales' version of the tale, Alice is not mentioned and the blame for the executions is placed squarely on Sir Hervey de Montmorency's shoulders. In my view neither source, given their bias towards Raymond, can be trusted

472

to tell the truth about this awful moment in history. I remain extremely doubtful that Alice ever existed as anything other than a patsy for Raymond and Hervey's crime. Her character in *Lord of the Sea Castle* is complete creation, as is her brother Geoffrey, and their alleged relationship to Sir William de Braose.

Basilia de Clare was actually the sister of Richard Strongbow rather than his illegitimate daughter. The historical figure only married Roger de Quincy (in reality, Robert) the year after her brother invaded Ireland.

Raymond's victory at Baginbun, in my opinion, did not win or lose Ireland as the famous verse claims, but the savagery and ease of his triumph must've shocked many of the local princes. Within a few weeks of Raymond's victory at Baginbun his lord, Strongbow, the most famous name to arise from the tale, would arrive on Irish shores. At his back was the biggest army yet seen in the story of the Norman invasion, and his eyes were firmly set on claiming both Waterford and Dublin as his own.

To my agent, David Riding at MBA, and my editor Greg Rees, as well as the whole team at Accent Press, my thanks for their vital contributions. I'd also like to express my appreciation to the Arts Council of Northern Ireland for their kind support, to Shea Cashman and the Deise Medieval Society for their information about life in Ostman Ireland, to Emma Barr for advising me about all things equine, and to my dad Ricky for keeping me right on ships and the tides.

Ruadh Butler, April 2017